About the author

Hedley Harrison graduated from London University and joined a major oil company, progressing to senior management and seeing service in the UK, Nigeria, Australia and the North Sea. He has published five other novels with The Book Guild: *Coup* in 2011, *Disunited States* in 2013, *China Wife* in 2015, *Sorak's Redemption* in 2016, *Sorak Returns* in 2018 and *Sorak's Legacy* in 2019.

COUP
ABORTIVE

HEDLEY HARRISON

The Book Guild Ltd

First published in Great Britain in 2020 by
The Book Guild Ltd
9 Priory Business Park
Wistow Road, Kibworth
Leicestershire, LE8 0RX
Freephone: 0800 999 2982
www.bookguild.co.uk
Email: info@bookguild.co.uk
Twitter: @bookguild

Typeset in Sabon MT

Printed and bound in Great Britain by CPI Group (UK) Ltd, Croydon, CR0 4YY

ISBN 978 1 91355112 4

British Library Cataloguing in Publication Data.
A catalogue record for this book is available from the British Library.

The good guys always
win out in the end

ONE

"It's always the same. There are never any taxis in London when it's raining."

But it wasn't just the weather.

Things had returned to normality surprisingly quickly after the abortive coup of 2022, largely as a result of the universal amnesty for all but the most unrepentant of the Nationalist elite. But labour shortages still existed in areas like transport that had always been dependent on a black and Asian workforce. As the former workers dribbled slowly back, and with bus and Underground services not yet fully restored, taxis were hard to come by rain or shine.

Mark Shortley's comment to his sister had a note of resignation rather than irritation as they waited under the canopy of St. Jerome's Hotel in Mayfair. Out on the pavement, his extravagant uniform becoming increasingly bedraggled, the commissionaire was making ineffectual and rather dispirited efforts to meet his clients' needs for transport.

Mark was ten years younger than his sister, although the age difference was well disguised by the discreet but effective use of the products of various cosmetics suppliers.

It was definitely a family day and Mark was keen to do his

only niece proud. It was for that reason that they were waiting for the elusive taxi. Mark was determined that Caroline would arrive at her daughter's graduation in as pristine a condition as possible. It was also for that reason that they were staying at St. Jerome's Hotel and not at Mark's perfectly serviceable flat in Herbert Street, Knightsbridge.

"Well, would you look at that?"

The commissionaire, like many of his breed, was Irish.

A taxi suddenly arrived. Standing back until the accumulated mess of rubbish and rainwater from the road had subsided back into the gutter, the commissionaire moved to open the door..

"Pardon me!" he said irritably as an Arab man of considerable girth thrust the door into his face and surged across the pavement, forcing both Mark and his sister to move aside.

Mark's equally angry exclamation died on his lips as the man was followed at a more measured pace by a young Arab woman completely enshrouded in the black, flowing burka now increasingly worn by Moslem women in Britain.

"I do beg your pardon," he said, moving aside for a second time.

The young woman followed the man into the hotel without apparently recognising that Mark had spoken. Both Mark and his sister watched her until she was out of view.

"Where to?" the taxi driver was demanding.

"Albert Hall, please; Kensington Road side; as close to the building as possible."

* * *

"Her eyes," Mark said as they made their way up the stairways of the famous building, "they were china blue!"

"What?"

"The Arab woman... at the hotel. Her eyes were china blue. Why did I suppose that Arab women should have brown eyes?"

"And she was wearing M&S sandals. Julie has a similar pair."

It was Julie's graduation that they were attending.

Mark had been pondering over the young Arab woman. Despite the mummifying effect of the head-to-toe black clothing she moved with boldness and vigour. And whatever impression the clear blue eyes, her only visible feature, had created, it was not one of submissiveness. This, he decided, was a woman of positive and powerful character.

He didn't doubt that his sister was right. Although the Arab/Israeli conflicts had largely ceased, for a strict Moslem to be wearing such footwear was certainly not usual.

* * *

The seats that they had been allocated in the Albert Hall were not ideal. They were a long way from the stage, but they had a panoramic view of the whole proceedings. Caroline was a little miffed with her daughter, however.

"Trust Julie," she said. "If she'd got the tickets earlier, we could've been closer and had a decent view."

Mark laughed; from what he knew of his niece she was definitely more laid back than her mother.

'She's very like me physically, but we're poles apart mentally,' Mark thought as his sister settled into her seat.

They both had the same colour eyes and they both had the same light brown hair, but whilst Mark's was showing the early signs of receding, Caroline's was well tended under the obscurity of her rather extravagant hat.

"I'm glad I got dressed up," she remarked as she scanned the audience.

Whilst his sister was taking in the haute couture, Mark was craning his neck too, but his interest was altogether different. Bred of early army and SAS training he was reminding himself of the layout of the Albert Hall and its means of exit.

"You could hide a whole army in here; who'd ever know."

But the ceremony was getting underway. The processional music announced that the colourful lines of the good and the great of the university, intermingled with an assortment of high-ranking police and military officers but a rather depleted retinue of civic dignitaries, were moving slowly through the seated mass of graduating students and onto the platform, shepherding the Chancellor with them. A junior member of the royal family, the Chancellor looked nervous and uncomfortable. Freshly appointed and more accustomed to a more active life, the media had rather scoffed at the prince's conversion to being a pillar of academia.

The opening speeches were largely unheard by the assembled gathering; everybody present was only interested in seeing their own particular offspring being honoured.

* * *

"In the faculty of science, the award of bachelor's degrees…"
The graduation had started.

Mark and Caroline watched the steady stream of youngsters make their way down the aisle and onto the platform.

"In the faculty of arts, the award of bachelor's degrees…"

"This is her lot," said Caroline in some excitement.

Mark focused on the platform and the faraway patch of light in the middle where the young people walked forward on announcement of their name and bowed with varying degrees of obeisance to the royal personage before moving away to collect the vital piece of paper at the other side of the stage.

"Michael Leaman… Carol Mace… Julie Mackenzie."

Even the normally calm and restrained Mark felt a little surge of pride at his niece's achievement.

The crocodile of excited youngsters continued across the stage.

"Andrew Warden… Muriel Wendover… Lawrence Wong."

Mark just had time to think that the lad was tall for being Chinese when he pitched forward and collapsed at the feet of the startled royal.

TWO

Even with his SAS training it took Mark a few seconds to register what had happened.

There was a corporate gasp and the forename of the next graduate hung in the air as the horrified announcer reacted.

After an uncertain pause, both noise and action erupted. As a body, everyone on the platform stood up. Instantly scurrying figures appeared from the wings and hustled the royal prince away towards the carefully guarded exit. The functionaries of the university coagulated around the space where the Chancellor had been seated, nervously avoiding the body. The few civic dignitaries fluttered about, unsure if they had any role to play. Only the police and military officers showed any signs of purposefulness. Rumbles of anxious chatter began to roll around the auditorium.

"Ladies and gentlemen, if I could ask you to please remain seated."

The calm voice of the Commissioner of Police cut into the rising atmosphere of anxiety, determined to prevent it from worrying itself into panic. Along with other police officers on the platform, he had forced himself forward and in front of the milling groups of academics and invited guests. As the other officers spoke into their mobile phones, the Commissioner took his position at the lectern and was beginning to pour out soothing words.

Meanwhile in front of him, the red flights of a crossbow bolt in his back clearly visible, lay the almost unnoticed body of the unfortunate Lawrence Wong.

"It's OK, it's OK, the students are all together, Julie'll be alright."

Mark's calmness reassured his sister.

But he wasn't just looking for Julie. He had been quick to realise, as the police had, that only a weapon fired from above and behind them in the gallery could have struck down the dead man. It was dark and empty up there, and an ideal vantage point. With the audience the size that it was, there was no need to use the gallery accommodation, and although the Royal Protection Squad had searched the area most thoroughly, they had seen no need to man it during the ceremony.

As Mark looked up, shadowy figures appeared in the gallery and quickly congregated at one point. Since this was where Mark had judged the shot had been fired from, he correctly deduced that they had found the crossbow. They had also found a forced door behind the firing position. However, their hope of finding the marksman had long since evaporated. And again like the police, Mark hadn't immediately assumed that the prince had been the target.

"I'm afraid I'm going to have to ask you to remain in the Hall for a while longer. My officers are beginning an investigation and I've called for additional staff to speed up the process."

It was the bland speech of a careful professional. The Commissioner knew that he couldn't hold the people for long; that would be both unreasonable and impractical.

Outside the Albert Hall the waiting media were surprised to see the rapid departure of the visiting royal, and the court correspondents were given a rare opportunity to report on more dramatic events. News of the shooting quickly filtered into the twenty-four-hour news services and, despite the efforts of the police, reports of an attempt on the life of the prince rattled around the world.

"Why would anyone want to kill him?" asked Caroline of Mark. "He's nothing special."

Steadied by Mark's presence, she had forgotten her own concerns and was beginning to join the speculation gaining strength in the Hall.

"Who says he was the target?"

Mark's response was rather sharper than he had intended, but he had switched into business mode, and from a professional point of view there was no immediate evidence to support such a suggestion.

"Thank you, ladies and gentlemen…"

Not many in the audience heard the Commissioner's pious assurances. Once it was clear that they were to be allowed to leave, the movement to the exits was immediate.

* * *

The snakes of people moved quickly, as everybody was keen to get away, but the sheer numbers still made it a long and tedious process. As Mark and Caroline emerged into the gloom of the early afternoon, Mark was relieved to see that it was no longer raining.

"Here she is."

Caroline had rapidly located her daughter at their agreed meeting place. Julie instantly hugged her mother and burst into tears. Both Caroline and Mark were surprised; it was not the reaction that they had expected.

"Oh, Mummy, it was so awful," wept Julie.

It was all that she said. But she kept on saying it as Mark took his bearings and decided the best way to get back to St Jerome's Hotel.

"It'll be quicker to walk; we'll never get a taxi in this lot," he said.

Caroline raised no objection. She put her arm around her daughter's shoulder; as hers and Mark's identical blue/grey eyes met, they both saw the same question in them: 'What's going on here; why is Julie so upset?'

The walk back to the hotel was readily accomplished with Mark forcefully manoeuvring them through the milling crowds of parents and offspring until they reached less crowded streets.

"We'll tidy up and join you for some tea," announced Caroline as they walked through the foyer of the hotel.

"OK."

Mark would have preferred something stronger, but he nodded his agreement and followed them to the lift.

* * *

'It's that ignorant bastard from the taxi,' Mark said to himself as he walked into the coffee shop of the hotel a few minutes later.

His tidying up hadn't taken very long.

In a corner by the window, the Arab man, still looking hideously overweight even in his closer-fitting European clothes, was sat before a plate of cream-laden cakes that gave the obvious clue to his substantial size. To his left and with her back to Mark was a young woman with long blonde hair. They were not a congenial couple. The woman's body language was dominant and her posture commanding. Sitting straight up in her chair whilst he slouched, she seemed both to intimidate the man and to ignore his existence. Mark could almost feel the contempt and resentment passing between them.

* * *

9

'So what the hell's all this about?' Mark said to himself.

With nothing else to do for the moment but await his sister and niece, he settled himself to a little self-indulgent speculation about Julie's distress.

He parked himself at a table with the Arab and the blonde only half in his view and set himself to reflect on the day. Caroline he knew would take an age to tidy herself and it was more than apparent that Julie was anxious to unburden something to her mother.

Mark was a conscientious, if sometimes bemused, uncle; he was very fond of Julie and he felt for her obvious suffering. From his years in the SAS, he was used to confronting unforeseen situations. Now within his own security company he was making a good living from this skill, but why the death of the Chinese student had so upset the girl he could only suppose was due to some emotional entanglement that clearly her mother knew nothing about.

"Oh well, I'll know soon enough when Julie gets here."

But since his mind usually resisted speculation, Mark soon moved on.

"'Nigeria denies a crisis' – they would, I suppose."

Having put the problems of his niece from his mind temporarily, he was scanning the complimentary newspapers thoughtfully left by the waiter.

'The rise of Moslem fundamentalism has continued from the late 1990s well into the new century, and if the fury of the zealots has abated in the Middle East (by 2024), the sub-Saharan states and the Indonesian islands have become the battleground. The mixed fortunes of Boko Haram in Nigeria and the increasingly effective government efforts to contain and defeat them in the late 2010s nonetheless could still occasionally lead to bloody confrontations.'

Mark read the words not so much in disbelieve but with a sense of time warp.

"The threat to Nigeria has been with us since at least 1998, for heaven's sake," said Mark half aloud, "and the subject 'has been of much concern in the corridors of power in the Nigerian capital Abuja and the ministries of the European Federation', of course it has!"

Mark discarded the paper, unclear why the columnist was raking over such self-evident truths.

Partly because his partner was Nigerian, but also with an eye to future business, Mark Shortley Associates had always been very interested in the progress of Moslem fundamentalism in black Africa and as a consequence all things North African, Arab and Iranian, even after Iran had imploded. The topic was being seriously researched in official and less official circles, and he well knew that the public pronouncements on Nigeria fell far short of the private anxieties.

* * *

"Julie and the dead man… they were friends," Caroline said as the two women eventually rejoined Mark.

His sister's carefully politically correct statement provided a caution to Mark; the situation was sensitive!

"Really? Poor girl, I'm so sorry. Boyfriend?"

Julie nodded forlornly. Mark felt an instant sympathy. Her mother's use of the word 'friends' had obviously been intended to cover something deeper. His niece, with so little experience of the adult world, didn't deserve such tragedy so early in her young life.

"Yes," she said, "we saw a lot of each other last year… but this year…"

She didn't finish. Her mother squeezed her hand.

Mark, sensitive to people and their unspoken feelings, and used to investigating out-of-character behaviour in his professional life, now recognised the situation, and why

Caroline was trying to protect her daughter. Poor Julie was still very fond of the dead boy, but his feelings had cooled and they had drifted apart.

"His name was Lawrence Wong," she said, adding unnecessarily that he was Chinese.

"Did he live in Britain?" asked Mark.

'They have complicated and widespread families,' thought Mark, knowing from his dealings with the latter-day Triads how obscure these family relationships could be, 'often with residences in several countries. Young Lawrence could easily have been an overseas student.'

"Lawrence's family live in Kent; there's a flat in London. He always seemed to have plenty of money. Lawrence didn't study much. He was clever... and, well, he was lazy. But he never seemed to want to go home. He spent most of his evenings at parties and most of his nights at other people's flats."

Julie didn't say 'including mine', but the expression on her mother's face said it for her. Mark thought it would be a good idea to get her to talk and gently try and give her a chance to work off her hurt.

"Did you meet any of the family?"

"No. He was always very cagey about them. I know he didn't have a mother. The way he talked about his father seemed very mixed up. He clearly respected him but was frightened of him, all at the same time. Whether he loved him I couldn't say. He had a sister, older. As far as I can remember, she's called Pearl. She seemed to be very hard, ambitious. Lawrence always said she would be better at running the business than him. He hated the whole idea of the business."

"Did he have a lot of other friends besides you?"

But Mark's 'get her to talk about it' philosophy wasn't working.

Much as she loved her mother and uncle, Julie didn't want to talk about Lawrence like this. She just wanted to recall the more intimate moments that she had shared with him, but she couldn't do that with her family; with the arrogance of youth she assumed that they wouldn't understand. Her mother and uncle had never met him; they had only known of his existence for a few brief hours.

"Oh, yes, he was very popular." She was proud of his popularity. "All my friends... our friends..." Her voice faltered. "Do you mind if I go back to my flat?"

The request was abrupt and so plaintive that Caroline could hardly refuse.

"Yes, of course, go and be with your friends." As Julie went off, she said, "The joys of parenthood."

Mark grinned.

* * *

Sudden action attracted Mark's attention to the Arab and the girl with him. They were conversing angrily if quietly, but from the man's body language, he wasn't enjoying the experience. Abruptly the woman stood up, threw some remark at him that made him cringe and marched out of the coffee shop. Like her every action, her demeanour was bold and positive. As he scanned her departing figure, Mark felt a sense of familiarity.

* * *

"I'll be off then."

It was Julie back. She was dressed in the casual uniform of the young woman of the day: leather jacket, tight jeans, boots. It was only as she walked away after the farewell hugs that Mark fixed the other young woman in his mind. Dressed virtually identically to Julie, her bold walk registered. Despite the cultural questions that it raised, it was obvious that the blonde-haired woman who had just passed from the room and the all-enveloped black-clad figure of earlier were one and the same.

"Oh, Mark, it's horrible when you know they're hurting and you can't help."

Mark's seemingly useless piece of deduction and the intrigue it caused him was pushed from his mind by his sister's anguished comment. He sympathised.

"I know," he said, giving her shoulder a gentle squeeze.

* * *

They relapsed into their own thoughts for a time. Caroline relived the day and gently chided herself for not being able to help her daughter. Mark in his turn allowed his mind to wandered homewards. It was Janine Effiong, his Nigerian partner, who filled his thoughts. He was missing her and her spontaneous warmth and affection.

'She would have known how to comfort the poor child,' he thought to himself. 'Not a lot fazes her.'

A gentle, warm smile, that surprised Caroline as she suddenly caught sight of it, rippled across his face.

'Janine's an active and intelligent young woman,' thought Mark, 'like no one I've met before.'

She was independently minded and very much her own person despite their intimacy. That was what he liked and what added to the excitement of her company. They didn't own each other and they were friends in a way that he had never thought possible with a member of the opposite sex. He wondered what more there could be in their relationship. Not only was she a partner in his life, but also she was very rapidly becoming an indispensable partner in his business. Past experience had proved that their relationship could withstand entanglements with other women; whether it could with other men wasn't something that had so far crossed Mark's mind.

An accountant by profession, Janine had brought computing skills and a knowledge of the business world to his activities that Mark was finding very useful and which was already bearing fruit. As he turned to respond to a question from his sister, he wondered how she was getting on at the Nigerian High Commission. It was rare that she had anything to do with the country of her origin, so being invited to the reception was a surprise to both of them.

"So how's your business?" Caroline was asking.

"It's thriving. I've been doing a lot of work for the military and the oil industry."

Caroline was aware of something of Mark's role in the recent past upheavals in Britain.

"And I've good contacts in Brussels. European fraud is big business and so is detecting it. And there are still dribs and drabs of Moslem Fundamentalists. Janine's very helpful here."

"Janine?"

Mark realised that he had never told Caroline about his partner. It was an omission that he was about to rectify when he was paged to take a telephone call.

* * *

"Stand by for more heartache," he said when he returned. "That was Julie. The Wong boy's place has been broken into and ransacked. Except that it isn't his, it's his father's. The police are bringing Julie back here."

THREE

Janine Effiong, Mark Shortley's partner, wasn't sure what to expect of her evening. The invitation to the Reception at the Nigerian High Commission was a complete surprise, and as she walked up the ornate staircase towards the function room, she recognised a feeling of apprehension. This was a rare sensation for her.

Janine was very much an expatriate Nigerian. Born in Lagos, she had been shipped to London when her parents had been killed in one of the periodic upheavals that Nigeria had once been prone to. It had been a traumatic experience and it had taken her many years to recover from the effects. Brought up in the family of a maternal uncle, she was classic British middle class with very little affinity with her homeland and, until recently, a fairly limited knowledge of it. That she was feeling the unaccustomed pangs of nervousness about entering a room that contained over a hundred of her fellow Nigerians, and most of them men, was hardly surprising.

"Miss Janine Effiong!"

The novelty of her name being shouted out by the scarlet-clad toastmaster abated her anxiety. By the time she reached the smiling figure standing waiting for her at the head of the queue, hand outstretched, her nervousness had all but disappeared.

"Glad you could come."

The High Commissioner had repeated the greeting many times during the evening, but the sentiment seemed genuine enough. It was also the limit of his conversation for ordinary mortals like Janine.

She headed for the throng. This was the largest gathering of black people that she had ever seen, and she doubted that she had anything in common with any of them. A dozen paces into the room, she was sucked, seemingly unnoticed, into the seething mass of people.

She began to cast about for some means of establishing communication with her fellow guests. It didn't seem likely to be easy.

A passing waiter – Chinese, like all of those that she saw – offered her a tray of drinks to choose from. She took a glass of champagne. Since a large proportion of Nigerians were Moslems, the bulk of the drinks on offer were non-alcoholic. As her hand closed around the glass, she wondered whether it was the done thing for women to drink in public even amongst the non-Moslems. With no other woman immediately available to refer to, she shrugged and drank.

* * *

"Janine?"

She was jerked out of her contemplation of the disparate groups around her by a quiet, enquiring voice. The man addressing her, in common with a sizeable minority of the male guests, was wearing the long, flowing robes and matching trousers which Janine at least knew to be the local dress of many of the southern Nigerian peoples. The embroidery was rich, ornate and complex, and it was mirrored on the small pillbox hat that the man was wearing. The effect was very pleasing, and when it was topped by the friendliest of welcoming grins, Janine warmed to him immediately.

17

"Yes, I'm Janine…" she responded calmly, making it sound like a question to him.

"I'm Fid Okeke; I was christened Phidelphus, but Fid sounds rather better. We're cousins. It's because of me you're here."

"Oh," said Janine.

* * *

When Janine had arrived, no one had taken any notice of her.

"Women sure as hell aren't equal in Nigerian society. There must be a dozen blokes within touching distance; they must be able to see me."

But the men carried on talking with varying degrees of animation, seemingly oblivious to her very existence.

The voices were harsh and the speech abrupt. Conversation was more by demand and counter-demand than by the easy flow and interchange that she was used to. And she could see no signs of any natural courtesy amongst them; speakers were frequently and continually interrupted. But it was all good-natured and never seemed to create offence.

"Mark's a total stiff beside this lot!"

The Nigerians talked with their bodies as much as they did with their mouths. By contrast, her partner was positively immobile. And his clothes were almost flamboyant compared with the sober suits of the men there in European dress.

"That's interesting."

Janine herself was a fan of the fashions of the 1960s, although her African origins tended to show themselves in her love of exotic jewellery. She was, however, pleased that she had chosen a dress of longer length than she was accustomed to wear for the Reception. Such women as there were present were all wearing national dress with no concessions to European style. A miniskirt might well have focused attention on her, but for reasons that Janine would not have appreciated.

"Much more colourful than the men," she said half aloud, "perhaps it's a small sign of rebellion?"

Eventually unsure of how to proceed, and not wishing to provoke a rebuff, she had slowly gravitated to the side of the room to watch and wait. Experience told her that she would eventually get drawn into the action. But her progress had not gone unnoticed and at the right moment the quiet, enquiring voice entered her life.

* * *

She wasn't quite sure how to react to Mr Okeke. That she should suddenly acquire a totally unexpected relative in the middle of London was not something that she could have reasonably anticipated. But at least there was now hope of an explanation of her invitation to the reception and, particularly, why it had been addressed to her at Mark's flat.

"How could they have known I was living there?"

Janine had moved in with Mark Shortley the year before when their relationship had been at its most intense and the upheavals of the previous eighteen months had abated. Over the months, although still very much in love, their feelings were not always so powerfully expressed now as they had been initially. Increasingly they took pleasure in shared friendship and companionship as much as in being fired-up lovers. Nonetheless, it had come as a surprise that the Nigerian High Commission knew of their cohabitation and had, so unexpectedly, invited her to the reception.

"Oh," she said again, "I've been wondering about that; especially as I don't know a single other Nigerian in London."

A feeling suddenly came to her that he knew a lot more about her than she would have expected. It was the appraising look in his eyes. But he smiled enigmatically and changed the subject.

"Our grandmothers were sisters. When your mother was killed, your grandmother came to live with us. My father was in the army, defence ministry in Abuja; eventually and unwillingly he was co-opted onto General Babangida's staff. I'm a civil servant. I've spent most of my working life in Abuja."

A jumble of thoughts filled Janine's mind. Her knowledge of Nigerian history wasn't that great. She knew vaguely who General Babangida was, a military dictator from the 1990s, and of course she knew that Abuja was the Federal Nigerian capital. But it was the first reference to a grandparent that had ever been made to her. In the light of her parents' deaths and her own experiences, ill-remembered as they might be, her relatives had thought to spare her and her sister painful memories.

"My sister lives in Abuja; she went there last year."

It was all that she could think of to say.

"Yes, I know, I've met her. She told me a lot about you."

He smiled again. Like Janine, a smile was never very far from his face. He continued the family exposé by sharing more information about their mutual relatives and antecedents. Janine noticed that it was carefully done; Mr Okeke was obviously a cautious person. Nonetheless she learnt a lot about her extended family and, by implication, about her new cousin. She felt that he was seeking to build her confidence in him but also trying to assess her. She wondered whether association with Mark's business was making her paranoid, but she found it very difficult not to be suspicious of Mr Okeke, relative or not.

It was not an easy conversation for Fid Okeke either; for all her skin colour Janine seemed like a European woman to him. He found as they talked that she was his equal intellectually, and that just as he was, she was also seeking to satisfy herself about his bona fides. And as with Mark Shortley before him, he found her direct approach rather challenging and he came away from the conversation with respect for her but very little of the reassurance about her that he was seeking.

* * *

"Alhaji, may I present Miss Janine Effiong."

The constant movement in the room had brought Janine and Okeke into the path of a group of men who were altogether different in dress and demeanour. The High Commissioner was with them. Consumed by what followed, Janine failed to be impressed that the High Commissioner had actually remembered her name.

He introduced Janine to a tall and austere man in his fifties dressed entirely in white with a turban-like headdress wound around his face as well as his head, exposing only a limited amount of his features. Janine held out her hand. It was ignored. She was greeted with a nod that barely recognised her existence. The man and his party moved on, leaving Janine fuming.

'Holy shit,' she said to herself, 'who the hell does he think he is?'

"Alhaji Mahomet Sullag. He's Federal Minister for Communications and a northern traditionalist."

The answer came instantly to her silent question.

It was a moment before she realised that it was not Fid Okeke who had offered the explanation but another woman. She turned to face the speaker and found herself looking into the laughing eyes of a female of her own height and of her own age.

"This is Victoria Akinbode." Okeke was still there and he hurriedly made the introduction. "She's also a civil servant."

Janine held out her hand again, but sufficiently tentatively to attract a fleeting grin from Victoria. The hand was grasped firmly although briefly. Somewhat to Janine's surprise, Victoria's hand was moist with sweat. It was unexpected and in marked contrast to her confident and open manner. Janine noted that Victoria was wearing a wedding ring, but unlike herself she was otherwise devoid of jewellery.

* * *

"I've got to go damn you, I've got to go!"

Her exclamation was playful enough; nonetheless, it had an urgency about it that her companion immediately recognised.

But he still didn't release her glossy naked body. He laughed mockingly at her, inviting her to struggle free. It was a game that they played. Normally Victoria enjoyed the violent rough and tumble of their lovemaking as much as he did, but on this occasion, things were different.

"I have to go," she repeated.

Her voice this time was colder and more measured. He rolled off her and allowed her to slide off the bed. He knew that he was no match for her and she had been known to use her fighting skills if she didn't feel in the mood for sexual adventures.

Victoria's affair with the Nigerian businessman, who now lazily watched her scurry around the hotel bedroom gathering up clothes discarded and clothes to be newly worn, was intense but intermittent. It was not often that their paths crossed, and even when they did, their meetings were rarely for more than a few hours. However, they were invariably passionate, if otherwise lacking in any deeper feelings. Victoria got a delicious buzz from the illicit nature of their trysting, although the liaison was by no means as secret as she supposed.

The vigour and the rapidity of her showering disposed of the old sweat and replaced it with new. As she poured and wound herself into the all-embracing lengths of a smart but heavy national dress, her lover watched her with his tongue as well as his eyes, and his salacious comments did nothing reduce the lather that she was in.

"Oh, do shut up!" she finally snapped at him, enjoying the banter but wishing that he would let up while she finished her high-speed toilette.

"You look wonderful."

He had finally obeyed her injunction to silence until her dressing was complete. His farewell comment was quietly spoken and genuine. She smiled her appreciation; such compliments did not often come her way.

She was gone within the space of a brief kiss and a wave of the hand. The hotel was not far from the High Commission, so she set off at as fast a shuffle pace as her constricting long skirt would allow. Fading into the circulating mass of guests at about the same time as Fid Okeke located his cousin, she in turn located Fid Okeke and the young woman whom she knew to be the object of her superior's interest, just about the same time as Mahomet Sullag flowed past them. She was secretly pleased to see the Alhaji; she was something of a closet admirer of his.

* * *

"You may not think his manners are too great, but he's a fervent believer in the old Nigeria and the need to defeat the Moslem Fundamentalists at all costs."

"What?" said Janine. 'God,' she thought, 'I've just found someone I can to relate to in all of this mob and I get the opening lines of an incomprehensible political lecture.'

"Never mind her," her cousin said, whispering rather familiarly into her ear, "that was just for anyone listening."

He gestured at the straggling entourage of hangers-on following the Minister around.

Janine shook her head in disbelief. "What is this?" she said.

Victoria Akinbode laughed. It was the sort of deep, gurgling laugh that so delighted Mark Shortley when Janine herself was amused and delighted by something.

"Nigerian politics," said Victoria, "what else? You've forgotten what a contentious bunch we are."

Janine grunted. She didn't like to say that she hadn't the least idea what the basic characteristics of Nigerians were, and she certainly hadn't forgotten something that she had never known. Apart, perhaps, from their tendency to treat women as lesser mortals, her country folk were still a mystery to her.

"The Moslem Fundamentalists have been causing no end of strife since before the 1990s. Some amongst the younger generation in the north have embraced their ideas, increasingly under the banner of Boko Haram, and there are real fears about whether it will be possible to release the movement's hold on these people. The traditionalists like Alhaji Sullag are determined to resist and defeat them."

It was Fid Okeke who gave the explanation, but Victoria who took up the story.

"But, of course, being Nigeria, it isn't as simple as that! What Sullag and the northern traditionalists really want is to preserve the status quo but with them in perpetual power. Inevitably that doesn't suit the south."

Victoria correctly supposed that Janine was aware of the perpetual political divide in Nigeria, and although she was, her knowledge was only recent due her studies of the encroachment of the Moslem Fundamentalists in general into black Africa for Mark Shortley and was coloured by that aspect rather than any north/south rivalries.

But Victoria didn't go on. Her eyes ranged over to two men in dismal European suits working their way towards them through the crush. Okeke followed the line of her glance.

'Who are these two then?' Janine wondered. 'Where do they fit into this Nigerian madhouse?'

It was the careful way that Victoria and her cousin switched off their previous conversation as the two came within earshot that told Janine that they were not necessarily the good guys. Victoria was right; nothing was simple about Nigerian politics.

"So, what have you been doing since you left your firm of accountants?" asked Victoria of Janine.

Janine, now past worrying about what they knew and how

they came to know it, gave a simple and uninformative answer, to which Victoria added an equally inane response.

"OK."

Neither Victoria Akinbode nor Fid Okeke offered any explanation for the little pantomime, nor for who the two men were. The danger, however, had obviously passed.

To Janine's relief, the conversation did not return to Nigeria's tortuous politics but stalled momentarily for want of another topic.

"Actually..." Janine said, shifting on her feet and gesturing towards the door.

"Excuse us," said Victoria to Okeke, having read the message.

She took Janine's arm and began to steer them out of the function room. As they walked away, they were distinguishable only by their dresses. Janine had already observed that the cut of Victoria's long dress was sharper and more recognisably Western than that of others on show, yet it retained the essential features of the national costume. It reached the floor, Janine's didn't. In every other respect – height, bodily proportions, hairstyles, even walk – they were as twins.

* * *

"The one on the right."

An attentive Chinese waiter whispered to a chef colleague as he restocked his tray of canapés. These small savoury and spiced offerings, called 'small-chop' in the old colonial days, were an essential accompaniment to drinking at all Nigerian functions. The chef nodded and readied his camera. As a consequence, he failed to notice that following the sort of entanglements that occur when so many people are forced together in such confined surroundings, the two women had switched sides. The photographs carefully taken through the one-sided mirror panel in the door to the kitchens, and equally carefully sent on to the headquarters of the Wong organisation, were, as a result, of the wrong woman.

* * *

In the ladies' room, Janine noticed, in a routine reminiscent of Mark's Shortley's behaviour on entering a strange place, that Victoria quickly checked for other occupants. There were none. She asked her new friend about the two men for whom she had put their earlier conversation so obviously on hold. Victoria was evasive.

"For heaven's sake, Victoria, you must know who I am, who I work for... his business... Otherwise how the hell else did I get here? You and my supposed cousin are no more genuine pen-pushing civil servants than I'm a high-class tart! What's going on? Who were those two men in their dreary little suits?"

The challenge put Victoria in a quandary. Janine was right; she actually worked for the Nigerian Security Service.

'I'm certainly not authorised to tell her what I really do,' she thought. 'No more is Fid Okeke, I guess, genuine cousin though he really is. Nor can I tell her that Falinde and Oje are security service as well, even if they are working illicitly for the southern Nigerian businessmen's group opposing the Fundamentalists.

'As for telling her that the northern Fundamentalists have recruited an operative from the remnants of one of the most feared and ruthless old Middle East terrorist groups to help them in their fight, which is why we're in London, she'd hardly believe me.'

Centred in Lebanon, the group, in its heyday in the last century, had been well known in Europe, and the operative had been specifically tasked with eliminating key Nigerian security agents and politicians. Victoria was aware that the remnants of the group itself had suffered in a battle with security forces in

Beirut the previous year, but the operative was still thought to be a very dangerous and elusive opponent for them.

"Janine, I really am a civil servant. You have to believe me; so is your cousin Fid Okeke."

Victoria had missed out Janine's key word, 'genuine'; Janine was quick to notice that.

"OK, I believe you."

She didn't, and she knew, as did Victoria, that Mark Shortley had the means of checking. That made Victoria's behaviour all the more odd.

* * *

Back in the function room, they rescued Okeke from the clutches of an enormously fat businessman.

"I'll leave you two to talk family talk," said Victoria when the three were alone.

She was anxious to get away and catch up on a little surveillance work.

Although the Reception had been going for two hours, the crowd showed little signs of thinning out, and Victoria supposed that it wouldn't whilst the food and drink kept coming. Confident, therefore, that the parties that she was interested in were unlikely to have left, she set to work.

And as Victoria went about her duties, Mahomet Sullag was focusing his attention on cultivating the northerners present to the cause of defeating the Fundamentalists and preserving the integrity of their country; at least, that was what he seemed to be doing.

"Let me remind you what happened in Iran many years ago and what was prevented from happening in Algeria, and in Egypt. The people of Nigeria do not want to survive in religious poverty, obedient only to the dictates of fanatics. We have been living by the Koran for centuries, and we have been living with our fellow Nigerians, if not in harmony, at least in a recognisable relationship, if not for centuries then certainly for decades. To abandon that, to try and force the non-believers to conversion, will be the end of our country. We will become a landlocked, impoverished mini-state no better than Chad with no future and only a past to make us regret what we had done to ourselves."

To Janine it seemed like a well-rehearsed speech. To Fid Okeke it was.

"I find it hard to agree with his desire to freeze everything in the past, especially as a woman, but the alternative, at least as practised in some of the other places around the world, seems much worse," Janine remarked as the speech came to an end.

"Janine," said her cousin, "it's a very complex situation. But if you listen hard to the Alhaji he can make the same speech sound good to southerners and to a bunch of fanatic radicals in a Kano mosque. Sometimes it's very hard to know what he's really saying, beyond what he thinks will please the audience of the moment."

* * *

Janine had had enough; she felt an urgent desire to be in Mark Shortley's arms.

"I think I've had my fill of Nigerian politics for one day. I'm sure they won't miss me if I leave."

"Of course not. I hope we'll meet again. I'm not often in London, but perhaps one day when you visit your sister."

Janine knew that his offer was genuine, but she seriously doubted that she would ever visit Nigeria; her and her sister were friendly but not close, and the incentives were otherwise not there. However, in her business nothing was ever too certain.

"My regards to Victoria."

"Of course. Her husband's around somewhere, pity you didn't get to meet him."

* * *

Janine's going was unnoticed, although she made no particular effort to make it so. However, Messrs Falinde and Oje, despite the close attention paid to them by Victoria Akinbode, did make special efforts and were eventually able to leave completely undetected. That left them free to undertake the meeting that they had arranged without interference. The middle-aged Chinese businessman whom they dined with was not good company, although they completed their deal readily enough.

Unaware of his private grief, the two Nigerians prolonged the meal until they were well gorged and thereby contrived to offend almost every sensibility that their host had. Neither of them had children, so they couldn't have comprehended his agony over the public slaying of his son and heir in the Albert Hall. Nor could they have comprehended the pain that was caused by his honouring his business commitment to them before retreating to share his suffering with his daughter and family.

FOUR

Mark Shortley's niece Julie arrived back at St Jerome's Hotel alone; the police would follow later, apparently. Finding Mark and Caroline in the lounge, she threw herself into her mother's arms and sobbed uncontrollably. The sophisticated undergraduate had given way to the frightened little girl as her distress overwhelmed her. Mark looked on impotently, feeling for Julie's anguish but powerless to assuage it. It was midnight, and the lounge was deserted; at least they were free to manage Julie's grief undisturbed.

"My poor darling," said Caroline, reverting to the role of all-consoling parent.

"Why, Mother, why?" Julie kept demanding, unable to comprehend this latest addition to her woes.

Caroline had no answers and made no attempt to provide any. She just gave her daughter shelter until she felt able to face up to what had happened. Drawing on almost-forgotten experience, she knew that only time would allow her daughter to recover.

It took Julie half an hour to regain her composure and be ready to move on. Then, disengaging herself from her mother's arms, she sat beside her and opposite her uncle and began to talk.

"Lawrence had this flat in Belgravia. At least, I always thought it was his flat. We were there once when his father arrived unexpectedly. He came with some people. Some black people, actually. We were obviously in the way. Lawrence was frantic. He just wanted to get out of the place. I was amazed. He seemed completely terrified of his father. Yet his father didn't seem unfriendly or to resent our being there.

"I didn't get much of a look around. The place is huge. The lounge and dining area were bigger than our whole ground floor! Loads of doors off the hall; I only went into Lawrence's bedroom and the bathroom."

Julie showed her first signs of renewed spark when she said this and realised what her mother might be thinking. Her grin was a little weak, but it was very much there.

"I only used the bathroom, Mother. He kept his computer in his bedroom, that's why I went in there."

"Yes, dear!"

"So why d'you suppose young Lawrence was frightened of his father?" Mark asked, both his natural and professional curiosity aroused.

He knew that the Chinese were patriarchal, but he sensed that there was something more than father/son growing pains.

"Goodness knows," said Julie.

She looked sad again and tears welled up, but she brushed them aside, both physically and mentally.

But her next comment said that somewhere in the back of her mind, she did know.

"Lawrence was a very weak person; maybe that was part of his charm. I guess his father knew that. His father didn't strike me as weak; anything but. Lawrence always wanted to be the centre of attraction... to be liked. He went to all of the parties and provided the booze as often as not, but he never drank himself. He was always bumming a night at my flat... despite the comforts of his own flat he never seemed to want to go home."

Julie's thoughts wandered off again and she stopped talking. Neither Mark nor his sister made any effort to bring her back to the conversation. Again, it was the passage of time that allowed Julie to regroup and resume her narrative.

"We only went there to stock up with food. He did that sometimes. It wasn't for him. He must have had messages from his father; he was expected to get stuff in. Mainly expensive Chinese prepacked meals."

A slight irritation crept into Julie's voice, as if this housekeeping duty should have told her the truth about whose flat it was.

"We got the timing wrong, I suppose, or his father arrived early – I don't know. All I know is Lawrence didn't want to be there once they'd arrived. He introduced me, or at least he tossed my name at his father as he pushed me out of the door."

She grinned wanly at the memory of the incident, all the deeper thoughts about Lawrence's relationship with his father forgotten again.

"Know anything about his father? What he does?" asked Mark, his professional brain for the moment overriding his family instincts.

'There was something about an incident in the Middle-East last year,' he thought. 'An arms dealer was briefly taken hostage by the "New Truth" terrorist group. He was Chinese. Wasn't there some sort of heavy-handed intervention and messy release that cost the lives of several terrorists?'

"Jason Wong, I think he's called. He had his name in the papers once, something to do with Lebanon, and Lawrence was really worried… although I thought he was more worried for himself than for his father."

Julie had another bout of sadness as she said this. Clearly her late boyfriend's weakness of character had actually been a cause of unhappiness for her.

Mark recognised the name; it made the link in his mind to

the Lebanese incident, Julie's reference closing the loop. He was not happy with the recognition.

'She could do without being mixed up with this lot,' he thought to himself.

Jason Wong was a secretive but enormously powerful international businessman whose activities were generally regarded as dubious, if not outright criminal, in most countries of the world. Mark didn't share his knowledge. He needed to double-check, and Julie had grief enough.

"I think Lawrence dreaded finishing college. He never talked about the family business, but I suppose the way these things happen he was clearly expecting to have to join it. But he hated…"

She went off into a long description of her dead lover's fears for the future as she understood them. Caroline listened, still acknowledging the continuing need for Julie to talk everything out. Much of the tale seemed to be a comparison of Lawrence with his much more powerful sister. Mark, equally aware of the therapeutic effect of such talking, listened but only picked out the salient points about the business relationships. Julie knew nothing of the real activities of the Wong senior, but a clear picture of his daughter definitely emerged.

"Pearl was everything that Lawrence wasn't. Well, so he seemed to think. And he reckoned his father was beginning to think so too. He was brighter than any of them, could have done pretty much anything he wanted. But he just wanted to be liked.

"His sister always knew her mind, according to him, always got her way, and not just because she was the eldest. She was always around her father, as they had no mother. He wasn't afraid of his sister; they seemed to get on… but I don't think I'd have trusted her. She's welcome to the business, as far as I'm concerned; Lawrence wouldn't have made a businessman in a million years."

Mark lost track of the conversation as Julie continued pouring out her angst by repeating what she had already said and pursued his own thoughts about Jason Wong.

'I guess the surveillance system will be picking up stuff on him,' he surmised. 'Since Janine upgraded it, the scanning programme must trawl just about the whole world's media and heaven knows what else. If Wong's on our list... I'm sure he must be, man like him... we'll know about him.'

The skills of his secretary, and now the much more sophisticated knowledge of Janine, had allowed Mark to gain largely unrestrained access to whatever routine intelligence that he wanted. The system searched for data on a variety of people, activities and political situations through the Internet and all of the major international computer communications systems, as well as more specifically searching 'noticeboards': blogs, tweets and other messaging facilities. And they were not above the occasional illegal access when the need arose. Not that the line between legal and illegal was necessarily all that clear at times.

'Janine'll have all the ins and outs on Jason Wong's affairs within minutes if I want them.'

And Mark decided that he did want them.

When it came to talking to Janine, his justification wasn't very coherent, but in their business anything that was obviously coherent was just as likely to be suspect.

Jason Wong was very much on their list and the data Mark was interested in was already accumulating. Even as Janine later shared this information, one of their sources was recording that Wong senior had made an online purchase of an airline ticket two days previously. The transaction was noted in the appropriate file within their database. The information was deposited next to the record of the purchase of tickets to Moscow on several previous occasions. The arms deal they were transacting, however, was hidden from Mark's surveillance.

FIVE

"I wonder if Russia will ever convert itself into a real twenty-first century country?" Jason Wong remarked to his daughter, his immaculate middle-England English belying his distinctive Chinese features.

In 2024, it seemed to him that nothing had changed from the early days of the Putin regime and that the upheavals of the mid/late 2010s had achieved very little.

Wong was recounting his latest arms deal to Pearl in the solid luxury of his own sitting room. Telling the tale took his mind off the tragedy of Lawrence's death.

"There's no evidence of the decay and the general rundown state of things from the old Soviet era, but you really have to wonder just how deep the modernity goes. Everything's there – the institutions, the regulatory processes, the basic commercial legal system – yet it still seems to work in the old clunking way that it did forty years ago. Money still talks, as it does everywhere; graft is no longer endemic; justice is definitely less arbitrary; their international status is no longer largely illusionary; but world-class efficiency – forget it."

Pearl said nothing.

"When I was a very young man, the Soviets were going to

rule the world! Now? Now there are so many rules to ensure that they don't break any rules they forget what it was they were applying the rules to."

But Jason Wong's chuckle didn't suggest that his perception of the shortcomings evident during his recent trip unduly bothered him in the completion of his deal. In fact, the official rules had very little to do with his transaction; he just found the present state of things in Russia amusing.

"It's all part of the game, I guess," he said.

He returned to his tale.

"They knew perfectly well what time we'd arranged to meet them. Noon; whenever we've met in the past it had always been at noon, but not this time. And why couldn't we meet at the usual hotel?"

"Do you suppose they were worried about the authorities?" Pearl asked.

"I doubt it! These days they don't pay off the authorities; they simply work round them."

Pearl was unclear what that meant, but her father was now in full flow.

"They'd given us the key to a flat, in a half-finished tower block on the outskirts of the Moscow. We'd no choice but to take a taxi. So we were stranded in this unheated apartment. It was obviously going to be a pretty fancy place when it was finished, but it had yet to be equipped with any of the normal amenities of a habitable dwelling. The living area boasted two ancient armchairs, clearly used by the builders for their tea breaks. Poor old Chang started to sit in one. It all but collapsed."

"So how cold d'you reckon it was?" Pearl wanted to know somewhat irrelevantly.

"It was about ten below, I guess. We tried to stamp our feet, but this caused a dust storm and the sound rattled around the empty rooms.

"One fifteen, and they finally showed up. There were three

of them. No apology, nothing – just checked who we were and got down to business. It was really only the woman; the others were bodyguards, the driver, whatever."

Pearl was interested in the woman.

"She was rather striking in a forgettable sort of way. She was largely hidden under an oversized military fur hat and a fur coat that would have been expensive wherever she'd bought it but which enshrouded her rather than reflected any appearance of femininity. Her English was a bit basic, but she didn't need much language to tell us we were off on a trip.

"So, back down the ten flights of stairs and into this brand-new state-of-the-art stretch Mercedes. What a contrast! Chang and I decided to talk in Mandarin Chinese since we didn't really know how much English she understood; the two bodyguards never opened their mouths."

"Weird."

"Weird, and something more, I can tell you, Pearl. At least the car was warm inside.

"The journey out of Moscow wasn't so bad as long as the road remained in a reasonable condition, which it mostly did. But after an hour we turned off somewhere onto what wasn't much more than a farm track. The woman kept saying we'd be there soon. Finally we fetched up outside this large, lit-up wooden dacha."

"I hope the arms dealer spoke better English than your woman friend," said Pearl.

"Oh yes. There was nothing wrong with his English, nor his booze! Great bear of a man, almost a caricature Russian. About the only one of them I've ever met who seemed to be genuinely welcoming. He was wearing this loose high-necked shirt, hideous design, and a pair of very English twill trousers. The room was like an oven. Everything about him exuded money and luxury.

"The woman handed out these huge measures of vodka.

Name of Natalia, apparently, but we never did find out what her role was. The old chap just introduced himself as Boris. We had no idea whether that was his actual name. The woman referred to him as General."

"Was he?"

"Oh yes. Even now in Russia these things are easy to check out if you put your money in the right place. He was the one-time head of their equivalent of the Ordnance Corps. God knows how old he is – probably in his eighties. He got into the arms trade years ago selling old Soviet weaponry without much regard to the niceties of ownership or the likely use of the weapons. In the immediate post-Soviet era anything seems to have been possible if you kept your nerve. Things have certainly changed, but they don't seem to have cramped his style any – made it easier, in fact; there's still an impenetrable bureaucracy and still a huge reservoir of unaccounted military hardware from amazing sources. He can even access modern Russian weaponry. His business is flourishing as never before."

"Nice guy," remarked Pearl.

"He wasn't a man for idle chatter, fortunately. Just downed his vodka and called in this guy in a sort of military uniform and presented Chang with an obvious AK47. He'd soon worked out who Chang was."

"Didn't suppose you'd be there without your own expert, surely?" his daughter said.

"No, my dear, he knew what he was up to OK."

"And?"

"Suddenly it was a total farce. You could see old Chang was disgusted. Told me the gun was ancient; maybe dangerous to fire. The old bastard, he was stringing us along. So I told him he was wasting my time; I wasn't there to buy second-hand junk."

"Bet he didn't like that!"

"He just laughed. He gave out this great braying laugh. Then this Natalia appeared with a second rifle, as new, still in its waxed paper wrapping. She just handed it to Chang. And the old boy simply said he hadn't asked us there to sell to amateurs! Must say he went up in my estimation. Bit theatrical, but the arms trade isn't big on trust. We still had to earn his trust, even us. And if we didn't know our business, how could he trust us?"

"So you didn't mind. I'd have been furious."

"Ah, but then I'm a bit longer in the tooth than you, my dear. Anyway, whilst Chang was doing his thing, out came more vodka. But I could see Chang was impressed. He said we should go for the deal if this was what was on offer."

"So what was so special?"

"Patience, girl. We still had to know if he could supply the quantity we needed and the ammunition."

"And they could, obviously."

"Oh yes. The old boy said he could deliver us up to five thousand, but it would have to be over a period. It was a big order; there might be transport difficulties. Five thousand rifles are a lot of weapons, that sort of thing; several shipments, especially with ammunition. He knew how many tons it would be, and Chang agreed the figure."

"That was it?"

"Well, he showed us a few boxes of them in his cellar. It seems that they were latest US issue."

"What! Not AK47s?"

"No. We'd heard about them, but we would hardly have expected them to come onto the market for a few years yet. But old Chang said the US had made vastly more than they needed since they'd run down their forces. However, the President also needed to keep the armaments workers sweet; it's an election year. They've replaced several of their overseas stockpiles, especially in the Middle East, and, my dear, you'll love this. The General was getting them stolen to order from these stockpiles, by... Moslem Fundamentalists! Well, some sort of rump-turned-criminal gang of Fundamentalists."

"He told you that?"

"Well, yes. He needs us to trust him too. But he won't need to 'liberate' any more, especially for us, it seems. He says he's got all we need in Russia already."

"And that really was it?"

"Oh yes. Wanted us to empty a bottle of vintage Scotch, but I wasn't having that. I told him I had to get back for my son's graduation on Saturday."

"Dad!"

The excuse seemed rather sour to Pearl now.

SIX

"Mark, any way we can find out when these wretched detectives will arrive? Julie's about done in; she ought to be in bed."

Caroline's wish was instantly fulfilled. She had hardly finished speaking when two men were shown into the lounge by the night porter.

"Miss Mackenzie? Mr Shortley?"

The two men produced their warrant cards, checked who Caroline was and then accepted an invitation to sit down.

"Sorry this is so late. We can come back in the morning if…?"

The detective inspector addressed his remarks to Caroline. The offer was an obvious courtesy, but Caroline had the distinct feeling that he himself would not have preferred it.

"No, no," Julie said before her mother could respond. "Let's get it over with. It'll be worse in the morning."

"Thank you. Miss Mackenzie, could you tell us what your relationship with the dead man was?"

The inspector started the questioning; the sergeant took notes.

"We were friends."

"Were you... er... intimate friends?"

Julie looked at her mother, took a mental deep breath and said, "If you mean was I sleeping with him, yes I was!"

The questioning went from there. What was Lawrence Wong's background; who were his friends? It got irritable on occasions when the information sought didn't seem relevant. Mark smoothed over several small spats. At the end of half an hour it was obvious that Julie could actually tell them nothing of any significance about Lawrence's life outside of college.

"Miss Mackenzie, d'you know who owned the flat the deceased occupied?"

"His father, I presume."

"And did you ever go there when his father was there?"

"He arrived once when we were just leaving."

"Did you know anything at all about the father?" said the inspector.

"Nothing. Lawrence and his father didn't get on particularly well. Lawrence never talked about him."

The inspector was not surprised; Jason Wong was known to be a very secretive and private man.

"Thank you, Miss Mackenzie."

"Anything you can tell us about what happened at the flat?" asked Mark once it was clear that the two policemen had nothing more to ask Julie.

Mark wasn't very hopeful, but the inspector seemed to know who he was and accepted that any information would be secure with him.

"The occupant of the flat below had returned during the evening and was surprised to find his own flat door open and his wife gone," the inspector said. "He thought she was probably visiting neighbours, so he went upstairs to find her. The door of the Wong's flat was also open. The place was in total chaos... it had been ransacked.

"The man thought he'd better not use the Wong's phone to

call us and was about to leave when he heard noises from the hall cupboard and found his missing wife. She was a bit battered but not seriously harmed and more excited than frightened. It seems she'd seen the door to the Wong's flat partly open and had simply gone in to investigate.

"Bit of a busybody," the inspector interpolated into his description, "lucky not to have been seriously hurt.

"We contacted the Wong's family home. Mr Wong and his daughter have agreed to come and check the flat in the morning. Naturally they're very distressed about the dead son and we didn't want to burden them unnecessarily. It seems that the old man didn't find out about the death until quite late as he had only just come back from Moscow, but he went to a business dinner even so. We only got hold of him just before midnight. That's why we were so late."

'Doesn't know much about the Chinese psyche,' thought Mark, picking up the inspector's bemusement at Jason Wong's seeming insensitivity.

"Amongst papers we found in what was presumably Mr Wong senior's study, was a dossier on yourself, Mr Shortley. Have you any idea why he would be interested in you?"

"You obviously know I'm in the security business," Mark said. "Perhaps Wong's interest had something to do with that?"

'I wonder who else he had dossiers on?' Mark asked himself. A man like Jason Wong he knew would be very interested in him, if, as was the case, he'd found that his son's girlfriend had such an uncle. 'Perhaps he just makes a habit of looking into the backgrounds of Lawrence's serious girlfriends. Wonder what he thought of Julie, apart from her not being a good Chinese girl of impeccable antecedents.'

The policemen left. Julie immediately retreated to her room, leaving Mark and her mother still sitting in the hotel lounge.

"Wonderful graduation," said Caroline with a touch of bitterness in her voice.

"I know."

It was a lame response, but Mark still hadn't got his feelings ordered over the events of the day. The Wongs were clearly not the sort of people that he would want his niece to mix with, and, sad as the reason was, Mark was relieved that it would put an end to the relationship. But the dossier worried him, not because of what it might say, more that his business activities had had an impact on his family. For all the murky world that he so often got himself involved in, posing any sort of threat to his relatives was not a part of the plan.

'Fortunately Caroline didn't pick up on the family background of Julie's late young man,' he told himself, putting thoughts of the day out of his head. "Bed, my girl, it's two o'clock in the morning!"

"There's that Arab woman again!" said Caroline in the hotel foyer.

"Where?" asked Mark, who had seen nothing.

Caroline gestured at the lift, its indicator signifying that it was heading for the top floor. Mark shrugged. He didn't need any more mysteries.

SEVEN

Mark met up with Caroline and Julie at breakfast. A good night's sleep, albeit a rather brief one, had refreshed them all. Mother and daughter were to head for the West Country on the ten o'clock train. Julie, for once, was only too happy to get away from London and its immediate memories. Mark, as the ill-fated episode with his relatives approached its end, found himself almost overcome by a desire to see Janine and to return to the more normal tenor of his life. Used as he was to the unforeseen and uncertainty, when it touched him so closely he had been surprised by how much he had been disturbed.

But before they made it to the station, they had another irritating encounter with the overweight Arab gentleman of the previous day. On this occasion he powered his way out of the lift, forcing the three of them to scatter. There was no sign of the Arab woman, or, as Mark supposed her to be, her blonde-haired incarnation.

"Ignorant bastard!"

It was a comment rather than a show of irritation. Upbringing, as well as years of duty in the SAS, had taught Mark to control his feelings. Anger for him was a rare thing.

Although he knew that Arab men had different rules of

behaviour towards women from people like him, Mark didn't see that as an excuse. When in Rome... seemed to him to a perfectly adequate dictum for the situation.

The man appeared to be alone; Mark accosted him.

"Excuse me!"

The Arab ignored him until Mark barred his way to the hotel door.

"That's twice you've forced us out of your way and twice you haven't thought to apologise. That may be OK where you come from; but it isn't here."

"You're wasting your breath. He doesn't understand English. He's too stupid anyway."

To Mark's surprise, the Arab's companion, this time in the form of the blonde young woman, materialised beside him.

The man stood between them, a look of confusion on his bloated face. The woman translated what Mark had said to him and then added a couple of venomous sentences of her own. His confusion turned briefly to defiance. A killer look from the woman astonished Mark, and he sullenly mumbled something that sounded to Mark like, "I'm sorry."

Mark nodded his acknowledgement.

"Thanks," he said to the girl.

* * *

In the back of the taxi that was waiting for them, the woman had more to say.

"You stupid, brainless bastard, that's the last time you do that to me!"

Lehia Said was furious. The harsh Arabic and the cold way that she delivered her rebuke cowed the man. The great hulking Saudi was supposed to be her cover, but his behaviour was making her stand out in lights everywhere they went.

The taxi dropped the woman at Armards department

store in Knightsbridge and at her instruction took the Arab on to an address in Kensington. It was only when the taxi had to pull up short to avoid another motorist that the driver, glancing in his mirror, noticed that his remaining passenger had disappeared from view. Stopping hurriedly, he found the Arab man slumped on the floor. Seeing that he was obviously dead, although from what cause wasn't immediately apparent, he alerted the emergency services. When the police investigated, they discovered that he had been neatly stabbed through the heart from under his left arm. The inspector in charge of the investigation, who as it happened had spent some time working with the French Police in Lyons, recognised the style at once.

"'New Truth'," he said, "it's their trademark, certainly it was 'New Truth'... Lebanese."

The information caused some consternation, especially as the taxi driver proved unable to given even the briefest description of the woman beyond her having 'lovely clear blue eyes'.

* * *

Mark would have been appalled by the outcome of his remonstration with the Arab. Assassination was certainly not the cure for bad manners that he would have advocated. He would also have been chilled by the ruthlessness of the young woman whom he had so briefly encountered. But as he accompanied his sister and niece to Waterloo Station, he only retained an impression of her as somebody physically attractive, of positive and decisive behaviour, and as a consequence perhaps worthy of better acquaintance.

Having seen his relatives onto their train, Mark headed back to his flat in Herbert Crescent and to a reunion with his partner. As the prospect came closer, he realised again just how much he had missed her straightforward and upfront attitude to life in contrast to the mire of poor Julie's feelings and shattered hopes. And he realised that when it came down to it, he hadn't been a whole lot of use to his sister and niece.

'Not quite the day we'd expected,' he told himself ruefully.

EIGHT

The detective inspector of the last evening shepherded Jason Wong and his daughter into the family flat. They entered almost as cautiously as the trio had the previous day.

Of that party, the two men were itinerant Romanian thugs working for their fare home. They gained access within seconds. One of Jason Wong's many complaints against his son had been his casualness and particularly his tendency to leave the flat's alarm system unarmed. Working quickly with a piece of electronic gadgetry, they scanned the flat for sound- and movement-activated devices, microphones or hidden cameras before entering. There was nothing other than the scanners for the alarm system. Checking the fire exit and finding it connected to a separate building alarm, they left the front door ajar. It was a precaution that the woman with them was not happy about.

"Milos, you start here. Jorge, the bedrooms. You know what we're looking for."

Like everything about her, the woman's orders were clear and precise. But the look of distaste on her face was hardly disguised. Not bothering even to ask the two men who they were and giving them names of her own, all she wanted was to be in and out of the flat. This sort of petty activity was not what she thought she was being paid for.

Almost like twins, the two Romanians moved about quietly and quickly. With nothing to do herself, she set out to explore the flat. Her interest in the kitchen, her first port of call, was minimal. A less domesticated woman would have been hard to imagine.

'Shouldn't take them long,' she told herself, suspecting that the reward wasn't going to be worth the effort.

She moved out of the kitchen, her heels leaving the faint indentations in the cushion-backed plastic tiles that attracted the attention of the scene of crime officers, and which, despite the clear evidence of two men, suggested that there must have been a third person, and that a woman. In the bathroom she paused to study herself in a gilded mirror. Smoothing her long blonde hair, she wrinkled her nose at her high cheekbones, a legacy of her Lebanese father as much as the china blue eyes were of her Swedish mother. The moment of vanity passed; she looked in contempt at the luxury around her.

"Greedy, selfish bastard," she muttered, all her hate for Jason Wong coming to the surface.

An article in the main English language Beirut newspaper last year had summed up the cause of her hate.

"The capture and then violent release of a Chinese arms dealer was an episode in the annals of the 'New Truth' terror group that the leaders of that group have no intention of forgetting. There were too many dead for that. Past history suggests that they will surely exact revenge.

"Amongst the survivors of the fierce gun battle in the Beirut suburb, Lehia Said was the most likely to be the instrument of this revenge. Although not a fanatical Moslem, she is a fanatical terrorist, and by the unholy standards of that calling, a very successful one. Powerful and decisive, she is anything but a traditional Arab woman."

Lehia had been vaguely flattered by the description, even if the ageing and largely ineffective leaders of the group hadn't been. Dealing with a woman who denied all the stereotypes of a religiously fanatical terrorist, whilst still being one, and who had announced her intentions of revenge when other commissions were in play wasn't to prove easy for the old men.

'She'd never make a male chauvinist Arab a good wife!' was Mark Shortley's conclusion when he saw her again on the day of his sister's departure.

The newspaper went on. "Her introduction to the world of organised terrorism was quick and brutal. A piece of unthinking savagery during one of Lebanon's many upheavals instantly changed her life. The power that she now displays in her present life satisfies her cravings for revenge against the world that she developed when her mother was killed in front of her and when she was subsequently raped by the American mercenary responsible. He was her first victim. At fifteen she was a killer."

A muffled cry attracted Lehia's attention. It came from the lounge.

"No!" she cried quietly but urgently.

As she bounded into the room she found Milos holding a middle-aged woman down on the carpet, back towards her, with his right hand raised to chop down on the side of her neck. Such a blow would surely have killed her. Jorge was beside his compatriot, ready to act in support.

The blow hung in the air. The woman subsided as though she had fainted.

In a pantomime of gestures to avoid her speaking again, Lehia instructed the two men to tie the woman up and find somewhere to hide her. Using a selection of the Wong menfolk's ties and sticking plaster from the medicine cabinet, they accomplished the task before the woman regained consciousness. Safely deposited in the hall wardrobe, the two

Romanians returned to the lounge, leaving the poor woman to recover as best she could.

"We're not here to kill, we're here for information! Finish the job; we're out of here in five minutes," the woman whispered.

The two men returned to their task, indifferent to Lehia's decision to spare the intruder.

As the detective inspector was later to remark to the Wongs, father and daughter, "As you probably know, Mrs Carwood seems to be the local busybody. And she finds plenty enough gossip to keep her happy, apparently."

He didn't say that he had discovered that, as her nearest neighbours, it was they who were her greatest source of conversational ammunition. Much of it was inconsequential, other of it, as events later revealed, would have been of great value to the various parties who were increasingly directing their attention to the activities of the Wong clan, and particularly its eldest member.

"You know," she would say to her husband or her other near neighbours, "that boy rarely sleeps in the flat…"

Her listeners never encouraged her, but she managed very well without their stimulation.

"I saw the two black men again today, and the boy, and a woman." Neither Lawrence nor Julie on that occasion had been aware that they were being spied upon. "He definitely has a lot of dealings with black people, and Russians."

As the victim herself told the inspector, "My husband worked in Russia for some years, and I speak the language fluently. Towards the end of last year, he was visited by some Russian soldiers."

In the course of her conversational elaborations, she had correctly characterised Jason Wong as an arms dealer buying weapons from the Russians. Unfortunately, as she had just found out, such people attracted a class of acquaintance that she was entirely unfamiliar with. So on the day in question with a lack of fear bred of ignorance, she had entered the flat above her own when she found the door open and saw a swarthy gentleman systematically rummaging through Mr Wong's desk.

Instinctively sensing her, the Romanian had turned and quickly advanced on her, emitting a low whistle as he did so. It was too late to escape. And it would have been too late entirely if Lehia hadn't heard the slight noise of her cry as Milos threw her to the floor.

Having saved Mrs Carwood from imminent destruction, Lehia waited impatiently for her associates to gather together the papers that they thought might be of interest. There was not much.

"Nothing about arms deals," she said on quick inspection.

But Lehia wasn't surprised by her lack of success. The flat was something of a long shot because she knew she had no chance of breaking into the Wongs' offices or home. She hurriedly thumbed through the small pile of dossiers that they had found. The only thing that attracted her attention was the details of a security firm and its owner. She was unaware that she had already met the security adviser in question.

They left the flat, leaving the door still ajar. None of them were concerned about their unexpected visitor. The old lady would soon be missed.

She was. Her returning husband, showing rather more caution than his wife, found the upstairs flat door open, then his spouse. To his surprise and relief, she was unhurt, just uncomfortable. It was an escapade that added to the artificial glamour that she had generated around the Wongs, and she revelled in it. But she also gave surprisingly accurate descriptions of the two men who had assaulted her.

* * *

Milos and Jorge were well out of the way by the time that the police were able to set a trace on them. Lehia Said took them to Heathrow and saw them onto the late-night Paris shuttle. They were aboard a flight to Sofia within an hour of arriving in France and had completely disappeared by the time the rather cumbersome European Federation processes had wound themselves up to seeking the aid of the Bulgarian and Romanian police.

Lehia, after collecting a holdall from a Terminal Five left luggage locker and secreting herself in the ladies' toilet for some while, returned to London. An idle young Australian, with time to spare in the silent hours, waited with increasing impatience and decreasing enthusiasm for her to emerge and be subjected to his overinflated chat-up routine. The only woman remotely near her in age to leave the toilet, however, was swathed in an all-embracing black burka and whose blue eyes were cast down and invisible to him. His interest in this apparition was negligible.

* * *

"Nothing stolen; no damage?" asked the inspector when Jason Wong and his daughter had completed their check of the apartment. "Have you any idea what they might have been after?"

Jason Wong shook his head. He had ideas, but he had no intention of sharing them with the police. Special Branch, he was sure, knew all about his activities – no point in feeding their curiosity. The police certainly did go through the catalogue of his perceived misdemeanours as they knew of them, but with so much to choose from they had a hard time fixing on any one activity that could account for the action against Mr Wong. Revenge wasn't something that immediately occurred to them.

"When you get to being as successful and wealthy as my father is," interposed Pearl Wong, "you attract all sorts of people who are jealous of your achievements."

'Hardly a justification for the murder of his son,' thought the inspector. 'A burglary, maybe. Still, I'm clearly not going to get much more here.'

"And Mr Shortley?" he said out loud, holding up the pages of the dossier.

"I was just checking up on one of my son's girlfriends. With an uncle like that, wouldn't you want to know more?"

Again Jason Wong saw no point in trying to deny his interest in Mark Shortley.

Lawrence was seeing rather more of Julie Mackenzie than he had of any other young woman, and although Jason thought her quite suitable, he saw that as all the more reason to know something about her background. He stumbled on Mark Shortley, the uncle, by chance, and being who he was, was naturally suspicious. His first thought, although not a very powerful one, was that she was a plant.

"Thank you, sir, madam, we'll be in touch if we turn anything up."

Back in his office, the inspector drew a line under the incident, although not under the affairs of Mr Jason Wong, and then tried to snatch something of the remainder of Sunday with his family.

NINE

Mark Shortley lived above the shop. He had acquired the lease on the premises several years previously when an infill building was being constructed in Herbert Crescent. It was narrow but deep and had four floors. The bottom two floors were offices for himself, Janine, the secretary and three other people. The top two floors were a spacious two-bedroomed flat. The success of Mark's business was putting pressure on the office space, but the living accommodation was more than adequate for the two of them.

"Mark?" A sleepy Janine struggled out of the duvet and sat up; the infectious grin that Mark so loved illuminated her whole face. It was nearly eleven o'clock. "How long have you been standing there?"

"Oh, not long, I just got back. They wanted to get away early and give Julie a chance to recover."

"What? What's wrong with Julie, what happened?"

Janine was alerted by the half-sad, half-anxious tone in Mark's voice.

"I've got a lot to tell you! Are you going to get up...?"

He left the question hanging in the air. He'd taken his jacket off and was unbuttoning his shirt, meaning to change into something more casual than the business suit that he had worn to the graduation. As he loosened his trousers, Janine lunged out of the bed and grabbed him. They tumbled together back onto the bed and then rolled off onto the floor with a loud thud. Janine giggled and gave little squeaks, seeking to kiss him on any available piece of body surface as she slowly and deliberately reduced Mark to the same level of nakedness as herself. Then, as she intertwined her legs with his, she let out gentle little moans as he moved his hands about her body, caressing her and savouring the silkiness of her flesh under his fingers.

It was the sort of boisterous lovemaking that they loved. Violated and physically abused in childhood during the military uprising that killed her parents, Janine had taken a long time to be able to accept so much as a touch from Mark. But with time, gentleness and the growing attachment that she felt for him, she had eventually overcome her fears and now enjoyed the contact, the sex and the intimacy as much as Mark did. Whether the memories of rape and death would ever be eliminated from her mind she doubted; she at least was able to deal with the pain.

"Missed you," Mark said as they subsided into a companionable stillness.

And he had done, even after so short a separation. Having no great love of his own company, Janine had become a friend, colleague, business partner, sounding board, lover and playmate, and a certain dependence on her was seeping into the relationship. That was not to say, when the need arose, that he wasn't capable of a very independent existence and capable of appreciating the charms of other women.

It was another hour before they emerged again from the duvet, or at least Mark did. He was shaved and showered and had breakfast-cum-lunch well underway before Janine finally appeared in the kitchen wearing only a pair of brightly coloured enamelled earrings.

"Practising for our holiday," she said with her deep laugh.

In the raw light of the kitchen, her dark skin sparkled. Mark had always been surprised by how much more glossy her body was than his.

"I suppose you're all packed and ready," he said, knowing how organised she was.

She didn't answer; she just set the table in the quick ordered and disordered way that a man might have done and sat down in her place. Mark was used to her tendency to eat naked and ignored her, trying to concentrate on the pan of bacon and eggs that he was preparing. It wasn't easy, as he knew that she was posing behind his back in the expectation that he would turn around and catch her.

"Here you go, last unhealthy eating for two weeks. It'll be fish and fruit from now on."

His efforts to avoid any recognition of her games caused her endless amusement.

"Missed you yesterday," she said.

"I'm sure you did. Especially whilst you were cavorting with all those handsome young diplomats!"

Janine laughed. Mark often made such light-hearted remarks to her, but occasionally she had sensed an edge to them. In this case it was as if he resented her having a good time. Mark himself was half aware that his own frustration at the way his family day had gone had crept into his response, but the words were out before the awareness had crystallised.

Janine reacted to the words, not the sentiment.

"Actually I met a cousin of mine. We nattered on for ages. There's a hell of a lot going on in Nigeria, more than we've discovered so far – maybe there's business there for us."

As she turned the conversation with rather more words than was her want, she also got up and collected the T-shirt that she had previously tossed onto a chair in the lounge. They both recognised the sudden cooling of the atmosphere but made determined efforts to ignore it rather than reinforce it;

nonetheless, the act of pulling on the T-shirt somehow did just that.

"Was that a surprise?" asked Mark. "I presume that you must have known that you had cousins, most of us do!"

Since it was his ill-considered remark that had provoked the faint chill, Mark felt that it was up to him to try and lighten things again. Only having lived in Nigeria briefly, Janine purported not to know any of her relatives there.

"This one's in the Nigerian Security Service, would you believe," she said in the same relaxed tone that Mark had adopted.

Over coffee she talked him through all that had happened.

"I guess there's nothing new, except the scale of things? Did they think that the Fundamentalists had gained serious support in the north?"

Janine nodded. "It seems they have. Everybody's agreed that they have to be defeated, the old-fashioned northern traditionalists and the southerners; it's just they have different agendas for doing it. The poor old security services are caught in the middle."

"We're going to have to give your research a bit more priority when we get back, wouldn't you say?"

"I reckon."

"What with this and Jason Wong…"

Mark knew that she wouldn't know what he was talking about. He was simply using the comment to move the conversation on to what he had to tell her.

Over more coffee he talked her through what had happened to him.

"Oh, Mark, I'm so sorry. I've been prattling on and you've had all this on your mind. Poor Julie, will she be alright?"

The warmth had crept back into the relationship with Janine's concern for Mark and his hurt over his niece's distress.

"I guess so in time; these kids are pretty tough."

Mark certainly hoped that Julie was tough. She had much of her mother's resilience and something of his ability to focus on the more fundamental things in any situation. Her handling of the police questioning told him that.

Concentrating on Julie, Janine's next comment caught him off balance.

"So you think the blonde is the woman in the Arab robes then? Intriguing. I get a complicated political scenario thrown at me and you get a couple of genuine mysteries. Aren't you the lucky boy?"

'Trust her to pick up on the Arab woman,' thought Mark.

He didn't say anything. He had no wish to cool the atmosphere again.

Janine had noticed his concentration on the blue-eyed young woman when he was talking. He had been interested in other women before, in passing, and usually like this, in a professional sense. It certainly alerted her to further references to this girl.

After their meal it was all activity. They were off on holiday taking an overnight flight and despite Mark's expectation, Janine was no more prepared than he was.

TEN

"Mark. Mark! Wake up, we're almost there!"

Mark could sleep through anything. The pilot's announcement of the imminent sight of Seychelles, which was exciting Janine, passed him by. He had heard the pre-landing gobbledygook so often that even on holiday and in a state of some anticipation, his subconscious failed to react.

'February's not ideal for a holiday in the Seychelles,' he thought when he was arranging the trip, 'but we need it. If we don't go now, we'll never go.'

His relationship with Janine was maturing in the business area but was suffering squalls on the personal side.

'Growing pains,' he told himself. 'It can't be red-hot all the time.'

Their relationship had certainly been intense when they had first met. Things had cooled, but in his heart Mark felt, or at least wanted to believe, that a deeper and more lasting union was being established that could withstand the 'slings and arrows' of their fortunes, outrageous or not. Not that his behaviour was always consistent with this belief.

'We don't own each other. We have to have space... both of us.' But the holiday was timely; it would give them the opportunity to recharge and to concentrate on each other, and they had both decided that they would make it as pleasant as they could. 'Well… that's the theory.'

As a consequence of his career as an SAS officer, Mark didn't tolerate negative thoughts any more than Janine did. The death of his wife in childbirth and the bitter enmity that that had generated in his sister-in-law were now part of a complex history that included the violence, entanglements and frustrated political ambitions that was the abortive Nationalist coup of 2022. Neither Mark nor Janine talked about that period of their lives, even if it had cemented their relationship. There were still too many ghosts.

With the brilliant vistas of an early-morning Seychelles unfolding as the aircraft landed, Mark's return to consciousness was as instant as it always was, if for once not as energetic.

"Mark!"

Janine had always been amazed at her partner's ability to sleep anywhere, even in airline seats. At a metre eighty tall, such seats were rarely comfortable for Mark.

"What?" he said in mock sleepiness.

Janine shrugged. The gentle bumping of the landing rendered the information that she had been so keen to impart redundant. They had arrived in the relative cool of a mid-February Monday morning. It was around six o'clock. It had just stopped raining; the clouds had cleared away.

But as they stood in the queue for Customs and Immigration, work problems and the stresses and strains of their relationship were nowhere in Mark's thoughts. He was already feeling relaxed, and as he looked at her he felt a surge of affection for the beautiful black woman standing beside him. Unfortunately the only surge that Janine felt was of sweat running down her back.

"Didn't think this out," she said, ruefully aware that the clothes of mid-winter London were not the thing for the tropics.

However, she shrugged again, mopped her brow and occupied herself in studying her surroundings.

She was not disappointed. Clear blue skies, palm trees and lots of warmth – that was what her middle-class British education had conditioned her to expect from such a place as Seychelles, and manifestly it was all there. An African she might be, but this was the closest that she had ever been to her home continent since the time twenty-five years or so ago when she had been hurried to Britain in shock with her sister on the death of her parents.

'Mark knows more about Africa than I do,' was her immediate thought as she took in the ambience. 'He's been here before and to other bits of Africa. Knows how it works, obviously.'

Well, perhaps not quite so obviously.

Notwithstanding the arrival of an ageing but refurbished Boeing 747-400 at least four days a week for countless years, Seychelles' authorities had never quite got round to matching the ground facilities to the sudden influx of nearly five hundred people. And Mark's laid-back approach to travel had left them at the back of the queue.

"Hey, look!" Janine said suddenly. "There's an Arab woman, like that one in London."

"What, where?" said Mark.

It was too late. Futilely Janine pointed out where the woman had been. Once through immigration control, the path of passengers was away to the left, and by the time Mark had reacted to her exclamation, the woman had moved out of their vision. By the time they themselves had been cleared, the black-clad Arab woman was inevitably nowhere to be seen. And, in Mark's case, inevitably forgotten.

* * *

"Got a bit of a journey; the hotel's on the western side of the island," Mark informed Janine.

Exhausted by the flight and their accumulated weariness, neither was very alert to the lush countryside of Mahé, the main island of Seychelles, gently steaming from the recent rain, as they passed through it. The taxi driver, of course, provided a running commentary on the glories around them, but they were not receptive.

The welcome at the hotel was friendly but mercifully not prolonged. They were able to retreat to their room fairly quickly. Barely pausing to investigate their suite, Janine, in uncharacteristic fashion, scattered her luggage and clothes all around the room in her hurry to climb into the huge double bed and let her exhaustion claim her. Mark, more practically, mastered the air conditioning before similarly stripping off and sinking down beside her.

"This is great," he sighed, but Janine was already oblivious to his reaction.

From a combination of jet lag and accumulated weariness, they slept the day through.

* * *

"Mark, wake up, Mark!"

Janine had been the first to stir and check the time. It was already beginning to get dark.

"Mark!"

Having met with no reaction, she gently shook him and then started to kiss his cheek. Aware that he sometimes woke up rather violently, she prepared to reassure him and mitigate the unconscious vestiges of his old army training.

"Hi," he said.

Feeling for her, he pulled her down on top of him. It turned out to be one of his more gentle awakenings, and she lay with him, watching the brief dusk pass into a deep darkness.

"It's gone six o'clock, you gorgeous hunk. Partying at seven. Can't miss that?"

"Oh wow… and free booze… we sure can't!"

She laughed and kissed him again, all her intense feelings for him stirring inside her. Maybe this holiday was going to be the renewal that they both wanted.

"Meet our fellow guests, you idiot!"

She slid off the bed and gathered up her strewn belongings from earlier. Then, in the dim light of the bedroom lamp, she quickly and efficiently stowed the strewn clothes and the other effects from her suitcase into the various cupboards and drawers. Mark watched the easy movements of her naked body with delight and with some of the same feelings that Janine herself was having moments earlier.

"Wonderful!" she breathed.

Unconscious of her lack of clothes, she had walked through the lounge room of the suite and out onto the balcony. Leaning on the rail, she looked down at the brightly lit pool area below.

"Wonderful," she said again, drinking in the scene.

Surrounded by palm trees and the fading displays of hibiscus and lilies, and a whole range of varieties of bougainvillea trees, the thread of bright blue water that had attracted her turned out to be a series of pools cascading down the gentle hillside. A few straggling adults were collecting their belongings and their reluctant children. The warm, scented air stirred by a gentle breeze off the sea carried the smells as well as the sounds to her.

"This is going to be great!"

Having absorbed the sights, slowly and joyfully, she headed back into the bedroom.

Mark was making his own, rather slower, efforts at stowing his belongings as she investigated the shower. Squeals and giggles suggested that the plumbing lacked the sophistication of the rest of the facilities. By the time Mark joined her, she had mastered it and they shared the refreshing deluge with the delight that they always got from such joint activities.

"I thought you said this party, or whatever, was at seven?"

The time was getting perilously close to the appointed hour and they were still dripping.

"Well," she said with a laugh, "don't want to be the first there, do we?"

* * *

They certainly weren't first. The hotel bar, entirely open along the seaward side to catch the evening breeze, was crowded with gaily clad guests. Most were dressed in the semi-formal style that people adopt when not certain of what is expected of them. Mark had opted for light grey linen trousers with a subdued flowered silk shirt. After the restrictions of his army years, he relished the freedom of civilian life but still found it difficult to be totally unconventional. Janine was wearing a bold trouser suit emblazoned with yellow and orange flowers with a half jacket that exposed several inches of her bare midriff. But it wasn't the clothes that stunned Mark.

"Holy shit!"

The reaction sent Janine into a fit of giggling that lasted from bedroom to bar.

The spectacular surprise was Janine's hair. Mark had vaguely been aware that she had been wearing a wig since the previous Friday evening when she had gone to have her hair done. It was a vanity that she had on occasions indulged in before. He had equally vaguely thought it had something to do with the High Commission Reception.

"Fantastic!"

Mark knew about African hairstyles but had never seen one as spectacular as this. Underneath the wig, her own hair had been pulled into a serious of carefully woven pigtails, with the partings generated by forming each plait producing an elaborate pattern on her scalp. The plaits themselves were twisted and intertwined above her head to form yet another complex design. With her hair pulled right back from her face and ears, she looked entirely different. Her long earrings, their large enamelled design matching her trouser suit, sparkled and jangled as she moved. Mark found the whole arrangement, when it was exposed by the removal of the wig, sensational and could hardly keep his eyes off her.

ELEVEN

"Like the hair," said a voice behind Janine.

It was a voice that brought instant recognition, but to her surprise the comment on her hairstyle was closely followed by a whispered caution: "Careful, don't overreact."

As she turned to face the group of people following them into the bar, she tugged gently at Mark's arm to carry him round with her.

"Victoria, is it really you? I don't believe it. But this is wonderful. Marvellous. You must've been on the same plane as us; how could we have missed you? Marvellous. Great to see you!"

The gush of Janine's greeting instantly put Mark on alert. She never used such language; something unusual was happening. Based on their previous conversations, he quickly and rightly guessed the woman to be Victoria Akinbode.

Mark lost it for a moment. His heart sank. This was not in his plan. The sudden interjection of something that belonged to his business life was anything but welcome. A quick suspicion that Janine might have known that Victoria was going to be in Seychelles came and went.

'She's just not that devious,' he told himself.

Nor was she. Despite her quick reaction to alert her partner, Janine was as surprised as Mark at the turn of events and no less disconcerted. In an instant, all of her daydreams of an escape to a tropical paradise were blown away as if by the breeze that was cooling the air around them.

'Oh, shit, shit, shit,' she said to herself with a venom that would have surprised Mark.

But Victoria was there. And it was apparent that she was insensitive to any of the thoughts that Mark or Janine might be having. Victoria was in business mode, even if they were not, and she was seemingly going to force herself onto them in pursuit of whatever activity she was engaged in.

"We flew to Nairobi straight after the Reception. Anyway, here's Silvanus, he was around on Saturday night, but he was avoiding me."

She introduced Janine to her husband. As they exchanged greetings, Janine noted a twinkle in his eyes that he was having difficulty in keeping under control. She liked him at once. Something of her irritation evaporated. Like Janine's cousin at the High Commission Reception, he was wearing the highly decorated but light and bright flowing robes of his national costume. Silvanus Akinbode was undoubtedly a more social person than his wife.

The next minutes were taken up in a confusion of further introductions. The Akinbodes were not alone. Where Silvanus was a slight, evenly proportioned man, his companion was a large, coarse-faced and rather flabby individual who from his very demeanour was overbearing and intolerant of the people around him. Also wearing the loose robes of his country, he seemed to have made no concessions to the holiday atmosphere. However, having come directly from Nigeria, he and his wife were the only members in the group not having to acclimatise to the warmth of the evening. Janine lost something of the lightening of spirit induced by Mr Akinbode.

"This is my brother-in-law, Chief William Adeko," said Victoria, "and my sister Grace."

The emphasis that she managed to put on the name as she introduced her relative was recognisably contemptuous. Adeko stepped in front of his wife and shook hands with Mark. Again, as with Mahomet Sullag at the High Commission, he made no effort to shake hands with Janine or even acknowledge her. But in this case, it was a deliberate piece of rudeness rather than the customary behaviour of a traditional Moslem leader. Sensitivity and good manners were not the Chief's strong points. Mark, by virtue of some footwork worthy of a champion ballroom dancer, managed to shake hands with Grace despite her inferior position at the back of the group.

"You're very like your sister," said Janine, who whilst seething inside at the husband, managed one of her more enchanting grins for the wife.

"How come you can get your hair done like that in London?" asked Victoria, who was genuinely impressed with Janine's hairstyle.

Janine made sure that the explanation included Grace.

"What d'you do?" demanded Chief Adeko of Mark.

It was debatable whether he was interested, but he knew that he was expected to make some sort of conversational effort, at least with Mark. Women could be ignored, but men couldn't.

"I'm in security," replied Mark.

Silvanus Akinbode, who knew precisely what Mark's business was, looked on, his face expressionless. His brother-in-law grunted.

* * *

"We need to get close to Adeko."

The decision to set up the surveillance on the Chief had been made by Fid Okeke some weeks earlier in his office in Abuja. The Chief naturally had no idea that his in-laws worked for the

Nigerian Security Service, nor did he know that they were not married, genuine sister-in-law though Victoria was.

"She's a hard-nosed bitch, Fid," Silvanus Akinbode had said to his superior. "She exploits her role as sister-in-law shamelessly and doesn't give a damn about the pain it's going to cause her sister."

Important as Adeko was as the leader of the southern businessmen intent on arming themselves ostensibly to resist the Moslem Fundamentalists in the north, the coldness and ruthlessness of Victoria's behaviour didn't endear him to his 'wife of convenience'.

"So what's your line of business then?" Mark in his turn asked the Chief.

The answer he got was not illuminating. Mark supposed that the Chief didn't want the true nature of his business and political activities to be widely known. His political influence in southern Nigeria was considerable. His particular strength was his ability to instil a sense of common purpose. Had Mark been more aware of the true nature of the man, he would have been less contemptuous of him for his boorish manners.

"The Chief is a power-hungry political opportunist, seeking where so many have failed before to achieve dominance of Nigeria from the south." So went the security service report buried deep in the safety of Fid Okeke's filing system.

The contrast with Silvanus Akinbode couldn't have been more extreme.

"An idealistic civil servant, he is seeking to preserve the coherence of his country and to introduce a level of integrity into public life that in the past has been wholly lacking. He is one of a new generation of administrators who grew up through the corrupting seesaw years of civil versus military power and who is striving for a more honest and responsible society."

The personnel report on Akinbode S. was held in a completely different part of Mr Okeke's system.

* * *

"They're creeping into every area of our national life, like some foul disease. What more can we do to stop them?" the Chief was demanding.

No one needed to be told that he was talking about the Moslem Fundamentalists.

"It's hard to say," said Akinbode cautiously. "How can we interfere with people's deeply held beliefs? Many more women are appearing in public wearing the niqab, or whatever they call it, whereas before the wives of the northern people were rarely seen at all. That ought to be a change for the better. But for whatever the reasons this is happening, there's nothing we can, or should, do about it. It's their choice.

"Alcohol consumption is falling. Even the brewery at Katsina is suffering. That's costing the government money in lost taxes; would you want us to encourage young people to drink alcohol? Yes, a more rigid political approach is developing. Yes, power has been significantly eased out of the hands of the emirs and the traditional leaders and into the hands of faceless young men. But only the northerners can do anything about that. There's tension enough between north and south as it is; any moves from the south are bound to be seen as provocative."

Adeko grunted irritably. The last thing he wanted to be told was that the south should not interfere.

"And what about all these young thugs spending months in Somalia and God knows where learning all the filthy tricks of their evil trade? What about them?"

"It's not a crime to travel abroad; how can we stop them? We can only deal with them if they commit a crime."

Chief Adeko didn't want to hear this either. Akinbode's even-handed legalistic approach was never going to find favour with him.

"What about this terrorist group they've hired? Aren't they

more thugs and killers? Are we supposed to do nothing about them too? Just wait until they kill someone?"

"I think we should eat. It's nearly eight o'clock."

The unexpected interjection from Grace Adeko spared Silvanus Akinbode the need to answer. Mark and Janine had long since decided to keep out of the debate.

The Chief was happy to eat. Not that he actually said so; he just forced his way towards the door, scattering the surrounding guests.

Janine held Mark back. Dining with a brute like Adeko was not in her plans for the evening. Victoria, noticing what was happening, allowed the gap between the two groups to widen. By the time that they had reached the restaurant entrance at the end of the covered walkway from the bar, the separation was such that the head waiter automatically led the Adekos and Akinbodes to a table for four. Ignoring the man's suggestions, Mark gestured at a table at the other end of the room. Janine chuckled quietly. She enjoyed Mark's small moments of masterfulness just as he enjoyed the occasions when she was equally as decisive.

* * *

Dinner was a great success. Janine's happy remark that their life together had always been punctuated by a succession of marvellous meals set the tone for the evening. Starting by sitting upright separated by the table's width, they slowly moved closer until, by the time the coffee came, their noses were only a few centimetres apart and they had their hands clasped like arm-wrestlers.

"Mark, I do love you," Janine said in a lazy whisper. "I know things haven't been so good recently; we've been tired, and maybe we're together too much at work. Perhaps we aren't giving each other enough space."

"I know," said Mark.

It was true. 'And I'm to blame rather than her,' he admitted to himself. In the office he was a different person; he obviously hadn't yet worked out how to reconcile this with his private life.

"I need something to be responsible for. Something I can be a success at. I know Helen's been with you from the beginning and she's very good at the electronic surveillance stuff, but I actually know far more about it than she does. When she leaves, how about if I take that on and develop it? You're only playing at it at the moment."

"Hey, you're talking shop! Verboten! This is holiday, remember... holiday!"

Janine exploded into gurgling laughter at Mark's mock severity. He joined in. He also got up and, pulling her to her feet, he swept her out of the dining room with his arm firmly around her bare waist. She tried to rest her head on his shoulder, but her exotic hairstyle didn't make for a comfortable cushion.

Mark and Janine's exit was noted by the Akinbodes and somewhat wistfully by Grace Adeko but in no way registered with the Chief, who was repeating for the umpteenth time, unheard and unheeded, his entirely well-known views on the question of Moslem Fundamentalist infiltration.

* * *

"Bit of a surprise seeing your friend Victoria," remarked Mark as they settled on the veranda of their suite.

"Certainly was!"

"Could just be a family holiday!"

With his face turned away from her in the dim light of the veranda, Janine couldn't be sure whether Mark was being serious or not. His sense of humour could be quirky on occasions.

"What! Nobody in their right mind would choose to go on

holiday with a pig like Adeko," she said, deciding to take the suggestion at its face value.

"Not even for the sake of your sister?"

Janine thought that possible but not likely. Her only knowledge of sisterly relations was with her own sibling. They were not close, although they were friendly enough.

Mark's more cynical thoughts were closer to the truth. Feeding off Janine's description, he had sensed that Victoria was very self-focused and supposed that she was using her sister to get close to Adeko, who, like Janine, he had categorised as a villain. It was behaviour that Mark, along with Silvanus Akinbode, found distasteful. He doubted that Janine would develop a liking for Victoria. Janine's own thoughts were identical to her partner's.

"Wonder what Adeko's up to? Where does Silvanus fit in? He's a nice enough guy, don't you think?"

Mark shared Janine's opinion but didn't get a chance to say so. There was a gentle knocking at the door. Mark moved to check if there was anybody there. As he did so, the door was pushed into his face and the slightly breathless figure of the very man they were talking about rushed into the room. Mark instinctively and quickly checked outside before he closed the door. He saw no one but couldn't be sure that his visitor hadn't been seen. Who might be watching didn't cross his mind; it was just an in-bred reaction brought on by Akinbode's precipitous entrance.

"Silvanus!" said Janine, who had followed Mark into the lounge from the veranda.

Silvanus Akinbode quickly composed himself. "I'm sorry to startle you. I was trying to get to you unobserved."

"Why?"

Mark's tone was sharp. Following their previous conversation, Mark had a sudden feeling of intense irritation at the Akinbodes' continuing intrusion into his holiday.

"We need your help," the Nigerian said simply.

It was hardly the answer that Mark or Janine had expected to hear, and it was certainly not one that they wanted to hear. They'd come to Seychelles specifically to get away from their work; to be abruptly drawn into some new intrigue within a few short hours of arrival was not a development that either of them welcomed.

However, Silvanus Akinbode was there now; they could hardly refuse to listen to what he had to say.

"What help?" demanded Mark, his irritation not lost on Akinbode.

Silvanus spent the next half an hour explaining why the Nigerian Security Service needed help and what he and Victoria wanted from Mark and his company. He formally offered to employ them. Then, leaving Mark to think about his proposition, he quietly slipped away without engaging in any conversational small talk. Mark was seriously put out, but he undertook to respond the next morning. He reluctantly had to admit that business was business, even if it did have the hallmarks of an opportunistic approach.

"Goddamn it," he said fiercely, "we're on holiday. Why the hell should we help him?"

"He isn't asking us to do anything now... here in the Seychelles, is he?"

Mark acknowledged that he was being unreasonable. Janine was secretly delighted that he was so worked up about the impact on their holiday. That meant that he cared more about their pleasure and comfort at the moment than his business. But she was also a realist. In the end, she felt sure they would work for the Nigerian authorities.

"Bed, my girl! We'll think about it in the morning."

Mark chased Janine into the bedroom. The guests next door speculated for some time on what was going on as the shrieks and giggles penetrated the intervening walls. Finally, with the bed crumpled and their bodies bathed in sweat, they slipped into an exhausted sleep. Not for the first time, Mark was amazed by the energy that Janine had for lovemaking and Janine at the tenderness that he could display in their foreplay.

TWELVE

The tropical dawn came quickly. The deep darkness was displaced by the first intense rays of the sun thrusting over the horizon. Many of the residents of the hotel were up and about, ready for their pre-breakfast swim almost as the sun's warmth touched them. The middle-aged German couple, the first to the poolside, were in for a nasty shock.

"We said we'd be up early," Janine reminded Mark with one of her more cheeky grins.

"We're on holiday."

Mark repeated his mantra. Not that he was ever amongst the earliest risers unless the need was especially pressing.

It was close to nine o'clock before they emerged from their apartment and headed towards the dining room and a breakfast that Janine was more than ready for.

"Wonder what's going on there?" she said as they emerged from the end of the covered way that linked the residential suites to the central amenities.

There was a commotion at the side of the upper swimming pool. Crowds of people were milling around. Janine could feel Mark tense beside her. The shimmering blue waters of the pool were barely visible through the barrier of anxious hotel staff and, as Mark had been quick to observe, people in uniform. There were no signs of any guests. As Mark hurried her into the bar to get a better view, Janine was distracted by a taxi that was pulling away from the hotel reception area at the other side of the covered way. She stopped short. The partial outline of a head and shoulders in heavy black robes flashed before her as the vehicle accelerated.

"What?" said Mark in question.

Janine told him what she had seen. Once again, it was too late for him to confirm the sighting, but he didn't doubt his partner. He was suddenly anxious about what was happening by the pool.

There was a policeman in the bar, his affable black face carrying a half smile. But despite his amiability, he wouldn't let them near the open side of the bar to see what was going on below.

"What's the problem?" asked Mark.

"They found a body in the pool," said the officer briefly.

Assuming 'they' to be the hotel staff, Mark paused to seek more information. But the policeman resisted his efforts to extract any further details from him and shepherded them firmly towards the restaurant.

"Better have breakfast; the superintendent will want to talk to everybody later."

"Sure you won't tell us who's dead?" said Janine, trying out her most winsome smile.

The officer grinned again and shook his head.

In the restaurant the waiter told them immediately. "Nigerian gentleman. Mr Akinbode."

The pronunciation was less than perfect but the name was clear enough.

"My God!" said Mark.

Both he and Janine were instantly taken up with their own thoughts.

Mark, who was already in business mode, quickly realised the implications of the waiter's announcement. And the first thought to occupy his mind was their clandestine meeting with Silvanus Akinbode last evening and where that now left them. Did they have a commission from the Nigerian Security Service and were they already embroiled in whatever it was that Mr Akinbode wanted them to investigate? And what about the local police? The last thing Mark wanted was to get involved with the police in Seychelles.

Janine was more concerned about the Arab woman. Was it a coincidence that an Arab woman kept appearing wherever she and Mark were? Had she anything at all to do with either Mark or the Nigerians? Why she made these links Janine couldn't have articulated; she tended to put such things down to an ill-informed paranoia generated by her growing involvement with Mark's business.

* * *

Breakfast was dismal compared with the dinner of the previous evening. The restaurant was silent. The waiter's gleeful reports on each stage of activity as he successively brought them the components of their meal were not met with any enthusiasm by Mark or Janine, but they were not inclined to discourage him. Details of each guest were carefully noted by groups of policemen as they arrived for their meal.

"They'll get to us eventually," said Janine. "I guess all we can do is try and enjoy our meal."

Mark, as ever, admired her down-to-earth approach to the situation. Hating inactivity and uncertainty, he was beginning to fret.

"We don't want to be drawn into all this," he said, still concerned that their precious holiday time was going to be eroded.

That Silvanus Akinbode's death might be anything else but murder never occurred to him. The secretiveness of the previous evening's visit would not have led Mark to any other conclusion.

Janine offered no comment.

* * *

"Mr Shortley?"

The enquiring policemen had arrived earlier than they had expected.

Mark noted that the two plainclothes officers and the uniformed policeman had come straight to their table, directed by some hidden denizen of the hotel who had obviously identified him. This was just the sort of attention that he had been dreading.

"Yes?"

"Would you like to join us in the manager's office?"

It had the appearance of a politely put question but was an undeniable instruction.

"I guess we have no choice," muttered Mark to Janine.

They followed the policemen.

"God, this is just what I didn't want to happen."

Mark's muttering to Janine continued as they left the restaurant, the curious glances of the other diners following them.

Mark took a sideways look at Janine. Head held high, she walked beside him with a calm but inscrutable expression on her face. The novelty of the hairstyle and the hidden view of her beauty that it exposed still sent shivers down his spine.

'Let's hope the local plod know their business and we can get it over with quickly!' It was a thought that Mark didn't mutter to Janine.

The route to the manager's office took them down to the same level as the swimming pools. Since they had so far hardly strayed from either their suite or the dining room, they had little idea where they were heading. As they skirted the bright blue areas of water, their surfaces for once unruffled by splashing children, they noticed that the body still lay where it had been deposited when recovered. Covered by a series of towels, it was watched over by a bored-looking policewoman who fiddled with her gun holster and paced a few yards each way from her charge. At no time did she let her eyes fall onto the body.

The hotel manager, evicted by the police from his office, was nowhere to be seen when Mark and Janine arrived.

"Mr Shortley?" said the superintendent. "And who's this?" The nod was in Janine's direction.

"This is Janine Effiong; she's my partner."

The superintendent sat behind the manager's desk. To his right and behind him in the corner of the room sat a second man. Slightly scruffy, with the look of an academic rather than a policeman, he studied Mark and Janine with bright, intelligent eyes. He had the sort of forgettable look about him that Mark instantly recognised.

The superintendent was ostensibly in charge, but it was soon apparent this was more a formality than a reality. Mark was aware of a third man seated somewhere behind them who took notes. Mark was the only white person in the room.

A slow grin came to the face of the man in plainclothes as Mark had responded to the superintendent. The uniformed officer, familiar with the politically correct parlance of Europeans, was aware of the ambiguity of the answer and gave a barely perceptible nod in acknowledgement. Both men correctly assumed the comprehensive nature of Mark and Janine's partnership.

"You are aware of the death of Mr Silvanus Akinbode?"

The superintendent knew that Mark and Janine could hardly not have been with the way that rumours spread in closed communities like hotels, but in the way of police enquiries the known usually had to be confirmed.

"Yes," said Mark simply.

"He was stabbed in the heart through the ribcage under the left arm. He didn't drown." It was the man in the corner who made the statement.

Mark was surprised; the police were not normally so forthcoming with such details. It made him wary.

"From the limited enquires we have made, he was killed fairly soon after midnight but was only dumped into the water just before dawn. What time did he leave you?"

"Around eleven thirty," said Mark, showing no surprise that they already knew about the supposedly secret meeting, nor at the quiescence of the superintendent now that the questioning was underway.

"Did he seem anxious or concerned about anything when he visited you?"

"No more than you would expect from a man who was making a clandestine visit to somebody."

"You know that Mr Akinbode was no ordinary tourist? Can I ask why he came to see you?"

The plainclothed officer was now sitting much more alertly.

"I'm aware that he worked for the Nigerian Security Service. if that's what you mean. He wanted our assistance in an investigation in Britain and Europe; nothing to do with Seychelles."

"Yes, yes," said the interrogator. "His visit to Seychelles was part of a domestic investigation. We've been assisting the Nigerian authorities. Some of their dissident elements have been using these islands as a staging post."

Again it was more information than Mark would have expected.

"We?" said Janine, almost without thinking.

Her query stopped the conversation for a moment. The

superintendent and the man in the corner exchanged looks. The uniformed officer gave a slight nod.

"I am Joshua Umberto, the Head of the Seychelles Security Service."

He presumed that the announcement would be enough to satisfy them. Like Silvanus Akinbode, he already knew about Mark and what his business was.

"Akinbode was here to keep an eye on his brother-in-law, Chief Adeko. The chief is building an organisation supposedly to resist the inroads of the Moslem Fundamentalists in northern Nigeria, but his real purpose is more likely to be engineering a takeover by the southern politicians in the wake of any upheavals in the north. Adeko has dealings with international arms dealers, some of whom use these islands as a meeting place with their clients."

Umberto paused to allow Mark and Janine to digest the information.

"So," said Mark, "are you saying that the adherents of Adeko's brand of politics killed Akinbode?"

"So it would seem."

"But couldn't it be just as likely that the northern Nigerians killed him, or their agents? The Federal Security Service are acting against them as well," said Janine.

Her query seemed sensible enough to her, but Umberto clearly thought he knew who the likely assassins were and didn't immediately want to hear about complications to his theory.

"There is no evidence of that."

"How do you know? The northern Fundamentalists have recruited an operative from a Middle East terror group to act on their behalf. You wouldn't be just looking for black people here," Janine persisted.

"There is still no evidence of that."

Umberto appealed with his eyes to Mark to intervene. Mark didn't.

"There was an Arab woman at this hotel last night. She left by taxi at around nine o'clock this morning. Heading for the airport, I'd say."

'She's making a huge leap in assuming a link between the woman and the killing,' thought Mark, despite himself impressed with Janine's intervention and the challenge it posed for Mr Umberto. He always admired her directness; it was a characteristic that he didn't see himself as possessing. 'The evidence is barely circumstantial.' And she could have had no knowledge of the suspicions of the police in London about the links between traditionally dressed Arab women and the old 'New Truth' terror group, or yet about their characteristic method of killing.

Janine's purpose was only to raise doubts in the official mind. She was successful.

Joshua Umberto broke off the questioning and moved into the outer office to make a long telephone call. He might have had trouble dealing with an articulate and powerful young woman like Janine, but he was good at his job and so had to be open to considering all possibilities, even if, as in this case, he had a strong preferred view on what had happened. The urgency of his demands on his subordinates, however, suggested the beginnings of doubts.

'Bit of a shock to the system, this,' Mark said to himself. 'Don't suppose there's a lot of international crime occurring in Seychelles, at least not violent crime. And I don't suppose he relishes the idea of Arab terrorists on his patch. He prefers a simpler and more palatable explanation, no doubt; who wouldn't?'

"OK," Umerto said, returning when he had finished his conversation with his headquarters in Victoria, "let's see."

Janine smiled sweetly at him.

"We've had a long discussion with Mrs Akinbode. She seems to be taking it rather well, really. Her interest is the southern

Nigerian businessmen. She clearly believes they've stepped a bit too far over of the self-defence mark and are arming themselves on a large scale. She didn't rule out their resorting to murder to protect their interests."

It was a statement. Umberto was still clearly going to be reluctant to shift from his theory. He gave no clue to whether he knew that Victoria's and Silvanus Akinbode's marriage was only window-dressing.

The conversation continued for a further quarter of an hour but added little to what had already been said. As Umberto was about to dismiss Mark and Janine, a uniformed officer entered the room and deposited a plastic envelope full of what were obviously Silvanus Akinbode's belongings in front of the superintendent.

"Not a lot here," said the superintendent. "Keys, wallet, nothing remarkable; Mr Akinbode seems to have carried the same amount of junk around as most men. Pocket diary, not many entries... This is more interesting."

Pushed into the pages for February were two scraps of paper. One was a rather soggy and torn newspaper cutting from an Arabic language journal with the photograph of a blonde-haired girl, and the other was the business card of one Jason Wong.

Joshua Umberto noticed that Mark looked surprised at the photograph.

"You know this woman?" he asked.

"Well, it could be the Arab woman that Janine mentioned earlier, but it's a bit too dog-eared to be really sure."

The telephone ringing cut off Mark's reply. The superintendent handed the instrument to the security service chief. The report lasted about five minutes. Umberto's face gave nothing away, but his changing body language suggested that he was increasingly unhappy about what he was hearing.

"No woman in traditional Arab costume boarded the flight

to London this morning. There were many women young and old, but no Arabs. However," he said, looking somewhat crestfallen, "a set of the black robes was found in the ladies' toilet at the airport. The police are making fuller enquiries."

"Thank you," said Janine quietly.

Nothing at all was said about the business card.

THIRTEEN

"God! I thought we'd never get away."

Mark and Janine were walking back to their suite after finally being released by the Head of the Seychelles Security Service. Mark had become increasingly irritated during the interview. The longer that he was in contact with the authorities the more he felt that their holiday was at risk, particularly as Silvanus Akinbode's death inevitably was not straightforward.

Whilst not prone to uncontrolled anger, Mark could get irritated when, as now, he had totally different priorities about how he wished to spend his time.

'I just want to be with her...'

He wasn't sure how to express the urges, mental and physical, that surged through him as he looked at Janine ambling amiably along beside him. Only vaguely aware of the contradictions within himself, he felt an enormous contentment at being with her yet was unhappy that he couldn't seem to engineer the opportunities to enjoy it. Janine, with a perception that surprised him, voiced the common-sense thoughts that he couldn't conjure up for himself.

"Mark, relax. It's over. We're on holiday. We've got to start enjoying ourselves. Forget the Akinbodes, and Arab women – concentrate on us, concentrate on me!"

Janine intended to be soothing, but as she let them into their quarters she was suddenly cautious. Mark chuckled. It was exactly the way that he would have reacted had he been first through the door.

"I've ordered a taxi for twelve o'clock," Janine said as she joined Mark on the veranda. "The girl at reception reckons we can still see quite a bit of the island in an afternoon."

"Great," said Mark.

* * *

'This is a Janine I didn't even know existed,' Mark thought as they scurried around in preparation. 'I guess the bright sunlight in the tropics makes for more colourful clothing; now suddenly it's all yellows and oranges, rather than black.'

Mark was impressed by her sure touch. 'Well, not to be outdone...' With an inner grin at his acceptance of the challenge, he went for a little flamboyance of his own.

So as they awaited the inevitable late arrival of their taxi and despite the earlier dramatic interlude with Silvanus Akinbode, they both felt physically comfortable, more at ease with the climate and increasingly exhilarated at the prospect of sampling the pleasures available to them.

Janine, in her turn, grinned happily at the yellow shorts that Mark was sporting, although hers were the briefer by several centimetres. Her T-shirt boldly and humorously proclaimed various environmental truths. Mark's, despite its more raucous hues, took a more serious tone. Janine had woven ribbons into her complex of hair plaits, and her earrings were amongst the longest and noisiest that Mark had ever seen or heard her wear.

"We're a great couple," she told the world at large.

They certainly attracted the appreciative glances of both guests and staff alike.

"Here we go!" said Mark as he handed Janine into the taxi.

The vehicle had seen better days and had a strong if indefinable smell about it, but they happily piled in and haggled with the driver over where they should go.

"I take you over the hill to the tea plantations and then to Victoria. You can lunch in the Botanical Gardens, see the coco-de-mer. I take you to the beach in the south, you can swim."

The route was obviously a standard one and the price was pretty well what the hotel receptionist had predicted once the haggling was over.

"Sounds great," said Janine, who had been wise enough to stay out of the financial bargaining.

Mark concluded the deal and they set off.

Apart from one small hiccup, the day was everything that they could have wished for. The taxi wound its way up into the hills that formed the spine of the main island of Mahé and meandered slowly through the hectares of tea gardens and coffee plantations. At the Plantation Visitors' Centre, they sampled the local produce.

"Isn't this divine?" Janine said as she drank in the sunlight, the all-embracing warmth and humidity, and the perfumes of the area, unperturbed by the approaching rain clouds.

As they sat enjoying the atmosphere, the inevitable crowd of small children materialised and crowded around them. Mark didn't shoo them away. Janine was particularly fascinating to them. Notwithstanding the African origin of most of the children, there was something unfamiliarly exotic about Janine to them. Such a hairstyle as she had was a novelty and they hadn't often seen a black woman so scantily clad before. Mark was amused by their interest; Janine herself was uncharacteristically delighted with the attention.

In the end a few coins, soon converted into shared Coca-Cola drinks, satisfied both children and visitors.

They moved on, pausing to climb a hill to get a view of the whole of the western side of the island. As the rain squall caught up with them, they sheltered under an old metal awning erected many years previously to provide protection for the old Queen on one of her visits to admire the vistas that they now marvelled at. On the way down through the dripping, steaming forest, chilled briefly by the downpour, the taxi driver led them to the base of a tall and ancient tree. Making a short cut in the bark, he released the blood-red sap.

"Weird," said Janine.

The grinning taxi driver shared the local legends that surrounded this curious tree.

'Bit of a contrast.'

As they made their way down the eastern side of the hills and along a road that took them through the diplomatic quarter, Mark was disconcerted by the splendid residences of the foreign dignitaries; they jarred with the more homely accommodation that they had previously seen. Eventually, having crawled their way through the mid-afternoon traffic of Victoria, the capital of Seychelles, the taxi driver deposited them in the main shopping street.

"Oh, wow," said Janine in yet further delight.

She'd noticed the miniature Big Ben that dominated the crossroads in the centre of the town.

Mark shared her pleasure. Then, behind the clock demanding his attention, he caught sight of a street name, and out of the corner of his eye he noticed a policeman apparently loitering in a doorway.

'That's where the office of our Mr Wong is, if I'm not mistaken. Forget it… you didn't see it,' he told himself, irritably trying to push the information from his mind.

And he had just about succeeded when he observed that he was not alone in showing an interest. As he allowed himself to be slowly dragged along the street by Janine, he just had time to see Victoria Akinbode slide by the policeman and into the offices.

"...the Post Office?"

Janine had set off across the street. With his attention distracted, he hadn't heard what she had said. Doing the tourist bit, they chose a range of postcards and, finding a pitch in the main post office, set about despatching them.

Then they wandered through the market area. Town-bred in Europe, Janine was appalled by the standards of hygiene at the fish and meat stalls. Mark, who had seen such things before, was less shocked. Having exhausted the delights of open-air trading and resisted every effort to induce them to buy things that they didn't want, they moved on and sampled the shops and stores, and became tourists again. Around three thirty, they headed back to rendezvous with the taxi.

"Mark," said Janine tentatively.

They were walking back along the street that housed the Wong office. The business card from Akinbode's pocket prompted Janine's recognition, just as the lumbering gait of the large African in front of them did.

"I see him," said Mark, his voice and his demeanour reflecting his sudden alertness.

He nudged Janine into the entrance of a clothes store where they took an excessive interest in the racks of T-shirts in the window. Minutes later, the less-than-proud owners of a shirt depicting two female wrestlers and one declaring the virtues of a reggae group that they had never even heard of had observed the casual and unobtrusive entrance of Chief Adeko into the offices of Mr Jason Wong.

"That was neatly done," remarked Mark as they resumed their progress towards the taxi.

"Did you know the office was there?" asked Janine, slightly miffed that they had apparently passed that way before without any recognition.

"Yes," said Mark, "and your friend Victoria went in earlier."

"What?!"

Janine was now really miffed. Despite agreeing that they would ignore the events of the morning, here he was doing a bit of surveillance without even telling her!

Mark sensed her annoyance. But before he could respond, they had arrived at the parked taxi and Janine was climbing in. He followed her.

"We go to the Botanical Gardens. You can have tea," said the driver as they moved off.

Both nodded their silent agreement.

'How can you win?' Mark thought ruefully. 'Tell her and I'm talking shop, don't tell her and I'm keeping things from her!'

They did have tea, but not before they had wandered around the Gardens for more than an hour, enjoying the splendour of the trees and shrubs and the relief of a slight breeze. After the rain, the atmosphere was less humid and sticky, and the movement of the air was welcome. Janine's natural curiosity and general interest in new experiences reasserted itself. They located the elderly coco-de-mer tree and marvelled at the huge fruit.

"Found only in Seychelles," the notice said, "they get their name from the outsized nuts that were found floating in the Indian Ocean and on the beaches of the countries surrounding it. The nuts can weigh as much as ten to twelve kilos and the trees can take hundreds of years to reach their full maturity."

"Wow," said Janine in mock surprise, "there're male and female trees and they only mate on stormy nights!"

Mark laughed. Putting his arm around her shoulder, he steered her back towards the restaurant. Janine followed his lead. Both were a little mortified by the speed with which their irritation had erupted in the town. To have reacted to such a trivial thing as Mark not sharing his sighting of Victoria Akinbode seemed, on reflection, to be absurd.

"Let's just forget it," was the message of the arm around the shoulder.

Janine was happy to do so, silently accepting Mark's gesture. But it illustrated just how fragile their relationship could be at times. And both of them instinctively were aware of this fragility. Their feelings of aggrievement melted away as they strolled and then scurried along the gravel pathways of the Botanical Gardens, their pace accelerating as they felt the spatter of the warm raindrops of the next shower.

"Good timing, sir," said Janine, with her infectious grin now returned.

They had to jog the last few paces as the downpour intensified. The resurgence of Janine's grin was very welcome. A weathervane for her spirits, Mark knew only too well that when it disappeared she was seriously unhappy about something. He had to admit that he still hadn't worked out how to deal with her hurt when some unintentional action of his had piqued her.

"This is a surprise!" Janine said as their tea was served.

It was a delicious English afternoon tea, complete with small sandwiches, scones with jam and cream, and Earl Grey.

With the clouds dispersed again, it had brightened up outside as the atmosphere between them had also lightened. With Janine back in effervescent mood, Mark was delighted to share her wonder at everything around her. He took his pleasures in a more staid fashion but never failed to be impressed by her enthusiastic enjoyment.

"Are we going swimming then?" she asked as they headed back for yet another rendezvous with their taxi.

"Sure, there's plenty of time."

The driver took them to a small but secluded cove about ten miles south of their hotel. The beach was deserted, even of the usual horde of inquisitive local children.

Mark enjoyed swimming. His lifestyle didn't give him as much exercise as he would have wished, although they had a mini-gym in the flat; boisterous lovemaking with Janine was not a serious alternative.

'Wonder how well she can swim?'

They had come prepared. At Mark's suggestion they were wearing their swimming costumes under their other clothes. Janine's outfit was sensible rather than stylish, and despite the stunning effect that it might have had on the average male, such a reaction was not something that she sought. As Mark had observed almost as he had first met her, Janine dressed to please herself; she never sought his opinion nor studied his preferences if he offered them unsought.

The sea was rough and the surf strong, but Mark was a powerful and competent swimmer. Janine, however, was not so capable, and after a rather cautious venture into the water that resulted in her being upended unceremoniously, she decided to watch.

"Mark, be careful!"

Having returned to the safety of the beach well chastened by the vigour of the waves, she was seized with anxiety for Mark.

She need hardly have worried. She knew that he was reasonably fit and accomplished in many physical pursuits; his time as an SAS officer had seen to that. What she didn't know, but was soon to learn, was that Mark had trained in underwater warfare and was as much at home in the boiling surf as in the innocuous surroundings of a swimming pool.

"Mark, oh my God?"

She couldn't see him. Gambolling in the breakers, Mark had disappeared. For what seemed like a lifetime in which her feelings for him asserted themselves painfully strongly, he was nowhere to be seen. And when he did emerge further up the beach, and obviously safe and well, she was angrier with him for frightening her than relieved at his return.

"Damn you," she said as he threw himself down beside her. "Don't do that to me!"

Realising that her anger and fear were real, he didn't go back into the water again. Letting himself dry, he lazed beside her for half an hour and then, carefully brushing the sand off each other like a couple of friendly cats, they rejoined the taxi driver and headed back to the hotel. It had been a glorious few hours and they both felt refreshed and happy; their earlier little spat now just a vague memory.

FOURTEEN

Unseen, Chief Adeko made his way back to his suite. Also unseen, Victoria Akinbode had recently returned and was busy typing her report into her laptop in preparation for despatching it to her Controller, Fid Okeke, in Abuja. She had had a satisfying day.

The death of her working partner had certainly been a shock to Victoria. Her relationship with Silvanus Akinbode was necessarily close, although not intimate. His wife and family in Ikeja near Lagos saw to that. For herself, despite her current boyfriend, the businessman who travelled a lot and who, as far as she knew, also strayed a lot, close personal ties were a disadvantage.

'"I guess his wife will find out what he really did for a living now,' Victoria said to herself as she read over her report. 'Just another casualty in the war that's raging.'

The real Mrs Akinbode's pain didn't raise any companion feeling in Victoria. In fact, her prime response, once the initial reaction had passed, was one of annoyance at the inconvenience caused to her by Akinbode's death and the extra work that it was going to impose on her.

"I guess she'd call it professionalism."

Fid Okeke made the remark to his own wife when the news of the death was known.

"It makes her a pretty determined and dangerous operator but hardly a warm or likeable person."

Although in normal circumstances Victoria's manner was pleasant enough. Physically similar to Janine, she was also as self-reliant, but being trained in different skills, she was more resourceful and more ruthless. In terms of personality, however, they were light years apart.

* * *

'Must get into town,' Victoria told herself after all the formalities had been seen to.

The aftermath of the death of her supposed husband was certainly awkward for her. On holiday with the Adekos to try and penetrate his relationship with the Wong organisation and their arms dealings, now having to act the grieving widow was a major constraint on her freedom of action.

Once the police and security services had departed after the interviews and the clearing up, Victoria began to plan her moves to maintain her cover but progress her activities. She ordered a taxi. The receptionist was rather shocked, and Victoria had to tearfully explain that there were legal things that had to be done and the death registered at the Nigerian Embassy. Joshua Umberto had fortunately given her an excuse to go into Seychelles' capital and she meant to take full advantage of that.

Victoria did go to all of the places that she had said that she had to, but for none of the reasons that she had offered. She also made an extra visit that she hadn't mentioned to anybody. At the Embassy the death had been registered without any action from her, but she did have a long conversation with Fid Okeke over a secure telephone to supplement her written report.

"The local police and security service think he was killed by the southern lot, or someone hired by them."

"But you don't?" queried Okeke.

"No," said Victoria. "I don't. This was an ultra-professional job. The business cartel has money and can buy most things, but it requires a bit more than just money to get an expert like this to do your dirty work for you. They wouldn't know where to look."

"Silvanus was getting close to the arms dealer. Couldn't it have been one of their people? It seems to me they had reason enough to kill him."

This was certainly true, but Fid Okeke was only seeing the immediate part of the picture: the impending arms supply to the southern conspirators. Victoria had concluded in the overall context of defeating the Fundamentalists that the motive was probably more complex.

"Fid, my gut feeling is that Silvanus was killed by the Fundamentalists. Or at least someone hired by them. I reckon the northerners wouldn't necessarily want the arms to be stopped. The traditionalists would, of course, but for the Fundamentalists the instability that would be created if the south had large-scale access to weapons would play right into their hands. It would focus all of the north on the southern threat and give the Fundamentalists a great rallying point."

'Tortuous,' thought Okeke, 'this sure is Nigeria!'

He knew that there were other possible explanations; Akinbode had made enemies over his efforts to be even-handed between north and south, for example, but he really didn't have time for such debates.

"Jesus, this gets worse by the hour! We have to stop the arms, even if your logic's right—"

"Of course we have to stop the arms; that's what I'm trying to do! But we can't afford to let the Fundamentalists get a real hold on power in the north either. Much more has to be done to stop them."

Victoria was getting passionate, but she realised that she was overstepping the mark by lecturing her superior. How deep-seated her passion was and how much it was more for effect with Okeke only she could know.

"Thank you, Victoria, I think I understand the problem."

Mr Okeke did, only too well.

Notwithstanding his terse reply, he also knew that the situation had now become much more dangerous for Victoria, so he was reluctant to admonish her.

The conversation reverted to factual reporting and then ended.

Victoria's subsequent visit to the offices of the Wong organisation was more secretive, but nonetheless rewarding. She had no difficulty in gaining access and, with the application of only a minimum of womanly wiles, had very little difficulty in obtaining information.

"Mr Wong doesn't come here very often. Usually it's Mr Xu," Wong's Seychelles man confided.

An austere man of indefinable age, Hector Xu left very little impression of himself when he visited, but in fact he was one of the most powerful men in the Wong organisation outside of the family. He was trusted by Jason Wong and had grown up with him in Hong Kong.

"It's just banking. The islands are an offshore financial centre. Clients deposit money in Seychelles and we shift it via our worldwide contacts to the places where it needs to go and turn it into whatever currency the client wants. Lot of the money used to be Russian; now it's Chinese."

The scale of this Wong activity was something that very few people understood.

"Big deal going through shortly," the local Wong representative went on. Flattered by Victoria's interest and attracted to her liberally exposed person, the man became positively garrulous. "Principal's due in ten minutes to set things up – a Nigerian gentleman."

The last statement was added by way of explanation. Victoria naturally hadn't been too generous with information about herself, so the fact that she also was a Nigerian had not been offered.

Broadly she had obtained the information that she was looking for, but if, as she supposed, her brother-in-law was due imminently, she hadn't time to tease out the details. In some frustration at being so close to a breakthrough, she prepared to leave.

"Oh well, I'd better let you get on with it…"

Victoria gave the man a smile that Janine would have been proud of. Then, with as little impression of hurry as she could manage, she left.

'Obviously doesn't know anything about what's really going on here or that it might not be legitimate. Otherwise why tell me so much? Couldn't just be my tits.'

She put the talkative young Chinese lad out of her mind.

Victoria's next meeting, with Joshua Umberto of the security service, took a little longer and involved none of the flirtation and coaxing that had been applied to the clerk at the Wong office. However, it was just as valuable. Proper surveillance of the Wong organisation's transactions was arranged, and as a consequence Victoria hoped the Nigerian Security Service would begin to get to know more of the secrets of both that group and of the southern cartel.

'Just one more thing to do,' Victoria said to herself as her dinner was delivered to her room by a waiter.

FIFTEEN

The atmosphere in the hotel restaurant that evening was loud and lively, fitting their mood perfectly. But the pounding background music didn't impede conversation. Janine reacted to it with relish and Mark noted that her African persona had steadily increased during the holiday. Unlike some rap and reggae, the local sega music was not unpleasant, and as he got used to it, Mark found himself being taken along by it.

"I enjoyed our trip," said Janine. "Maybe we should hire a car and revisit some of the places."

"Could do," said Mark, although he fancied another lazy day.

He was as pleased as Janine that the holiday was beginning to take off. His slow processes of relaxation were underway, and he could feel himself mellowing.

On top of the underlying weariness that had prompted the holiday, the swimming had made him surprisingly tired, so he was definitely adverse to too much strenuous activity for a day or so. He said as much to Janine.

"You poor old fella," she said, giggling loudly. "Maybe we'll sit by the pool and nurture your grey hairs!"

Her giggles developed into a deep, gurgling laugh that

rumbled up from somewhere inside her. Mark joined in, and they laughed so much that their meal went uneaten for some considerable time. Around them people looked on in amusement. The inhabitants of the next suite, used to such boisterousness filtering through the walls of their room, viewed their merriment with some apprehension. They clearly anticipated another rowdy night.

But they didn't have to suffer it. Although Janine's outburst set the tone for a joyful evening, and their intimacy was never more complete, their elation was killed the moment that they arrived back at the door of their suite.

"It's open," whispered Janine.

She froze. No mean judo performer, she was happy enough to take on anybody that she could see and get a measure of in the open, but walking into a potential ambush, that was something else. They exchanged silent looks. Mark knew that this was work for him.

Holding his hand up to caution Janine not to speak or make any noise, he eased past her and moved quietly into the darkness of the hallway. He paused to allow his eyes to become used to the gloom. There was no moon, and only a limited amount of light from the hotel areas below filtered up. As he waited, the lighter area of the exposed veranda doors formed into a backdrop. Beyond the sense of his own breathing, Mark could hear nothing. The silence was complete. Bracing himself and adopting as comfortable a combat position as was possible in the confined space, he moved forward. As he cautiously rounded into the lounge area of the suite, he halted. Sat in front of the doors to the veranda with a silhouette dimly but clearly visible was their visitor. Mark was relieved. He moved to switch on the lights. There was no danger; no one with evil intent would have positioned themselves in such a way. Whoever it was wanted to be seen and to be seen as soon as Mark and Janine entered.

"Victoria!"

It was actually Janine who voiced the recognition.

As the lights revealed her, Victoria, with one sweeping movement, jerked the curtain nearest to her across and hid herself from any possibility of outside observation. Mark closed the opposing curtain and flicked the switch on the air conditioner. The machine's noise would serve to cover their speech as much as the cooling would compensate for the night air being excluded.

Victoria sat down again. Janine dispensed beer from the fridge. Her actions were purposeful; her face was a blank. Janine rarely exercised any domestic skills and on this occasion did so with more than her usual reluctance. Her body language told Mark at once that she was not happy at this intrusion. It was a feeling that he shared.

"OK, Victoria, what's all this about?"

The question was blunt and harsh. Victoria could hardly have failed to notice that her visit was not welcome. In their position she would have been equally as unenthusiastic. But she still had a job to do. Her apology wasn't very fulsome, but it sufficed. She stated her business.

"I'm sorry for the intrusion, but despite Silvanus's death, or more perhaps because of it, we still need your help."

'There's a surprise,' thought Mark. Despite their desire to be left to enjoy their holiday in peace, both he and Janine had mentally been expecting something like this to happen. 'Why the cloak-and-dagger stuff? Everybody knows we know Victoria. I suppose it's the Adekos being here. Shit, the tortuous toils of Nigerian politics… Can't back out now.'

"You know what Akinbode asked us to do?"

Mark assumed that she did but felt it better to re-establish the ground rules. His tone was civil but not friendly.

"Of course, we worked together. He wanted you to help prevent arms from Russia getting to Nigeria."

Mark made no effort to help the conversation along.

Victoria hurried on. "But there's more than that. There's a complex political game in play: to defeat the Moslem Fundamentalists in the north and prevent dissident politicians and businessmen from southern Nigeria exploiting the situation."

"With the Federal Government and its security service holding the ring," finished Mark.

He and Janine knew all of this.

"Right. But this is Nigeria. The southern agenda is more than just about preventing the Fundamentalists taking over the north and then the Federation; it's also about using the turmoil to shift the power to the south. Maintaining the status quo, which is the Government's objective, is not what they want."

"And the northern traditionalists," said Janine, picking up the tale, "want to prevent their power being usurped by the Fundamentalists but to still hold the power in the Federation."

"So?" said Mark.

"So," repeated Victoria, "the southerners, through a cartel of businessmen, have started building an arsenal of weapons both to resist the Fundamentalists and to increase their clout in the future debate. My brother-in-law, and he's for real, is the power behind the cartel. The holiday's a cover. He's really here to arrange payment for a huge shipment of arms, the first part of which is due shortly."

"And the arms are being supplied by the Wong organisation from Russia?" said Mark.

"So we believe."

Thoughts of Wong's dead son and the Arab woman flashed through Mark's brain, but he suppressed them.

"What about the two guys at the High Commission?" asked Janine; if they were in a mood to share confidences she thought she might satisfy all her curiosity.

"Falinde and Oje. Fixers for the southern cartel. Go-betweens with the Chinese, we believe."

They also worked for the Nigerian Security Service, but Victoria didn't seem to think this worth mentioning.

"OK," said Mark, wanting to get the conversation over with, "So who's driving the Fundamentalists?"

"We're not really sure, although one of the sons of the Emir of Kano is known to have spent a lot of time in Iran; but that was some time ago. More significantly, perhaps, his father has repudiated him. A growing number of young northerners are being trained in the bad lands of Somalia. And large numbers of disaffected men from the Middle East, Yemenis and Saudis, are appearing all over the north. Hard to penetrate these groups since they aren't black."

"OK, hear all that," said Janine. "Presumably the Federal Government knows what's going on, though. That's why your lot are involved."

"Of course. And our Minister's right behind us, and there are others. You met the Alhaji."

"What, Mahomet Sullag? He's a traditionalist!"

Janine wasn't surprised.

"Yes, he is; but he knows that things have got to change. He doesn't want them to, and he might not interfere with those who resist. Nonetheless, he's a realist."

Victoria's admiration of the Alhaji was clear. This grated on Mark, although he couldn't put his finger on why. He hoped that this Alhaji Sullag was all that Victoria cracked him up to be; he sounded like a personality who could have great influence on the outcome of the Fundamentalist question and that was key to the campaign against the Boko Haram group.

"Enough of this," Mark said, interposing in the conversation, his desire to be rid of Victoria rising again. "Let's get back to the point. You want us to prevent the arms shipments. That'll upset the Wongs, the southerners, the Fundamentalists… Do we have any allies?"

"Only us, and we won't acknowledge you. Hiring Europeans to help us is a sensitive issue."

"So why hire us?"

"Mark," Victoria said, "you're white, we're black; isn't it obvious?"

"Money?" said Mark.

Victoria didn't haggle much, as Silvanus Akinbode had already outlined the figures, and a deal was soon struck.

"Anything more?" asked Victoria, suddenly mindful that her sister and the Chief would soon be back from having dinner in town. "I have to take Silvanus's body home tomorrow. We'll all be leaving. I'll be in contact in London. I think Janine might like to see rather more of me for a while, to console me, you understand."

She grinned. Janine's enthusiasm wasn't immediately apparent.

* * *

After breakfast the next day, Mark was called to the manager's office and another interview with Joshua Umberto.

"Won't keep you long. Thought you might like to know we believe Mr Akinbode was killed by a Moslem Fundamentalists operative from the old 'New Truth' group."

"What?" said Mark in some surprise at the completeness of the statement.

"We contacted London. Seems a Saudi businessman was killed in a taxi in the same way. No Arab woman there, though. The London police believe that we're dealing with the same terror group or, more to the point, one of their key operatives. At least the woman in the photograph has nothing to do with it. Apparently she was killed in a gun battle with the Lebanese police last year."

Umberto opened out his hands in a rather French gesture to signify that that was all he had to say.

Mark offered no comment. He was convinced that the young blonde-cum-Arab woman he had met was involved in what was going on, even if he wasn't sure how or whether it was her who had just flown out of Seychelles. He looked forward to encountering her again. Her perceived prowess with a knife didn't bother him too much.

SIXTEEN

Despite her origins, Janine's knowledge of her homeland had only become anything like comprehensive when she had been asked by Mark to build a database on Nigeria in the face of a resumption of the Boko Haram's efforts to radicalise the north of the country. Violent, sectarian and amateurish efforts had been made in the first two decades of the century by this group, but now in 2024 there was a sense of something much more sophisticated was being attempted. Not that the public evidence was any the less violent and simplistic than before; it was, as Janine had discovered, the underlying organisation that was different. The shift of the remnants of the old al-Qaeda to Somalia from Afghanistan and Pakistan towards the end of the 2010s and the final implosion of that country had forced an apparent strategic rethink. The evolution of the terrorist structures into local autonomous groups accelerated. But because of the deep-seated traditionalist culture of northern Nigeria and a reluctance to share power with an external hegemony, the Fundamentalists weren't making much progress. And the large-scale killings were alienating the people, irrespective of their religion.

"When you break it all down," Janine had said to Mark,

"Nigerian politics is very simple. It's about which out of the north or south runs the country and as a consequence has first chance to get their noses in the trough."

"That's a bit hard."

"Maybe, but the history of the past decades does rather suggest that material benefit and politics are joined at the hip in Nigeria."

"Except," said Mark, "didn't you also say that the younger generation, the sons and daughters of the Big Men of the past, are beginning to forge an economic base for themselves and the country that is much more inclusive and doing it with far more integrity than their parents?"

Big Men was the universal African description of the rich and powerful, the political patrons, the successful monopolistic businessmen, the super-class wheelers and dealers and fixers. For Mark it was a term of contempt.

"There are certainly such signs, but old habits will take a time to die. Perhaps more importantly, and according to people like Fid Okeke, the public servants are beginning to turn their backs on the sort of graft and corruption that has always been endemic."

"Why?" asked Mark.

"Fid was a bit bemused by this, I have to say."

In such free moments as Mark had had for thinking in the last few days, and as a result of the feedback from the Akinbodes, what he thought was beginning to happen was also, as Janine had implied, very simple. The Fundamentalists in the north were trying to destabilise the rule of the traditional and paternalistic Islamic-based sultanate government, a tactic made much more difficult to combat due to the multi-state nature of the Nigerian Constitution, whilst the vested interests in the south were gearing up to take advantage. In the end, both groups wanted the same thing, notwithstanding their different reasons, national power.

"Simple, but potentially destructive," Mark had concluded.

"But how many times has Nigeria been to the brink and back?" Janine had asked. "And how robust has the country proved to be despite the military/civilian yo-yo of power, civil war, local insurrections, tribal and religious massacres? You name it. And it's all been happening within boundaries that have no regional or ethnic logic drawn up by some high-handed and ignorant European elitist group who had never been to Africa nor showed any sign of wanting to."

"Wow, Janine; that was a bit passionate!"

Janine herself had wondered where the sudden intensity had come from.

And now on holiday on the edge of Africa, she had to admit that something was stirring inside her, and it wasn't just Mark's and her exuberant lovemaking!

* * *

"They've gone, that's it – the police, Victoria, the Adekos, the lot of them!" Mark said when he returned to the suite after his conversation with the Seychelles' security chief. "Now let's really enjoy this holiday."

The conversation with Joshua Umberto had drawn a line under the whole episode in his mind. He was relieved. Now it was going to be pleasure all the way.

And it certainly was. It was Thursday morning when Mark announced his determination, and for the next ten days, they gave themselves over to total enjoyment. When they returned to London two weekends later, they were both physically refreshed, mentally renewed and more at ease with each other than they had been for some time. And Nigerian politics had receded in their minds to something like its proper pace, or so they hoped.

* * *

"Let's island-hop," Janine had suggested.

"What a great idea. We've explored just about all there is of the scenery, beaches and restaurants of Mahé, how about Praslin, or La Digue island, or Fregate Island?"

They went to all three. They walked and fossicked on the beaches, picnicked, ate only local produce, and lived a lifestyle that was totally different from anything that Janine had ever experienced before. And her unending delight and wonder at the limitless range of wildlife was a real joy to Mark. Although perhaps not jaded, his senses were certainly conditioned by several visits to Africa and the tropics.

"Oh my God!" Janine had exclaimed.

They were on Fregate Island and they had been startled by the silent appearance of one of the ponderous giant turtles that reside there.

Mark was convulsed with laughter.

'How can she be so streetwise and effective at living in a big city but so ignorant of the natural world?' he had to ask himself.

When the mood took them, they swam in the sea and Mark taught Janine how to manage the big breakers. And when the mood took them, they made love, in the sea, on the beach and even, on one occasion, high up on a rocky outcrop on La Digue Island.

On their last day, they returned to the beach at the south of the main island where they'd first swam. Stripping off, Janine headed for the sea the moment that they arrived. Mark didn't see her enter the water. It was only when she swam up beside him and pulled him into an excited embrace that he realised that she totally naked.

"Come on, old man!" Janine challenged him.

It was only the arrival of a young family of local people that forced them into behaving with a more normal level of decorum.

"That was wonderful," said Janine, now firmly back in her red satin strip.

'It sure was,' Mark thought. 'We've moved together at lot more in the past two weeks.' The relationship had deepened and become more tolerant and less demanding. Janine had been the first to recognise the importance of having space in the partnership and of having room for other relationships; in his heart Mark agreed with her. It seemed entirely likely to her that in their line of work they would meet and possibly be attracted to other people. Although, conditioned as she was by living as a black woman in a white-dominated society, she thought the probability to be rather less in her own case.

'She's the only girl for me; we could certainly manage our working relationship better… but…'

The fact that his thoughts had more than once strayed to the blue-eyed blonde woman didn't register with him in the context of Janine. Had he been confronted, he would have called it professional interest, but the visions that broke into his lazy thoughts on the Seychelles beach were anything but professional.

"What you thinking about?" Janine asked, propping herself up and peering down at him.

A small surge of disloyalty had ended her own thoughts and she was keen to be at one with Mark again. His answer wasn't quite what she had expected.

"How we can get in touch with that blessed blonde woman?"

"Mark! Goddamn it, we're still on holiday!"

Her anger was more theatrical than real and deliberately overacted.

Mark pulled her down onto him and quieted her protests by gently kissing her. But despite the frolicking children nearby, the embrace didn't remain gentle for long.

"I'll buy you champagne at dinner," he said as a final palliative when he eventually released her.

"Oh, wow!"

She grinned her delighted grin; their last lingering dinner was now to be crowned with the ultimate in luxury. At least from being a small child and brought up by her careful rather than parsimonious relatives, such was her definition of luxury.

SEVENTEEN

Lawrence Wong's death had been a bitter blow to his father. The public nature of the killing was a deep and painful humiliation. To slay the youth with such casual ease was both a gesture of contempt and evidence of his father's vulnerability, something that he would find it very hard to come to terms with. In the ultimate event, the Wong organisation's power had proved no protection to his family. It didn't help that neither the police nor his own organisation had produced any evidence of the identity of the killer. But Jason Wong himself was very clear who had carried out the evil deed.

"'New Truth'," he said to his daughter Pearl the day before Lawrence's funeral.

Pearl knew perfectly well who 'New Truth' were and she knew why they might want to kill her father.

"Are you sure?"

"It was a revenge killing, what else!"

Unfinished business is what Lehia Said would have called it; to be completed before she fully settled to her real purpose for being in Britain.

* * *

"My father has several houses," the late Lawrence had once told Julie Mackenzie, Mark Shortley's niece, in a rare moment of unburdening, "apart from the flat. He has one in the Seychelles; not that he ever goes there. My real home's near Canterbury. I like it there. So does my father."

It was from his permanent base in Kent that Jason Wong and his daughter were now preparing for the funeral.

Pearl Wong had had no illusions about her dead brother, however much she loved him and however well she got on with him. Clever he might have been, but to her in her innermost thoughts he was lazy and feckless. Her father's disappointment concerning his son had been expressed more frequently as Lawrence had approached graduation, but she hadn't been inclined to become an advocate for her brother; her own best interests in the Wong empire would not have been served by that.

'Maybe it's for the best,' Pearl said to herself as she dressed for the funeral. 'With Lawrence in charge, our side of the family would soon have lost control of the business.'

The recently engineered demise in a car accident of one of her more able cousins had made her position more secure, but being a woman, she had to demonstrate her power very clearly if she was to be accepted as Jason's successor.

She joined her father in his ancient and valuable Rolls Royce.

The Wong house was well secluded, but nonetheless very close to the centre of the small village and consequently to the church. Although long since notionally converted to the Christian faith, the Wong family could not have been classed as regular churchgoers, but as the richest family in the neighbourhood, they were not unknown to the church and its untiring band of fundraisers.

"Mr Wong... Miss Wong..."

The waiting vicar of the parish led the way into the Norman church.

The array of parked cars would have warmed the heart of any BMW salesman and encouraged the vicar's expectations for the collection. It occurred to Pearl that the Wong family retainers were getting paid too much. But she didn't stint herself either; her clothes were at once fashionable and expensive.

Pearl quickly noted the make-up of the congregation. In front were three rows of impassive Chinese faces, all men, then a group of awkward but sad-looking young people, the most prominent of whom was Julie Mackenzie. Recognising her, Jason Wong inclined his head in silent acknowledgement of her presence. Pearl, taking in the university delegation as a whole, missed this little passage. At the back, finding it impossible not to stand out, Pearl observed the brooding figures of Messrs Falinde and Oje.

'Like obscene vultures,' she said to herself, hating them for bringing business once again into their grief.

The service was short, and as so often happens, young Lawrence turned out to be a more worthy person in death than in life. Apart from quiet sobs from Julie, the proceedings were largely uninterrupted by any contribution from the gathered mourners and the vicar's droning oratory didn't disturb the silence for very long. The private parts of the funeral were carried out with equal facility and the mourners were soon congregating at the Wong's country house.

* * *

The still of the Wong's spacious and luxurious sitting room, however, was well and truly disturbed when the small party of guests gathered back there, and it was apparent that Falinde and Oje had gate-crashed.

"Don't you two bastards have any respect?" demanded Pearl.

She confronted the two Nigerians before the servants

could begin distributing drinks and canapés. There was an embarrassed shuffle from the other guests, all family and all Chinese. Everybody else at the church had melted away.

"We have business," said Falinde, oblivious to the reactions of those around him.

Pearl's outrage was palpable, but it was also well acted. The scene was for her father as much as it was for the Nigerians; not that she didn't think that they were being both rude and insensitive.

"Hector," she said to the diminutive Chinese man who had by now insinuated himself into a position beside her, "take these two to the back study and see they get food and drink. There will be no business for at least an hour."

Hector Xu, Jason Wong's most trusted associate, gestured to the two men to follow him. They shuffled aggressively. But the body language of three burly Chinese men dressed in waiter's uniforms but carrying no trays was giving clear signals that even the Nigerians couldn't fail to understand.

"Thank you, Pearl," said Jason.

He was impressed.

The wake got underway and, true to Pearl's predictions, it lasted an hour. As the family and associates began to drift away, they all felt that they knew how the void left by Lawrence's death was going to be filled. Reaction was mixed, but the mystery surrounding the death of the cousin when his particular BMW left the road with apparent brake failure had added spice to the mixture. Amongst her own generation, Pearl had universal support, but it was the old men who decided these things.

"They've gone, Father, I'll get those two wretched black men back here."

"No, no, get Hector, we'll confront them in the back study. They'll be outnumbered; they won't give us any trouble."

Hector Xu was not hard to find. Ever the diplomat, he'd spent much of the hour's mourning carefully nurturing the more volatile and recalcitrant of the Wong family members. The Wong organisation was an ill-defined corporation with all of the shares being held by the several branches of the Wong clan. Its management was vested in the members considered most fitted to exercise the considerable power that the organisation had. Jason Wong's position was unassailable, but his successor was not preordained.

"Hector, we're going to confront those damn blacks."

'She'll do,' Xu thought as he quietly escorted Pearl to join her father and the two despised Nigerians.

As the ultimate fixer in the Wong organisation, his politicking during the wake was very much in support of Pearl, whom he saw as a natural to succeed her father. He had no qualms whatsoever about advancing the interests of a woman, once he had decided that she was the best leader available.

'Lawrence just didn't have what it would have taken.'

Devoted as he was to Jason Wong and his family, like Pearl he had no illusions about the capabilities of the late Lawrence Wong. Respected and feared within the Wong empire, despite not being a family member, and within the wider Chinese business community, support from Hector Xu was a great prize for Pearl.

"Gentlemen, I do not take kindly to this further intrusion into my family's grief."

The words were cold and hard.

"Our apologies and condolences, Mr Wong," said Falinde, "but we do have a great deal of money tied up in your activities on our behalf, and—"

"And no trust!" snapped Pearl, interrupting the speech.

"...and we must protect our interest."

The Nigerian's words were equally cold, but manifestly insincere.

Falinde finished his sentence with a twisted suggestion of a smile on his face. His contempt for Pearl was more than obvious.

Nothing of this frigid passage escaped Jason Wong and, more particularly, Hector Xu.

"It's most important this first shipment is successful," Falinde continued. "The political situation in Nigeria is uncertain and the south needs to assert itself."

'The last thing we need is a lecture on politics,' thought Pearl.

"Gentlemen, a deal has been done. My contact has the goods in his possession and we have agreed a delivery programme."

Jason Wong explained the outcome of his visit to Moscow and the arrangements for the transfer of the arms and ammunition from Russia to Nigeria. He was necessarily vague on some of the details and resistant to pleas for clarification, but he told the two men what he thought they needed to know and they eventually had to be satisfied.

"Why can't there be just one shipment?" asked Falinde.

It seemed an obvious enough question to the Nigerian.

"Clearly you've never seen five thousand rifles," said Pearl, the tone of her voice almost unbelieving of their ignorance.

"Hector, can you initiate the payment arrangements? They've been set up in the Seychelles. We need the money."

Falinde was inclined to argue; he still wasn't getting the detail he felt he needed. His concentration on the minutiae of the deal had already considerably irritated Jason Wong.

"Pearl, it might be a good idea if you delivered these gentlemen back to Heathrow yourself."

It was the end of the meeting. Jason Wong had had enough of the Nigerians and wanted to retreat to the solitude of his own study and to be alone with his grief again. And he wanted to be sure that the wretched Nigerians were truly out of the country.

Messrs Falinde and Oje protested. They had their own arrangements already in place. At least Falinde protested; Pearl was beginning to seriously wonder whether Mr Oje wasn't mute.

The arrival of the three burly Chinese men again, with coats, resolved the matter.

* * *

"Interesting goings-on in the Seychelles," remarked Pearl after they joined the M25 near Maidstone.

"What goings-on?" asked Falinde, the abruptness of his speech almost stifling Pearl's first effort at conversation.

"One of your colleagues was killed. Stabbed, I believe. At an island hotel."

Calling Silvanus Akinbode a colleague was a fortuitous display of courtesy by Pearl; it spurred Falinde into a prompt denial. It was clear that he had no idea that Pearl knew the truth of his and Mr Oje's employment situation.

"He was no colleague of ours! Akinbode worked for the Federal Security Service. He's been trying to get close to Chief Adeko for ages. It was a very difficult situation when they were on holiday in the Seychelles."

Falinde thought it better not to say too much without realising that saying anything at all would tell Pearl a lot more than he would have wanted, the reference to Chief Adeko being entirely gratuitous. How she knew about Mr Akinbode's death didn't seem to have occurred to him either.

'Seems to be well informed,' thought Pearl, although she in her turn didn't bother to wonder how he got to be so.

"Akinbode's death sorted the problem, though," she said aloud. "Killing the man certainly broke up the happy holiday."

The callousness of the remark was lost on Mr Falinde, who was immediately trapped into saying more.

"Akinbode wasn't the key player; the dangerous one is his wife!"

Somewhat taken aback by the unnecessary disclosure of yet

more information, Pearl went on alert; the fact that Falinde felt the need to say what he had focused her instantly.

'He obviously doesn't have a very high regard for women,' she thought, 'that's for sure, but that was respect – grudging, maybe, but respect nonetheless – for Victoria Akinbode.'

Pearl had only recently heard of the young Nigerian woman, but she had been impressed and thought she might relish the possibility of doing battle with her. Her father, she had discovered, already had a file on Victoria, complete with recent photographs.

"So why would anyone else want to kill him?" she asked innocently.

"How should I know?" Falinde's response was sharp, sensing at last that the conversation was not wise. "Dirty business security and intelligence... could be any number of reasons."

'He's right,' Pearl conceded in her head, 'but to carry out such a killing in the Seychelles requires sophistication and skill; it was hardly a casual murder.'

The reports of the killing from the Wong's Seychelles office were accurate enough in the absence of access to information from the police. The report of the visit to the office by a young black woman asking all sorts of well-informed questions she was less sure about. For a start, the report didn't provide any names. Pearl suspected that the information that it contained was understated and the young woman had been more successful in her probing than was indicated.

'Has to be Victoria Akinbode,' she'd said to herself when she read the details and compared them with her father's files. 'Our Victoria would be better out of the way rather than being around to play games with.'

It was a typical ruthless thought from Pearl. Encroachment from the Nigerian Security Service was not in the Wong's plans and disposing of Victoria if, as Falinde seemed to be saying, she was a key figure, was the sort of direct action that Pearl was becoming known for.

However, for Messrs Falinde and Oje, she moved the conversation on.

"Your northern compatriots would have a reason to kill this man?" Pearl asked.

They had just entered the access tunnel at Heathrow and were heading for Terminal Three.

"Might have," said Falinde.

But he got on further. Something about the car in front of them suddenly fazed him.

"Keep going, keep going. Round again if you have to."

The tone of voice was more panic than urgency.

Pearl did as she was bid, in some surprise, causing consternation and chaos to the cars following them. If Falinde had been spooked, she assumed that she might have cause to be cautious as well.

"Problem?" she said.

"Mahomet Sullag, he mustn't see us."

Pearl hadn't a clue who Mahomet Sullag might be.

"Could he be on the same flight?"

"We'd have to get another one."

Falinde and the silent Mr Oje both became more animated than Pearl had ever seen them.

"It's not the Alhaji, it's his security staff," Falinde said. "if they recognise us, we risk being forced to stay in Nigeria."

That was the last thing they wanted.

The Wong organisation had a legitimate cargo forwarding business at the Airport with offices and, more importantly, computers. Within seconds, Pearl was able to check that Alhaji Mahomet Sullag and a party of six were on the same flight as Messrs Falinde and Oje. She invaded the Nigeria Airways computer and erased all record of the two men ever having been booked on the flight. Routine checks at Lagos later confirmed to the Nigerian Security Service that no one that they might be interested in was on the flight. They noted, however, that two of their agents were arriving on a British Airways flight from Gatwick overnight.

* * *

On her way back from Gatwick, several hours later than expected, Pearl began to plan her next moves, both to further her ambitions for control of the Wong empire and to protect their investment in the arms shipments. There was no doubt in her mind that the Nigerian Security Service would be attempting to prevent the weapons arriving in their country. That would have to be countered vigorously.

"Pity about Victoria Akinbode, I think I could have liked her!"

EIGHTEEN

Following Lawrence's funeral, the Wong household attempted to settle back into a normal lifestyle. None of them found it easy.

That is not to say that in the more private parts of the various participants' brains some thoughts about the future weren't going on. They all knew about the abhorrence of vacuums.

And it was Hector Xu's thoughts on the new situation that very much reflected the prevailing views of the organisation at large.

'Lawrence didn't have a role in the business, as yet, so there's no practical gap, just a hole in people's expectations. Don't think the vacuum will last very long. It's pretty obvious where Jason was coming from; otherwise why pull Pearl into the dealings with those two abominable Nigerians? Doesn't seem to be too much objection to Pearl being Jason's number two... . Or universal enthusiasm either! I guess some of the old fools are still a bit sexist. Still, she'll have to prove herself. Need to knock a few rough edges off. At least we know her faults; not that there's anything desperately wrong with her. The young are always intolerant of those less capable than themselves; she'll have to hide her contempt for the old men, though. Ruthlessness combined with sensitivity; that's what's important.'

"She'll do," Xu said aloud.

It was his current mantra to be preached to the decision-makers of the Wong clan.

For others, the thoughts were rather less political.

To the bodyguards, Pearl was already something of a cult figure. Fit and proficient in the martial arts, they had collected many a bruise between them to attest to her similar passion. Had she known of Victoria Akinbode's accomplishments, Pearl might have relished a more basic form of combat with her, but the decisions on Victoria were already made.

* * *

Despite the frequent urgings of Mr Falinde and even Chief Adeko, the arrangements between the Wong organisation and the Nigerians for the arms shipments took their time. It was almost a month before Hector Xu could be despatched to Moscow to make the first payment. It was also a month since Pearl had begun to regularly shadow her father's business activities. Notwithstanding Xu's confidence, the seniors in some of the other branches of the family still tried to convince themselves that Jason Wong was only paying lip service to the notion of promoting his daughter. But Pearl slipped easily into the role of Chief of Staff to her father.

If the truth were known, Jason Wong genuinely welcomed Pearl's more intimate involvement with the business. Although his disappointment at the loss of his son was still acute, the daily cut and thrust of his activities quickly reawakened him to the realities of life, and the possibilities arising from having Pearl permanently with him began to occupy his mind increasingly.

* * *

"I don't believe it!"

Victoria Akinbode was reading the newspapers on the morning of her return to Abuja.

Several Christians in Katsina had been beaten up and at least one beheaded for apparently defiling the Koran. The suggestion, albeit untrue, that his wife had used pages from the holy book as toilet paper was sufficient for the poor man to be decapitated. Sharia law had prevailed in Katsina for many years, but in this instance the due processes of religious or civil law had little opportunity to be enforced. Mob violence prevailed.

The incident served to alert non-Moslems again to the fragile nature of their residence in northern cities, and if it didn't reopen old wounds, it undoubtedly reminded people that they were there. In this case, the incident seemed to be contrived, which was the cause of Victoria's exclamation, and a part of a more widespread Boko Haram effort to raise the religious temperature again.

In Kano, a number of young women, all of whom were Christians, had been beaten through the streets by groups of both men and women fanatics for various crimes of lewd behaviour, particularly going bareheaded or wearing mini-skirts. Dress styles in most northern cities had conformed to traditional Moslem standards for many years, but it had been rare in the past for these standards to be forced on Christians.

"Devious bastards," said Victoria with a chuckle. "The women were breaking the existing edicts of the city, so the authorities couldn't object!"

But the Fundamentalists didn't always have it all their own way.

"Groups of Fundamentalist youths who tried to force the already segregated state high school in Sokoto to banish its female pupils to some distant and dingy back area of the campus were resisted by the school's students, both male and female," reported the main Sokoto daily newspaper, also in Victoria's pile of reading. "The riot police responded with a severity that certainly cured the zealous youngsters of any desire for further confrontation. However, armed with the counsels of their more thoughtful and consequently more dangerous elders amongst the Fundamentalists, they have now resorted again to harassing tourists and other foreigners."

'At least they didn't try to shut down the women's classes completely,' Victoria said to herself. 'too provocative, I guess, for the moment.'

Under the influence of such men as Mahomet Sullag, the response to this renewed outbreak of violence and mayhem was vigorous, but because the Minister appeared to be reluctant to cut off the Fundamentalists' access to the media, the results of his actions were limited. However, both sides knew that they were only witnessing the opening skirmishes of a renewed and more determined power struggle. Criticism of the Minister for the ambivalence of his actions was muted, but nonetheless people like Fid Okeke again wondered where his loyalties truly lay. Victoria had no such doubts in her mind.

"Looks like the early days in Somalia," Fid Okeke said to Victoria Akinbode when she later reported to his office. "we ought to have learnt some of the lessons."

"Maybe. Shortley's research into the spread of the Fundamentalists would certainly suggest Boko Haram have learnt a lot from old al-Shabaab tactics."

Okeke was interested. More business seemed likely to be coming Mark's way as the conversation developed, although some of Victoria's suggestions seemed to Okeke to be missing to the point of what he was seeking. But Victoria's perspective was often different from his, as he was well aware.

"At the suggestion of Alhaji Sullag, the Federal Government has reintroduced visas for non-African Union citizens," the Sokoto newspaper had continued. "This is intended to force the increasing number of people of Middle-Eastern and North African origin moving into Nigeria into the open. However, the difficulties in stemming the existing illicit immigrants who flock into the country to seek their fortunes indicates how difficult a task the authorities will have."

Again Fid Okeke and Victoria took different inferences from this proposal.

And within a relatively short time, even more subversives were flooding in through the porous borders of Katsina, Kano and Borno States, and the Sullag's traditionalist credentials were again under challenge.

* * *

Pearl Wong, with the newfound freedom that her latest role gave her, had decided to overhaul her father's intelligence machine and widen its areas of interest. In view of the size of the pending arms deal, she not unnaturally included Nigeria and its multiplicity of political activities within her net. She was conscious that if the deal didn't come off or was fouled up in some way it would have a major impact on the credibility of the Wong organisation and her father. Having staked her future on succeeding him, she did not intend that this should happen.

Pearl also admitted to herself something of a fascination for all things Nigerian.

NINETEEN

"We'll have coffee in Canterbury, talk a little, plan a little, and then we'll go back and give 'em hell!" he said.

Jason Wong didn't specify who it was he was planning to give hell to.

Pearl laughed; this was a side of her father that she knew existed but which she had never shared before. It wasn't quite as casual as it sounded, telephone calls were made, urgent matters were dealt with, and half -an -hour later, Jason Wong, hanging on his daughter's arm, was striding up Canterbury High Street with all the gaiety of a schoolboy genuinely playing truant from school.

"This is wonderful. I haven't seen you like this for years!"

Pearl was both delighted and bemused. In her more serious approach to the family business, she found such unpredictable behaviour unsettling. But her father intended it to be. It was one of the ways in which he kept the staff of his empire on their toes. If he were always to be predictable, life would have been both boring and threatening to him. Keeping his internal, as well as his external, enemies guessing, he reasoned, made good sense.

'Pity we have to have Tang One to make way for us, and

Michael and Tang Two always in the background,' thought Pearl.

"Why not! why not...!"

Jason Wong's delighted chuckle at his daughter's pleasure suddenly turned into a rasping gurgle as he struggled unsuccessfully for breath. Pearl felt his light touch turn into a dead weight on the arm that he had hooked through hers. Pivoted by his grasp, he slewed round as he stumbled forward, impelled by a force that had struck him from behind and which took Pearl entirely by surprise. He fell to his knees and then forward onto his face, coughing blood over her legs and feet as he did so. It was a horrific split second of action.

Shocked bystanders took in what had happened. There was a concerted silence, broken only by Jason Wong's short desperate struggle for his last breaths. Within seconds he too was silent. From below his left shoulder blade, the red flights of a crossbow bolt stood out against the delicate colour of his camel-hair coat.

The three bodyguards crowded around Pearl and her fallen father, their weapons drawn. Caught utterly unawares, they searched nervously up and down the street. But they saw only a mass of stunned people, each focused on the cameo group that had formed in the middle of the road just past the old Post Office building and where the paved walkway rose for the bridge over the River Stour.

Away from the more immediate vicinity of the killing, people moved about their business, unaware that the tragedy had occurred. Prompted by some instinct known only to their breed, two policewomen appeared from somewhere in the kaleidoscopic mass of people. As the pair of neat figures in blue ran into Pearl's frame of vision, she refocused on the distance. Her eyes had been mechanically scanning the backcloth of colour and movement, but the images hadn't registered in her conscious mind. Her subconscious mind inevitably had recorded more. Even the Arab woman in long, black robes, her face almost completely obscured, had passed before her eyes without her knowing at the time that her brain had registered her existence.

* * *

"That was one hell of a good shot," the detective inspector in charge remarked.

His comment had been made to a colleague ten minutes later as they tried to piece together what had happened. The bolt, they surmised, had been fired from a small percussion-type weapon rather than a traditional crossbow, which would have been far too cumbersome to hide. The range they computed to be no more than thirty metres.

"Dead risky with all those people about," said the colleague. "As the bodyguards tell it, the gap between them must have only opened up for a few fractions of a second. Felt the draught of the bolt, one of them. The killer must've been watching for a hell of a long time to be able to take such a sudden chance."

The two policewomen shepherded Pearl away to the seclusion of a small public garden nearby to await the arrival of a car to take her from the scene. As their colleagues poured onto the murder scene, they undertook the impossible task of comforting Pearl. They recognised the futility of their efforts, but they stuck to it as best they could.

Jason Wong was, of course, well known to the local police. They made no effort to protect him. But they did make it their business to keep track of his activities, and as a consequence they were in immediate contact with their counterparts in London checking the details of the death of the son. By this time the Metropolitan Police had followed down all of their leads and had largely satisfied themselves that Lawrence Wong had been killed by a terrorist, probably a Moslem Fundamentalist.

132

They were also satisfied that the act was unrelated to any more general threat to the population at large.

"Some shoppers saw an Arab woman and the victim's daughter thought she did too."

The detective inspector was reporting to his superiors.

"We've recovered the weapon, a one-shot pistol of Iraqi manufacture, easily disguisable in the sleeve of Arab robes. And we've recovered the robes too. But that's it. Like the son and the Met, we've got a pretty good idea who did it but not a lot of chance of proving it."

At home, Pearl retreated to her bedroom, utterly bereft. Unable to comprehend the full enormity of what had happened at first, she sat alone in her room, her soiled clothes hurriedly consigned to the furnace and her mind crushed by the horror of what she had witnessed.

'First Lawrence and now this God, what's happening to me?'

The staff left her to herself. As evening closed in, family and business associates began to arrive, but Tang One and Tang Two steadfastly refused to allow anybody near their mistress. Borne down by their own failure, the two men showed a pathetic determination to protect her to the last and stolidly announced that she was not to be disturbed. They blocked the way of any who felt inclined to challenge their edict. None did. Conscious of how much face the two men had lost, the visitors accepted their restriction rather than risk more violence. Michael, the third bodyguard, overtaken by shock, was nowhere to be found.

TWENTY

The news of Jason Wong's death travelled quickly; the instant information transmission capabilities of the Internet saw to that. But in Russia, the General, like Hector Xu, didn't rely just on the Internet and had his own satellite telecommunications system that gave him access to various useful parts of the world. In London, he had a relative who had long since established herself in the upper reaches of the Moscow-Kiev Bank. She was aware of Wong's death as soon as the news services were. The General knew minutes later.

"Welcome, Sir."

Hector Xu was met from the London flight by a rather young and worried member of the extensive Wong family. Recently deposited in Moscow as a postbox and listening post, Leonard Wong was informed of the news via the organisation's private worldwide communications network and had been asked to advise Hector Xu. It was not a task that the young man relished. Unaware whether his visitor would have watched the airline news channels, Leonard Wong assumed that the arriving Xu would not know. He didn't. He thrust the news onto his senior almost as they first shook hands.

"Killed," said Hector Xu in disbelief, "in the street, in Canterbury!"

But Hector Xu was nothing if not a professional and a seasoned businessman, so having worked with his pain at the death of his old friend for a while, he almost visibly switched the grieving off and turned his attention to the job in hand.

"We have work to do," he said with renewed vigour.

Leonard Wong was torn away from his own thoughts. Although a close member of the family, he was too young at nineteen to be concerned with the innermost workings of the Wong empire, but that didn't prevent him from speculating on the likely outcome of the latest tragedy.

"We have work to do," said Xu again. "where are we to meet with the General?"

Mindful of Jason Wong's and Chang's treatment on their previous visit, the old man was anxious not to have to endure the same experience.

"At his dacha in the country. I had to telephone when you arrived; I've done so. There'll be a car soon."

Leonard Wong was more dynamic than his late cousin Lawrence, so he had asked for directions in order that they could make their way in his own car, but the request was rudely rejected. Young Wong doubted that he would get lost in the snow and so rightly assumed that the General and his staff were not anxious for the whereabouts of their base to become too well known.

"The Russian authorities have been making some belated but largely ineffectual efforts to curb the General's activities," the youth reported to Hector Xu, by way of explanation for the secrecy.

"There could be problems then," said Xu, more as a statement than as a question.

Jason Wong had warned Xu about the slippery nature of their contact.

'Take the arms in stages, keep the money as long as possible,' thought Hector Zu. 'not surprising he wasn't saying much to the Nigerians hardly confidence-building.'

"There's the car. I doubt if it will be a pleasant trip. The roads are heavily congested and the Russians drive like maniacs."

Young Wong's prediction proved to be accurate. The driver managed to avoid a collision with an army truck by millimetres within minutes of collecting the two Chinese. An angry altercation with a taxi driver followed before some semblance of driving competence emerged. But to Xu's astonishment the incidents did absolutely nothing to curb the driver's crazy enthusiasm and they set off again, achieving the same manic pace once they were outside the city.

"They're all mad," said the younger man in Mandarin Chinese to his senior.

But they survived and were eventually shown into the jovial presence of the General. It was just on noon when they arrived.

Firmly planted in front of one of two enormous log fires, the Russian awaited the two men's progress towards him. With a fine recognition of his own supposed worth, he took only one pace forward to shake Hector Xu's hand. He nodded coolly at Leonard Wong. None of this play-acting escaped Xu. But it put Xu firmly on his guard despite his host's opening remark.

"Sorry about Mr Wong," the General said rather gruffly in his fractured English but in a genuine attempt to be sympathetic.

Both Xu and Leonard Wong acknowledged the General's condolences.

But it was business as usual instantly afterwards.

"You have the money?"

The General had asked for a down payment of one hundred thousand dollars. Hector Xu had only brought eighty thousand dollars. This was still more than Jason Wong had wanted to pay. However, Xu, long in the tooth when it came to negotiations, knew that the General would be looking for reassurance after the death of the heir to the business. The continuing effectiveness of the Wong organisation would be very important to him. So at the last minute Xu had instructed Leonard Wong to bring more money from Moscow. What the General's reaction to the death of the head of the organisation now would be, Hector Xu knew that he would very soon find out.

"I have the money," he said.

"I think we trade less rifles," the General said.

He was still being jovial, but as Hector Xu supposed, he was testing them out. It was the sort of reaction that he was expecting.

Leonard Wong, who had opened the briefcase of money, snapped it shut as the General spoke and as the beautiful Natalia appeared to take it from him.

"We have a deal. The rest of the money will be transferred the moment the arms are checked in at Felixstowe in England and loaded onto the ship for Nigeria. That was what was agreed! That is what will happen!"

Hector Xu was not angry, just unyieldingly firm. A mahjong player of immense skill at the age of sixteen, Hector had spent a lifetime in negotiations and in wheeling and dealing. With fifty years of experience since the heady days of his first friendship with Jason Wong, negotiating with an inveterate rogue like the General was almost an affront to his dignity.

Like Jason Wong before him in similar circumstances, he was not ready for the General's reaction.

The old Russian roared with laughter. The lovely Natalia reappeared with vodka and they all drank; but warily. The rapport that Jason Wong had achieved was not there on this occasion. Leonard Wong oozed suspicion from every pore and Hector Xu was clearly uncomfortable.

"The General is known as a man of his word. He is shifty and crooked in negotiations, he bargains and cheats all the way, but once his word is given, he keeps it. And he expects others to keep theirs."

If Hector Xu had had time to read Pearl's new intelligence digest he would have been reassured.

* * *

The death of Jason Wong was hot news for most of the Monday. The media were universal in predicting that Pearl Wong would follow her father as head of the organisation. They had even managed to dig out some very flattering photographs of her. Internet chat was perhaps less unanimous with the suspicions over the death of the cousin again being revived, albeit in rather guarded terms. Pearl, generally speaking, ignored the twittering.

"Very tasty, I think you'd call her!" remarked Janine as she deposited the media digests and a sample of the pictures on Mark's desk later on the Monday afternoon.

Pearl Wong was undoubtedly a very attractive young woman. And because of the sad relationship of his niece with Lawrence Wong, as Janine was well aware, Mark knew exactly who she was.

"But not as tasty as you, eh?" he said aloud.

Janine's grin lit up in appreciation. Mark wasn't usually one for extravagant compliments.

"I need to talk to Victoria; better find out what she knows about this."

Mark had regular conversations with Victoria Akinbode over a secure telephone line and Janine had had several meetings with her in London. The business relationship was developing well. A rather broader contract than originally proposed had finally been agreed, and Janine in particular, had been presented with some pretty challenging objectives. However, the high level of surveillance of the various key figures required by Victoria was speedily and successfully established. And closing the links to the Wongs via the Mark's family connection and the business card found on Silvanus Akinbode in the Seychelles had been one of the first activities of the new partnership.

"Nigeria is one hell of an enigma," Janine had said to Mark when she'd finished the basic surveillance system. "Until recently it's been as peaceful and stable as it had ever been, which doesn't say too much. But the re-emergence of Boko Haram has put this peace and stability into question."

But as Mark and Janine well knew, in a country with such a vast population, they could only gather a limited amount of information. The Big Men syndrome was still very important, but the younger, computer literate and Internet-wise, more international generation, were asserting themselves and behaving very much as any similar group in any other country would. But the breakdown of the cultural stratification was still only happening slowly.

"The money's pouring in," Janine continued. "Much of it is still going into IT and other infrastructure. High-speed broadband is available in all states and all big towns and is widely used socially as well as for business. Outside the population centres and in the villages it's anyone's guess what the penetration is. How much it is being used with the sort of openness and integrity that applies in Europe is equally anyone's guess."

"And below the surface?" said Mark.

"You tell me," responded Janine, picking up on the religious/tribal/racial inference, "more stresses and strains than I ever imagined possible in one country."

By taking advantage of the developments taking place, Janine had readily been able to tap into the computer systems. By also exploiting the greyer areas of international law on data transmission and security, which the Nigerian Government had now belatedly implemented, she was able to monitor virtually anything she wanted to about Nigeria and be aware of the movements of virtually anybody – including, as she admitted, Victoria Akinbode – if they accessed or were identified on any computer.

But Victoria, on her visits to Janine, didn't spend all of her time on business matters; they also spent leisure time together and had enjoyed some vigorous workouts at Janine's judo club. This was very much at Victoria's instigation.

"I don't know," Janine said in frustration after one particularly long session with Victoria, both at the office and in the gym. "She's really likeable, so why don't I like her?"

"Do you have to like her?" was Mark's response.

Victoria was business as far as he was concerned. There was no reason why she should be anything else, so Janine's wariness about their Nigerian Security Service contact surprised him. But something in his head also told him not to discount her reaction. Janine's judgement of other women was usually sound.

"She's OK," was Victoria's judgement in turn on Janine. "We get on well enough."

But that was as far as it went. Victoria was as forthcoming and informative about her work as she felt she needed to be. But she was also very competitive and self-focused. She would have hardly succeeded as she had if she hadn't been. Almost unknowingly she classed Janine as a rival in her mind and had no more special liking for her than Janine had for her. She had no concept of loyalty in her relationship with Janine.

"You don't think Victoria's lot killed Wong, do you?" asked Janine, reverting to the topic of the day.

"I very much doubt it. Everything seems to point to the Moslem Fundamentalists again."

"I guess so. Still it makes no odds to us, I suppose."

As well as her work for Victoria, Janine had spent many hours trawling for information about Jason Wong and the Wong organisation. 'I guess he has to be right,' she thought, acknowledging Mark's judgement of the likely killers. 'Nonetheless, this guy's got an amazing array of enemies. But the Fundamentalists have to be suspect number one, if only because of the Beirut fracas last year.'

Janine was aware that there were several unsupported

assumptions in her mental meanderings that Mark might not have approved of, but it was a scenario that fitted the facts as she knew them.

* * *

"Victoria, good to hear from you."

Mark was on the telephone to the Nigerian security agent in Abuja.

"We've just been talking about the murder of Jason Wong. I guess you've heard?"

With the Internet agog with rumours about the whole Wong enterprise, Mark knew that it was a rather facile question, but it opened the conversation on his terms.

"We certainly have."

"Any likely impact you can see?" Mark then asked.

"No, not really; the Wongs will want to carry on with the deal. There'll be a lot of money in selling arms to the southerners. Mind you, Falinde and Oje scurried off to London pretty damn quick; that shows what confidence those two little shits have in the Wongs."

Victoria chuckled; the antics of the two southern fixers were totally transparent to their colleagues in the security service. So far these antics had had no impact on what Mark was doing or had been asked to do, so he didn't seek any enlightenment about Falinde and Oje. They would keep.

"Worried about the Wong empire being run by a woman, I shouldn't wonder," said Janine to herself with her usual delighted grin.

Victoria was voicing something similar to Mark over the telephone, as she had already done to Fid Okeke. It was another conversational passage that Mark let pass without response.

* * *

Both Victoria and Janine were largely correct in their separate assumptions. As the gloomy figures of Messrs Falinde and Oje were invited into the Wongs' residence in Kent, Pearl Wong had a major problem controlling her anger. The very presence of the two men was an obvious vote of no confidence in her. That they regarded women with contempt she was already well aware of. What they weren't aware of was that arousing Pearl's animosity was not necessarily good for their long-term well-being.

Her day had been all angst. She had awoken from the sleep of exhaustion that had overtaken her in the small hours with a feeling of anger and resentment against the nameless assassins who had first taken her brother from her and now her father. Her anger continued to simmer over a rather dismal breakfast when it was apparent from the seating preferences and the body language that the older members of the family were still not yet reconciled to her assuming the position of power. Never one to avoid such a challenge, she confronted the problem immediately by demanding the Will be read at nine o'clock and then the business day be resumed.

"It will be better if Miss Pearl attends the reading."

Even by Jason Wong's enlightened standards, Pearl might not have been involved in what everybody else saw as man's business, but the family solicitor, an ancient Chinese man whose word was deeply respected, had insisted. The proceedings were brief, irritable and at one stage noisy, but in the end, Pearl emerged as the head of the Wong empire, and by ten -thirty the party dispersed.

'Silly old farts,' Pearl thought as her elderly uncles and not-so-elderly cousins finally gave up huffing and puffing in the face of both Pearl's obvious determination and of her father's clear preference. But she was on trial. 'The vultures will gather soon enough if I make a fist of it.'

But she had no intention of that happening, and although

she didn't yet know it, she had some powerful allies in the shape of Hector Xu and his more compliant cronies.

By eleven-thirty Pearl had made a number of adjustments to the hierarchy of the organisation which were seen as shrewd but mindful of the sensitivities of the older members of the family. In the middle of this process, she received a telephone call from Hector Xu reporting the success of his mission. Taking the opportunity to confirm him in his position, she also sought his advice on Leonard Wong and then determined that that young man would remain in Moscow for some time longer. Pearl wanted to be sure that the resentments in that branch of the family remained as remote from the centre of things as possible. Had she known, Leonard Wong harboured no resentment of her, just respect verging on adulation.

By twelve-thirty Pearl was reminded that the two Nigerians had been waiting for more than two hours and were showing signs of anger.

"Gentlemen, I'm informed that your patience is running out!"

Pearl, who shared Janine's penchant for the clothes of the nineteen sixties, marched into the back study where the two Nigerians were fretting and startled them both by the harshness of her tone and the brevity of the body-hugging black dress that she was wearing.

"We've been here since just before ten o'clock and there's a limit to how much coffee we can drink!"

In the face of Pearl's obvious body language, Falinde's reply was more surly than angry. Oje, as always, said nothing but stood up as if to reinforce his colleague's point.

"So why is that my problem? I didn't ask you to come here."

Her dark eyes held theirs only briefly; neither man could sustain the cold, hard stare that she directed at them.

"Chief Adeko " started Falinde.

"I don't give a shit about your Chief Adeko. You lot are the worst customers I've ever had to deal with."

Pearl's anger was real on this occasion. She knew that her language was offensive to the Nigerians, but since the deal was done, she didn't really care.

"Don't tell me. You've got a lot of money at stake. And in case you hadn't noticed, so have we, and we don't want to lose it by the actions of two halfwits who traipse halfway across the world every time somebody in the Wong organisation sneezes."

Falinde was on his feet beside his henchman. He was shaking with anger. But he was also without words. He had no idea how to deal with the situation. It was beyond his experience. Women in Nigeria had increasingly invaded the men's world, but this woman had power both in language and in the business activities that they were overseeing and knew how to use it. She had apparently stepped into her father's shoes without even faltering and had a whole worldwide organisation at her fingertips. She was the one who was going to deliver their arms to them, yet she didn't seem to understand that the people they worked for didn't trust anybody, woman or not, when the sums of money involved were so great.

Pearl briefly felt sorry for Falinde; since he was so obviously a messenger boy. But it wasn't a feeling that lasted for very long.

She walked up to him and faced him; with her high heels they were about eye to eye.

"Look, Mr Falinde," she said patiently, "the deal is underway, the first instalment is paid and the arms are on the move. The people in the Wong organisation who arrange these things are the same today as they were yesterday. You've got to trust us."

"Chief Adeko,..." he started again to quote his principal.

"Mr Falinde," she said again with the same level of patience but with a frigidity in her tone, "I repeat, you have got to trust us!"

"You might remember," Pearl then continued, giving her anger more rein, "that every time you fly on a 'plane the whole world knows. Every security service under the sun monitors the airlines' computers. A whole lot of people will be wondering why you're back in Britain again and what deal the Nigerian Security Service has got going with the Wong group. All this frantic flying around the place is creating a security risk for us that I don't like. Once the arms move into western Europe, the last thing we need is any attention drawn to us. So, if you won't trust us, at least stay at home and stop jeopardising the whole deal!"

Her final outburst seemed to have hit some sort of a mark. The two Nigerians sat down. Following their example, Pearl perched on the edge of a table. As her words sank in, the atmosphere became less fraught. Her anger departed as she repeated the progress of the deal and added a little more detail. She also talked about establishing a secure communications system in an effort to find a route to providing them with reassurance without opening up another opportunity for penetration by the Nigerian or British security services. She thought that she was getting somewhere.

The meeting broke up at two o'clock and the Nigerians left. Pearl made no effort to offer them more hospitality.

"We will report your concerns on security to Chief Adeko," Falinde promised.

The Chief's demand that the arms shipments be taken over and managed by a senior man in the Wong organisation was unmade. It was clear that Pearl was very much in charge and unlikely to be interested in Chief Adeko's antiquated views on the role of women. However, the necessary contacts between the Wong organisation and the southern Nigerians were conducted on a much more professional basis thenceforth. The change frustrated Victoria Akinbode for a period, but after consultation with Mark Shortley, who had been committing significant resources to the problem, namely Janine, other avenues had been opened up and the tracking of the arms shipments took another direction.

"We'll never be able to tackle things from the Chinese end," Mark advised Janine. "my experience is that the Chinese criminal organisations are virtually impenetrable unless you can attract an informer. We'll have to go for the transport system. I've a few SAS colleagues who'll be able to help here. If you can keep getting your fingers into everybody's secret computer files and telling us what's happening, we should be able to crack it."

"The only thing that we don't know," Mark said to Janine later as they relaxed in his office at the end of the Tuesday following Jason Wong's death, "is who else knows about the shipments."

It was a question that they didn't find the answer to for some time.

TWENTY-ONE

March 22nd was Mark's birthday. He regarded birthdays with mixed feelings. They were occasions when he thought about his dead wife, but Shelley's image was overwritten by that of her sister after the events of the 2022 Nationalist coup and Mark no longer had a clear picture of her. The only pain he felt was over his dead child and the fact that he never saw his son. The legacy of Shelley was a submerged feeling of impermanence in his relationship with Janine. He could never articulate this, but it did occasionally inhibit his response to her displays of passion.

But this was not one of the occasions.

Janine was going to Armards department store later than she had intended as a result of some rather exuberant early-morning lovemaking. Her presents to Mark had been well received but the celebration had ended on a mildly discordant note when the mysterious blonde/Arab woman again somehow crept into the conversation.

"Why do we always end up talking about her?" she demanded of Mark.

The woman had become a source of good-humoured banter between them, but Janine sometimes felt irritated that he talked about her at all.

Anxious that nothing should spoil the day, he merely shrugged by way of reply. His interest was purely professional, or so he always told her. Janine's head said something similar, but a quirky little feeling on occasion got in the way of her common sense.

"I must get on," she said, breaking off the discussion.

Mark's lack of serious reaction made her feel foolish, and fearing that her annoyance with herself might be sparked into a more resentful outburst, she headed for the safety of the bathroom.

As so often happened when she was in a relaxed mood, Janine had come to the breakfast table naked. Mark's bemusement at how the atmosphere had altered faded as he watched her glossy body move sinuously around the table and then out of the room. As a gesture of appeasement, he trawled his hand over her bare buttocks as she slipped past him, but she didn't react.

Moments later, she returned fully clothed to go out. Her long, electric blue coat covered her down to the ankles of her sensible boots, and she had a huge black and white scarf wound around her head against the chill morning air.

As she marched into the famous store, briefly acknowledging the almost non-existent contribution of the commissionaire to opening the door for her, her anger had abated but had not completely gone away. She was rarely angry for long, but on this occasion, the last shreds of her irritation were more resistant to reasoning than was customary with her.

'Stupid idiot!'

As she walked the short distance to the store, she rebuked herself for succumbing to a male chauvinist attitude. She was deeply attached to her partner and there was nothing new in Mark's interest in attractive women.

'It proves he's alive and well. If I were to be angry with every woman that Mark comments on I'd be in a permanent fury. Despite our closeness and my feelings, he's still a man of his times and early twenty-first century man isn't so different from his predatory predecessors!'

That was not to say that Mark wasn't aware of the hurt that he had caused and that he didn't regret his throwaway reference to the Arab woman.

'Can't have it both ways, I guess,' he told himself when she had gone.

But in the depths of his mind, something said that he could. His relationship with Janine was secure, of that he was convinced.

'But we still don't own each other.'

It was a recurrent thought that provided justification when his eye strayed and his adrenalin surged.

'There must be other men that she fancies!'

But Mark wasn't sure that there were or how he might react if he came across one. About the only certainty for him was that he wouldn't react in the same way as Janine would, she being a woman.

'For heaven's sakes, keep your mind on the job! Defeating the Moslem Fundamentalists is what this is all about for both of us. Stopping the arms and not giving the Fundamentalists a pretext for a takeover. She's the computer wizard, not me; without her, where would I be?'

A surge of excitement flowed through Mark. Where his life would be without Janine he couldn't imagine. The joy and intensity that she brought to his existence overwhelmed him momentarily. The desire to have her back in his arms was almost physically painful. His dead wife didn't reappear in his thoughts.

* * *

"So what's bugging you then?"

It was a quietly spoken, educated voice.   When Janine

turned she saw to her mild surprise, that it was a fellow African who had addressed her.

"Nothing to interest you," she replied with a grin.

It wasn't the face-enlivening grin that she might have had for Mark, but it was friendly enough. It acknowledged that she was miffed about something and it encouraged the man.

"Try me. It's not the obvious place for soul-searching, but…"

They were in the fish department of the Armards Food Hall; hardly an inspiring setting for an exchange of confidences nor yet a romantic encounter.

"It's good for buying fish, though!" said Janine, trying to stifle a giggle.

The man's body language was relaxed and unthreatening, so she found it easy to respond to his approach.

If she really was there to buy fish, there was no obvious cause for her amusement, and her unexplained merriment bemused the newcomer. He clearly hadn't seen anything incongruous in making his approach amongst the piles of ice and dead piscine flesh, but being propositioned in such a place struck Janine as hilarious.

"It's my partner's birthday," she said with a wave of the hand between giggles that conveyed that the fish was for him.

"Ah."

He obviously hadn't expected her to be so immediately open about her status.

'I wonder if she's planning to cook,' Mark had thought as Janine had set off for Armards. 'Not sure why we have a deal on the chores, since it's rare that I catch her carrying out her side of the bargain. Domestic duties are definitely not her thing.' Generally, if Mark wasn't in the mood to prepare a meal, they ate out. 'Still, it's my birthday; she does make an effort for things like that.' Janine's cooking was basic and of negligible gastronomic merit compared to Mark's accomplishments, but he would have died rather than admit that to her.

Having made her purchase, Janine drifted idly around the food hall until she was opposite the coffee shop that sat in the middle of the grocery section. Then, without giving any indication of her intentions, she marched into the brightly lit area, sat down at an empty table, and waited. After some hesitation, the man followed her.

"I guess that was an invitation," he said.

He was finding Janine's direct approach to him rather disconcerting. She was treating him as an equal and conducting their relationship as if there was no sexual difference between them.

'Why am I doing this?'

He momentarily questioned the wisdom of having approached her. But then, with a chauvinism that Mark would never have evinced, he decided that the challenge of getting her into his bed was too great to be passed up. Since he and his partner were used to each other's infidelities, he had no qualms about pursuing Janine.

'I can always just walk away.'

Janine was also having her moments of doubt about the meeting. As they talked, she watched his sexist arrogance grow with horror. Eventually she knew that she would get too angry and that would be it. In the meantime, her thoughts were more benign and her inaction carried things forward.

'I like his style,' she thought. 'He's clearly well into the charm bit! And his pitch is obviously talk about her, don't say a lot about yourself.'

However, the joys of the chase were not to last long. In probing her background, her companion let slip that he too was a Nigerian. Alarm bells instantly rang in Janine's mind.

'So why pick on me in the whole of London? Some coincidence!'

As she pondered this new situation, she automatically switched into work mode. All thoughts of philandering disappeared from her brain.

"Do you spend much time in Nigeria?"

Janine picked up on his inadvertent reference to his origins and ignored his efforts to keep the conversation personal to her.

"Not a lot, most of my business is in Europe."

The ever- present smile was supposed to convey the message that he didn't really want to talk about himself. He moved on quickly.

"D'you get out in the evenings much?"

"Oh, I play squash, I work out... I'm into judo."

She didn't tell him about her new passion for kick-boxing. It was something that Victoria Akinbode had introduced her to, but she thought it might be overdoing it. But he wouldn't have been surprised; his own partner was an exponent of the sport.

"Fascinating!"

It seemed to him that she was deliberately emphasising her least attractive points. Delightful as she was, she was anything but the sophisticated young woman-about-town that he was looking for. As he smiled his synthetic smile, his second thoughts became stronger.

Sensing this, and conscious that the morning was rapidly passing, Janine decided that it was time to end the conversation.

"I'll have to go. It's been great – maybe another time."

"Maybe," he said.

Now that she seemed ready to leave, he was suddenly anxious to get away. Janine's misgivings about the meeting being contrived returned.

She walked slowly through the store, carrying her long coat over her arm. Oblivious to the admiring glances of the younger salesmen, she watched her late companion out of sight through one of the side entrances. Only then did she pull on her coat and hide the brief leather miniskirt that was causing all of the interest. She headed for the Knightsbridge entrance. Concentrating on watching her man, she was totally unaware that she herself was being watched.

But as she left the coffee shop, her movements were observed with intense interest. The prediction of which exit she would emerge from may have had the appearance of some sort of gambling game, but forecasting of the right answer was fundamental to her Chinese watchers' plans. Janine's wanderings amongst the endless array of cosmetic displays were not appreciated. Not that Janine was much interested in the sort of products on display; as Mark had quickly noticed when he had first met her, beautiful as she was, she was totally oblivious to the effect that she could have on people and made no effort to artificially enhance her looks. However, as she wrapped her long scarf around her head, the watchers knew that the end was in sight.

TWENTY-TWO

The entrances to Armards were cavernous and used as meeting places by many of the customers of the shop. The marble-floored entrance porticos gave way to the carpeted luxury of the ground floor shop on the inside and to the canopy-covered pavement on the outside. All of the world came and went this way in the hurried unhurried way of shoppers, both of the money-spending type and the sightseeing type. The loiterers in all the entrances were unseen by Janine and by all of the other people trafficking in both directions. Interest in Janine, however, heightened as she marched across the marble and headed for the pavement through the central entrance.

Why the presence of a taxi, with its door already open, caused her to pause, she was unable afterwards to say, but pause she did. As she did so, she became aware of movement very close behind her.

"Oh shit!"

She had half turned and taken a hurried pace into the middle of the pavement before the man launched himself. Her movement forward had taken her closer to the waiting taxi, but it had also given her room to manoeuvre. The stocky Chinese man projected himself at her in a hunched shoulder charge. She had little time to react. He struck Janine in the small of the back, momentarily forcing the breath out of her in an agonised gasp. However, since she was off balance already as a result of her instinctive half turn to protect her rear, she was not thrust into the gaping side of the taxi but sprawled across the pavement beside it. Her assailant was carried passed her by the momentum of his charge.

With her trained-in judo instincts coming to her aid, Janine hit the hard pavement safely and flipped herself onto her knees, ready to face the renewed attack. The Chinese man pulled himself up short and turned swiftly on his heel to face her. The look of surprise that had taken over his face as he bounced off Janine was replaced by a look of malevolent anger at being thwarted.

"Oh, shit," Janine panted again as she struggled to get up, encumbered by her long coat and the scarf that she had so recently flung around her head and shoulders.

As her opponent moved forward to grapple with her, she struggled to get mastery of her breathing and to untangle herself from the coat. Totally surprised by the unexpected assault and not wanting to have any part of a confrontation, she stepped back to try and keep the man at a distance. But the movement took her into the arms of a new assailant. The driver of the taxi, a young, muscular Chinese woman, had come to her colleague's aid. Trying to shake off the woman's grasp Janine also observed a group of three or four other Chinese people emerging from the department store. The potentially overwhelming odds served only to galvanise her into even greater effort.

Unaware of anyone else but the Chinese people around her, Janine took the offensive.

"Sorry, girl," she muttered, crashing her heel down painfully onto the young taxi driver's foot.

The responding scream gave Janine satisfaction as well as relief. Twisting herself from her attacker's loosened grasp, she shed her coat. With an eye on the Chinese man standing uncertainly in front of her, she aimed a rapid backwards elbow jab into the woman's midriff and then concentrated her attention on her original opponent. Tossing the coat that she had been left, grasping onto the pavement but still clasping Janine's shoulder bag, the young Chinese woman hobbled back to her taxi, retching and vomiting. She was out of the game.

Devoid of her coat and scarf, and slim and body-honed in her tight sweater and short skirt, Janine faced the Chinese thug in the middle of the pavement. Planting her feet firmly and bending her knees in readiness for the renewed attack, she raised her hands defensively and waited. It seemed like slow motion to her at the time, but Janine readied herself in split seconds.

"Come on then," she muttered under her breath.

The man's rush was quick and uncoordinated, and it was solitary. It was only later that Janine realised that the mob of Chinese people who had spilled out of Armards hadn't joined the battle. In fact, nothing in the background impinged on her as the man charged forward. Completely focused, she adjusted her posture as the man projected himself at her.

Sidestepping easily, Janine aimed one of the kick-boxing kicks that Victoria had taught her at the man's rib-cage. Regaining her balance, she waited for the next attack. It didn't come. Intended for barefoot warfare, the kick delivered by Janine in her heavy winter boots had shattered three of the man's ribs. Coughing blood, he staggered into the taxi at the urgent demands of the female cabby and was driven off before Janine or anybody else could react.

A ragged cheer greeted her success. Refocusing on her surroundings, Janine observed the small knot of soldiers who had been holding back the now rapidly dissolving group of Chinese people in the store doorway. It was then that Janine understood how the odds had been levelled.

"Fantastic!"

The only woman amongst the soldiers was full of admiration as she draped Janine's coat over her shoulders. Janine clawed her arms into it. Snatching up her scarf from the gutter, she looked for her shoulder bag. It was nowhere to be seen.

"You OK, miss?"

The soldier had given place to a policeman. Janine quickly explained what had happened. Unharmed, her only loss was her bag. The female soldier reported what had happened to it.

"A purse with some small change, a couple of business cards and a make-up mirror," she said in response to the enquiry, "I don't normally carry much with me."

The sparseness of the contents of her handbag was something that set Janine apart from the rest of womankind.

"Oh, and there was a half a kilo of salmon."

The policeman raised an eyebrow.

"Well," said Janine with a rather jaundiced smile, "I only came out to buy fish."

The police didn't detain her long; nor did her elation at her success in the encounter last long either. As Janine walked disconsolately towards Mark's office and flat, her hands thrust deeply into her coat pockets, her hyped-up confidence ebbed away at every step.

"Oh, Mark," she said dolefully when she had reached the safety of home.

Triggered by her hangdog expression, he had followed her upstairs from the office. It was a little while before he could work out whether she was more upset by her now inevitably failed birthday surprise, or the assault on her person.

TWENTY-THREE

It was also a little while before Pearl Wong was advised of the outcome of her planned attack on Victoria Akinbode. The leader of the gang charged with making Victoria disappear was in no rush to report his failure. Having dispatched his two battered foot soldiers to hospital with a clear understanding of his views on their failure, he set out to confront Pearl in her office. His obvious reluctance was marked by his decision to walk rather than take a taxi.

Pearl, who was dressed almost identically to Janine, was creating the same sort of mayhem amongst the hormones of her male employees as Mark's partner had done amongst the salesmen of Armards. However, the admiration she received was less verbal.

"So, Mr Chang…?"

Sat behind her desk, she looked almost benign. Chang wasn't fooled. Her father was only days dead and not yet buried, but the Wong world surely knew that he had gone. Chang's expression and his body language told her that he had failed; he hardly needed Pearl's raised eyebrow to ask the question.

"She got away?" she said.

The thug nodded.

"Put two of mine in hospital."

"God damn it, you knew she was a hard case before you attacked her."

"Some soldiers got in the way."

Pearl wasn't interested in Chang's defence. She was interested, though, when she discovered that Victoria had apparently escaped without so much as a scratch. However, on that subject she expressed herself in the gutter Chinese that the street gangs understood but which her father never knew that she had mastered.

"We have her handbag," whispered Chang at the end of the diatribe.

He was ordered to dispatch it to her home and then ejected from her office with another blast of the vernacular that amazed even the most worldly-wise of her subordinates who happened to overhear it. But the loss of face at his failure was probably Chang's greatest punishment.

* * *

Chang gone, Pearl turned her attention to more pressing matters like the pressure developing at the United Nations to combat the escalating illicit arms trade. Past efforts had failed, so she was interested to know what was different. It turned out to be very little. As always, the rich European nations were trying to impose their one-sided solutions on the poorer countries, but they were having none of it.

"The Nigerians supporting the Europeans," Pearl remarked to her otherwise-empty office. "They'll be looking for cut-price supplies for their military as a payoff!"

It was pretty close to the truth. In return for trying to suppress illegal arms shipments into Nigeria, the Abuja Government was agreeing to purchase weapons from the European Federation. Whilst paying lip service to their ban on offensive weapons systems, the Europeans were quite happy to supply small arms and anti-riot equipment. With the increasing trouble being fermented by the Fundamentalists, particularly in the northern cities, this was just the sort of hardware that the Nigerian authorities wanted. Their vote was easily secured.

"The debate must still be going on," Pearl said as she called up the United Nations TV channel on her computer screen.

She was in time to cut into the last moments of the discussion. As she watched, it wasn't the pious outpourings of the elderly and self-satisfied leaders of the European Federation that finally riveted Pearl's attention; it was the glimpses of the Nigerian delegation. Such had been their prominence in the debate, the world's media had concentrated on their leaders for several minutes after the formal session had ended. But Pearl's attention was concentrated on the undeniably living and active figure of Victoria Akinbode as she restlessly policed the fringes of the group. Study of her father's files had imprinted the features of the young Nigerian woman firmly on her mind.

"Holy shit!" she exclaimed.

They'd attacked the wrong person. Her intended target was in Munich, to where the United Nations had moved, very much alive. That meant that somewhere in London was another, no doubt seriously aggrieved, young woman, of the same calibre as Victoria. The carnage she had created amongst Pearl's thugs certainly spoke volumes for her fighting skills.

Pearl backtracked the TV broadcast on the replayer channel and froze on the best still of her intended victim. Reaching into her desk drawer, she pulled out the bundle of photographs of Victoria that her father had been given but which until that moment she hadn't looked at.

"The idiots," she said out loud.

The photographs taken at the Nigerian High Commission

were certainly not of Victoria Akinbode, although Pearl would have conceded the possibility of confusion if she had seen the two women from behind.

"Problems?"

It was Hector Xu. He wandered into Pearl's office late in the afternoon because he had just heard about the attack on Victoria Akinbode and he was unhappy. After he had returned from Moscow, he had spent much of his time quietly reinforcing Pearl's grasp on the Wong empire and he saw the action against the Nigerian Security Service as a mistake.

He sat back in one of the luxury armchairs in her office, confident of his welcome, and watched her pace back and forward. He said nothing for several minutes. Nearer eighty than seventy, his hormones were immune to the images passing in front of him.

"We have to concentrate on getting the arms delivered," the old man finally said. "We can't beat the Nigerian Security Service; we can only outwit them. Killing one of their agents will only heighten their interest in us."

Pearl felt herself rebuked; which in truth she had been. Killing Victoria Akinbode had been her idea based on the antipathy that her father felt for the Nigerian Security Service. They, he knew, would be the most likely group to interfere with their arms dealings. But it had been a superficial judgement on Pearl's part and the action had failed. Worse still in Xu's eyes, an innocent person could very well have been killed instead. They certainly needed to get the Nigerians off their backs, but as Hector Xu was implying, there were other ways. She stopped pacing and stood in front of him.

"I guess I've learnt a useful lesson today," she said with the sort of humility that she was unlikely to display to anybody other than Hector Xu.

He smiled a weary smile. He knew that she would have to learn many more. But his smile was almost paternal. Hector

Xu had a strong affection for the daughter of his old friend and knew that the Wong empire would collapse if she were unable to control it. He knew she had what it would take. And he meant to see that she succeeded. He owed that much to his murdered friend. Loyalty was everything to Hector Xu, and loyalty to the oaths that he and Jason Wong had sworn as very young men was still his main motivation.

* * *

"Mr Falinde, how are you?"

Pearl made the telephone call to Abuja with some reluctance. As he answered, she wondered whether the ever-silent Mr Oje was standing beside him. She talked for a long time, briefing Falinde as she had promised and exploring the workings of the Nigerian Security Service. It was not a fruitful conversation. Falinde was of equivalent seniority to Mr Okeke, Janine Effiong's cousin and Victoria's controller. But as Pearl listened, it was obvious to her that he felt that his seniors were suspicious of him and he was being isolated and insulated from the areas of work that Victoria was active in.

* * *

On the way home with the two bodyguards Tang One and Tang Two, Pearl said almost nothing. Forewarned of her apparently unsuccessful day, they made no conversation either. Experience had told them when to encroach on their mistress's patience and when to stay quiet. And they didn't look forward with any relish to an agreed training session in the Wong's private gym. They tended to suffer when she was in a bad mood, even if her skills did improve.

In the privacy of her bedroom, Pearl opened Janine's shoulder bag.

"Oh, my God," she said, hurriedly shutting it again before the smell could pervade the room.

In the scullery, with a less-than-enthusiastic Tang Two now doing the investigation, the contents of the bag were laid out on a draining board.

"Fish," said Pearl with some distaste.

She couldn't somehow relate the sharply dressed young woman in the photographs with the domestic duties associated with a package of fish!

"Ten euros and sixty-five cents, no make-up, name of Janine Effiong...... . I wonder who Mark Shortley Associates are," she muttered when Tang Two had completed his search.

It was the sum total of knowledge that the shoulder bag yielded about Janine apart from an obvious liking for salmon. She picked up the business cards and headed back to her bedroom to change.

"Burn the rest," she said as she passed by the bodyguard.

Later in the gym, she duly worked off the tensions of the day.

* * *

If the blow that split Pearl's lip brought tears to her eyes, it was the blows that her inept Chinese thugs had inflicted on her that eventually brought tears to Janine's eyes. As she lay in Mark's arms, with the bruises in her back and forearm beginning to come out, she wept silently until her angst was worked off. Sprawled fully clothed on the bed, Mark looked down at the slender body of the black girl who was sobbing quietly beside him, and all the love and anxieties he had for her poured out in the words of comfort he offered her. He was thankful that at least she was weeping; it was something that she hadn't always been able to do in his presence.

Knowing how she coped with such stress, he let her cry until she was empty, and then with careful questions, teased out the whole story. When she had told it to him three times, he knew that she was on the mend.

"Strange this Nigerian bloke came straight up to you," said Mark, seeing the event only from a professional point of view.

"Guess I was the only black woman around the place," said Janine.

"It's still too neat," said Mark. "How do we know he wasn't there to point you up to the Chinese? Chat you up… give you coffee."

"Coffee was my idea," Janine said.

"Well," he said after they had debated for another half -an -hour, "we shouldn't ignore the possibility that you were decoyed."

"Nor, that there isn't any obvious motive that I can think of."

"They stole your bag," said Mark.

"And our dinner," said Janine.

Mark tried to look grave, but it didn't quite work. Janine, to his immense relief, giggled and, beating him on the chest, berated him for his contempt of her cooking. In the ensuing brawl, they both ended up half naked before Mark managed to convince Janine that it was only late afternoon and their office was still open.

Alone again in his private office, Mark's conscience niggled at him. The idea that Janine might get hurt working for him had occurred to him before, but now it had happened.

'That's not what it's about,' he pondered. 'She's too precious to be put at risk!'

The thought troubled him as he sat there. For him, a trained soldier, and a special services one at that, the risk of injury was a fact of life. For her, it was something that he would rather not have happened.

Later they headed for a nearby Chinese restaurant and still celebrated Mark's birthday.

"Better enjoy the food," Mark said. "The first shipment of arms has probably crossed into France by now, so regular meals may not be on the agenda for a while!"

TWENTY-FOUR

"You really are something," he said.

Janine's ever-present grin lit up her entire face. It was one of the happiest that Mark had ever seen.

"You like this place?"

"Sure. I like this place."

Mark was worried as he said it that she might be offended at his enjoying eating out in the Chinese restaurant when she had clearly planned a meal at home. Janine showed no signs of such a feeling.

"It's great when it's half empty like this," she said., "can't be more than half-a-dozen people left."

'Certainly is,' thought Mark, 'and it's great when I can see all of you curled up like that on the settee.'

Janine was still wearing black, as she usually did, but she had replaced her tight skirt with a pleated one and her serviceable boots with an elegant heeled pair. And as usual, only her earrings gave a splash of vibrant colour. Mark had every bit of her within his vision.

His adrenalin level was rising. Janine laughed the deep, gurgling laugh that had always so entranced him and gave him an unashamed leering look.

'She's stripping me off, I can see it her eyes.'

She was. Her vision of him without his neat, tailored, double-breasted jacket and wide-bottomed trousers, sober, smart and stylish, made her eyes dance with extravagant delight. Always with a subtle and harmonious match between the colours of his tie and shirt, she admired his taste.

"Mark, you're gorgeous," she said softly.

"And you're a luscious tart," he said, ogling her with an outrageous leer.

She exploded into giggles and sobs of laughter that attracted the attention of the remaining guests and waiters alike.

'But you're more than gorgeous,' Mark thought, lost for suitable superlatives to express the almost overpowering surge of desire that flowed through him.

As he watched her reach forward for her coffee cup, her whole body fluid, he wanted to reach and wrap himself around her. Her movement was neat and economic, but her smile had a gentle edge to it that crept in when she was truly relaxed and contented.

"God, I'm stiff," she said after a period of comfortable silence, referring to her earlier exploits.

Mark wasn't surprised. She'd taken a bit of a battering, more, perhaps, than she had realised, but thankfully it was not as bad as it could have been. He was happy that she had now mentally put the episode behind her.

* * *

The other parties to Janine's little escapade, in their separate ways, were as thankful as Mark was that she had come to so little harm. Pearl Wong, now preoccupied with her father's funeral, was relieved to be spared an unnecessary death.

"I reckon that should've been me," Victoria had said to Mark in a brief telephone call from Munich.

She knew that Janine had been mistaken for her before, especially from behind. It had happened quite recently at Janine's gym even when they were both dressed in the briefest of training gear. But of course neither Victoria nor Janine was aware of the mix-up during the photo session at the Nigerian High Commission.

* * *

It was during the call from the United Nations that Victoria had alerted Mark to rumours in the intelligence community that a big arms shipment was underway.

"Anything else I should know?" Mark had asked.

"Background mainly," she'd said, "from an unexpected source in Abuja. Fearing the Fundamentalists, whatever they say in public, were using drugs to corrupt youngsters in the north, Mahomet Sullag had set up a number of undercover operations. They quickly exposed a secret brotherhood of Hausa truck drivers who've been running a smuggling network for many years. You know the Hausa are the main northern tribe; they get everywhere. They aren't political, just smugglers, the transporters of illicit goods for money; no surprise they were shifting drugs then. The surprise was they were shifting the drugs into the southern heartlands and these drugs were being paid for by weapons that they then shipped back to the north."

"What? I thought the Fundamentalists' arms were coming across the desert from North Africa?"

"So they are," said Victoria. "But these arms are being bought by southerners living in the north, presumably to protect themselves if the Fundamentalists manage to stir up enough trouble. It's just another twist. It's Nigeria, remember."

'So it is,' thought Mark, 'but it's a side issue. The situation is complicated enough with the politics without the normal criminality getting in the way of clear thinking!'

Whilst not explicitly wondering why Victoria had raised this potential red herring, in the recesses of Mark's mind a caution was entered alongside Janine's partially articulated concern about Victoria's sincerity in opposing the Fundamentalists' cause.

'Another piece of unverifiable intelligence down to this man Sullag,' Mark thought when Victoria had finished.

'Muddies the waters,' was Janine's cousin Fid Okeke's reaction, and, like so many things Sullag's done recently, it doesn't actually have an adverse impact on the Fundamentalists'

He didn't share his steadily increasing concerns about Mahomet Sullag with Victoria.

* * *

"Are you still with me, Mark?"

Janine, who had been lost in her own thoughts for a while in the restaurant, had suddenly noticed the silence again.

If he hadn't been mulling over his conversation with Victoria, Mark might have noticed that Janine had had a broad smile of quiet satisfaction on her face for some time.

'I think I enjoyed that,' she'd been saying to herself about her little set-to with the Chinese gentry.

The feeling of physical power that her judo gave her had now been enhanced when she saw how devastatingly effective Victoria's kick-boxing moves had been. She was quietly proud of her prowess.

'Not so sure about my other escapade. Mark's wrong about the guy in Armards, though. It was just a pick-up attempt. It certainly didn't do anything for me at all.'

Janine could be a passionate and extremely physical lover when she was aroused, but that was a separate side of her character not available to anybody but her partner. Mark had come to terms with her being self-contained and seemingly often negligent of her own femininity, but he could certainly vouch for her appetite for the sexual side of their relationship! What Janine's reaction might be if the Armards Nigerian crossed her path again she gave no thought to. It was a pleasant interlude to her and just that.

'Pleased he tried, though!'

Whatever the man's motives in attaching himself to Janine were, with the benefit of time and maturity of thought, she was gratified that she could still attract such an attempt and she was in no way contrite about her original decision to encourage him.

'Sod the Arab woman; he's a gorgeous old fart, even if he is miles away in his own thoughts.'

With the mellowing effect of good food and wine, she felt well content. All it needed was for Mark to be with her mentally as well as physically, so she recalled him from his ponderings and made him share his world with her again.

It was then that he told he that the arms shipment was on its way and that their services were in serious demand.

TWENTY-FIVE

The Eurotransit depot at Ashford was one of a number of trans-shipment areas scattered around the Kentish countryside. Anybody with the time and energy to trace through the Byzantine complexity of the ownership arrangements amongst the consortium that operated the depot would have eventually discovered that the Wong organisation was the sole shareholder. However, for various reasons, most of which were of debatable legality, the only role that the Wongs publicly undertook was that of leaseholder of one of the warehouses at the depot.

It was into this warehouse that two six axle trucks roared and hissed to a standstill at around three-thirty in the morning of the Friday following Mark's birthday celebration.

"The TransChannel ferry operators like to balance the payload of the ships on the Dover-Calais route whenever they can, since it's a twenty-four-hour operation. Given enough notice, they are happy to consign the heavier vehicles to the night-time runs."

Hector Xu's forwarding agent in France was reporting to his principal.

"I made it my business to let them know about two

171

particularly heavy vehicle loads of machine-tool parts that would be arriving in Britain in mid-March."

"And?"

"Like I expected, Mr Xu, they let us choose our own departure time."

The forwarding agency was, of course, of as obscure ownership as the Ashford depot. In other words, it was another Wong offshoot.

"Good, thanks."

The arrival of the trucks was reported to the Wong's night manager; he was relieved. The constant demand for information from Pearl Wong's assistants was becoming a trial to him.

* * *

But the Wong organisation wasn't the only group of people interested in the safe arrival of the arms shipment in Britain. The inhabitants of the houses surrounding the depot were so used to the comings and goings of vehicles of all shapes and sizes at all hours of day and night that almost anything would normally have got past them without attracting even the slightest notice.

The appearance of the faint glow of night-sight equipment in the back room of one of the houses nearest to and overlooking the Wong warehouse would certainly have attracted attention if the watchers hadn't been so careful to ensure that they went unobserved.

* * *

"Right, let's get to it," said one of Hector Xu's minions who had arrived at the depot to take charge of handling the two trucks, "just check the details on the crates; they need to match the manifests I brought with me. They've already been entered into the Tranship data-base for onwards transmission."

The man satisfied himself that the crates contained what he expected them to without the assistance of the depot staff; he then resealed the crates and had the containers reloaded.

"Come on, we haven't got all night," he snapped. "We need to get the trucks away by six o'clock at the latest."

The three or four normal depot staff who had been given only the more menial tasks in receiving and processing the two trucks were irritated by the intrusion of the abrasive Chinese man who had arrived with the warehouse manager. Theirs was a high-security business, but the precautions in this case seemed to them to be excessive and unnecessarily secretive. The lack of trust rankled and, not unnaturally, they wondered what was so special about the cargo that the two trucks contained and which they had been denied even a glimpse of.

* * *

"OK, they've just left."

The identical message was passed on by both the Wong night manager and the watcher in the adjacent house. As the two trucks, now equipped with new papers for the next stage of their journey and with new drivers, headed up the M20 towards London and the Dartford Crossing, a small procession of motor vehicles also headed away from the Eurotransit depot and the nearby housing area. They travelled at a discreet distance behind the trucks and between each other.

The Wong manager made it to his bed in the Annex to Pearl Wong's country home after a solitary journey.

* * *

"Janine, you OK?"

Suspicious of his partner's rather torpid state, Mark prepared himself for bed. Even more suspicious of the apparent

173

lack of activity from the bedroom, he cautiously returned to investigate what Janine was up to. Somewhat to his surprise, she was in bed. Even more to his surprise, she merely rolled her naked body against him and gave him a lingering but otherwise innocuous kiss.

Next morning, it was different.

"Come on, you idle sod, get with it!"

Janine's jeering set the tone. Refreshed from a solid eight hours' sleep and still on something of a high from her fighting success, she tumbled Mark out of bed whilst he was still half comatose and set about arousing him. She was quickly successful. As their passions subsided, Janine crept away to start the shower, but her back was still sore and stiff, and she was, for once, reluctant to repeat the lovemaking in what was usually one of her favourite places.

Victoria Akinbode called just as Mark was drying himself off.

"If she says she hopes she's not interrupting anything, tell her the truth!" said Janine.

"And what's that?"

Mark could hardly reply to Victoria as he exploded into laughter at the sheer vulgarity of Janine's suggestion. The conversation, however, was business-like and detailed.

"That's great," said Mark. "Janine's done a lot of ground work and we've a pretty good idea about most of the Wongs' facilities. There aren't many options, but it'll take a while to fix on a specific depot. Once the trucks get to the docks it'll be easier."

"OK," said Victoria, aware that things were now out of her hands, "let's keep in touch."

Mark was also quick to notice that Janine had skipped her almost habitual Saturday-morning nudity. She was wearing a loose black and red tracksuit and designer trainers. Mark had opted for lightweight jeans and the monstrous tee-shirt depicting two female wrestlers that they'd bought in the Seychelles. Janine had also laid the table and, uncharacteristically, was well into the scrambled eggs. By her rare incursion into domestic duties, Mark acknowledged that she was signalling a more serious intent for this Saturday.

"So what did Victoria have to say?"

"The French Regional Government have told the Nigerians that the arms are being handled by a forwarding agent in Paris. It's a Wong front company."

"And?"

"And, the agency has one hundred and seventy eight trucks en route for Britain in the next seventy-two hours."

"Looks like a fun weekend!" said Janine.

* * *

"We've obviously got to eliminate as many as possible as quickly as possible," Janine said, as much to herself as Mark, as she disappeared downstairs to her computers.

Mark wasn't sure whether she meant depots or trucks, but since it was ultimately about individual trucks to a specific depot, equally he wasn't sure that it mattered which she was referring to.

A couple of hours later she resurfaced in the flat. The sheaf of printouts in her hand was witness to the complexity of what she was attempting.

"Manifest summaries for fifty-eight trucks fresh from the Tranship data-base," she said, waving the papers.

"The rest?" asked Mark.

"Refrigerated, carrying livestock, carrying bulk vegetables or other perishable goods. There are too many regulations and too many inspections for such vehicles to be able to hide anything. It would be much too risky to use them. And the others are fixed vehicles, not container trailers."

Janine grinned her incredible grin as Mark nodded his appreciation for her efforts. He was pleased to see that her spirits were high and the challenge was invigorating her.

"It's really only fifty," Janine continued. "There're eight containers from a travelling circus, would you believe! I've kept them on the list because they haven't been across a public weighbridge."

"OK, so what's next?"

"Narrow down the number of trucks some more. Look for the unusual. Things like weapons, machine -tools, other metallic manufactured goods, are very heavy."

By the end of Saturday afternoon, she was down to twenty-seven. By working through the manifests, she had eliminated the containers on a set of fleet-owned trucks carrying flat-pack kitchen units, nine containers that were replenishing a German supermarket chain's warehouse, several container-loads of furniture, which didn't seem heavy enough, and the household effects of two returning diplomats.

"So why keep the furniture wagon on the list? They would hardly be likely to use something so obvious as some civil servant's second-hand heirloom dining-room suite to stow rifles and ammunition in, would they?" asked Mark, looking at the papers as she returned once more to the flat for another caffeine fix.

Janine's grin was more arched this time. It was obvious that Mark hadn't quite grasped what it was she was looking for.

"Can't find the weighbridge they used on any official list."

"Want to call it a day?" asked Mark.

"Not yet. I want to sort out any pairs if I can."

"Pairs?" said Mark.

"Yes, Victoria said there were two trucks. Can't decide in their shoes whether I'd disguise the fact or simply schedule them together? And why send the trucks to a trans-shipment depot?"

"It's the only information we've got."

Janine draped her arms around Mark's neck and gave him a brief but sensual kiss that sent shivers down his spine. But she had disengaged before he could react.

"Sure," said Janine, back in business mode instantly, "Let's work backwards for the moment. The next ship to West Africa from Britain sails at eight o'clock on the Monday evening, from Felixstowe. There are twenty-eight containers booked to be loaded on the vessel for on-forwarding in Nigeria. Twenty-six have weights registered at the time of booking, two don't. Out of my twenty-seven vehicles, five are scheduled to deliver containers to Felixstowe for Nigeria. There has to be that sort of cross link."

'How the hell can she be so bright-eyed and bushy-tailed after what she's done today?' Mark asked himself.

Janine sensed not his admiration for her stamina but Mark's frustration.

"We're nearly there, Mark."

Just before midnight, Janine invaded the TransChannel operator's computer and pulled out the ferry manifests for the night and for the next day. The information was sparse. By the time she had cross-referenced such vehicles as she could, been into the Tranship database again and invaded the computers of three transport companies and two forwarding agents, it was two o'clock in the morning.

"We're down to nine, at least two of which are carrying oil field equipment and probably going to Aberdeen or Yarmouth direct. I think I know the two trucks now."

Exhausted, Janine flopped into bed beside Mark and was asleep before he could even say goodnight.

"What an incredible woman," he said to her sleeping form, his admiration welling up again to be overwhelmed almost immediately by his feelings of desire for her. Not ready for sleep, he pushed the desire to the back of his mind; its fulfillment would have to wait.

Not so readily able to switch off as Janine, Mark pondered the action that they had got themselves into. He found it impossible to share Janine's excitement at the challenge of pinning down the two arms trucks. He didn't rise to such challenges. He was much more hands-on.

'I need to do something,' he kept telling himself during the day as she painstakingly put together her jigsaw puzzle. 'I need to get out there and chase down the trucks for real!'

Janine had laughed at his fretting. She couldn't understand how he got his satisfaction from purely physical things any more than he could her delight at teasing out the details of truck movements.

But next day it was the same. Janine was up and about early, none the worse for her exertions of the previous day. Apart from having filched the wrestling tee-shirt from Mark, she was just as she was on the Saturday. She got cold sitting long hours at her computer terminal and had cheekily grabbed the first available garment to add to her tracksuit.

"I reckon it's Ashford," Janine said as they broke for lunch. "There are three trucks and containers scheduled for a depot near Faversham in Kent, and two seemingly unrelated containers to be checked over and re-documented at a depot at Ashford. Both depots are owned by the Wongs and both are within spitting distance of the Wong headquarters. All I need to do is match the two containers to the ship at Felixstowe."

"Yeah, my money's on Ashford," she said, after another flurry of post-lunch activity seemed to finally satisfy her.

"Why?"

Janine wasn't sure whether Mark's relief was at the final knowledge that had emerged or that her period of immersion in computer minutiae was at an end.

"The container weights are identical to two booked on the ship, but the details were only entered into the Tranship database at the last minute, in fact overnight from the Ashford depot. That was the clincher. If the containers had been loaded in Eastern Europe, the details would have been known well in advance. I'd say the information was being held back as a precaution."

"I'll back your judgement, Janine, but I think we'll still keep a tag on the Faversham depot."

"Absolutely," she said. "The Wongs are a devious bunch; there's plenty of chance for them to try and fool us. A whole lot can go wrong yet."

Janine was well pleased when a recheck of the database told her that the trucks they'd been hunting had indeed turned up at Ashford and been re-documented for Nigeria via Felixstowe.

"Can't worry about that now," said Mark. "It's Monday morning; we've got things to do."

Warnings were issued to the small group of operatives monitoring the truck movements. Mark revisited the intervention plans and made a number of calls to his police contacts. Following Victoria Akinbode's instructions, he also made a coded telephone call to the Nigerian High Commission.

* * *

Mark had eight people working for him on the job. All but one were moonlighting SAS personnel. From past experience the SAS authorities tended to turn a blind eye to his poaching of their personnel, provided he didn't interfere with their availability for official duties; the senior officers saw such extracurricular activities as providing needful training. In cases like the present where there was every chance that the operation would end up by being official, the police were relaxed about the SAS presence, again, provided that they stayed within the rules as essentially private citizens.

As Mark had said, it was Monday morning and life had to go on. His other business activities took over. He had to deliver a report to a client. Since Janine had a lunch appointment, they set off, sharing a taxi. As Janine skipped lightly out of the cab, Mark observed that beneath her long coat she was wearing a skirt of surprisingly demure length. He couldn't help wondering whom she was lunching with. But as the taxi pulled into the entrance of St. Jerome's Hotel, other thoughts crowded into his head and Janine was relegated to that special part of his mind kept exclusively for her. And in the active compartment of his brain, Mark was now alert to anything, and perhaps anyone, that might be relevant to the work he had undertaken for the Nigerians. Although the client he was visiting didn't fall into this category.

* * *

Mark felt decidedly overdressed when he was shown into his client's suite to deliver his report. His host seemed to be attired only in a flamboyant and hideously vulgar dressing gown. Mark's company had done some investigatory work into a complex VAT fraud case that Mr ver Ellst's partner was perpetrating. Janine's accounting skills had contributed significantly to the success of the investigation. The evidence was contained in the thick volume that Mark presented to him once the civilities were over. They were joined by an attractive young woman, equally scantily dressed, who was introduced as the ver Ellst company accountant. As he began to present his findings, he soon discovered that the young woman was highly intelligent and very well informed, whatever else she might have been. Instinctively he found himself explaining the details to her rather than the older man. At around twelve-thirty, and with a very satisfying cheque in his pocket, he was dismissed.

TWENTY-SIX

Emerging from the lift into the splendour of St. Jerome's marbled foyer, memories of his last visit and the dejected face of his niece flooded back to Mark. Glancing into the crowded restaurant, however, other memories and then a set of quite different feelings chased the thoughts of young Julie from his mind. There at the very table that she had occupied before was the young blonde woman who had made such an impression on him.

"It's very crowded, can I join you?"

Lehia Said looked up at the intruder, her eyes were even clearer and bluer than Mark could have imagined. Rejection started to form in her face, but in the event, it was an invitation that was offered.

"Of course, do sit down."

Mark was relieved. The surge of excitement that coursed through him as he approached the young woman was nothing like the feelings that Janine induced. It was more the adrenalin surge that he felt when he was in action against a resourceful enemy.

Yet the involvement of the young woman in the affairs of the Nigerians via what he was convinced was her alter ego was an opportunity that he couldn't ignore.

181

There was little warmth in the woman's smile, but as he soon discovered, there was little warmth in the woman anyway. She had passion, and some rather primitive lusts, but not much in the way of finer feelings.

"I'm Mark Shortley."

She grasped the proffered hand firmly and then relaxed her grip almost to a caress. Surprised, he quickly slid his hand away, giving her the friendliest grin that he could muster.

"Lehia Said," she said.

Her English proved to be almost perfect, with only the faintest occasional hint of a Scandinavian accent. A smirk rather than a smile acknowledged that he had reacted to her gesture. She didn't make any move to follow up her signal until they were free of fussing waiters and only Mark was in her immediate space.

'No shrinking violet, this one,' Mark realised as they studied each other frankly. The undisguised sexual challenge could hardly have escaped him.

Lehia was bored.

'I need a man,' was the very thought in her mind as Mark hove into view.

Her appetite as a full-blooded young woman had been easily satisfied with healthy and virile young men in the Lebanon. It made her unpopular with the older and more religiously committed members of her group; the wiser of them, however, allowed her scope in return for the ruthless devotion that she showed to her calling.

'Stupid bastard though he was, Faid was shit hot in bed.'

The Saudi man, who until recently had been providing her with cover, despite his size and unpleasant nature, had proved a vigorous and satisfying partner, and she had more than once regretted her action in removing him.

'Still, if it hadn't been for him, I wouldn't have come across this one.'

Hidden behind her expressionless features, a surge of desire was beginning to build up in her. She recognised that she had seen and met Mark before in the hotel. But driven by her more basic feelings that was all that she recognised. Mark's name didn't register.

'He's got to be good in bed,' she said to herself.

It was both a hope and an expectation.

Mark's thoughts hadn't got anywhere near this point. 'She's certainly attractive. It's hard to see her as a terrorist.'

The evidence that she was was circumstantial.

"So how d'you get that fantastic suntan in mid-winter?" she asked, shattering his train of thought.

"Just had a couple of weeks in the Seychelles," he said.

"I was there recently."

Alarm bells tinkled rather than rang. Janine had seen an Arab woman at their hotel and Silvanus Akinbode had been killed by a known Moslem terrorist technique. Both of these things could have been down to the young woman artlessly looking at him across the restaurant table. Signals to be careful were activated in the depths of his mind, but they were, as yet, unrecognised.

No alarm bells at all rang for her. The Nigerian operative that she been sent to eliminate had met with a British Security Service agent who she knew, but she made no link to the man that she had been seeking to stimulate for the last few minutes. Nor did she make any link to the information that she had gathered at the flat of Lawrence Wong.

"Wonderful place," she sighed distractedly.

The look of passion now clearly in her eyes seemed to detach her from her surroundings.

"Bronzed bodies...... .!"

With her excitement mounting, it was Mark's bronzed body that was filling her thoughts. Crushing her legs against his, her hand searched for his genitals, and as he gently tried to fend off her probing fingers under the table, her thoughts became words.

"I want your body!" she breathed urgently. "Now!"

The voice was low and insistent. It was all happening at astonishing speed. Such a blatant piece of sexual domineering was way beyond Mark's experience and he was totally at a loss. His original intention of just getting to know the woman and to determine whether she and the Arab woman truly were one and the same had been driven totally from his mind. The sheer animal passion she was evincing almost destroyed his powers of coherent thought.

"Come on!"

She was coming on so fast he didn't know what to do; but she knew. Standing up, she grasped his left wrist and pulled him to his feet. She then towed the unresisting Mark out of the restaurant and into a convenient lift. As the doors closed, she cupped his cheeks in her hands and kissed him repeatedly and with bruising energy until the lift halted at the top floor. Back in the restaurant the other diners registered nothing of the drama that had developed in their midst. The atmosphere was intimate to more than just Mark and Lehia Said.

"Come on," she said, hauling him almost frantically into a room opposite the lift.

Her body was gyrating with increasing urgency as she kicked the door shut behind them. With extraordinary speed and facility, she shed her clothes all around the bedroom. Then, completely naked, she began clawing at Mark's trousers.

"Come on, come on!" she said again and again; a manic passion had taken her over.

Mark wasn't allowed to hesitate.

* * *

"This is Daniel Onifade."

Janine had gone to lunch with her cousin Fid Okeke at the Nigerian High Commission, both as a family and social meeting, but also to provide an update on the situation with the arms shipment. Neither she nor Mark had known that Fid was back in the UK until the High Commission texted Janine. If Victoria had known, she had made no mention in any of her conversations with Mark from Munich.

But as she walked with him into the Hhigh Commission dining room, the unexpected happened.

'I know that back!'

As he had left her at Armards, the Nigerian businessman hadn't looked back, and her last view of him was from behind. It was that back that was presented to her and which materialised into a smiling face with a name as it turned to confront her.

Fid Okeke had thought from Onifade's rather bemused description of her that his friend's mystery woman might have been Janine. Onifade had come away from the meeting in the department store with no illusions about his prospects with Janine, and although the thoughts of getting her into his bed hadn't been banished, a more undemanding liaison seemed possible and he was, in ignorance, exploiting Fid Okeke's chance presence in London to pursue his quarry.

No such thoughts were occurring to Janine. She had another, much more powerful, relationship, as Daniel Onifade and her cousin well knew, and that was very important to her. But as she chatted over a drink, her thoughts were not really on either Mark or Onifade. She was still mentally immersed in arms shipments.

"Let's eat," said her cousin.

It was a pleasant and relaxing meal, and one that provided the two men with considerable entertainment. Fid Okeke deliberately chose a meal of traditional Nigerian dishes, because that was what he himself liked, but he was amused and amazed to discover that Janine, of course, was completely unfamiliar with such cuisine.

TWENTY-SEVEN

"Nothing happened! I tell you, nothing happened! Nothing!"

"Mark, you were stood there. You had your trousers round your ankles. Something was going to happen!"

As Janine sat beside him in the speeding car, her anger and hurt had been in serious competition with her sense of the ridiculous. The idea of her tough and resourceful partner, reduced to his shirt, quavering before the oversexed and overexcited young Arab woman was almost too much for her; it was something that she couldn't help but find funny. And even as they went over the episode again, Janine was hard pressed not to laugh.

"Janine, I didn't touch her, I wasn't even......"

"Oh, spare me, please," she said, interrupting as much to suppress her rising giggles as anything.

'The last thing I need is a sordid description,' she thought, trying once more to take the situation seriously. 'going over it all again can't change anything.'

She hadn't wanted to be pained by the scene being too real for her and she didn't want the ludicrous images that Mark had recalled to her mind reduced to their actuality; that might have killed her amusement. The situation had certainly been hilarious to her at a superficial level, but it could all too easily have been turned into something desperately serious and fatally threatening to their relationship if it had become too tangible. She hadn't wanted that.

They drove on in silence. Janine was relishing Mark's discomfort and he was feeling unutterably stupid.

'God,' he'd told himself after the event, 'how could I have been so gutless! Of course she's a killer, but where the hell could she hide a knife when she's naked? I wasn't frightened by her with her clothes on; why did I go to pieces when she'd got them off?'

Somewhere in the depths of his mind, he thought he knew the answer. Fascinated by the sheer ruthlessness of the woman, frustrated by the inaction forced on him by the way events were unfolding, he was only too ready to react to a new situation. Shut away in a separate corner of the male mind, the impact of this or any other sexual adventure on his relationship with Janine only became real when it was forced on him. It had been here. That he himself had initiated the whole debacle by approaching Lehia Said in the first place wasn't something that Mark was too ready to acknowledge.

'I guess I have to respect his honesty for telling me,' Janine had told herself, acknowledging that Mark had done so even at the risk of damaging their relationship. 'I would hardly have been likely to find out after the spats we've already had over the wretched woman. Still, just because the whole thing turned out to be a farce, that isn't an excuse.'

But it did prevent her from any damaging overreaction. However, Mark's mortification was palpable, and she tried to contain her mirth for as long as she could to make him suffer as much as possible.

"I had lunch with Fid Okeke," Janine had said when her turn for confiding had come. "And he brought the mysterious Nigerian from Armards with him. Daniel Onifade; he's an old school friend, it seems. I rather think Fid has overplayed my little set-to with the Chinese. It seems to have cooled Onifade's ardour somewhat!"

To his credit, Mark had made no effort to minimise his own transgressions by focusing on what he might have said were hers.

* * *

The whole episode in Lehia Said's hotel room had come to an absurd, anticlimactic end. In a frenzied state and desperate to be satisfied, she had grasped at Mark with the intention of dragging him onto the bed. But as her hands reached out, the insistent and discordant bleeping of her mobile phone erupted from somewhere in the piles of her scattered clothes. She stopped dead, looked confused, recovered and then began to scrabble frantically amongst her cast-off garments.

Mark muttered a prayer and a curse and hurriedly started to get dressed again. Angered by his own capitulation and humiliation, his determination to escape was instantly fired. But Lehia was off the boil; after studying the newly arrived text message, she scurried into the bathroom.

"Another time!" she shouted from the shower.

Mark's response was incoherent. He was convinced that she had no idea who he was, but he was equally sure that she would very soon find out. Since she was bound to think that he had been trying to take advantage of her, a venomous reaction was inevitable.

* * *

It was almost three o'clock when Mark had arrived back at his office. He had waited long enough to see Lehia picked up by two swarthy gentlemen in a hired late model BMW. He noted the number. He also noted that although Lehia may have seemed to be a careless dresser, her clothes were all of the chain store, nondescript type that made her readily forgettable. Without his knowledge of her alter ego, the black-clad traditional Arab with china blue eyes, Mark wouldn't even have noticed her.

Janine arrived back from her lunch-time jaunt in something of a state of excitement. Whether it was because of their impending involvement in the final stages of the arms shipment, or because of the success of her assignation, Mark couldn't fathom. She reported her conversation with Mr Okeke but left open the opportunity to tell him about what else she had been doing for later.

TWENTY-EIGHT

"We'd better get started," Janine said the moment Mark had completed his dressing.

Their exchange of confidences had commenced whilst they were both changing into more practical outdoor clothes. Mark found it easier to mask his continuing mortification when he was actively doing something. The episode with the Lehia Said had dampened the effects of the adrenalin build up he usually felt when getting into real action, but that was only going to be temporary.

"So?" said Janine.

She always dressed quickly with no seeming hesitations over her choice of clothes. She sat on the bed to listen. She didn't make Mark's confession very easy for him, but to his relief she didn't make it any worse by displays of anger or jealousy. She made her own contribution to the soul-searching in her usual matter-of-fact way and was, in her turn, pleased to receive no criticism from him.

"The car's out the back."

Mark didn't own a vehicle; in central London it didn't make a lot of sense. However, he had a contract with a local garage to supply his transport needs. On this occasion he had secured a comfortable but powerful run-of-the-mill Ford that he knew that he could depend upon.

"I'll pick up the latest information," said Janine.

She trawled through her voice-recording system as Mark checked the back-up procedures with a couple of his subordinates.

As they worked their way out of London through the normal early-afternoon tangle of traffic, Janine reported that the two trucks were holed up at a service area outside Colchester. With plenty of time to arrive at Felixstowe and no doubt with orders not to draw attention to themselves, the truck drivers were meticulously obeying the myriad of European Federation regulations that ruled the lives of people such as them.

"Taking the A12, Ipswich bypass and presumably the A14," Janine said, "they picked up an escort somewhere near Chelmsford. There are at least two cars of Chinese thugs according to our man. They've advised the police."

"What's the latest they need to be at the docks?"

"Around seven, I'd guess. It's three-thirty now; they wouldn't need to leave the service area until six if they didn't want to hang around at Felixstowe.

"So what about this Arab woman then?"

Mark knew that she would revert to the subject eventually.

It was then that he pleaded that nothing had happened, and Janine had voiced her disbelief.

"Janine, she didn't do anything for me. If her goddamn 'phone hadn't gone off... it would have been a disaster!"

He took his hand off the steering wheel and made a gesture. Aware of how powerful he was when he was making love to her, his hand picture of limp ineffectiveness was more then she could bear. The vision burst the barriers of her self-restraint. She simply exploded into shrieks of laughter.'

"Oh, Mark," she said, gasping for breath after several minutes of being completely out of control.

He listened to her in total amazement, her inarticulate splutters hardly necessary in explanation of her hysterical outburst. She repeated his gesture to herself and that set her off again. It was many more minutes before she began to calm down. Mark felt utterly deflated.

"Mark, I'm sorry," she eventually said when she could manage something like normal speech. "But the idea of you being unable to perform in the face of any woman…"

The giggles and shrieks started again, and they were only cut off, as with Lehia Said, by the gentle bleeping of Janine's laptop. Plugged into the car power supply and using a private radio channel, Mark's office was transmitting an update of the situation.

"The trucks are moving again; one lot of Chinese minders has gone on ahead."

Now in command of herself, Janine was reading the messages as they came up on her screen.

"The patrol at Chelmsford has picked up this late model BMW on the bypass. It's heading up the A12 at high speed."

The car make registered with Mark, but making a direct link to Lehia Said was too tenuous a connection to take root in his brain at the time – BMWs were hardly uncommon.

"The police are ready to start their action. They don't want the SAS people in sight.

"The European Federal Police have told the Nigerians that they've no claim on the weapons; they still belong to the Americans."

"What!" said Mark in response to the last of the messages.

"It seems that the Nigerian Government had asked for the arms to be returned to them since they were paid for with Nigerian money. I told Fid they hadn't a chance, but he didn't see the arguments."

It wasn't an issue that Janine felt much interest in, but she had asked for the information as it was an outstanding point from her lunch-time meeting.

"So what about this bloke Onifargo then?" Mark pulled the conversation back to the personal once the messages had been dealt with.

"Fancies me in bed…,or at least he did 'til Fid told him about the Chinese man. He can't work me out and that bugs him. I guess he'll be good for the odd dinner or two. And his name is Onifade, Daniel."

Janine chuckled at the recollections of her two meetings with Daniel Onifade and how her views had changed. But what she really liked was the gentle way that Mark reintroduced the subject of her recent informal activities in contrast to her rather heavy-handed reference to his.

"Pax," he simply said.

She leant over and kissed his ear.

"Pax," she replied, and it was all over.

* * *

"They not here!"

The Romanian driver of the late model BMW had just dawdled past another row of trucks at another service area and reported the obvious in his fractured English.

"This is pointless!" Lehia muttered to the two East Europeans, but they had no knowledge of Arabic.

If her frightened contact in the Nigerian High Commission had had more specific information, things would have been better.

'New Truth aren't spies!' Lehia told herself, 'and why destroy the arms? Hijack them, trade them!'

She didn't like her group being used as general dogs-bodies by the northern Nigerians and couldn't understand why her Fundamentalist bosses had offered their services. Dealing with the Nigerian Federal Government agent in the Seychelles was fine; chasing lorries just to destroy them was as tedious as it was pointless to her.

"Now what?"

She had been brought back from her musings by a shouted obscenity from the driver. They had run into a traffic jam. Lehia's day had started in farce with her failed attempt to get Mark Shortley into her bed and now it was going to end in farce with the Romanians' inability to get them anywhere near the vehicles that they had come to deal with.

* * *

Janine's computer terminal erupted into frantic life again as they pulled onto the A14 for the final stretch to Felixstowe. The police were in action and a string of messages detailed the status of the situation. More importantly, a route was identified for Mark and Janine that would bypass the inevitable traffic jams.

"Bucklesham, Kirton, Falkenham.," Janine was counting off the villages on their private route as they passed through them.

* * *

"Why the hell do we have to get there so bloody late?"

Each of the drivers of the two trucks had asked the other that simple question a thousand times over their hands-free communication link.

"Gawd knows," said his compatriot.

The two drivers were not from the Wong organisation. Piloting vast juggernauts all over the face of Europe was not an occupation that found much favour with the Chinese community, so they had no choice but to hire Europeans. Not that in the present case the two drivers were venturing very far. The trip from Ashford to Felixstowe was not particularly exacting, but as a result of their incomprehensible instructions, it was taking the two men far longer than they thought that it should.

"The lorries are the most vulnerable when they're stood still," was Hector Xu's instruction to his planners. "There's a miss-match between the cross-Channel ferry arrival and the departure from Felixstow, you've got to keep the trucks moving. Short stops, move slowly."

Hence the meanderings that were so irritating for the two drivers. Why they hadn't been allowed just to stay at the Ashford depot was another unanswered question to the two men.

"Need to stop at the next service area and take the security guards on board," the driver of the first truck said to his colleague.

"OK."

For their own reasons, neither man voiced the obvious question of why they needed security guards anyway. And if the two drivers were expecting any sort of companionship for the final kilometres of their journey, they were disappointed. Both the Chinese guards were surly and largely silent.

"The trucks are on the move, line astern," reported the police observer. "Car two has fallen in behind; we'll keep him company."

A little procession involving the two trucks formed at the exit of the service area and once again set out. There was a third car here also, but after a short exchange on the radio it headed away back to Ipswich. Janine reported that the last of the SAS had now withdrawn.

"Problem up front," reported the first driver as they entered the approaches to Felixstowe.

As he came around a gentle curve into a straight section of road, the unsynchronised flashing of an array of hazard lights on the vehicles ahead of him warned him of some obstruction.

"Keep moving," said his Chinese passenger.

The driver shrugged. Of course he would keep moving as long as he could; he wanted an end to this journey far more than the security guard did.

As they crawled forward, they saw that the police had erected a roadblock of their own cars but also of a number of other larger vehicles. Recognising that the trucks were powerful enough to ride over their vehicles, they had decided to go for something more substantial as back-up.

"Keep moving!" shouted the guard, as a policeman in a reflective jacket began waving the truck towards a lay-by.

The gap in the carriageway had been closed by a road roller. With the second truck and the tailback of traffic behind him, the driver knew that he was totally boxed in.

"Keep moving!" screamed the guard again, urging the driver first with his bare hand and then with a handgun.

"You bloody mad? There's nowhere to go!"

The driver was more angry than frightened.

"Move over, move over!"

Even against the throbbing whine of the truck engines, both drivers could clearly hear the instruction blasted at them over the police megaphone.

The bodyguard in the first truck showed his weapon as a spotlight flashed into the cabin. Mark and the senior police officer had a rapid conference. Threats to the drivers were an eventuality that they had foreseen. Floodlights were switched on and both vehicles were illuminated. Armed marksmen covered both cabins.

"Bugger this!" exclaimed the first driver, an ex-paratrooper.

In one sweeping movement, he flicked his cabin door open and rolled himself out. Landing on his feet, he ducked close to the side of the truck. The guard's shot flew harmlessly through the open door and on into the dark night at the other side of the highway. The return of fire wrecked the windscreen and the driver's cherished photograph of the Manchester United FA Cup-winning team but otherwise did no physical harm to the gunman.

"Throw out your gun!"

The man did so, and the crisis was over.

The roadblock was opened up. The second car of Chinese heavies was pulled to one side and the three occupants joined the two security guards in the police van. The truck drivers were not arrested.

"They'll not know what they're carrying," Mark said to the police superintendent. "The Wong's don't work like that."

* * *

As the roadblock was dismantled and the traffic speed increased, the disgruntled Lehia Said and her two tame Romanians got to the action. Seeing the two trucks that they were hunting pulled up at the roadside and surrounded by police, she knew at once what had happened. Any attempt at sabotage would now be suicidal. Her original plan was abandoned instantly. The arms would be denied to the southern Nigerians that at least was a success, but a victory for the authorities did not please Lehia.

"Slow down!" she suddenly demanded, but it was too late; they were past.

But she'd seen enough. There, clearly in some sort of authority, was the man who had, only hours earlier, stood in her bedroom with his trousers at his feet. As Mark had predicted, Lehia Said had pretty soon found out about him. Feeling used and humiliated by her lack of success with him, she swore vengeance.

"The police report that the suspect Ford-BMW has just passed the roadblock; what should they do?" said Janine as Mark rejoined her in the car.

"Let them go," he said. "There's nothing they could hold them on."

That the late model Ford-BMW had been a part of the action the police had confirmed to Mark by passing on the registration number. What Lehia Said had been planning to do, however, neither Mark nor the police bothered to speculate on, since in reality they had done nothing. But Mark was all too aware of Lehia Said's resilience and toughness; some further action was inevitable.

* * *

Both Mark and Janine exalted over their success, Mark particularly. They knew it was only a partial achievement, there were many more weapons yet to intercept, but they had cause to be satisfied.

'Different bloke when there's action about,' thought Janine as she looked at Mark's profile with a surge of affection.

Mark himself felt the tingling of excitement diminish as they left the police to tidy up the details, but there was a warmth that he always felt when he had been successful that would last for some time. He wasn't quite an action junkie, but he was certainly happier when there was action, and now especially because he knew that a whole sequence of events had been started.

"Don't think this day's work's going to improve relations between the Wongs and the Nigerians," remarked Mark as he settled into the drive back towards London. "Either their clients, or the security service!"

"It'll set things back a bit for the southerners," said Janine. "Just hope it doesn't make it easier for the Fundamentalists, … since they're the real enemy."

Mark drove into the car park of a pub that he had noticed when they were edging their way through the countryside around the roadblock.

"What a good idea!" Janine was delighted.

* * *

Janine and Victoria Akinbode were the only two of the women involved in the armaments action who were pleased with life.

Lehia Said was angry about a day wasted and more especially about being made a fool of by Mark; Pearl Wong was angry because of her organisation's failure to deliver the arms and ammunition to their customer. Pearl was at home when she had been informed. With her father's funeral the following day, she had been busy and, as usual, had worked off her tensions by giving Tang One and Tang Two a hard time in the gym.

"...you mean the police knew about the arms? How could they have done? You can see the Nigerian Security Service a mile away!"

Her anger boiled over.

Hector Xu let her rant and roar. Long in the tooth, he knew that she would calm down and be better able to accept the news that the Nigerians had recruited a British security company to handle the European end of their affairs. Xu still believed that it was fruitless to fight the Nigerians – circumventing them was a better strategy – but the problem had now become much harder.

"I should've killed her," Pearl insisted once she had finally listened to the old man.

Pearl credited every success the Nigerians had to Victoria Akinbode; it gave her something to focus on. In this case, she did so with some justice. Victoria had spent her time well when she was ostensibly overseeing the security of the Nigerian delegation to the United Nations. She had quickly built up good relations with the European Security Service and her growing rapport with the French had proved particularly rewarding. The French authorities had easily picked up the arms trucks as they had crossed Europe.

"I guess a hiccup like this won't change things much in Nigeria, and there's still the rest of the arms."

Having talked out all the implications with Hector Xu, Pearl felt better. The next shipments had to be arranged and life in the Wong empire had to move on. A few angry Nigerians were just part of the risks of what they did.

TWENTY-NINE

"We need to learn from our mistakes," Pearl said after Hector Xu had finished briefing her on the arrest of the two trucks. "if only for the organisation's credibility."

It was Janine's business card that provided the clues.

"Mark Shortley Associates," Xu said, "firm of security consultants; they seem to be the key to this."

After the Armards incident, he had taken the card away and made enquiries. A contact in the Metropolitan Police with an expensive gambling habit supplied the basic details.

"Very well regarded by the British authorities, and with strong contacts in the military, especially the SAS," he continued.

"And the girl?"

"Live-in girlfriend."

Xu had become well briefed on Mark Shortley. He saw him as a very resourceful and tenacious opponent. He didn't share the concerns that gave him with Pearl.

"Couldn't find much about her at first, but working with your photos, and checking with the company who provided the catering at the Nigerian High Commission. Definitely knows Victoria Akinbode, ... not hard to see how the confusion arose."

Pearl understood the point; she'd also compared photographs.

"They've been spending a lot of time together; after the husband was killed. And she's on good terms with the man we suspect is Victoria Akinbode's superior."

Again Xu didn't share the knowledge that Janine was an accomplished computer wizard.

"And you reckon this Shortley is working for the Nigerian Security Service?"

"The High Commission aren't paying Shortley's invoices for nothing!"

A young Nigerian clerk, far gone in his heroin addiction, was a regular source of intelligence to anybody prepared to indulge his habit. Despite her scruples, his clients had also included Lehia Said in the recent past.

"And Shortley's got the resources and contacts to detect and intercept the arms shipment?"

"No doubt of it."

'And,' thought Pearl, 'if he's got the resources to intercept one shipment, he's got the resources to intercept the others.'

That was something that she needed to think about.

* * *

Mark certainly had got the resources, and he and Janine had spent much of the week following the arrest of the trucks in preparing the ground for the counteraction against the next movement.

On the Tuesday morning, Janine, who was basically the resource in question, sauntered into Mark's office and perched herself on his lap. Having completed her task, she was feeling content with herself and ready to share her conclusions.

"We've cracked it!" she said with her brightest grin.

"Oh, great," he replied, unconsciously running his hand backwards and forwards across her buttocks. "So what have we cracked?"

"The arms route."

"OK then…"

Mark withdrew his hand, much to Janine's disappointment.

"Working from what we gathered during the first shipment and errr, … and some hacking into the customs records of a couple of friendly countries, I reckon I've sorted the entire route of the shipment. Better still, I've sorted something that's been bugging me in all of this! There's a Wong company in Paris we didn't know about. It looks like they're masterminding the whole thing."

Mark wondered why Paris, but he was well aware of the Wong's penchant for dispersing their activities to preserve their security.

"And you think they'll use the same route again?"

"I reckon; maybe with variations. But it's such a complex job I doubt they'll switch to something completely different."

Unknown to her, Janine's view was supported by a frosty conversation between Pearl Wong and Mr Falinde. The southern Nigerians greeted the loss of the arms with dismay. However, the outcome of the conversation put some renewed urgency into the delivery schedule and, as a consequence, seriously cut down on the Wong's flexibility. Chief Adeko was not a happy man.

'If that's the case,' thought Mark, 'maybe it gives us some new options.'

It was against his nature to be as passive as he was required to be at the current time, and he'd been looking for ways to take a more active role in countering the arms movements. However, he needed to test his ideas with Janine, and probably Mr Okeke. Victoria had plenty enough to occupy her, and the less people who knew about his thinking the better. Mark was conscious that this conclusion reflected Janine's reservations about her friend.

"Victoria's in Paris," Janine remarked, still sitting companionably on Mark's lap.

She sounded wistful.

"Someone has to go to Paris and talk to the French authorities; that's obvious. I could fancy that… she and I could have a great time. Still… makes more sense for you to go, I suppose."

"Oh, I think so," said Mark.

'He seemed pretty sure about that!'

Sensitive after the affair with Lehia Said, Janine thought Mark had agreed rather too readily.

'Maybe he's expecting a great time with Victoria too!'

The idea of Mark and Victoria in Paris grated with her, but she was quick enough to admit that it was a feeling against Victoria rather than Mark.

'Well,' she said to herself, 'maybe our Mr Onifade will have to earn his keep!'

She was aware that Onifade was spending a rather longer spell in London than was his normal habit, so she assumed that he would be available if the fancy took her.

The arrangements for Mark to meet up with Victoria in Paris were readily made.

* * *

"Janine, we're going to be late."

They had an appointment with an academic at nine o'clock and needed to get across to Bloomsbury through the usual early-morning morass of traffic. Janine was even more meticulous about appointments than he was, so when he saw her, a study of absolute concentration, scanning her computer monitor intently, he knew that something was wrong.

"What is it?"

She didn't respond; she simply raised a hand to acknowledge his presence. Then as a lot more of what she called computer gibberish passed over the screen, she gave a grunt. It was followed by a second one as she went back and rechecked something that she had seen before. The last grunt was one of satisfaction, but it was not accompanied by one of Janine's more usual displays of pleasure.

"Well, now," she said.

"Janine! What is it?"

"Somebody's hacked into our systems. Your meeting with Victoria is already known to whoever it is."

"Serious?"

Mark was concerned because Janine was concerned.

"Maybe. Can't be sure yet."

He wasn't quite the computer ignoramus that he made out to be, but he did like to be told things in plain language.

"We'll have to upgrade the security of our routine systems and change the office procedures," she said in response to his plea for enlightenment.

But as Janine had been quick to note, the attack had only been against their lowest-level communication systems.

"Can you tell who's hacking us?"

"The impossible…," she said with a shrug, beginning to quote a well-known adage, "if you want me to come with you to the professor, the miracle will definitely have to take a little longer."

* * *

'He's not much older than Mark,' Janine thought as they were shown into Professor Iain Jordane's office, 'nor is he my idea of a typical academic!'

He was dressed expensively. His office was equipped expensively but with the sort of furniture more likely to be found in a corporate chairman's inner sanctum than in the workstation of an expert on Middle Eastern terror groups. The walls were lined with books. His enormous desk was almost totally devoid of paper.

"This is Janine Effiong, my business partner."

The professor took Janine's long coat and deposited it on a spare chair. He gestured his visitors to seats around a glass-topped occasional table and in turn introduced the research student who had joined them.

"Knew each other in the SAS," remarked Jordane, by way of explanation to both Janine and Sara, the research student, who, despite her Afro-Caribbean appearance under her all-enveloping clothing, was actually a Kuwaiti. She was carrying a small folder of papers and seemed to be somewhat nonplussed by Janine's rather exotic appearance.

"Sara?"

"The Moslem Fundamentalists, as you are no doubt well aware, have been expanding into black Africa and Asia for some considerable time. Using the springboard provided by al-Shabaab in Somalia, they have sought to spread their doctrine into Mali, Mauritania, Niger, Chad and, we believe, parts of Uganda, but particularly Nigeria. The Fundamentalists have gained some sort of a foothold in all of these places and have fermented the sort of fanatical anti-secular revolution that was more typical of the Afghanistan of old than, say, Iran in the early part of the century. The Iranians focused their attention on the Middle East and, being Shia Moslems, tended to keep their distance from the remnants of al-Qaeda and the like.

"In addition, over the last six months a very substantial renewed campaign to subvert the traditional rulers of northern Nigeria has been underway. This is by far the largest attempt at Islamic revolution in Nigeria. And it is organised, unlike the disorganised creeping subversion of the past ten to twelve years. There's a determination about what's happening that was absent before. Boko Haram have been revitalised, reorganised and definitely upskilled."

There was more. Sara's presentation was earnest and precise.

"All of this said, the evidence is that despite its greater

urgency, planning and coherence, the incursion is not working well. The leaders of the Fundamentalists, like Alhaji Mahomet Sullag, are proving too cautious, and the Somali leadership has recently dispatched a large number of their own supporters, largely of dissident Middle -Eastern origin, to try and inflame the situation and build a momentum. They have also introduced some of the remnants of the old Lebanese and Palestinian terror groups in an effort to eliminate some of the more persistent opposition. So far they don't appear to have had much effect there either. The most prominent…"

Janine, who had already gleaned much of the information from her own studies, came to life at the mention of the Alhaji. She was only waiting for a pause in Sara's presentation but in the end couldn't contain herself until one came.

"Hold on. You just said that Alhaji Mahomet Sullag was one of the leaders of the Fundamentalists?"

"So he is."

The research student was adamant

"According to our information," Janine said carefully, "he's a leading traditionalist seeking to resist the Fundamentalists."

"That's Nigeria for you," remarked Iain Jordane. "Nothing is quite what it seems."

"We'd like sight of your evidence," said Mark.

The information needed checking with Okeke. From her conversations with her cousin, Janine had gained the impression that the Alhaji was regarded with suspicion in both the traditionalist and the Fundamentalist camps. Against this, Victoria seemed to have every confidence in him.

"The most prominent of the old terror groups recruited is 'New Truth'. Their remit seems to be to operate outside Nigeria. The group was thought to have been destroyed last year following a gun battle with the Lebanese Police and the members of an international arms-dealing organisation; Chinese, supposedly. However, there is clear evidence from news reports and other sources that it's still active, albeit on a much-reduced scale and almost on an individual terrorist basis."

The young Kuwaiti woman reached into her folder and pulled out a set of photographs. They were all of the same young woman.

"You know who this woman is?" asked Mark.

He'd recognised her, and so, by inference, had Janine.

"Lehia Said. Said to be twenty-five or -six, part Swedish. She has eleven murders supposedly to her credit, including the man who killed her mother and raped her. She is known to be currently living in London. She has proved very adept at exploiting her European appearance and it has been very difficult to associate her with many of the incidents that she is suspected of being involved in. She is said to be without compassion."

Again there was more, but the research student seemed reluctant to continue.

"She's a woman with a very short fuse and a very large sexual appetite," added the professor.

"Isn't she just!" muttered Janine.

"Lehia Said," repeated Mark, not hearing this exchange.

"Well," said Janine quietly, "we've surely got ourselves one hell of an enemy!"

"We've prepared a dossier," said the professor. "Sara has already given you the flavour of it. We'd be happy to follow up any questions. It's not exhaustive, of course; it's only based on published data. We don't have access to intelligence service information."

'Not that you'd admit to,' thought Mark.

THIRTY

"Hi, pleased to see you."

Victoria hadn't entered Mark's thoughts again until he emerged the next day from a Eurostar sleeper and the young lady herself stood two feet from his nose to greet him.

'She's not as beautiful as Janine,' Mark thought. 'There's a sort of Asian look to her features and her hair's not as luxuriant.'

Her clothes were practical. She favoured the same sort of sensible boots as Janine but would never have worn the minuscule skirts that her friend usually preferred. Her own calf-length skirt, quilted jacket and pert Parisian beret were serviceable rather than tasteful.

'Just like Lehia Said's clothes, they're eminently forgettable.'

"Hi."

Victoria's greeting had been surprisingly warm and friendly. But, starved of masculine companionship since the death of Silvanus Akinbode, and with a partner forever travelling the world, Victoria was drawn to Mark as much by Janine's description of him as by his obvious charms as a wholesome and virile male of the species.

"We're staying in this little hotel off the Rue Rivoli. And we're meeting two French Security Service guys for dinner.

There's a bar at the corner of the street that overlooks the square; you can see all the approaches to the restaurant. It's a good place to watch and wait."

Mark's opinion of Victoria rose. She gestured at the restaurant as they got settled into the bar. A festoon of coloured lights obscured the name, but it looked like just the sort of place that Mark, who had been to Paris many times, loved.

Around them the bar filled and emptied as customers passed in and out, some on their way home from work, some meeting with friends for the casual gossip that the French so much enjoyed, and some like Mark and Victoria, just idling the time away. The young Nigerian studied each customer unobtrusively, trying to discern if any of them were potential watchers of themselves.

"I'm afraid my visit's known."

Mark had noticed her surveillance.

"Somebody's hacked into our computer system. Janine doesn't know who yet."

Victoria didn't seem surprised.

"Inevitable, I guess. Everybody's watching everybody else."

'That's assuming,' Mark thought, 'we know who everybody actually is!'

* * *

"This is Léon and François," Victoria introduced the two French agents.

Neither Mark nor Victoria supposed that they were christened as such.

The Frenchmen were reluctant to discuss any business until the proper rituals of eating were accomplished. Mark, naturally, was familiar with all the menu analysis and the rather strident questioning of the waiter that formed a part of this process, but Victoria was less patient. He was obliged to quell her frustration under the table, but the gesture was at first misinterpreted and he found his foot trapped between her ankles. Eventually supplying the information that he had wanted to convey by the exaggerated use of his eyebrows, she released his leg with an arched grin.

'Oh God, not another one!' he said to himself. 'First Lehia Said, now Victoria.'

The Frenchman Léon, having then safely piloted an uncomprehending Victoria through the pitfalls of the menu, broached the subject of the Wong organisation.

"We have a contact," he said in slow, careful English., "He works for L'heure du soleil, a firm of travel agents who never arrange any travel."

"But who do arrange shipments of merchandise?" said Victoria.

"Quite so."

Léon broke off for the meal to be served. Poor Victoria, who lacked Janine's sophistication after lifelong residence in London, looked on in horror as quails and rabbit were served to the three men. Her relief when her dish of plain turbot was presented to her made even the rather taciturn François chuckle.

"We will meet with him tomorrow," he said, picking up where Léon had left off, "in the Louvre."

Even in winter, the Louvre was a favoured meeting place. Its ready access by foot, taxi or Metro was the principal reason for its popularity, but its sheer size and the cosmopolitan nature of its clientele meant that a group of Europeans, Chinese and an African woman would not excite attention.

"We'll need to take special precautions," Mark said.

He explained that his presence in Paris was already known. The Frenchmen immediately assumed that it was the Wong organisation; to them that was logical.

"The French Regional Government is not happy with arms

movements on such a scale taking place through its territory," Léon remarked rather primly.

"Neither is the British Government," said Mark sourly in response.

A chief superintendent of the Eastern Counties Police had recently made the point rather strongly to him.

"The worry is the Moslem Fundamentalist terrorists will return to France. We understand they're helping the Nigerians."

Léon was articulating the French Government's greatest fear.

Having expended a tremendous effort and not a few lives in the mid-1990s and onwards expelling the terrorists, the French authorities were naturally sensitive to a return. It was only after years of effort that an understanding had been achieved with its Islamic population and France had settled into a wary coexistence between its faith groups.

"We've prevented one arms shipment and we'll prevent the others," Victoria said, trying to reassure them. "The most useful thing that the French Security Sservice can do is let the weapons through France as quickly as possible and not give the Fundamentalists the chance to interfere."

There was much shoulder-shrugging and hand-spreading at this, but the arrival of coffee distracted the two Frenchmen and gave them the opportunity to resume their good-humoured wrangles with the waiter over the liqueurs. The French Security Service realised that the Nigerian authorities were doing their best to deal with the situation and that their problems were current and real rather than being more perceived than actual, as was the case with the French authorities.

"So what about Marseille then?" said Mark by way of both distracting the Frenchmen from what was likely to be a fruitless discussion and signalling that the business session was over. Marseille had been beaten in an extremely exciting but ill-natured cup tie the previous evening.

There was an instant and opposed reaction from the two men.

"It was a terrible game," said Léon with some heat, his remark almost drowning out the enthusiastic appreciation of his colleague.

They all laughed. The Frenchmen knew that the British always made fun of their football fervour, despite being pretty excitable about the performances of their own teams. The good-humoured football talk continued for a while; it was a light-hearted way to draw the evening to a close.

"We see you tomorrow," said Léon.

They went through the arrangements again and the Frenchmen departed.

* * *

"Why do they always seem to be criticising us?"

Victoria's remark was a little peevish, but he could understand why. The fact that half of her country was tearing itself apart and the other half was waiting to pick over the bones was not a good image to present to the world. But at least the French authorities understood the imperative of defeating the Moslem Fundamentalists.

"More coffee?"

Mark was not keen to get back to the hotel.

Victoria shook her head. In her focused way, she was pursuing another train of thought and had had more than enough to eat and drink.

"Some lady, this Pearl Wong," she said. "A real tough nut by all accounts, and she seems to be very much her father's daughter."

Victoria had heard stories about Pearl when she was researching the Wongs but hadn't taken them very seriously at the time.

"I guess we'll come across again her at some stage," Mark responded.

He was unenthusiastic. In his turn he had had enough of powerful woman for one day.

Unfortunately Victoria hadn't had enough of powerful men, and she made a calculated if uninspiring effort to get Mark into her bed that night.

There was no finesse about her approach. Victoria was clearly not a world-class lover like Janine, who enjoyed the sport beforehand every bit as much as the eventual lovemaking.

'Why the hell didn't I just walk away?' Mark asked himself later when he was back in his room. 'It was so obvious what she had in mind when she asked me into her room for a drink. I suppose I went there in the interests of good relations.'

Janine would have had apoplexy at such a suggestion, knowing how determined Victoria could be and how naive Mark sometimes was when faced with womanly wiles.

The drinking didn't take five minutes. As he sat on the end of the bed, Victoria started to undress in front of him.

"Relax, Mark," she said.

He couldn't; he was feeling too uncomfortable.

"No, no, this is not for me," he said rather limply.

Victoria stripped herself straight down to her tights in a series of practical movements that left Mark with no feelings of excitement at all. She had had an urge to make love and she was pursuing it. It was nothing more. When satisfaction was denied to her, she shrugged, kissed Mark on the cheek and let him go. It didn't mean enough to her to try to arouse him in some other way.

"Another time," she said, closing the door behind him.

Where had he heard that before!

In his own room, the Victoria stepping out of her clothes in front of him seemed so different from the Victoria he was in a working partnership with. It was almost as if she was another person. But he was tired and didn't dwell on the comparison for long.

Next morning, thoughts of Janine and the certainties of her boisterous and physically exciting approach to lovemaking invaded his mind, carrying with it a twinge of guilt that he had even allowed himself to get into the situation he had with Victoria. The guilt didn't last, and the male mind moved to comparisons. Between Janine, one frenetic encounter with Lehia Said, and one rather mechanical one with Victoria, he knew which he preferred!

* * *

If Victoria's sexual appetite hadn't been satisfied overnight, neither too was her more usual one in the morning. The one thing that she really hated about Paris was the dismal breakfasts that she was offered.

"How are you supposed to survive on this?" she demanded of Mark as he joined her rather warily.

He laughed, he found the rolls and croissants equally unfulfilling, but accepted them as part of the environment.

"We'd better go," she said moments later.

The trip to the Louvre was deliberately tortuous and took in a fascinating detour through the Les Halles area. It was Victoria's attempt to throw off any pursuit. As they finally emerged from the Metro station right into the heart of the underground entrance hall to the museum, they were both relieved. It was a bitterly cold morning and all the dodging in and out of the chilly air was quite wearing, particularly for Victoria, whose life was split between London and Abuja and who, as a consequence, was never really acclimatised to either place.

"Ah, you've arrived."

The two Frenchmen materialised precisely where they said they would be and exactly on time.

"Our friend has a passion for the *Mona Lisa*," said Léon.

'Or at least for the most crowded areas of the museum,' thought Mark.

The man was easily found. A lone Chinese gentleman was a comparative rarity in the Louvre. He was very nervous and flitted around the edge of the group, surrounding the celebrated portrait like a startled butterfly. Once he had received reassuring signals, Victoria approached him. In a rather inept switch of museum catalogues, he passed on his information and received his payment. Victoria pushed the brochure into her shoulder bag and made as if to talk to him. The man panicked.

"We leave him," said Léon, steering Victoria away.

Victoria was angry.

"But we need to know more about what the Wongs are doing."

"He will tell you nothing about the Wong organisation."

Léon was adamant.

Whatever hold they had over the man, and were using to get details of the arms shipments, it would only be enough for such minor infidelities. Mark agreed with the Frenchman; as they talked the frightened informer quietly slipped away. With no other reason to be there, the two Frenchmen faded away as unobtrusively as they had appeared.

"A thousand dollars and we don't get chance to check the merchandise until it's far too late."

Victoria was still angry.

"Yeah, OK, I'm not so happy either, but the main thing is for the man to get away undetected. He's not a lot of use to us dead."

The man's weak spot was gambling, and he was known to be well in debt to moneylenders, so the money, if found on him, would not necessarily cause surprise. It would if he had been seen talking to strangers, one of whom was black. If anything could force the Wongs to change the arms delivery route, it would obviously be if they suspected that it had been compromised.

"Coffee," he suggested, keen to distract Victoria.

He'd noticed a café on an upper landing with tables laid out in an open area. Conversation would be reasonably secure there. He pointed it out to Victoria. She signalled her agreement by leading the way.

"If we've got timings, we've got all we need," said Mark as they sat down. "Janine's got all the details of the previous route and we reckon they'll use the same one again. Thing is, even with the Wong's resources, they'd find it extremely difficult to run a different route for each shipment. Why should they, unless they suspect we've sussed it?"

"OK, but suppose you're wrong?"

Mark didn't think that they were and said so. Victoria began to argue and then stopped. A little vision of Mr Okeke flashed though her mind, and she reminded herself that they were paying Mark and Janine to prevent the arms getting to the southern Nigerians and she should let them get on with it.

THIRTY-ONE

Mark and Victoria had been talking for half -an -hour, and having completed their intended tasks, they had no cause to remain in Paris. However, rather than rush for a train to London, Mark proposed some sightseeing. Despite having been in Paris for some days, Victoria, it seemed, had seen very little of the city.

"We lost them," the Wong's Paris organisation reported to Hector Xu. "They must have known they were being watched. We picked them up at their hotel , that was easy enough; then they started dodging in and out of the underground shopping areas around the Les Halles; that made things more difficult. And they kept mixing with the black people around there. We lost them."

Mark had been confident that they had arrived at the Louvre undetected. But he was not so confident that they had got away equally undetected.

"We're virtually in the Place de la Concorde, let's head for the Arc de Triomphe," he suggested.

They set off to walk across the square and then on up towards the famous monument. Despite the harshness of the weather, there were plenty of people about, so it was some time before Mark detected any signs of their being followed.

'Looks like company,' he thought as he became aware of a group of three well-muffled individuals who were walking in parallel with them. 'Reckon they were there when we left the Louvre, ... certainly when we were at the end of the Rue Rivoli.'

As he watched, they were apparently scurrying around the edge of the square in order to keep up with them as they wandered across the middle.

He alerted Victoria.

"Group of three to the right," he said.

She quickly saw them.

"Let's head for the left-hand side of the road," Victoria suggested.

That made the trio's efforts to stay abreast of them much more difficult and forced them to expose themselves by having to run.

As they left the Place and crossed onto the wide gravel verge that ran alongside the street at the other side, two of the three appeared in front of them. The need to thread their way through the mass of traffic had slowed Mark and Victoria down and given their pursuers time to catch up with them and then to overtake them.

"They're not going to let us pass," muttered Victoria, making space between herself and Mark, ready for any action.

"Oh, no you don't!"

Victoria was holding her shoulder bag tightly, forcing it down and making it difficult to pull off. Suddenly she felt a thump in the small of her back and the pressure eased. The strap had been cut by a powerful slash of a sharp knife.

"Mark!" she yelled in warning.

She swung around, still holding the soft leather body of the bag. She sharply tugged the cut strap from her attacker's grasp.

She was confronted by a person of her own height who was so well wrapped up that she had no idea whether it was a man or a woman. It was the third of the three people who had been following them.

Victoria saw the knife, but she didn't wait for it to be employed. She adjusted her balance and aimed a rapid kick at the wrist behind the knife with her left foot. The weapon skied on contact and struck one of the other attackers behind Victoria. Disarmed, her assailant hesitated and then came at her in a rush. Using the same kick that she had so successfully taught to Janine, her opponent crumpled. Ignoring any sporting rules, Victoria then aimed a follow-up kick at the jaw. The figure collapsed and rolled over, revealing that it was, in fact, a Chinese woman of about thirty. Behind her, Mark was dealing with the rest of the group. With his attention distracted, he hadn't seen the ruthlessly efficient way in which she had dealt with her opponent.

With one of his attackers effectively out of the battle with the knife impaled in his leg, Mark had an easy enough time with the other. In any event, the arrival of two gendarmes, who had seen the whole incident from the other side of the street, cut short any serious action.

"You OK?"

Victoria nodded. Whether or not Mark was she didn't concern herself with.

Victoria's padded coat had an unlooked-for slit in it and she would probably have a bruise in her back, but otherwise physically they were none the worse for their escapade. The gendarmes dealt with their assailants in a rather heavy-handed manner, apparently recognising them as part of one of the many gangs who dogged well-dressed tourists like Mark and made themselves a nuisance to Parisians alike. Only the woman was Chinese. She sat in a daze on the ground until she was roughly hauled into a police van.

"So it wasn't the Wongs after all."

* * *

219

By the time they had returned to the hotel, Victoria was in mild shock and Mark comforted her much as he would have done Janine. She recovered quickly enough, but the comforting still ended up as it would have done with Janine. This time it was a softer and far less driven Victoria. But for Mark the sex was, nonetheless, still mechanical.

'I'm not sure the trip was the success she seems to reckon it was,' Mark thought as the train carried them back to London. 'She pretty soon forgot about the set-to with the muggers. Janine would've been more agitated. It's not hard to see why she says she could never really like Victoria; cold-hearted bitch.'

It was a small paragraph on the inside page of one of the lesser French dailies that convinced him that the trip definitely had not been worthwhile.

"A middle-aged Chinese man, an employee of L'heure du soleil travel agents, was attacked and robbed in an alleyway close to his place of work. He died from his injuries on the way to hospital."

Hector Xu didn't think that the trip had been a success either. His minions had failed to keep Mark and Victoria under constant surveillance in Paris. Pearl's invasion of Mark's computers had been a short-lived achievement, and the Wongs consequently didn't know that Mark and Victoria had both identified their control centre for the arms shipments and had received confirmation of the timing of the next movement. And the death of their key operative in Paris had set back the management of the further shipments until Xu could get a reliable replacement in post.

* * *

"Victoria, wow!"

Janine had come to meet Mark at St. Pancras and had

embraced her friend with all the signs of real delight at seeing her. But her enthusiasm was more the product of conscience than of any genuine pleasure.

Sensing that Mark was vulnerable to any sexual advances that Victoria might make, she knew her friend was every bit as full-blooded as she herself was , she had encouraged Daniel Onifade to the extent of being invited back to his hotel room. It was a sign of defiance that she couldn't readily explain to herself. Just as Mark had at first been turned off by Victoria's mechanical approach to sex, so had she been discouraged by Onifade's rather crude, even brutal, approach. Unlike Mark, she hadn't as yet had a second bite at the cherry, but her conscience had at least given her enough trouble to induce her to come and meet Mark, and be particularly attentive.

Concerned to shield Janine from his own exploits, Mark failed to notice his partner's unusually hyperactive interest in his well-being and her rather wary behaviour towards his companion. Victoria, who seemed to have no qualms at all about climbing into bed with her friend's partner, was all sweetness and light and greeted Janine like a long-lost friend.

* * *

"Worthwhile trip?" asked Janine as they set off in a taxi, leaving Victoria to her own devices.

"Not especially."

Mark handed her the envelope that the now-dead Chinese man had given to Victoria. Janine studied the contents and looked satisfied. The data that they had obtained was invaluable for their activities, but he couldn't help feeling that the price for it had been much too high.

Alone in the taxi, they each sensed a reticence on the other's part; each also supposed the reason to be their infidelities.

'I shouldn't have given in to Victoria,' he told himself yet again. 'I know how Janine reacts under stress; I could have avoided the whole situation.'

A thousand times' telling unfortunately couldn't undo what had been done.

And Janine told herself just as many times that she could have avoided the situation where she had had to literally jump out of a man's bed. They were both contrite and both determined to make it up to the other. Their stories untold to each other, they both suspected what had happened and, consumed by guilt, the night's lovemaking was one of the most intense since the early days of their relationship.

THIRTY-TWO

Lehia Said was not consumed by guilt, she was consumed by lust. But unlike her encounter with Mark, she now had a certainty of satisfying it. She was meeting an incoming flight at Heathrow. The two former members of 'New Truth' who emerged into Lehia's waiting arms were companions of her bed as well as of her terrorist campaigns.

"Let's get back to the hotel," said Lehia, her excitement rising already.

Next morning Janine was exhausted and happy; Lehia was just exhausted.

* * *

Along the street, eating in the seclusion of his own hotel suite, Alhaji Mahomet Sullag was not pleased. The arms shipment had been intercepted, but not by his emissaries. The success of the Nigerian Security Service did not make him a happy man.

The woman dressed in the flowing full-length black robes of the strict Moslems shown discreetly into his drawing room precisely at ten o'clock was a picture of decorum. The material of her headdress was pulled tightly around her face. All that was visible were her penetrating pale blue eyes. As she raised her head after making a deep obeisance, those eyes surprised even Sullag. This was the first time that he had encountered this woman directly and he was having more than a little trouble hiding his distaste.

"Your Excellency," she muttered.

"So what happened? It was not you who stopped the arms!"

The voice was harsh and demanding, the English perfect.

The contrast between Lehia, in her all-enveloping black, and the northern Nigerian patrician, in his all-enveloping white, could hardly have been starker. Normally he would not have addressed a woman so directly, but in this case, despite his distaste, the woman was the only person he could address. Lehia was irritated but not intimidated by the man who sat in front of her.

"The British police interfered," she said.

"The British police, working with our security service, interfered," he replied coldly. "Our excellent security service has recruited the assistance of a British firm of security consultants. They did so without authority, I'm told; but the Home Affairs Minister has not objected."

The Nigerian Home Affairs Minister was another northerner but, unlike Sullag, was not a closet Fundamentalist. He was their fiercest opponent. The mixture of sarcasm and cold anger still didn't daunt Lehia. Sullag to her was an anachronism, something from a past that she had spent much of her life trying to destroy. But she and her group had to live.

"It's not easy to work in this country; the British police are very alert."

"The British police are overstretched and under strength, their morale is poor," remarked Sullag.

Lehia didn't say anything. What was the point? The man opposite her was knowledgeable and she had no answers. But despite what he said, the British police had been very effective.

"'New Truth' was recruited to undertake certain tasks," Sullag continued. "They were not recruited to carry on a private feud with members of the Wong family. From now on, you will concentrate on preventing arms from getting to our southern friends and you will eliminate certain people who we will specify when they visit London, and that is all that you will do."

"Very well," Lehia said.

She not pleased to be rebuked in this way. But at least he wasn't telling her how to do her job.

Sullag had moved on, unconcerned by whatever reaction she might have had to what he had said.

"From time to time you will come into contact with the Nigerian Security Service and their new British allies. From now on you will not make general war on them. They should be resisted where necessary; they should not be attacked."

The fact that he had ordered the earlier death of Silvanus Akinbode was completely forgotten.

The Nigerian disdainfully tossed a photograph onto the table in front of him. Lehia moved forward to retrieve it. Her attention was immediately engaged. A cold anger welled up inside her.

"Shortley!" she breathed.

This man had taken advantage of her when her lust was getting the better of her. As the Alhaji produced two more photographs, Lehia vowed vengeance on Mark once again.

"...they are also officials of the Security Service, but their loyalties are to the south. More important, they are working with the Wong organisation; they, however, may be eliminated if they come to Britain."

Lehia had no doubt that she would recognise Messrs Falinde and Oje if she came across them, but her focus was on Mark Shortley.

But the interview was over. The Sullag had other meetings

to attend to, and the presence of a hired killer, and a woman at that, was offensive to him.

* * *

At the time that the interview was taking place, a much more amiable conversation was going on.

"Mark, Fid Okeke. I gather the visit to Paris was successful. The French are being very supportive according to Victoria."

"Hardly surprising, they don't want the Fundamentalists back in their backyard."

"Who does?!"

Mark reported his plans for dealing with the next arms shipment and shared the information he'd obtained from Professor Jordane.

"Sullag is being isolated. A caucus of Federal Ministers and a 'Club' of influential civil servants have come together, committed to the long-term future of the country. The Young Turks of the north aren't buying Fundamentalism, they think they can work with the southern states, so long as they aren't threatened by them."

"Not quite as I heard from Chief Adeko."

The background that Fid Okeke was describing was new to Mark. Janine's researches had highlighted the burgeoning middle class in Nigeria, particularly the sons and daughters of the old-fashioned Big Men, who were no longer in sympathy with this older generation. Educated abroad, this education had backfired amongst this rising generation, the children of the age of the Internet, mobile 'phones, etc. With more in common with their banking and management peers in Europe and America than with their parents, they were steadily forcing a slow but irreversible change in the culture of the country. That the public servants, or at least some of them, and some of the politicians were embracing the same cultural change was encouraging to

Mark. His largely unspoken concern about what he was doing was that it might somehow cement the system in the past. Fid Okeke gave him hope that it might not.

"Stop the arms, Mark. Fundamentalism can be beaten, but there's only a future if north and south can live together."

"That's what you're paying me for."

THIRTY-THREE

"Victoria's coming here?"

"Yes," said Mark. "The next arms shipment's due at the weekend, remember. We need to plan how we're going to deal with it."

It was two weeks now since Mark's trip to Paris, but in her usual straightforward way Janine hadn't let her suspicions fester for that long. She had put the question bluntly to him on the Saturday after his return whilst they were dawdling over their coffee after breakfast.

'It's obvious what this is about,' he had thought. 'The signals are clear enough. No lovemaking and she's wearing a tee-shirt.'

It was all that she was wearing, but it was a definite hands-off message.

'Wonder if there's any significance in the two women fighters on the tee-shirt?'

"Well, did you?" she had eventually demanded.

"Yes, I slept with Victoria."

There was no challenge or innuendo in Janine's question, nor defensiveness in Mark's answer.

"She's not in your league in bed."

"Neither's Daniel Onifade in yours," said Janine.

Her grin had appeared and her eyes were twinkling, but it was a more restrained sort of response from the one that she usually had for Mark.

"Actually, we had two goes at it…"

Janine had been surprised that Victoria was so mechanical and unemotional; she had credited her with more fire.

"Perhaps she keeps it for this partner of hers," she said.

'At least he didn't get anything out of it,' she told herself.

It made her feel better about her equally unsuccessful exploit.

"You mean you actually leapt out of the poor guy's bed?"

Mark had surprised himself, and Janine, by being rather amused by what had happened. Previously he had been more resentful of her dalliance with Onifade, now his own transgressions seemed somehow diminished by it.

After the exchange of confidences, the conversation stalled, and Janine finally wandered off into the bedroom. Keen to brief himself fully before Victoria arrived, Mark had planned a trip to the Kent coast to reconnoitre the ferry terminal and the access to the Wong's depot at Ashford. But when he followed her to the bedroom, he found Janine waiting for him and charged up to the full! Their departure was delayed. But the trip to the Kent countryside proved to be equally rewarding.

When Victoria eventually arrived, Mark had briefed Janine on his plans; she even added some suggestions of her own.

'I have to be a bit circumspect here,' Mark told himself, 'since I've got to spend so much time in Victoria's company. I'm not sure Janine's as detached about all of this as she makes out!'

Nor was she, but whether Victoria sensed any of the subtle changes of attitude towards her was debatable. One thing that Mark and Janine were agreed on was that Victoria was not a sensitive person.

* * *

"Nice place!" Victoria said as she was shown into Mark's office. "And you live upstairs!"

"Hello, Victoria."

Warned when she had arrived, Janine joined them in the office.

"Hi!"

To Victoria's surprise it was Mark who got the coffee.

"I gather you've spoken to Mr Okeke," Victoria said.

She'd had a long conversation with her superior, who had told her as much of Mark's proposals as he thought she should know. This didn't turn out to be very much. Victoria sensed that she was not being told everything but doubted whether she could wheedle out any further information from Janine, let alone Mark.

"Mr Okeke has talked to the Head of Security and the Minister for Home Affairs. He's going to talk to other members of the 'Club'."

Victoria assumed that they knew who the members of the 'Club' were. Nonetheless, Mark's puzzled looked forced Victoria to explain. As he was expecting, her slant on the 'Club' was rather different from Fid Okeke's and infinitely more sceptical. Mark's plans depended on support from within Nigeria and he needed to be sure that it would be forthcoming. His confidence in Mr Okeke was not matched by a similar feeling for Victoria. As she watched, Janine sensed Mark's shifting opinion of her friend.

"It seems there's been leakage of information to the Fundamentalists. Orders have apparently gone out to destroy the weapons in transit. And 'New Truth' has reinforced itself in Britain."

"What about Sullag?" asked Mark.

"We can't confirm he's a secret Fundamentalist. But non-northerners are never really likely to know where the real sympathies of people like him lie."

Fid Okeke had talked to Victoria about the information

from Professor Jordane, but knowing that she was an admirer of the Alhaji, he had tended to discount what she had told him in response. He had already privately shared his own views with Mark.

"So," said Mark, "the picture's as confused as ever. At least we know we're definitely up against our friend Lehia now."

"That'll be fun," said Janine.

"Surely will," agreed Mark.

The animosity that Lehia Said was expected to display towards Mark, once she had realised who he was, was a complication that they could have done without. With both the Wongs and the Fundamentalists in action, Mark expected a very challenging few days. That Lehia Said had definite views on the best way to handle the problems of the arms shipment was unknown to him.

"I've recruited the necessary help from my army friends," Mark said when his turn for reporting came. "Not so easy. Fortunately it seems my credit's still good. There's a party of twelve SAS types standing by. I know the lieutenant; she's good –tough and resourceful."

"Do they know there might be opposition?" asked Victoria.

"Not yet, we'll brief them this afternoon. I've arranged to meet them at the zoo park."

Mark had suggested that they gather at a celebrated private zoo just outside Canterbury because it was open all year round and not likely to be too busy at the time of year. The chances of their being observed there by anybody from the opposition were not high.

Victoria accepted the plan without comment, zoo parks not being a part of her normal life. Janine, whose interest in the wildlife of her home continent was minimal, secretly gave thanks that she was to spend her afternoon in the warmth of the office, notwithstanding her reluctance to see Mark and Victoria together again.

"The arms shipment has left Russia," she said when the other two had finished their briefings. "It's another two-truck convoy travelling via Poland."

"Is that good?" asked Victoria, whose knowledge of European geography was fairly limited.

"Yes," said Janine. "Poland's a member of the European Federation. It means that we were able to arrange for the vehicle movements to be recorded along the way. They should be well across Germany by now. And the Wongs have learnt a thing or two from the last run. The timetable is incredible tight – no stopovers, no opportunities for the trucks to stand around."

"Anything else?" asked Mark.

"Each truck is carrying a relief driver, according to Russian Customs, but the journey times and records continue to show the statutory routine stops."

"What does that mean?" asked Victoria.

Her knowledge of European bureaucracy was no better than her geography.

"It means that the relief drivers aren't doing any driving," said Janine.

"Guards?" suggested Mark.

"I would reckon."

Janine gave them the expected journey times and the most likely TransChannel ferries that the trucks would be loaded on to.

"The payload of one is much higher than the other. The manifest says it's small parts and fastenings; I'd say it's ammunition, more like."

"Do the Fundamentalists have access to this sort of information?" asked Victoria.

Janine shook her head. She was very dubious about the involvement of the Fundamentalists but didn't discount them. Lehia Said definitely had a high reputation for resourcefulness, but her computer skills and those of her newly arrived colleagues were unknown. For Mark, it was one more factor to be taken into account.

* * *

"Remember I'm out to dinner tonight," said Janine as the two headed off to meet up with the soldiers.

Mark grunted. She'd mentioned that she had a date but not with whom. She'd only agreed to dine with Daniel Onifade because she felt that she had treated him badly. She wasn't actually looking forward to the meal. True to her conversation with Mark, she had no interest in the man any more; his sexual demands on her had sickened her. But when she caught herself wondering whether Mark would now have dinner with Victoria, she knew that detachment had yet to be achieved.

* * *

The trip to the zoo park was uneventful. Victoria asked questions about the places that they passed through or, more often than not, that they had by-passed. Mark took a less direct route to Canterbury than he might normally have done, continuing on the M20 for longer in order to give Victoria some sense of the area surrounding Ashford, before eventually heading for the zoo.

"Looks like the SAS party have all arrived," Mark said.

The soldiers had taken full advantage of the spider's web of lanes and byroads that surrounded Canterbury and which stretched out as far as Ashford. Following a pattern laid out by the lieutenant, they had between them settled on a comprehensive series of routes that would take them to the Wong depot with as little risk of detection as possible.

"This is Victoria Akinbode... Lieutenant... Smith."

Mark made the introductions. They were not introduced to the rest of the party. The lieutenant was the only other woman.

"Some of the guys were involved with the previous shipment, and we've done the odd job together before," Mark continued by way of explanation for the lack of names.

The party gathered around a group of adjacent tables in the almost-deserted cafeteria. Mark quietly organised the briefing's walkabouts.

"OK, we'll split up. The surveillance group goes with Victoria, the depot party with me. We'll meet at the gorilla enclosure in an hour."

Victoria led the way from the restaurant with her group. As she passed, Mark noticed somewhat irrelevantly that the slit in her padded coat had not been repaired.

"Right, Lieutenant, let's go and admire a few tigers and allocate a few duties."

Mark led the second party off.

"When's the action?" asked the lieutenant as soon as they were out of earshot.

"Friday. We don't have much time. Things are heating up pretty quickly. The trucks are already on the way; they'll be in France around nine o'clock this evening."

As the party of five soldiers ambled along beside Mark, he gave them the information that they needed to carry out their part in the planned action.

"The employees at the depot are innocent parties. So are the truck drivers. None of them will have a clue what's going on. If we need them out the way, no violence, OK. There's a guard on each truck; they can be treated as potentially hostile. Members of the Wong organisation are definitely hostile, but we don't want to arouse any suspicions. OK?"

The soldiers asked various questions of clarification.

"The bad news," said Mark, "is... we're not the only ones who don't want these arms to get to Nigeria. A bunch belonging to the old Middle Eastern terror group 'New Truth' will be trying to stop them as well. They must not be allowed to interfere! And the subplot, we suspect, is ; they'll be trying to kill me."

The soldiers' interest in the job perked up at this revelation.

"There's not a lot to go on. Apart from their leader, one Lehia Said, we've no idea who any of the others are. All we know is the group has recently been reinforced."

At the appointed time, the two parties arrived at the gorilla enclosure. Ironically, Victoria, the eastern part of whose country was once a gorilla habitat, was the only one of them who had never seen such animals before. She looked at the huge beasts in a mixture of wonder and horror. The lieutenant, forestalling any ribald or racist comments, asked her troops if they had any questions. There were none.

"Right," said Mark, "we know what we have to do. We'll disperse and get ourselves ready for action. Hopefully things'll be peaceful, but there are no guarantees."

Looking at them, Victoria thought the last thing that the soldiers wanted was a peaceful time.

"Might be worthwhile checking out the route from the ferry terminal to the depot, you'll have the full picture then," said Mark as they returned to their car.

"Sure, OK."

Victoria accepted the suggestion. This was a different Mark from her previous experience, clear-eyed, confident, and enthusiastic. With action pending, even she had noticed that he had come alive. But this wasn't the only reason why he was being so zealous. Deep-seated in his brain he hadn't forgiven himself for his transgressions with Victoria. In consequence, the poor girl was overwhelmed by the minutiae of the job; but Mark felt better.

* * *

Unfortunately his determination to include Victoria in

everything led to consequences that he hadn't foreseen. They were observed as they headed away from the TransChannel Terminal by one the Wong organisation's operatives. Or at least Victoria was observed by the young Chinese man. Of Mark he knew nothing until he telephoned Pearl.

"You're sure it's the Akinbode woman?" Pearl demanded.

"I've seen the photographs. It's her; the one in the long dress at the Reception. It's not the one who beat up old Chang's thugs at Armards."

'I was there,' young Marcus Ho said to himself. 'I'm sure.'

After watching her in action, Janine had almost replaced Pearl in the lad's affections as the perfect fighting female. Brought up on an unrestricted diet of computer games and late-night satellite television, minimally-clad heroines beating the living daylights out of large and ugly men was the stuff of his dreams. Pearl and now Janine brought that to reality for him; Victoria didn't, and he knew the difference!

"Describe the man," demanded Pearl.

Marcus Ho did his best from the vantage point that he had. He was travelling at speed behind Mark, and although he had a far more powerful car, he was anxious not to be detected. A Chinese youth driving a BMW sports coupé and driving behind him, however, was hardly likely to escape Mark's notice.

"OK, could be Shortley. Follow them, tell me where they go."

"Will do."

Ho settled to his task with some pleasure. But the feeling didn't last.

"Shit, he's trying to lose me!"

"Looks like we got a Chinese tail," Mark said to Victoria as he slowly accelerated along the M20 towards Maidstone.

"Soon fix you, my lad," he muttered, setting about losing the trailing BMW with much the same relish as Marcus Ho showed in following him. "I reckon I know a thing or two about

Maidstone you won't… wasn't stationed at the RE barracks for nothing."

Mark was well aware that to the unfamiliar, the complex of one-way streets that comprised the centre of the town could be very confusing. And once he got there, he knew exactly how to exploit the confusion.

"Hang on, Victoria!"

Mark pulled off the Motorway at the last minute.

Picking up Mark's late decision late in his turn, the young driver of the BMW almost lost control of his vehicle as he braked and slewed the car onto the hard shoulder and then onto the slip road.

"Jesus, Mark!" Victoria gasped at the suddenness of Mark's manoeuvre.

He accelerated along the country lanes, working his way through the villages of Bearsted and then Penenden Heath. Then, turning sharply back towards the town centre, he headed for the most complicated area of Maidstone. As he twisted his way through the side roads and around the back of the prison, Mark checked behind him.

"Still with us, but at least we're separated now."

Praying for a green light, he cut back past the old County Council offices. Trapped by a red light, Marcus Ho didn't see where Mark went. Employing his superior knowledge, Mark was through and onto the huge central roundabout and back on himself before there was any sign of the BMW.

"That's him," exclaimed Victoria as Mark headed back towards Chatham and the M20 junction as young Ho dithered about which lane to be in at the roundabout.

"Wonderful what a little local knowledge can do for you," Mark remarked coolly.

They were soon back on the London-bound Motorway.

* * *

"You lost them; how the hell could you lose them?!"

Tolerance of incompetence, and patience, were not Pearl Wong's strong points.

"Hector, Marcus Ho just spotted Victoria Akinbode and Mark Shortley on the road from the TransChannel Terminal to the Ashford depot. I guess we have to assume they know something."

Pearl had called her counsellor in as soon as Ho had rung off.

"Our friend in Special Branch tells me that the 'New Truth' group has been reinforced from the Lebanon. Lehia Said was also seen heading out of London on the M20; quite a busy road!"

Hector Xu was pleased to see that Pearl's reaction was suitably muted.

'She's learning,' he thought.

"And we're sure it was Victoria Akinbode and Mark Shortley?" asked Xu.

"Young Ho's convinced about Victoria," said Pearl. "Said it definitely wasn't Shortley's girlfriend. He didn't get much of a look at Shortley himself, but from the decisive way he sorted Ho out, if it wasn't Shortley, it was someone just as good as him."

"That young man would certainly know the difference between the Akinbode woman and somebody as exotic as Janine Effiong," Xu remarked dryly.

"Oh, I'm sure he would," said Pearl with a grin.

She knew something of Ho's admiration of ferocious females.

"We should get a warning out for extra vigilance; the next forty-eight hours or so are going to be very demanding!"

Xu agreed with her.

THIRTY-FOUR

"Mark!"

Mark was heading for a small restaurant in Bayswater. They had turned into Lancaster Gate and he was looking for somewhere to park. Victoria's tone alerted him. Something had attracted her attention that was obviously of concern to her.

"What?"

He glanced across at her as he responded. By chance highlighted outside a convenience store, he saw the placards: 'Massacre of Nigerian Bus Passengers'.

Ignoring the angry honking of a taxi behind him, he pulled sharply into the kerb and rushed into the shop. Returning with two copies of the *London Evening Echo*, he handed one to Victoria and hurriedly started to scan the other. They didn't make very good reading.

* * *

"A bus travelling from Kaduna to Zaria in northern Nigeria was savagely attacked yesterday by a group of men armed with automatic weapons."

The *Echo's* front-page story repeated the Nigerian News Agency report.

"The vehicle was raked from front to rear with machine-gun fire and two grenades were thrown into the wreckage. Forty-seven people , men, women and children – were killed. There were five survivors, of whom only two were adults. All were seriously injured, with the exception of one of the adults whose wounds miraculously were only superficial. Eight of the dead passengers were foreigners, three Britons, a German and four people from Dahomey.

"The police have been able to build up a reliable picture of what had happened, largely because one of the survivors was a sergeant major in the Nigeria Army with service with UN Peacekeeping forces. Inured to scenes of horror and mutilation, he was able to give an accurate description of the essentials before the severity of his wounds overtook him. The second survivor was able to add very little to the details provided by the soldier."

"I'd been asleep when the attack started."

Fid Okeke gave his story to the police in the security of their barracks in Zaria.

"The atmosphere in the bus was stifling. I guess I'm too used to air-conditioning. Eventually I must have dozed off. I didn't want to have to talk to anyone; people up here are suspicious of southerners, so I sat next to this large lady who wouldn't have wanted to talk to me anyway."

The police were only too aware of the new restrictions being forced on northern women in some States.

What Okeke didn't make the police aware of was that he was in the north because one of the sons of the Emir of Zaria, whom he had known at University, had volunteered some information about Mahomet Sullag whilst on a short trip to Abuja. To hear more, he had invited Mr Okeke to visit Zaria.

"A trap?"

It was the obvious explanation to both Fid Okeke and the Head of the Security Service, to whom he thought it appropriate to report the contact.

"Most likely, but we have to take the risk. We don't have a lot of choice. Sullag's up to something. We must know where he fits into all of this."

So he had flown to Kaduna and taken the bus to Zaria. The bus trip had started out pretty much as Fid Okeke had expected. Used to either his own or a government car, he found the chaos and general frenetic clamour of the Kaduna Television Garage, the general Motor Park that serves Zaria, rather intimidating until he switched himself back into his boyhood mode and allowed himself to be carried along by the seemingly incomprehensible processes of getting the bus he needed. He had decided to use this Motor Park, which wasn't the biggest in Kaduna, rather than the others and to avoid the direct minibuses to Zaria in order to avoid having to have too much conversation with the local people. His accent would instantly give him away.

By just listening Okeke was able to locate the required bus, it was large, already overfull and ready to leave as he boarded. He was carried forward in the crush induced by the efforts of the driver to pack yet more people into the body of the vehicle. Failing to be intimidated by the vast lady seemingly monopolising one of the rows of seats in the middle of the bus, he scrambled over her and forced himself into the crack of the seat that she wasn't occupying. At no time did he have to stand around waiting in the Motor Park or ask anybody for directions. Yet his every move Pwas being watched by a small team of Fundamentalist foot soldiers.

Urgent mobile phone conversations were had between a scruffy pale-skinned man who had been taking considerable interest in the silent Fid Okeke, and a group of people on the Kaduna/Zaria road followed the clanking, smoke-billowing departure of the bus. Dispositions were rapidly made and an ambush set up.

"It was a trap. Somebody knew I was on the bus and it was attacked," Fid Okeke continued to the Zaria police superintendent. "I'm on the Fundamentalists' hit list."

He didn't make any effort to explain why.

At the unintended expense of her own life, the large lady provided Okeke with protection by absorbing both the bullets of the attackers and the force of the explosion. Her body, hideously mutilated by the terrorists' actions, slumped on top of him and hid him from view.

"The sergeant major found me as he tried to check the ghastly remains in the bus. I was almost unconscious; the poor woman's dead weight was steadily crushing the life out of me. Once I was free, I called for help on my mobile phone."

The police doctor had treated his wounds, bullet gouges in his left arm and lower back, deep but not life-threatening.

"I finished the checking; the sergeant major was totally exhausted, still bleeding heavily and close to collapse. There were only five of us alive. Without medical supplies, there wasn't much I could do. The three children were traumatised and couldn't respond to me. I got what I could of the story from the soldier.

"According to him, the bus had been stopped by a truck parked across the road. Four men appeared and opened fire without warning. The attackers all wore army fatigues. Their faces were covered, but he was convinced only one of them was an African."

With some omissions, the sergeant major's report formed the basis for the subsequent news stories and the report that Fid Okeke made to Mr Aminu, the Minister for Home Affairs, when he returned to Abuja. His escape was greeted with consternation by his opponents, but attacking such buses was a part of the Fundamentalists' terror plans, so they didn't see the incident as a failure. With his functions in life well understood by the Fundamentalists, Mr Okeke knew that further attempts on his life were to be expected.

* * *

The newspaper story that Mark and Victoria were reading of course made no mention of Fid Okeke's involvement in the incident. His more detailed description of what had happened was communicated to both Victoria and Mark later.

"It's beginning again," muttered Victoria. "Just like Iraq, Afghanistan, Egypt. Attacks on buses, women and children, tourists… Boko Haram!"

Another thing not reported in the media, along with the sergeant major's identity, was that eight of the bus passengers were Nigerian special forces troops on a covert exercise. At least two of these soldiers had returned fire before they died. There was evidence at the scene that their fire had had some effect. Although their main target had escaped, the Fundamentalists had reaped an unlooked for, and, for them, an unknown bonus in the deaths of these hardened and experienced soldiers.

"We've been expecting something like this," Victoria remarked.

Mark had moved the car to a more sensible parking place and they were walking slowly back towards the restaurant. It was well after eight o'clock, the appointed time, but their table was still available.

'It'll be all over the media for a while,' Mark thought as they had been walking. 'Janine's monitoring service will have picked it up.'

The news agencies had had reports of a series of such outrages over many months, particularly during Ramadan, a period favoured by all Islamic terrorists, and Janine had been keeping a file on them.

'I guess the extent of the death toll and the heroics of the sergeant major will keep it newsworthy for a day or so.'

Responsibility for the attack was immediately claimed by Boko Haram. An al-Qaeda style video was posted on theIinternet. The graphic nature of the video caused widespread condemnation. The positions taken by the various northern Nigerian leaders were of considerable interest to Fid Okeke in Abuja.

"The Alhaji called it a most unfortunate incident."

It was the weakest comment by any Nigerian Government Minister. To Okeke, it was further proof of where Alhaji Sullag's loyalties lay.

"Not a very good start to the evening," Mark said.

Victoria was quiet for some time after she'd finished reading the reports of the massacre, although Mark sensed that she was thoughtful rather than distressed. He recalled Janine's suspicions of her want of finer feelings.

But, like Janine, it wasn't in Victoria's nature to be miserable, so in the end she became more talkative than she'd ever been before. Mark discovered some interesting things about her, as much by the way that she reacted, as by what she said.

"My father, like Janine's, was an army officer. One of the many who found themselves caught up in the hangover from the Biafran episode."

Victoria took it for granted that Mark was familiar with the past upheavals in Nigerian history, but she didn't pursue her personal story immediately.

"With our past," Victoria continued, "you can see why it's so remarkable that Adeko's built such a strong cross-tribal interest. And it's dangerous. It's always been the numerical strength of the north against the commercial strength of the south. Every time the south felt itself politically strong enough, there's been trouble. And with weapons... It's back to 1967, civil war..."

There was much more.

But Victoria made no mention of the emerging consensus amongst the enlightened public servants and politicians and the growing urban and outward-looking middle-class professionals. She made no mention of the BRICS group (Brazil, Russia, India, China, South Africa) now becoming BRINCS with Nigeria's burgeoning influence worldwide. And she seemed unaware that what she was saying was both anachronistic and out of touch with the younger generation and the ordinary people in general. Despite her involvement with the evolving situation, the new Nigeria seemed to have passed Victoria by in some way.

In his turn, Mark was surprised at Victoria's sudden surge of feeling.

'She knows her history, but this isn't what it's about. The threat is Fundamentalism destabilising the north. That's the issue, that's what will destroy Nigeria. Why's she so steamed up about this rather archaic view of the political scene?'

"So how'd you get into all this?"

Mark thought it better to change the subject; an excited Victoria was something that he felt he couldn't handle any more.

"My father was a visionary. He was an army surgeon, and a Christian who married a Moslem. My mother was from a good northern family. He believed in a Nigeria for all its peoples. After every swing of the pendulum from military rule back to civil, he thought at last it was happening."

Mark found himself surprised at the sadness in Victoria's tone.

"But when General Abacha seized power, it was a disappointment to many, and he committed suicide."

Mark was aware of something else now, a fervour, a hardness.

"I was devastated. I was only five, and the horror of my father's action stayed with me. At school, I was going to be a lawyer. But with the Obasanjo period, I guess my father's ghost reappeared, military or civilian rule, nothing changed. I felt I needed to do something more positive. So... I joined the security service."

"Hardly the place for an idealist?"

Mark sensed that Victoria wasn't quite telling him everything, but he wanted to keep the conversation going. This was the nearest he'd ever got to Victoria's true feelings; maybe her true political views would also surface.

"It's the only bit of government that's above tribal hatreds. The security service takes all tribes; on merit. It works to its own Nigerian vision; whoever's in power. Like all security services, it's a law unto itself!"

She seemed to have conveniently forgotten Messrs Falinde and Oje, and their attachment to the southern cause.

Mark laughed. "Never heard that from an insider before!"

"I started in anti-drugs," she volunteered, "dangerous and violent."

She didn't say very much, but from what she did say, Mark gathered that she had had to kill at least twice in the course of her duties.

'So matter of fact,' he thought to himself. 'Just like Janine, but there's an underlying callousness that's light years from Janine's approach to her fellow human beings.'

* * *

The meal was over and Victoria clearly wanted to leave. Mark's discomfort increased again, but he needn't have worried; Victoria wasn't interested in further sexual exploits.

THIRTY-FIVE

"Janine, what a surprise; what are you doing here?"

Victoria caught Mark's astonished expression as she had led the way into the Astoria-Regina Hotel where she was staying in more luxury, as Mark noted, than her security service status might have suggested. Janine was marching across the foyer, pulling on her long, blue coat. When he had fully focused on her, Mark was surprised to see that she was seriously agitated. It was something that he wasn't sure that he'd ever seen before.

"I was just leaving!" Janine said sharply, giving Mark a venomous look that surprised him even more than the signs of her agitation.

Victoria shrugged and headed for the bar. Her relationship with Janine was friendly but with no real depth of feeling. And it certainly didn't preclude a little rivalry for Mark's attentions. Mark himself, aggrieved by Janine's reaction to him, followed Victoria automatically, his concerns about her predatory intentions not entirely allayed by her targeting the bar rather than the lift to her bedroom. And underneath, his anxieties for Janine tried desperately to claim his attention.

"Excuse me!"

Much to Victoria's irritation, the barman ignored her until

Mark's arrival. The man seemed much more interested in a fracas that had apparently occurred only moments beforehand between two guests. As Victoria was obliged to hear it, it seemed that the couple had come into the bar very much against the man's wishes. He clearly wanted to take the woman to his room. She was having none of it. In the end, he appeared to have grabbed at her and she to have landed a punch on his chin that met with the clear approval of the barman, a serious fight fan.

"Would you like to serve the lady?" interrupted Mark.

Even more furious that Mark had intervened, Victoria had, however, heard sufficient to recognise that they had just parted from the woman in question. Janine's penchant for abbreviated skirts was well known to both of them and was a prominent feature of the barman's description.

* * *

The incident had been worthy of the man's description. Janine had decided to risk another dinner with Daniel Onifade, as she felt that her behaviour at their last outing had been a little unfair. Not that she had any intention of ending up in his bed again; she merely wanted to end their relationship on a friendly note.

'I guess he's going to misinterpret the gesture,' she said to herself, but confident that she could handle the situation, she made the contact.

The dinner was fine.

'Like the previous little contretemps had never happened,' Janine thought.

Even in the taxi back to the hotel, he kept his distance and she began to hope that the evening would go the way that she had wanted it to. In the bar, unfortunately, and after having resisted pressure to go straight upstairs, came disillusionment.

"That was a great evening, Janine; we're a natural couple."

'Like hell we are,' she thought.

"The other night… maybe I was too quick. I should've given you more time. You obviously come on more slowly than I do."

"No way, Daniel, no way. Being slapped about does not turn me on!"

Janine immediately saw where the conversation was going, and she wasn't going with it.

"I'll be more gentle then."

Mr Onifade was clearly a man of some arrogance and not much sensitivity.

'He's not hearing me! I'm out of here.'

If he'd been more wide awake, he would have noticed some very clear warning signs from his companion, the key one being that she had stood up and moved away from the barstool.

"Daniel, no! We've got absolutely nothing going for us. This evening is about goodbye. I'm not going anywhere near your bed. You'd better believe it."

It was this last statement that had been picked up by the barman's ever-curious ears.

"Janine…"

Onifade moved to put his left arm around her waist.

He had seen the punch coming too late; it was the next day before he could use his jaw with anything like its normal facility. By the time he had recovered his equilibrium, Janine was on the way out. And by the time Victoria and Mark had arrived, Mr Onifade had beaten a rather ignominious retreat.

* * *

"It sounds as if Janine had a bit of bother!" Victoria said.

She had eventually got served. Mark placed himself opposite her in the lounge area in much the same way as he liked to sit opposite Janine, but for totally different reasons.

Mark nodded miserably. They were both wondering about the overeager man. After what Janine had told him, Mark assumed that it was Daniel Onifade, which was why he was depressed. She had gone back to him. It didn't occur to him at the time that in Janine's eyes he'd 'gone back' to Victoria. Victoria's own thoughts didn't dwell on the man with the sore jaw for very long. Nor, for that matter, did they dwell on Janine either; her interest in Mark, however, was not rekindled.

"Great evening, Victoria!"

Neither thought it had been, but Mark had at least made his escape unscathed. Janine was not in bed when he got to the flat; she was up and waiting for him.

* * *

'Not surprised she should thump him,' Mark told himself during the short trip from the hotel to Herbert Street. 'What's this guy Onifade up to?'

In a thought process that Janine herself had gone through more than once since she had met Onifade; he was still niggled by whether the man's interest in his partner was more professional than recreational.

Victoria had none of the relationship problems of Mark and Janine. When she called her partner, he was in no mood for conversation, let alone anything else. Assuming from his slurred and mumbled responses to her that he was drunk, she didn't prolong the conversation. Amused, she slept alone.

Janine's expression when Mark arrived home suggested that he might be spending the night alone as well. It wouldn't have been the first time. They'd had their share of lover's tiffs and nights apart, but they were always resolved the next morning in a round of rumbustious lovemaking. Such spikes of anger and reunion seemed to arouse Janine more than normal.

She was rarely contrite if the initial cause of the rupture had been hers, but she was always honest in accepting the blame.

"I trust you had a good evening?"

The question from Janine was conversational but laced with sarcasm, and Mark knew from past experience that it was the way that the opening sparring went that would decide if he was to sleep on the couch or in his own double bed. His nod was intended to be neutral.

"Did you?"

She didn't answer at once. Mark attempted to concentrate on her body language; it wasn't easy. She'd thrown off her jacket and was clasping her hands behind her back as she moved backwards and forwards across the room. Her mobility, rather than her usual static composure, didn't encourage Mark.

"No, I didn't! It was a disaster."

The anger he had seen in her at the hotel returned. Mark suspected that she was angry with herself, but he saw her stiffen and prepare to do battle with him over whatever he said.

"You chose to meet the wretched man, what did you expect?"

"You chose to be with tha..." She was going to say, 'slut Victoria', but as the words formed they seemed too crude, so she didn't utter them.

"Victoria's business, you know that. We'd had a long day....."

"And a few drinks and quick bang in bed to relax are OK?"

"Janine, we..., no.... ,"

Mark wasn't sure what to deny first, but he didn't get the chance.

"God, Mark, you hopped into bed with her in Paris, and you said you wouldn't again.... ."

Mark's guilt for that incident was instantly reawakened.

"Damn it, Janine, you don't know I leapt into bed with her again. You know what we were doing today! She's paying us to do a job. Don't judge everybody by yourself. She isn't forever wanting sex!"

It was a cruel remark that Mark instantly regretted.

"I'm not forever wanting sex! And I don't drop my knickers just because we have a contract."

"But you drop 'em for any old stranger who chats you up! You haven't a clue who that Oni-whatever-his-name-is is. You'd look a right idiot if he was part of Adeko's mob, or one of the Wongs hangers-on, wouldn't you?"

Mark was getting angry too.

"Nothing happened with Daniel. I keep telling you! Sure, I dropped my knickers and I got into bed, but... I got out again. He's into all sorts of crazy kinky things."

"What! Then why the hell go back to him? He'd only think you'd be wanting it after all."

Janine's anger gave way to a look of sheepishness.

"I thought I could find out who he was," she said.

"And who is he then? I suppose he told you he was a spy for the Fundamentalists?"

Janine's anger was back.

"Of course he didn't, because he isn't. He's a businessman who can't keep it in his trousers for very long after he meets a woman he fancies. And he fancied me!"

If Mark had been thinking rationally, he would have picked up on the real reason behind Janine's exploits with Daniel Onifade. It was a piece of assertiveness made into a piece of defiance by his own challenging of her.

"And Victoria," she continued, carrying the fight back to him, "is a woman who can't keep her knickers up when she meets someone she fancies too. And she doesn't meet that many people to get the chance with! She's frustrated. She only sees her partner once in a blue moon and I'm not sure he's up to her appetite. She just grabs at every opportunity. And in Paris you walked right into it. How the hell could you... again. It's so obvious."

Janine paused before she went on. But Mark missed her following remark.

"You get enough from me, I'd have thought."

"I guess I felt sorry for her; she'd just half killed somebody," he said.

"For Christ's sake, she's a killer by trade. She's quick enough to tell you that. So she's stressed out and her boy-friend's never around when she needs it. You could've walked away,;- you didn't have to console her."

Janine wasn't going to be sympathetic to Victoria whatever Mark said. Her own life had been on the line because of her and it wasn't what she was paid for. That didn't entirely endear her to Victoria. And she'd had enough of self-justification.

"Hell-fire, Mark, if you want it, it's always here."

It was said in anger, but there was a softer feeling struggling to get through to him. Mark knew then that he wouldn't be sleeping on the couch! Janine clearly didn't want a breach over Victoria and he certainly didn't!

They didn't make it straight to bed. That wasn't their way. All that they had done was break the logjam. Sharing their bodies with each other was precious to them both, and they needed to feel right about it.

Janine's own valuation of Victoria was an important part of her healing, and her rising distaste for her supposed friend somehow helped her to diminish Mark's infraction in her mind. But she knew that Mark forgave more slowly and needed more time than she did. She could talk out a problem two or three times and then be happy to move on from it. Mark needed to brood, and it was important that he set off on his brooding in the right frame of mind. If he did, he soon rationalised away any hurt from Janine's actions and was as ready for the bouts of sexual activity as she was; if he didn't, it could take him days before he came round.

"Victoria really is only business," he said partly to himself.

Janine nodded, the final conversation, and then the acceptance had started.

"And Daniel Onifade really is nothing."

It was well after two o'clock before they crawled into bed, mentally as well as physically exhausted. The only anger left was for later when the strident chimes of Mark's alarm summoned them back to the real world.

But Janine wasn't the only young woman whose unrelenting activity was a cause for remark.

* * *

"Don't know where she gets the energy from," Hector Xu had bemoaned at an intimate gathering of Chinese business colleagues in London that lasted well into the small hours.

Pearl had always been hyperactive, but now that she was running the Wong empire, she seemed to have gone into overdrive. However, much that that pleased Hector Xu, it also exhausted him. He missed the rather more subdued pace of life under his old friend and companion Jason Wong.

Under Pearl, he had risen to new heights, both in the organisation and in her trust, largely because she was not yet ready to share her new-found power with other close members of the Wong clan.

'He's never judgemental,' she thought. 'He doesn't criticise me or tell me what to do like the other old fools, he just tells me what the options are as he sees them. But he's a terrible slow-brain. I guess it worries him that I always want the answer yesterday, without due time and process!'

At least Hector Xu would have been pleased that Pearl understood her own weaknesses.

"She's not a proper young woman," remarked one of his dining companions.

Like Xu himself and most of the others present, the speaker was elderly and belonged to a rather different world from the one that Pearl inhabited. For them, women stayed in the background and certainly didn't head up large business corporations. Hector Xu said nothing; to disagree would take the conversation away from the areas that he wanted to go to.

"Needs a husband," said a nonagenarian and the head of a business organisation almost as extensive as that of the Wongs.

'We've put several "suitable" young men in front of her over the years,' thought Xu. 'Wouldn't have any of them; frightened them off, more like. She's one powerful young lady.'

He was aware that one of Pearl's favourite tricks was to encourage her suitors to come to one of her workouts. After that, they tended to creep away, feeling rather like the male spider destined to be his mate's next meal after copulation.

But Pearl and her marital prospects was not the prime reason for the gathering.

"What about the Fundamentalists and the Nigerians then?" said Hector Xu as they sipped their tea and smoked.

The close-knit Chinese community often acted as an intelligence clearing house, and Xu had called for information some days earlier. It was mutual thing that served them all very well.

"'New Truth' have reinforced their group in Britain."

Peng Xiang was the ninety-five-year-old who was so keen to marry Pearl off.

"They did some odd jobs for us recently. Interesting what they're into!"

Religious purity for the terrorists had long since given way to a more practical approach to the employment of their dubious skills.

"The leader, Lehia Said, is not trusted by other groups. She's too independent. And she's a woman," Peng Xiang continued.

It was clear that the old man shared the prejudices of the more chauvinistic terrorists. However, it was more Lehia's pragmatic approach to her activities rather than the rigidities of the older terrorists' approach that made them wary. Lehia herself would have said it was a generational thing.

"You shouldn't have much trouble with the 'New Truth' lot. They're hired killers. That's what they do best. Protect the key people from them; that's all you need to do."

The speaker was the youngest man present and Peng Xiang's chief of staff.

Hector Xu was satisfied; he'd come to the same conclusion, but his real interest was with the southern Nigerians; his original question had been just to get the conversation going.

'This lot will understand the complexity of Nigerian politics; their own interrelations are probably more tortuous!'

"Chief Adeko's capable of bankrolling a whole army," Peng Xiang's man said, "and he's got some limited support in some sections of the military and among some civil servants. But it's not very extensive, nor does it include the young echelons, apparently. Nor has he widespread support among the general population, as far as we can tell. The age-old tribal animosities are still felt by the ordinary folk and what's the southern consortium to them, the Big Men, the old-time money-grubbers – why should they support them? In the more cosmopolitan and sophisticated cities like Port Harcourt, Ibadan, the consortium has barely taken root at all. And perhaps more worryingly for Adeko, the Nigerian Government, and especially the real decision-makers of the civil service, have got their act together and are no longer just interested in the loot. The southerners will find it very hard to exploit any instability in the north."

There was more opinion and background from others of those present. At no time did anyone seek to enquire why Xu wanted the intelligence.

"Our information," said Xu himself, "is that the Fundamentalists are increasingly meeting with indifference among the northern Nigerians, if not active resistance. That's why they're escalating the violence. Attacks on buses and non-Moslem targets are likely to increase."

There was more tea- drinking and smoking.

"This Mark Shortley," said old Peng Xiang, eventually reverting to a previous conversation amongst the group. "He's good."

"Something of a favourite... for a European!" his minion added with a grin. "We used him to sort out who was siphoning funds from one of our companies."

It was a throwaway remark rather than a major point of discussion, but the comment didn't send Hector Xu off to his disturbed night's rest with any feeling of comfort.

And as he slept fitfully, the arms shipment was heading inexorably for Calais. He had made his plans, and he supposed that Mark and the Nigerians had too. But in his heart, he seriously wished that the Wong organisation wasn't supplying the weapons at all; the risk was too great.

THIRTY-SIX

Both Mark and Fid Okeke knew that the complexities of Nigerian politics and the historic baggage that always accompanied any discussions of them inevitably led to a frustrated disengagement in all but the most committed insiders. And since the impending arms shipment to the UK resulted from the convoluted interactions between both the political and religious aspirations of the various traditionalist parties in Nigeria, that it was happening at all signified that the new younger, worldly-wise and technology-connected generation had still not yet got its message across internally. For Mark and Fid Okeke, the arms shipments were the catalyst for the activities necessary to defeat the various reactionary forces seeking to destabilise the country and thereby provide the opportunity for the Young Turks to make Nigeria a truly twenty-first century state.

For Mark in Europe, it allowed a simplification of the objectives for the law enforcement agencies involved and a focus on a clear-cut set of actions. Arms smuggling was illegal and had to be suppressed, and for the UK police and security services, it didn't really matter on whose behalf the smuggling was taking place.

For Fid Okeke in Nigeria, where arms smuggling was

equally illegal, it allowed a focus on the loyalties of the leading politicians. No politician was going to publicly support the supply of arms to ferment unrest. The security services were, nonetheless, on high alert to detect the private positioning of people like Chief Adeko, who was hardly shy about his views, and, more particularly, the more cerebral leaders like the Alhaji Sullag, whose ambivalence Okeke hoped to challenge.

The southern business consortium, hoping to gain an edge from the supply of the weapons, and the Moslem Fundamentalists, hoping to frustrate the supply and profit from it, were both aware that the next action would unfold in the UK. But the situation there was much more complex. With the Nigerian Security Services via Victoria Akinbode and Messrs Falinde and Oje playing a both public and private game, the Wongs only seeking profit, and Lehia Said and the leftover Middle East terror group playing an open game to halt the arms and a closed game of revenge, Mark and the forces of law and order were left to concentrate on dealing with the arms movement.

* * *

"Today's the day," exclaimed Janine as she leapt out of bed in response to the alarm.

"It sure is!"

Mark was normally the slower of the two to greet the new day, but with the prospect of action and a plentiful supply of adrenalin fixes, he was as full of the joys of spring as she was and as ready to take on the world. That it was four -thirty, well before dawn, and silent apart from Janine's tuneless singing, bothered him not at all.

'Great,' thought Janine, stimulated even more by Mark's controlled excitement. 'It's so much more fun when he's hyped up!'

The grin and the glossy black figure scampered around the bedroom, gathering clothes and jewellery before disappearing into the bathroom.

"Jesus, Janine!" Mark's buoyant feelings weren't going to be disturbed by his partner's excruciating rendition of her latest iTunes gem.

Emerging fully dressed after her shower, Janine met Mark in the bathroom doorway with much exuberant pushing and shoving. She didn't often abandon her skirt, but tight trousers and solid, sensible footwear seemed more appropriate for the activities of the day. Mark himself favoured well-used jeans and a nondescript jumper. Janine noted when he reappeared in the kitchen that he even managed to make these look smart and somehow distinguished. He seemed incapable of dressing down.

After a rapid breakfast, they set off for the Eurotransit depot at Ashford in Kent. It was essential that they arrived at the precise time agreed.

* * *

"I guess we really don't have much of a clue what it would be like living under the Moslem Fundamentalists," Mark remarked as they emerged onto the M25 and headed for the M20.

"Oh, I don't know! You're a man, you wouldn't notice the difference; I sure as hell would!"

"Yeah, I guess it isn't much of a woman's world!"

"It isn't much of any sort of a world. It's a living death, unremitting, hell, or the Moslem equivalent."

"But the women go for it just as much as the men; don't they?"

"Who says? Women hardly exist to the Fundamentalists, they're property, they do chores, have children; they're things, not beings. I can't believe it's like that in the Koran. How can women survive behind closed doors without choices? And this is what they've been trying to impose in Nigeria for years? Sharia law, primitive punishments... denied even the simplest of levels of human contact outside of the family. How can it work? Nigerian women have had a taste of the twenty-first century, Moslem and Christian alike, in a modern state. You can't take that away from them, it's reality. But that's what these fanatics want to do!"

"Pardon me!"

"Mark. You're not a woman; you can have no idea what it must be like to have your status so debased, to be totally disempowered. That's what Fundamentalism means for women. Remember the Taleban, Afghanistan, the country went backwards centuries from a woman's point of view. This is what Boko Haram want to do in Nigeria."

"With the benefit of hindsight, I shouldn't have started this conversation; it's not the best topic for a pre-dawn debate!"

"Certainly isn't, Mark," said Janine, her grin sufficiently present to convince Mark that her anger and frustration were directed at the Moslem Fundamentalists, not himself.

And he had to admit, living under such a religious totalitarianism would be pretty grim.

* * *

Friday morning was a busy time for everybody. Victoria Akinbode, Pearl Wong and Lehia Said were all in play early.

"There's no way we can prevent the arms leaving Britain," Lehia Said told her foot soldiers. "They'd be better hijacked in Nigeria anyway. So... if we can't meet the Alhaji's requirements here, we'd better try and see that nobody else gets to them. Problem is, with the vessel calling at Hamburg and Lisbon, and an endless string of African ports, there're far too many opportunities for someone like Mark Shortley to interfere."

Hector Xu would have been pleased with Lehia Said's

conclusion if not her thoughts on spiriting the arms away once in Nigeria.

"We'll base ourselves in Ipswich," Lehia continued. "One of you can watch at the Dartford crossing and the other at the docks at Felixstowe."

Having satisfied her sexual appetites at Dartford on the Thursday night, she was heading to a promised liaison with her other acolyte as Mark and Janine headed out of London.

* * *

"We're on our way; we'll be at Ashford by six -thirty. The timing's tight, but we'll make it. Where are the trucks?"

Janine was talking to Victoria on their private link.

"They're due at the ferry terminal at six. The Wong's forwarding agent informed the TransChannel operator at the last minute. One of the trucks is on the axle weight limit for the ferry. Anxious moment, but the French have been trailing the two trucks ever since they've been in their territory and told the TransChannel people not to impede the vehicles."

"OK," said Janine, "I'm using the same tracking system as before, so we've got surveillance all the way. The French were able to identify the trucks immediately. The Wong lot have tried to compress the timetable to minimise the opportunities for interference, but the details supplied by the Chinese informer before he died told us pretty well all we needed. Doesn't look from their actions that the Wongs know their security's been breached. Where'll you be?"

"At the TransChannel depot. The French police will be in touch when the trucks are on the ferry. I want to be sure the arms have left France. Once they are on British soil, things will be easier."

Victoria, who was the best known of the Wongs' opponents, was aware that she needed to keep out of sight, but she couldn't quite manage the trust necessary to leave everything to Mark. Most of the action of the day would be undertaken by the moonlighting SAS soldiers, supervised by Mark from a suitable distance, so once the trucks were on the ferry, Victoria was redundant. That was something that worried her.

"OK," said Janine, "see you when it's all over."

They arranged a rendezvous meeting place.

* * *

"I need to be there," Pearl had insisted with Hector Xu. "After the last fiasco…"

Xu found it hard to dispute her arguments.

She had arrived in Calais on the previous evening and had spent the time quietly checking that everything was in order. The most recent coded telephone message from the lead bodyguard on the trucks said that they were on schedule and would be at the terminal in time to drive straight onto the ferry.

"The Café St. Germaine, any idea where that is?"

Pearl was driving back into Calais with Marcus Ho. They'd changed from his rather conspicuous BMW to a non-descript Fiat family saloon. Despite the early hour, Pearl was irritatingly cheerful.

"Yeah, I had a scout around before I picked you up," Marcus said.

"I'll take Marcus," Pearl had also agreed with Hector Xu as she left, "I need a bag-carrier to provide backup and ensure the payment for the arms is safely made. The Brits and Nigerians are bound to be active."

"All future shipments will be paid for in our backyard, not in the wilds of Russia," Pearl had insisted, and Xu had forced the point on the Russians.

The General, who couldn't travel abroad as a result of numerous past misdemeanours, was not happy at this but eventually bowed to her demand. Natalia, the original intermediary when her father was setting up the deal, was to receive payment on his behalf. They had a detailed description of the Russian woman from Hector Xu.

Inevitably Natalia was late.

"She's here now," said Marcus.

He pointed to a woman of striking beauty who was carefully making her way through the tables towards them. Natalia had had no difficulty in locating the two Chinese people in the busy restaurant. Her approach was leisurely but still purposeful.

"Miss Wong?"

Natalia didn't offer to shake hands; she just accepted Pearl's acknowledgement and sat down. She assumed that Marcus was a bodyguard and ignored him. That suited him; he wanted to remain in the background.

"We eat first," said Natalia, revealing the limitations of her English.

She hadn't travelled very much outside of Russia, but when she did, she always feasted herself as well as she could. The simple fare on offer in a minor French café was a welcome change from the over-rich offerings available in many prestigious Moscow restaurants.

The breakfast was leisurely and largely silent. But it wasn't unobserved.

"A bit like Bastille Day," was how the senior French security service officer described it after the day's events had been unscrambled. "The Russian woman had a couple of bodyguards, a child could have spotted them, watching from another café opposite. There was a Moroccan street cleaner who was so thorough our two patrolling gendarmes were immediately suspicious. But the Fundamentalists at least knew where Pearl Wong was. And there were a couple of Nigerians tucked away with the black workmen in the corner of Café StGermaine itself."

It was Mark Shortley who identified these two. Mr Falinde's distrust had clearly not gone away! The two French security service agents, who were also there, were rather harder to detect than their more amateurish competitors.

'God,' thought Pearl as she and Marcus watched the Russian woman eat her way through two breakfasts, 'is she ever going to finish?'

Mindful of the time of their intended ferry, Pearl had set herself a mental deadline beyond which she was not going to be so acquiescent. She need not have worried.

"You have the money?" asked Natalia.

It was a ridiculous question in the circumstances, but it signalled that Natalia had eaten her fill.

Pearl nodded. "Yes, we have the money."

"OK, I take it. It is all there?"

"Yes, it's all there," snarled Pearl, becoming less enamoured of the statuesque Russian woman at every conversational passage. "Receipt?"

Natalia handed over an envelope. Marcus intercepted it and checked the contents. His eyebrows told Pearl that all was in order. She stood up and nodded her thanks. The watchers all became active and prepared to make their own exits as appropriate.

"Let's get that ferry," Pearl muttered as Natalia preceded them from the café and was immediately joined by her two sullen bodyguards.

Mobile phones buzzed as the security service men reported and the two Africans headed for their car. The knowledge that Pearl was heading for the ferry terminal was soon widespread.

"Goddamn it!" exclaimed Marcus Ho as they approached their parked car. The cause of his anger was instantly apparent.

He had been careful to leave the car in a nearby street, well positioned for a quick and smooth getaway. Locating the vehicle at the extreme end of a street parking zone, his plan had been to simply drive off without hindrance from other parked cars. His curse was in recognition that his intention had been thwarted.

A battered and elderly Citroën had been parked behind their car with barely a couple of centimetres clearance. Beside the Fiat, a large fruit lorry, jacked up and with one of its wheels missing, prevented any sideways movement, and parked on the pavement, actually touching their front bumper, was the service vehicle of the tyre company. No one was working on the lorry.

"I don't believe this," said Pearl, furiously looking at her watch.

Two disinterested-looking gendarmes were taking details but were not making any serious attempt to deal with the problem. Inevitably, as Marcus protested, neither gendarme appeared to understand any English, although his gestures must have made it abundantly clear who he and Pearl were and what they wanted.

"Ten minutes," snapped Pearl. "Otherwise we miss the ferry the trucks are on."

With only two unhelpful policemen to rely on, they had no chance.

Along the road, the two French security service agents watched the pantomime with increasing amusement, although at one point one of them had to leap out and intercept a cruising taxi before it came within hailing distance of the two Chinese people. By the time the taxi had been round the block, all chance of Pearl and her henchman arriving in time for the requisite ferry had safely been eroded. On confirmation that it had left, the two agents radioed the garage to get the fruit lorry attended to.

"That was too convenient!" snapped Pearl as they eventually got underway.

They made the next ferry but with a wait that did nothing for Pearl's temper.

* * *

The arms-carrying trucks themselves had made their scheduled ferry, but only after their own share of disruption.

As they drove into the ferry terminal, a TransChannel security guard waved them down and ordered them to halt rather than move straight through the check-in booths and into the loading area.

"What now?" demanded the lead bodyguard over his radio.

His colleague in the second truck could offer no explanation. The driver, who spoke very little English, shrugged. This sort of thing happened all the time; all that was needed was patience. Conscious of their tight timetable, the two Chinese guards knew that their masters in the Wong organisation were lacking in such a commodity.

"Get out of the truck."

The demand was made to the driver by a less-than- friendly French Customs official.

The driver climbed down and joined his confrère from the other truck. Approaching the vehicles from the other side, two French gendarmes simultaneously demanded to see the papers of the bodyguards. After a lengthy consultation, during which customs officers inspected the trucks and their loaded containers, the senior policeman announced that the papers of the two guards were not in order.

"What do you mean, not in order? Of course they are," snapped the leading bodyguard, fluent in French if not apparently in English.

"Not in order," repeated the officer. "You stay!"

The policemen and customs officers gathered up the two drivers and headed towards the terminal office building. The bodyguards were obviously required to remain with the trucks, that much, at least, was very clear. The arrival of a gendarme cradling a compact machine gun in his arms reinforced the point.

Inside the terminal building, the security agent whom Victoria and Mark knew as Léon was being briefed by the customs officers.

"Separate Pearl or any other minders from the trucks," Mark had told Victoria and Janine, "then deal with the drivers. The police always keep an eye on long-distance drivers like these, especially if they cross a lot of borders. There's always plenty of chance for a bit of business on the side. And even if they are honest, there's always something they could question them about."

Mark's plan was to exploit this minor aspect of trucking.

"You've been to Moldavia and back seven times in the last six months," said one of the customs officers. "And our colleagues in Poland say there's been an increase in black-market cigarette movements from Russia during that period. We're questioning all drivers who regularly use the routes through Poland."

Both drivers protested their innocence of anything to do with cigarette smuggling. The customs officers were naturally unimpressed. The two men were invited to join them in discussing the matter further.

"But what... the trucks?" said the older man, straining his limited English to breaking -point.

The man had no idea what was in the containers, but he knew he was to attract a handsome bonus for their delivery on time. What's more, parked where they were, they would be causing chaos if they didn't soon take their places on the ferry. But the customs officers had a solution to the problem.

"We have replacement drivers," the senior official said.

The bodyguards were suspicious when the little party headed towards them from the terminal building. Aggravation was already developing as the build-up of traffic increased and the agitated TransChannel officials tried to get the armed gendarme to allow the trucks to move.

"You'll have new drivers," announced the customs man

when the group arrived at the waiting trucks, his English improving to meet the occasion.

"New drivers, why?" demanded the lead bodyguard, who discovered some English as well in the stress of the moment.

But the bodyguards were distracted by another piece of theatre that was going on at the same time.

"This is wholly irregular..."

A rather portly gentleman was protesting in rapid French as two men moved from behind the group and headed one to each truck. They were obviously the replacement drivers. The lead guard demanded to know what the hell was going on.

"They are not the relief drivers," the fat man said in his own version of fractured English.

Slowly the bodyguards picked up the story. Everybody seemed very concerned that they should fully understand.

"This gentleman is the local representative of UFTR, the French Transport Workers Union," the customs official said, gesturing at his angry companion. "His Union is required to provide standby drivers for vehicles if the existing drivers can't continue. These spare drivers are at the Union's offices in central Calais; it would take time for them to get here. And we have orders not to disrupt the ferry traffic so the TransChannel officials can find two drivers of their own."

It was against this intrusion that the Union man was protesting.

"Never mind, we go, we go," said the lead bodyguard.

And go they did. Within minutes, the trucks were on the ferry and the Union official was heading back into central Calais with a fat cheque courtesy of the French Security Service to swell his branch funds. The new drivers, who had learnt their skills at a British Army training school in Herefordshire, settled to the task of delivering the two trucks to the Wong depot in Ashford.

The lead bodyguard hadn't been able to report the change

of circumstances from the ferry. When he eventually did make contact, the information did nothing to allay Pearl's ill-defined feelings of concern. Was it another coincidence that the drivers had to be changed? Whether it was or not, the trucks were already at Ashford by the time she was told, and the Wong organisation had other problems there.

THIRTY-SEVEN

The day shift were just arriving at the Eurotransit depot when the first signs of trouble were detected, a breach in the fence near the Wong warehouse. The depot manager Alan Jenkins, as was his habit, arrived early. The overnight security guards sheepishly reported the gaping hole in the fence. Jenkins set out to investigate. He found as the front door of the Wong office came into view that it had been forced open. It was just coming up to eight-thirty and he knew that two special trucks were due any time.

And at precisely eight-thirty the conflagration started.

The damaged office door was propelled towards Jenkins by the force of a muted explosion from within the building. A blast of hot air preceded the flying debris. His efforts to escape the speeding door were rewarded, but he took a hard tumble. Bruised by his fall, he gathered himself to take stock of the situation. As sections of doorframe crashed into the side of his car, he reached for his mobile phone.

His calls for help made, he cautiously edged back towards the building. He could feel the heat, although no flames had so far broken out of the shell of the building. A continuous wall of escaping hot air and fumes confronted him from the space where the door and the flimsy offices had been. He could see through into the storage area. It was a mass of flames reaching upwards with ever- increasing intensity.

"God," he muttered, holding back.

He tried to recall if he knew what was being held in the various sections of the warehouse overnight. Almost everything he could bring to mind was hazardous in some way.

'OK, Alan, you can't do anything. Better move back and let the fire brigade deal with it.'

Jenkins nodded and walked away with Shen Lee, the Wong warehouse manager, a stocky, balding Chinese man of indeterminate age.

Equally aware of the important consignment of machine tools arriving imminently, the warehouse manager had also arrived early. The first explosion had occurred as he pulled up at the depot security gate. As Jenkins and he got back to Mr Shen's car, a second explosion punched a ragged hole in the roof of the building, sending wreckage in all directions and allowing an escalating column of flames to reach a hundred feet into the sky. In the back of the manager's car another obviously elderly Chinese man looked at the blazing warehouse with an expression that showed neither surprise nor concern. Hector Xu nonetheless was deeply troubled.

"Sounds like the fire brigade," said the depot manager.

The distant wail of the emergency service vehicles began to fill the air, getting louder and then seemingly to stall.

At the depot security gate, the two trucks now with SAS drivers arrived at the same moment as the three fire engines. The traffic snarl took several minutes to sort out. Once inside the depot, the fire-fighting vehicles were quickly deployed. By the nature of the site there was plenty of room for them to manoeuvre into strategic positions to attack the blaze. Having verified the well-being of his staff, Mr Shen made himself available to the senior fire officer and identified as much of the contents of the warehouse as he could.

"Mr Jenkins, our two expected trucks have arrived. They are causing chaos at the gates. The police want us to move them inside and free the area. Can you find another warehouse for them to be checked over in?"

His liaison duties complete Mr Shen's normal composure was breaking down.

The first spate of emergency service vehicles had arrived, but the backup crews and the precautionary ambulances were having difficulty in getting into the depot. The Eurotransit depot manager was under pressure to relieve the situation. The police were unsympathetic to the truck driver's difficulties; if they couldn't access the Wong warehouse, they must either be allocated another one or leave the site.

* * *

"Standby, Janine, they're coming in."

Mark and the SAS lieutenant were holed up in the back bedroom of one of the houses overlooking the depot and were watching as their plans unfolded. Janine was already installed in her vantage point. The Eurotransit depot manager was privy to something of what was to happen but was playing his part with some reluctance. The fire at the Wong warehouse didn't appear in the script that he had been given and it didn't improve Alan Jenkins' toleration of what was happening at his depot.

"Talk to the police," Mark had told him at the initial briefing. "They'll provide you with evidence that the Wongs were using their warehouse, and your depot, for the movement of prohibited chemicals, possibly even drugs."

Later sifting through the wreckage, the Kent and Sussex Police forensic officers confirmed that significant traces of the chemical intermediaries for producing some sophisticated and pretty unpleasant chemical warfare agents had been found. Nobody believed that the arbitrary decision to destroy the warehouse was justified by what was discovered, but not many tears were shed over it either. No claim for damages was ever received from the Wongs.

"The other warehouse will do," said Hector Xu when consulted. "Anywhere that's private. We have all the documents with us; we only need space."

Mr Shen advised Jenkins of the decision and the two trucks were finally driven into the nominated building. The warehouse was at the opposite end of the site from the Wong premises. The police had carefully isolated the area of the fire and had opened up the rest of the depot. Once the question of the two Wong trucks had been resolved, the activities unaffected by the fire were allowed to proceed.

"The Newson warehouse has its own staff, so you won't need to release your own people."

"We only need to do a limited check. I can manage that easily enough. We have to get the vehicles away to Felixstowe by one o'clock at the very latest; that's the only thing that matters. The delay over the fire has already seriously eaten into the time."

Hector Xu just wanted the job done, and an hour or more had disappeared with sorting out the arrangements with the police and depot staff.

"The Newson warehouse is of a different design to the Wong's building," Mark briefed Janine. "There are offices upstairs overlooking the storage area and a plant room. You'll get a good view of the action through the ventilator grill and the troopers can keep out of the way until they're needed. There'll be stacks of crates and other stuff around, but that won't get in our way."

"Things are happening," Janine said quietly into her radio. "The trucks have arrived. Two people, both Chinese, one's elderly. The old chap's giving the orders."

Two of the warehouse workers unloaded a selection of crates from the two containers.

"Not very trusting, this Wong lot," remarked Janine as she watched the chosen crates being unloaded using a forklift truck.

The two SAS men doing the work moved about quickly and efficiently under the urging of Hector Xu.

"Our guys are releasing the crate lids but not opening them. Now they've been sent away. Clever. They're inspecting the crates without taking anything out. Can't see what's in 'em."

As Janine watched, Hector Xu and the warehouse manager Mr Shen delved into the crates and compared the contents with the papers that Xu had with him. They worked quickly. Mr Shen, now fully aware of the contents of the crates, showed no surprise. His business was always a mixture of legitimate and illicit activities.

"They've finished," said Janine. "They've called the guys back to fix the crates and return them to the trucks."

It had taken barely ten minutes.

Under Hector Xu's instructions, the crates were reloaded and the containers resealed.

"OK, go," said Janine urgently.

There was a pounding on the outside door of the warehouse as the two Chinese men tidied their papers and a senior policeman let himself in.

"Yes?" said Mr Shen rather sharply.

"The fire is out at your warehouse, Mr Shen. But there are a number of things that we need to clear up with you," said the officer, a superintendent.

He was careful to ensure that Hector Xu was included in the invitation to return to the site of the now-destroyed building.

"We must see these trucks off first."

"Mr Shen, I'm sure that some subordinate of yours can do that, I wish to release some of the fire service units so... shall we go?"

The superintendent was not to be denied. As Mr Shen departed, he instructed the two SAS soldiers-cum-warehousemen to remain with the vehicles and await the arrival of the drivers and the guards. Twenty-five frantic minutes later, after the bodyguards had been located in a local hostelry with the two SAS drivers, the two trucks set off on the next stage of their journey. It was just after half-past twelve.

* * *

"So what the hell happened?"

In the police incident caravan, Mr Shen was being questioned about a number of interesting things that had been found in the remains of the building. Hector Xu had been excused and had located Pearl Wong. They were discussing events in the back of Marcus Ho's car parked in a remote part of the depot.

"The warehouse exploded. It was firebombed. The police say it was broken into during the night. It was set to go off at eight -thirty by the look of it."

Hector Xu had managed to get the information without having to explain who he was and why he was interested.

"Sun Lee will know more. But I think they have found some of the chemicals from the Azeri cargo, so he may be delayed."

Pearl waved the information aside. She only wanted to know about the arms.

"And the trucks, where are they?"

"They're in a warehouse at the other end of the site. They arrived at the same time as the fire engines and the police wanted to turn them away. The depot manager offered us this other warehouse. We had to take it."

"Hector!"

Pearl stopped. Was it yet another coincidence that they just happened to have a spare warehouse available?

"We opened a selection of boxes. The arms checked out with the Russian lists."

As they talked, the car 'phone rang. It was the lead

bodyguard. He reported that they were just about to leave and explained about the hang-up at TransChannel Terminal and the relief drivers. Pearl expressed her anger at not being told about the changeover earlier but realised the futility of such a protest.

"OK, you're making good time. Watch out for any problems at roadworks or areas where you have to slow down. The escort will pick you up as you leave the depot. Good luck."

Pearl and Hector Xu watched the convoy of two trucks head off.

"We can only wait and see. OK, Marcus, let's go home and see what the rest of the day brings."

* * *

"Oh..."

In deference to Hector Xu, Pearl stifled the expletive that formed in her mind.

"Did you see that?"

Hector had. Parked in a lay-by only yards from the main gate of the depot was a large black car. In the back, clearly preparing to leave, were the unmistakable gloomy figures of Messrs Falinde and Oje.

"Still the bastards don't trust us," howled Pearl, her older companion's sensibilities ignored this time.

"No indeed," he replied grimly.

The rest of the trip was silent, but for their own reasons the two principals of the Wong organisation seethed. Whilst Mr Xu focused his aggrievement on the two Nigerians, Pearl was still trying to come to terms with the feeling of unease that kept coming back to her.

'It's not only the coincidences,' she told herself. 'It's all going too well. Shortley's too good to be so apparently inactive. What's the bastard doing?'

But she couldn't put her finger on where Mark's organisation might be in play.

* * *

"What a gorgeous little place," said Janine in some excitement.

She'd noticed the pub in Bearsted near Maidstone when she and Mark were on their earlier recce visit. Victoria, brought up on a diet of curiously outmoded images of Britain, shared Janine's delight. Nestled into the vast inglenook, they ate a late lunch and reviewed the action. All three were in high spirits. Mark was physically squeezed between the two girls, his adrenalin still running high, and a sense of anticipation pervaded him. The game had started, and the chase to him, as always, was every bit as good as the elation at the final outcome.

He was happy to be so close to Janine, but he was unsure about her reaction to his being in such intimate contact with Victoria. She was unconcerned. Excited by being involved in the action of the day, she was oblivious to the presence of her fellow Nigerian as a rival.

"Well," said Victoria after they had ordered drinks, "to our success."

The meal was lively and light-hearted. Sandwiched between the two black women, Mark found himself a bystander to much of the conversation.

"So what really happened in Calais?" asked Janine.

Victoria filled in the details of what had occurred at the TransChannel Terminal. Her vivid description of the antics of the French Security Service in delaying Pearl sent Janine into near hysterics. Mark shared her delight. Some of Janine's wariness of Victoria faded over the meal, although her insensitivity to personal tragedy still struck her as odd.

"You knew about the car bombs?" Janine asked when the conversation began to flag.

"Lagos?"

Victoria knew that there had been incidents in Lagos and Enugu.

"No, these were after that. There was one in Abuja and another at the Airport at Kano."

Janine gave the details; they were not pleasant.

"There weren't many casualties in Abuja," she said, "but there was outrage and anger as they were mainly amongst a party of school children visiting the Federal Parliament."

Victoria shrugged whilst Mark, who was equally unaware of what had had happened, muttered an angry curse.

"The demonstration that followed got out of hand," Janine continued, "grew into a major riot and the property of a number of known supporters of the Moslem Fundamentalists was attacked. Only promises of firm action by the Home Affairs Minister quelled the mob."

"Interesting," said Victoria, "just the sort of opportunity that the Minister would have wanted. Give him a pretext to act against the influx of Middle Eastern people."

That Victoria should pick up on a political point rather than show sympathy once again struck Mark as a bit cold.

"In Kano, the bomb went off next to a bus-load of returning pilgrims. Mainly elderly and all from a mosque known for its strong support for the traditionalist approach to Islam. The riot that followed here was much worse than in Abuja. The police lost control, or maybe let go. Two Afghans and an Algerian were beaten to death."

Janine had invaded the computers at the Nigerian High Commission to see an intelligence briefing for the High Commissioner, but she thought it better not to tell Victoria that.

"Seems to me," said Mark, "the Fundamentalists aren't making the headway they hoped they would."

"Takes time," said Victoria. "The Fundamentalist leaders are looking for a quick win in Nigeria, and it doesn't look as if they're going to get it. Nigeria is a big prize, but it's also the first time they have tried to take over in a country that's not overwhelmingly Moslem."

She was quoting from an internal security service appraisal of the situation which suggested that the instigators of the spread of Fundamentalism in Nigeria believed the country had been ripe for a take-over. This was now seen as a misjudgement. A religious coup required far deeper and far more widespread support than was apparent. However imperfect Nigerian democracy was, the average northerner seemed to like it as the devil they knew.

"I guess the worst development was the demonstrations in Lagos and Ibadan Universities against what was happening in the north," said Mark.

"The students have always been the first to protest in our country," said Victoria.

"Hey," interrupted Janine suddenly, "this is getting a bit deep. I wish I hadn't said anything now."

* * *

'We must settle this thing with the 'New Truth' lot once and for all,' Pearl said to herself as she settled into her home office and prepared to pick up her day's business.

The police enquiry into the two family deaths had been inconclusive but Miss Wong knew better.

As Hector Xu and Marcus Ho headed back to London and affairs unrelated to the Nigerians and arms shipments, Pearl set her mind to avenge the affront the killings had caused.

Lehia Said would have agreed with Pearl. When she had satisfied herself that she'd done the barest minimum to fulfill her obligations to the northern Nigerians, she fully intended to return to what to her was her prime activity. She had a couple of scores to settle before she left Britain.

THIRTY-EIGHT

"That's it," said Lehia Said.

The second arms shipment was loaded on board the Freightroute vessel at Felixstowe at seven o'clock on the Friday evening. After a clear, warm April evening, the ship finally left port at midnight. Lehia and her two accomplices watched the sleek vessel pull away from the dock and head out into the North Sea.

* * *

"Well, that turned out to be pretty uneventful," the SAS lieutenant said.

She and her team had settled into a country pub, unlikely to attract any attention from the returning Chinese escort party or the Moslem terrorists, for a debriefing, and to consume the proceeds of Mark Shortley's personal generosity.

"The ship's gone," reported Marcus Ho to Pearl as the SAS drivers and surveillance teams had just about got into their first pints.

The two parties of Chinese thugs had had a boring and undisturbed trip to the east coast. They waited to pick up the two bodyguards before setting off back to London at break-neck speed.

"It's Lehia Said, Ma'am, and a couple of Middle East types."

One of the SAS corporals had been on a weekend school run by Professor Jordane and had earlier recognised the 'New Truth' operative as she headed back past the unobtrusive checkpoint towards London. It was only then, having checked off all the other players, did the troopers headed for their chosen pub.

"We'll pass the information on to Shortley," said the lieutenant. "He'll let the anti-terrorist squad know if he thinks it's important. Lehia Said is police business."

After her debriefing, and a very modest celebration by their standards, the lieutenant took her troops back to their barracks and they faded from the action.

* * *

"We've a few days before the next stage in the action," Mark said to Janine as they eventually made it back to their flat. "Fun time!"

Janine wasn't too hopeful that Mark would practise what he was preaching. He was still hyped up in anticipation of the trip to Nigeria, the implications of which had barely registered with Janine. But a fiercely competitive game of squash on the Saturday refreshed them both and by Sunday the prospects for a lazy and relaxing day were infinitely better. Any mention Mark made of the Wongs, the Moslem Fundamentalists or the Nigerians was instantly reproved by Janine; and she confined herself to a short period of routine surveillance activity via her computers before closing her mind to everything but pleasure.

"Come on, you idle sod....."

Around eight o'clock on Sunday morning, Janine dug Mark awake by chewing at his ear and running her hands in and out of his crotch. Still in a state of half stupor, he eventually tumbled her out of bed and pulled the covers back over himself. Rising to the provocation, she leapt on his back, and a round of the riotous lovemaking that they both so much enjoyed in the morning ensued. Finally, after one last bout in the shower, they turned their attention to activities for the day.

"How about we have a picnic in Kensington Gardens?" Janine suggested.

She was watching Mark work his usual magic with bacon and eggs, semi-nude, chin in hands and elbows on the kitchen table. Mark sensed that she was uncharacteristically pensive. But she was simply savouring a glow of silent pleasure inside herself, both at the intimacy that they had just achieved and at their lack of inhibitions, despite the upsets over Victoria and Daniel Onifade.

"You move like a dream," she said quietly.

Mark, as she intended, didn't quite hear what she had said. She was leaning back in the chair now, her naked breasts thrust out in front of her. Had he looked, her enormous grin would have told him that the words didn't matter; she simply wanted his attention. He dumped the plates piled high with food on the table and sat down. As she often did, she skipped around the table and sat, little girl-like, on his knees. She had his attention.

"Gorgeous one," she purred through the kisses she was planting all over his face and then on his lips.

She knew that she was having an effect on him; she could feel it through the brief linen skirt that she was wearing. Finally she was still, and he sat with her cradled in his arms, rocking her gently backwards and forwards. It was a moment of great tenderness between them that spoke for her anxieties about the next few days and about the battering that their relationship had taken over the last few weeks.

"I love you, Mark."

It wasn't something that she said very often. She was

almost as sparing with her words of affection as he was. He acknowledged her declaration with a gentle and delicate kiss.

"And I love you too, Janine."

His feelings were confused. It was his behaviour rather than hers that had provoked the upheavals and it was her forgiveness that usually got things back on to an even keel. Not wishing to lose the moment, he didn't say anything; he wasn't even sure what he could have said. Ever the matter-of-fact one, it was Janine who eventually broke the spell.

"Better eat this lovely food."

She moved from his lap and sat down again opposite him. They were silent for a period as they ate. Mark wondered, as he had done many times, about her ability to express herself so wonderfully in her vibrant and exciting lovemaking, and her inability to express herself with the same fluency in words. He could usually find the words but was slower to be aroused sexually.

'Better get the monitoring checks done,' Janine told herself, her stomach full of Mark's cooking and a feeling of well-being beginning to invade her brain. She got up and silently went downstairs. Mark let her go.

'Can't blame her if she's anxious,' he thought. 'It's bound to be traumatic.'

Mark had shared the final stages of his plans with her. They involved a reversal of roles and Janine making the trip to Nigeria with him.

The news that they were going to Africa was more a shock to Janine than a surprise. It wasn't that she wasn't expecting it; with everything that had been going on, it was inevitable. It was simply that she now had to confront the reality, whereas before she could avoid it.

The past didn't immediately flood back. It was too long ago for the images to be clearly resurrected. But she knew that when the trip became a reality, things might come more into focus.

"For the same reason the Nigerians can't operate very easily in Europe, I'll have to stay in the background when we get out there," he had explained. "It's vital we have good communications. You'll have to act as the link with Victoria and the Nigerian authorities anywhere that we are exposed to public gaze, which will be pretty well everywhere."

Mark was well aware that to accompany him to Nigeria would place an unlooked-for burden on Janine. Even during the horror days of the abortive Nationalist coup in 2022, Janine had maintained a positive and optimistic outlook. Worse things had happened to her. She had been assaulted as a small child by a drunken Nigerian soldier. The intervention of a Moslem sergeant, deeply offended by the soldier's conduct, saved her physically, but it had taken many years for the psychological trauma to dissipate.

And now she was being asked to return to the country of her birth; the scene of her violation.

'If I don't make a meal of it,' Mark had told himself, 'neither will she.'

He hadn't really given her an option. He needed her in Nigeria; it was a simple matter of skin colour.

Janine herself was determined not to give credence to her anxieties or let them get in the way of the job. She had moved on.

But as she called up the first media trawlings onto her computer screen, she could have been excused for feeling anxious. The situation in Nigeria was worsening almost by the hour.

"The car bombing campaign and the demonstrations and counter-demonstrations have intensified over the last few days."

BBC/CNN's *Planetcover* twenty-four-hour news analysis channel said it all.

"A pattern of violence is feeding on itself with the Moslem Fundamentalists furiously stoking passions.

"A junior Federal Nigerian Government Minister has been assassinated on a trip to his constituency in Bauchi State, one of the more populous areas of the north. Quick reaction by the local police and his own bodyguards resulted in the death of one of the assassins and the capture of the second. The parading of the detained man, believed to be either Iranian or Iraqi, on television, caused an enormous outcry, in both the north and the south of Nigeria.

"The reaction in the south," the *Planetcover* reporter said, "was a new departure and a step change in reaction to Fundamentalist activities.

"Chief Adeko was quoted as saying that the troubles in the north were entirely fermented by foreigners, as no native Nigerian extremists seemed to have been arrested."

Janine switched to a report in the *Eastern Nigeria Post*.

"Chief Adeko has demanded action on the violence in the north and has proposed that the states where the troubles are the most serious be placed under direct Federal Government rule."

Being a supporter of the Chief, the paper sidestepped the provocative nature of the statement, and concentrated on the upsurge of protest in the north, which in turn provoked a supportive response from many of the southern states.

"The oil workers, virtually all southerners, threatened to strike unless the Federal Government took a firmer line with the Fundamentalists," the *Post* concluded.

"What's the old shit up to?" muttered Janine. "The oil workers are a key group. Mark won't like this."

Returning to the *Planetcover* report and the latest analysis, Janine discovered that the Chief's speech had been met with a mixed reaction.

"Behind the comparison between the unruly north and the coherent and peaceful south, there is a sense that the Chief is really seeking to excite the Fundamentalists to greater activity."

However, the news channel appeared to doubt whether the Chief had a clear grasp of the hold that the Fundamentalists had in the north. It was the *Planetcover*'s view that this hold was much more fragile than he and the external agitators imagined. That was not to say that the threat was not still formidable.

The other piece of news that Janine spotted was evidence that Chief Adeko's southern consortium was suffering stresses and strains of its own. Scanning through another purloined brief addressed to the Nigerian High Commissioner, the Chief's almost complete lack of manners and total insensitivity to the feelings of others was creating tensions.

"The Chief's associates," the brief said, "have no quarrel with what he was doing, more with his tendency to assume that his were the only views on any topic of merit."

However, not a man to let such minor inconveniences get in his way, the Chief, according to the brief. was close to his target of five thousand recruits for his paramilitary organisation. Fortunately, as Janine was well aware, he was not yet in a position to provide his troopers with weapons.

"Don't think the old pig'll be having it all his own way for much longer!" Janine muttered to herself with some satisfaction.

Chief Adeko was not one of her favourite people, although she did feel sorry for his wife. Even on brief acquaintance, Janine liked Grace much better than her sister Victoria.

THIRTY-NINE

"Aren't you ready yet, woman?"

Tired of waiting, Mark had come to find her. Grasping her around her bare waist, he carried her bodily back upstairs and dumped her on the bed. Giggling, she hurriedly covered her remaining nakedness and declared herself ready as required.

"No point in getting all hot and bothered," Mark said, so by the time that they had found themselves a spot in the rather crowded Kensington Gardens, it was nearly eleven o'clock.

Mark dumped the inevitable trappings of the picnic down and prepared a comfortable pitch for them to settle on. Janine watched his lean and tight body with obvious delight and gave him giggling and unhelpful instructions. He largely ignored her, but when he had finished his preparations, he unceremoniously tumbled her onto the ground and then threw himself down beside her. Janine wriggled herself very close to him and, uttering exaggerated sighs of contentment, settled and lay still.

"This is heaven," she murmured.

Mark's grunt was confirmation enough for her.

The sky was cloudless, the sun hot and the whole atmosphere around them relaxed, lethargic and peaceful. Even the chatter and restless disruption of nearby children seemed to fade into the background, although Mark's trained-in instincts meant that he was unlikely to do more than doze in such surroundings. Janine laid her hand gently on his arm, anxious to have physical contact with his body, and began to drift into half sleep.

For nearly an hour, the world slid passed them unnoticed.

* * *

"Oh, look, Mummy, it's a nun! There's a nun over there, Mummy!"

The excited urgency of the child was enough to recall Mark to consciousness. He opened a lazy eye and rolled his head around to look about him. The strident child's voice was hushed by an equally reluctantly aroused parent. But the little exchange between mother and daughter was sufficiently close to Mark to ensure that he was alert to his immediate surroundings. Janine stirred because he had stirred.

It was not a nun.

"Oh, shit!" muttered Mark, instantly awake.

The figure in long, flowing black robes was standing about ten paces from where Mark and Janine were laying. With the full headdress, all that Mark could see were the piercing china blue eyes.

"Lehia Said!"

He'd have known those eyes anywhere, having so recently stood within a very few centimetres of them when they were illuminated with the same intensity. But this was not sexual excitement. There was only pure hatred in the eyes now.

Control mechanisms deep inside his brain took charge. The cameo action in front of him was almost in black and white so dominated was it by the Arab woman.

"Mark?"

Janine's whispered anxiety and her cautious movements

beside him were momentarily blocked from his mind. He was totally concentrated on Lehia Said.

The Arab woman's right arm came up, exposing the opening in the voluminous sleeve. Mark didn't know that it was a hand-held rather than shoulder-held crossbow, but he did know that it was a weapon. The blue eyes sparkled and then went dull as the woman took aim.

With nowhere to hide, Mark flung himself sideways, away from Janine.

As he propelled himself, he had a vision of the red feathered crossbow bolt streaking towards him. He felt it tear at his flesh and then his body was jerked back to the ground by the force of its impact. Gouging a path along the edge of his chest, the bolt had pinned the loose material of his shirt to the ground. As he felt it, so he wrenched the bolt free. It was an action of desperate strength.

With blood seeping rapidly from the wound, Mark was on his feet in one movement. Unconscious of any thought processes, his actions were entirely instinctive.

"Mark!" exclaimed Janine sharply in warning.

It was the first time that he had been aware of his partner during the split second of the action of firing the crossbow. As he oriented himself, Janine moved between him and the Arab woman. It was another split- second action that seemed to take an age. Janine coiled and uncoiled.

"Bitch," she snapped, but it was an exclamation in her head rather than in the face of the woman in front of her.

The high-pitched grunt that escaped the Arab woman as Janine loosed off a savage and well- aimed kick at her wrist was the only sound that she made during the whole of the episode. The crossbow arced in the air and landed three or four metres away, narrowly missing the young girl, whose excited cry had alerted Mark to his danger in the first place.

"Mark, you OK?"

Janine threw the query urgently over her shoulder as she watched the black-clad woman intently for her next move. She was a competent judo exponent and had learnt a thing or two from Victoria about less lady-like fighting, but that was the limit of her skills.

'If she's got a knife…' she thought in sudden panic. She knew she had no skills in that department; that was one for Mark, as he'd been trained in almost every form of combat.

The woman did produce a knife. For Mark, as he saw it suddenly appear in her right hand, it was the final confirmation that the mysterious Arab woman was indeed Lehia Said.

"Oh my God," said Janine, her courage ebbing.

But she didn't have much time to dwell on her fears; Lehia advanced on her immediately. Janine avoided the first thrust, her abbreviated clothing giving her an advantage in mobility.

The second thrust never came. The disadvantage of the long robes was immediately apparent to Lehia as she observed the ease with which Janine evaded her.

'Bastard! Another time!' she thought, or at least that was the meaning of the rapid Arabic that flashed through her mind.

Never foolhardy in what she did, Lehia realised that against an obviously active and aggressive opponent, and with Mark still in play, her only sensible option was retreat. So she hoisted up her skirts in one sweep of her left hand and set off at an astonishing pace across the gardens towards the Serpentine, and escaping in the direction of Bayswater Road. Perhaps with a touch of desperation to aid her progress, the speed of her withdrawal amazed both Mark and Janine.

"Leave her," said Mark before he realised that Janine had no intention of pursuing the retreating Lehia.

"Mark?"

Janine repeated her anxious query, seeing him clutching his side and the blood escaping through his fingers.

Other picnickers gathered around them, momentarily

curious about the extraordinary scene that they had just witnessed. An off-duty nurse offered her assistance, but without the necessary equipment, there was not much that she could do.

Janine quickly gathered up their belongings and urged Mark to head for Kensington Road and the refuge of a taxi to hospital. Recovering the crossbow from the little girl who was playing with it, they set off for the nearest section of thoroughfare. The onlookers drifted away as they left, their interest already fading.

"I'll put that in my bag," said Janine, relieving Mark of the crossbow. "Doesn't look so good, you carrying it in your hand!"

Mark laughed; that encouraged Janine.

A taxi was easily found, although the driver was wary when he saw Mark's blood-soaked shirt.

"The nearest casualty hospital," demanded Janine.

Like the taxi, the hospital was also readily found.

"Nasty! How did this happen?"

Mark didn't think the young doctor really wanted to know. Once the wound was cleaned and stitched up, it certainly wasn't as bad as appearances would have suggested. It was only a flesh wound, albeit a tear rather than a cut, and Mark had had many such in his time.

* * *

"I'll call George," Mark said back at the flat.

Janine didn't fuss around him; it wasn't her way, and she knew that he wouldn't take kindly to it anyway. He never wanted attention when he was hurt; he always preferred to cope with his injuries in his own way.

"I'm OK, just a bit sore," was the sole comment that he made on his wound.

George was one of Mark's contacts in the Metropolitan Police Anti-Terrorist Squad. He'd been in touch with him and his detective inspector quite frequently in the days since the first arms shipment had been intercepted. After their visit to Professor Jordane, they had been specifically feeding him all the information that they could about Lehia Said. The news of the attack on Mark with the chance of a positive identification would be welcome.

Being Sunday, Mark had some difficulty making contact; however, it was the detective inspector who eventually called back at around five o'clock and arranged to visit.

"She'll be here around half six," Mark reported to Janine.

"She?" said Janine with her grin now returned.

* * *

With time to spare, Janine carefully sat beside Mark on the settee and curled herself up against him, avoiding his injured side.

"That was horrible," she said in a low voice.

"Hey now, don't get all upset. I've been in worse scrapes than this. I'll be fine tomorrow. Well… almost fine."

He leered down at her in such an outrageously suggestive way that she exploded into the deep, gurgling laughter that always excited him so much. Any anxiety she had about his well-being was dispelled before it even had a chance to take hold.

"I can't wait," she said before going off into more rumbles of laughter.

But there was something else that Mark wanted to say.

"You were really great in the park. Where'd you learn that kick? No judo instructor ever taught you that."

His question was admiring as well as curious.

Janine's concern for his injury was in danger of obscuring the fact that it was she who had disarmed Lehia and put her to flight. He didn't want that to happen.

"Victoria. She's into kick-boxing. She showed me a couple of unauthorised attack kicks when I took her to the gym."

293

She was pleased by his interest.

"Saved my life," he added thoughtfully. "If she'd come at me with the knife, I mightn't have been quick enough..." He left the thought hanging in the air. "Thanks."

Janine showed signs of tears. Her feelings for Mark had been much more exposed by the incident than she usually allowed them to be, and his quiet gratitude, so simply stated, really touched her.

"I wish it hadn't happened with Victoria," he said.

"And I wish it hadn't happened with Daniel Onifade. But we don't own each other, we have to have space if we need it... ."

But neither really believed that, nor wanted to.

"You're all I need, Janine. You're enough of everything I want. I don't want anyone else!"

"I'm glad!" she said, hugging him until he winced.

"Janine," he said quietly.

The tears came for real this time as she realised with horror how her exuberance was hurting him. She pulled away from him and looked so crestfallen that he couldn't help but chuckle himself.

"We must never let anybody ever get between us again," she said rather primly.

"No, ma'am," he responded with another chuckle.

"I couldn't bear it without you," she whispered.

It was the sort of declaration that they had never felt the need to make before.

"I couldn't bear it without you either!" Mark said.

* * *

"Inspector, it's good of you to come on a Sunday."

Inspector Wilke acknowledged Mark's greeting and, seeing him move stiffly, asked about his injuries.

"Not too serious, only a flesh wound. Soon heal."

The inspector read something different in Janine's eyes but didn't pursue the subject.

Between them, Mark and Janine explained what had happened. The policewoman looked at Janine with renewed interest as the story unfolded.

"And you're sure this Arab woman was Lehia Said?"

"Oh yes, I'm sure. I've seen her so many times now; I'd know her whatever she was wearing."

Mark was adamant.

"OK, but why would she suddenly decided to try and kill you?"

"Oh, come on," said Janine, answering for him. "It's a power game. She didn't get Mark laid when she meant to. But she didn't know who he was then. When she found out, she'd naturally assume Mark had known who she was. So it wasn't she who had used him; it was he who had used her and made a fool of her. Who wouldn't be angry?"

"And she'd kill for that?"

Mark was incredulous.

The two women weren't. Knowing how dominant Lehia was in her group, to be so easily undermined, and by a mere man at that, she would have been furious. The inspector, who had seen a psychological profile of Lehia, had very little difficulty in accepting Janine's theory.

"She's checked into St. Jerome's Hotel until tomorrow. She's with two men; they're sharing a room, the two men."

"If she's supposed to be supporting the Fundamentalists, she's a very funny way of doing it," said Janine.

The police inspector didn't say anything; the intelligence that she had about the long history of conflict between 'New Truth' and the Wong organisation told her something else.

FORTY

"The Portuguese Security Service reports the arrival and departure of the container ship," Janine told Mark. "They also say that an inconspicuous Chinese woman and a very conspicuous African man made separate checks of their own, ostensibly sightseeing in the dock area."

"Par for the course," remarked Mark.

"Since the containers are safe in the hold according to the manifest," continued Janine, "and since Port Harcourt's the last port of call, the ammunition and weapons are as secure as they are ever likely to be."

The excess of zeal by the Wong organisation and the excess of distrust by the southern Nigerians were more a tangible tribute to the reputations of Mark Shortley and the Nigerian Security Service than any genuine need for reassurance.

* * *

"You feeling OK?"

Janine's gentle enquiry came as she felt Mark stir beside her.

The sunlight was flooding into their bedroom; it was another brilliant spring day. She'd been reluctant to move too much until she was happy that he was comfortably awake.

"Stiff and sore. Still, I had a reasonable night's sleep."

'Eventually,' she thought.

The early part of the night had been disturbed, and he had tossed and turned feverishly. In the small hours, his temperature had abated, and he had finally settled into a deep and obviously refreshing sleep. Later, as the pressures of the business day developed and he forced his body to be active, the stiffness left him, although the soreness persisted all day.

* * *

Mark gathered his small staff together the Monday following the Portuguese feedback.

"The ship arrives in Port Harcourt lunch-time Friday," Janine reported. "The timing is good, although it wasn't planned. It's a local holiday and the docks won't be very busy with most people taking the day off."

"As far as the situation as a whole is concerned," Mark said, "all we need to know is that the efforts to destabilise the country are proceeding apace. The attempt on the life of the Home Affairs Minister and the deaths of the Chief Ministers of Bornu and Yobe were sadly predictable; they strongly opposed the Fundamentalists.

"The army's too thinly spread. But on the plus side, the plans of the 'Club' of loyalist civil servants and local politicians to counter just such activities by the Fundamentalists are working. There's been continuity of government in the two states despite their Chief Ministers' deaths, and with control of the media, limited as it is in some of the remoter areas, the 'Club' members have been increasingly successful in influencing the hearts and minds of the populace against the Fundamentalists.

"Chief Adeko and his southern friends," continued Mark, "haven't been quite so successful. The Nigerian News Agency in Lagos reports bodies of well-disciplined youths orchestrating demonstrations. And in Benin the youths wore distinctive armbands to identify themselves. These groups are the likely recipients of the weapons that the southerners are trying to buy."

There was concern about attacks on northerners in the south and the risk of reawakening old animosities, but Mark felt that that was more information than his staff needed. All that mattered was what would happen in the few days after the arms arrived in Nigeria. Mark concentrated on that and then ended the briefing. Defeating the Fundamentalists was always the long-term objective, but in the short term, denying the southerners the means to engineer a coup was the priority.

"You OK?"

Janine had seen a flash of pain cross Mark's face as he moved sharply. The wound caused by the crossbow bolt had been jagged and had penetrated further than they had at first realised. The healing process was slower than Mark would have wanted.

"Never better," he said with a grin.

Janine's matching grin was a delight to him. The closeness of the previous weekend had not been lost in the mounting tension and in their preparations for the arrival of the weapons in Nigeria.

* * *

'That was the last thing I expected,' Lehia Said thought to herself in her bedroom at the St .Jerome's Hotel. She was flexing her right wrist and working her fingers open and shut. An ugly bruise had spread down towards her fingers and up her arm where Janine had kicked the crossbow from her grasp.

'Knew her stuff!'

Her wrist had stiffened considerably during the night despite her efforts and although she was sure that it wasn't broken, it was certainly of little use to her when she first got up.

"I guess we're safe enough in the hotel," she muttered to herself. "The sooner we're on the flight to Damascus the better."

Lehia's trip to London had had a rather mixed success. She'd settled with the Wong organisation, but her pride, as well as her arm, was still seriously hurt over her affair with Mark Shortley. He'd made her look foolish in her own eyes, and worse, he'd escaped her vengeance!

"Another time, when he's forgotten all about me," she announced to the room around her.

Along the corridor, the telephone rang in the room of her two henchmen.

"This is Lehia. When you're packed, I want you along here."

She rang off before any reply was possible.

The man who answered, Amin, put the telephone down painfully. A trickle of blood from a cut over his eye had passed from his hand to the telephone handset.

"Well?"

The quiet dispassionate voice of Hector Xu demanded to know the content of the conversation.

"She wants us in her room. She said no more."

Amin and his compatriot were cowards when faced with superior force, as bullies often were. They had been separately ambushed on their way back from breakfast. His companion had been struck down silently by one of the four Chinese heavies, but Amin himself had attempted some modest resistance. He had ended up being rescued by Hector Xu.

"He's no use to us dead," the old man had snapped.

The two men were dragged into their hotel room and dumped on the floor. Amin at least had recovered by the time Lehia had called.

"OK, but this has to be the end of it," Hector Xu had said when Pearl had made her proposal.

By no means innocent of acts of violence in his younger days, he had grown fastidious in his old age, and had long since put such things behind him.

'This continuing feud with 'New Truth' is absurd, and a wasteful distraction.'

But Mr Xu kept his thoughts to himself. He knew his young friend had a blind spot on the subject, so he was doing his bit to bring the feud to an end as quickly and as discreetly as possible.

"She's called these two to her room," Mr Xu said, telephoning Pearl Wong.

The Wongs had secured the entire floor of the hotel with Pearl herself next to Lehia. By dint of particular generosity, they ensured that the Filipino chambermaids were unlikely to interrupt them.

"OK, use one of them to get the door open. I've got Leonard back from Moscow. This is a family matter. All you've got to do is give me time and space. Keep watch in the corridor; you will certainly know when it's over."

Hector Xu acknowledged Pearl's instructions. One of the Chinese heavies cleaned up Amin's face and propelled him along the corridor. The heavy's robust pounding on Lehia's bedroom door put her on alert.

"Who is it?"

She was suspicious. Her minions would never have made such a noise.

"Amin," he said.

She looked through the spy hole. It was certainly Amin, but the distortion of the image hid his battered face. She was puzzled; the voice was in alarm, yet he was there at the door. She supposed that he might not be alone, but there was no way she could have seen the two Chinese thugs flattened against the wall each side of the door.

She grunted. She had to do something; she couldn't just let him stand there.

Lehia quietly unlocked the interconnecting door to the next room and eased it ajar. She had checked that the room was empty the previous day and, with her own largesse to the maid, secured the keys. She wasn't to know that Hector Xu had proved to be rather more generous. On the other side of the door and out of sight, Pearl tensed ready for any action. Also out of sight, his back to the door into the corridor and his hand on the weapon in his jacket pocket, her cousin Leonard Wong waited. He no more relished his part in the enfolding drama than Hector Xu did.

"OK," said Lehia, and slowly opened her door.

Amin didn't move forward into the room. Lehia instinctively braced herself for what she sensed would happen. As one of the Chinese toughs spun around and crashed the door open, she leapt back and out of the range of both the door and the man's flailing fists. With her escape already planned, she was through into the next room almost before the first man was across the threshold.

"Lehia," said Pearl Wong quietly. "Not quite a surprise; we've been rather expecting you!"

"What?!"

Lehia's exclamation was in Arabic. Her surprise was complete.

The room was a mirror image of the one that she had just left. She quickly orientated herself as Pearl stared at her malevolently. Leonard Wong stood in the doorway, tense and intent.

"Don't interfere unless my life is at risk!"

Pearl had been very clear in her instruction.

Since his fighting skills were strictly limited, Leonard had armed himself for the ultimate intervention. Lehia observed his bulging pocket and interpreted it correctly. At the other end of the room, a glass sliding door opened onto a balcony and then to a fire escape. Pearl observed the direction of Lehia's glance and smiled. She'd left the door open a crack to make her own escape if the need arose.

'She's a professional, this one. She's in one hell of a corner, but she's still checking her options,' Pearl said to herself, impressed.

'And she's injured,' Pearl said, continuing to address herself.

She'd noticed that Lehia was carrying her right arm rather oddly.

'Some bruise!'

As her adversary moved, she saw the hideous discolouring.

'Hang on here; this isn't going to make things easier. She's cornered – that makes her dangerous enough; being injured makes her doubly so.'

As she took in the scene, Lehia noted that the room furniture had been cleared back against the walls, leaving an open space of about three metres square. It was obvious why. Pearl was waiting for her with her arms hanging loosely by her sides but not relaxed. Dressed in black, her clothes were close-fitting but wouldn't inhibit her movements. She was wearing heavy, thick-soled boots. It was a set piece for a battle.

"We've a score to settle, I think," Pearl said quietly.

"We do, yes," Lehia replied calmly in English.

It was the first time that she had ever spoken to Pearl.

"You killed my father and my brother?"

Pearl knew perfectly well that the young Arab in front of her had, but she had an emotional need for the crimes to be admitted to her face.

Lehia sneered in defiance, switching back to Arabic again suddenly. The colourful expressions were lost on Pearl.

"And you'll die like them," she said with a look of triumph that ill-befitted her seemingly dire circumstances.

Her defiance didn't surprise Pearl. She told herself for the millionth time to keep cool. The battle was as much about confidence and personality as physical prowess. Lehia was a fanatic; dying was not such a fearsome outcome to her.

Lehia back-heeled the interconnecting door closed and moved into the space that had been cleared.

'We can do without interference,' she thought.

Pearl backed away before her, watching and waiting. She had no weapon but assumed that her opponent had. She, like Mark Shortley and Janine, was well acquainted with Lehia's prowess with a knife.

It was Leonard's gasp that signalled that the weapon had been produced. The knife had a slender double-edged blade about fifteen centimetres long. Lehia was holding it in her uninjured left hand.

'Keep your arm in!' she told herself.

She'd learnt a thing or two from her encounter with Janine in Kensington Gardens. As she grasped the well-worn leather handle, Lehia kept her arm close to her body, giving Pearl less of a target.

'Watch her feet.'

Having observed the heavy boots, she correctly assumed that the Chinese girl was just as proficient at fighting with her feet as her fists.

Nothing happened. It seemed like a lifetime to the observers. As Leonard Wong watched with ever-increasing anxiety, and Hector Xu and the others in the next room strained to listen for any sound, only the gentle hiss of the air conditioning broke the otherwise complete silence.

It was Pearl who eventually made the first move.

"Come on then!" she said, gesturing towards herself with her hands.

Lehia ignored her.

'Take your time!' she said to herself in her turn, continuing to talk herself through the action.

With her feet planted wide, she just waited. She tried to meet Pearl's eyes, but Pearl was avoiding all such contact. It wasn't weakness and her opponent didn't take it as such. Pearl was aware that Lehia wasn't going to attack her with her eyes; there were more important things that needed to be kept in view.

Pearl gestured again.

The Arab girl came this time. In two quick movements she advanced about a metre, flicking the knife out and across Pearl's face and then back again. She held it high; another thing she had learnt from her episode with Janine.

Pearl shuffled. The glittering blade had passed within a few millimetres of her cheek, but she hadn't flinched. She felt pleased about that. But she had to move again. She knew her survival depended on her mobility; being hemmed in against the pile of furniture behind her was certain death. Her instinctive avoidance of the steel had carried her backwards.

Lehia was quick to notice.

'Again,' she told herself.

She took another pace forward and flashed the knife across Pearl again. Moving the slender blade in an 'S'-shape pattern, she came within a centimetre or two of her stomach. Pearl chopped down on her wrist with her right hand, catching Lehia's arm in a glancing blow.

The Arab girl sneeringly shrugged off the contact.

Pearl's response was to aim a kick with her right foot at Lehia's left knee.

Lehia saw it coming, but having moved her weight forward onto her right foot, she was unbalanced. She managed a two-footed hop backwards, but Pearl's heavy boot caught her to the side of her kneecap. The pain was intense.

And she hesitated long enough for Pearl to grasp her left wrist with both of own her hands.

The interconnecting door was pushed ajar as Hector Xu urged one of the Chinese heavies to see what was happening. He hurriedly jerked the door shut again as the grappling girls headed towards him. There was another gasp from Leonard Wong.

Lehia was propelled backwards by the pressure of Pearl forcing her arm up and back. She had no more time now to issue herself with instructions. Crashing against the hurriedly closed door, Lehia gave a strangled groan as the protruding knob was jammed into her kidneys. But she didn't relax her efforts. Seeking to protect her injured right wrist but still making use of the arm, she brought her forearm down on Pearl's face with the powerful smash used by all-in wrestlers. It had little immediate effect, although moments later a trickle of blood oozed out of Pearl's nose. She nonetheless held her ground.

They stood straining their faces within a couple of centimetres of each other. This time Pearl did look into Lehia's eyes, but all she saw were two cold blue stones devoid of any expression.

"Murdering bitch," she muttered as she gave another heave and smashed Lehia back against the door again.

As a consequence of her regular workouts, her upper-body strength was much greater than her opponent's, but Lehia's more primitive emotions meant that she could summon up huge reserves of energy, injured as she was. At no time was the grip on the knife relaxed.

The slow-motion trial of strength continued, neither girl being conscious of the banging and shouting that emanated from Lehia's former room next door.

Leonard Wong, tense enough in his present situation, heard the noises. He moved a pace forward in an agony of indecision. The words 'under arrest' filtered through the wall and into his consciousness.

"Aaah!" A grunt-turned-scream escaped from Lehia.

Her arm, forced up and round, and now down the wall against its natural movement, cracked and dislocated at the shoulder. In the final moments of the downwards pressure, Pearl released her left hand and, levering herself sideways, crashed a short, stabbing punch into the Arab girl's abdomen below her ribcage. Her expelled breath covered Pearl with a mist of foul-smelling sputum. She collapsed at Pearl's feet.

"Hold it!"

The interconnecting door had been splintered from its mounting and a large policeman burst into the room. Pearl, on one leg in preparation for a last vicious kick to Lehia's head behind the jaw, froze, hobbled to regain her balance and took a pace back.

* * *

Inspector Wilke's plan was being enacted. After she had left Mark and Janine following the attack in the park, she had set the final arrangements in place to capture Lehia Said at the St Jerome's Hotel. But when she arrived there, she discovered a second action in play.

"Not sure what it might mean," the Hotel Manager said, "but all the remaining rooms on floor you're interested in have been taken in the name of a Chinese company. As far as we can tell, only two of the rooms have actually been used. And there's a bunch of unsavoury Chinese people up there now."

The Mmanager and other staff gave the best descriptions that they could of the various Chinese people who had been sighted.

"Young Chinese woman of commanding appearance out of character with her clothing, you say, and an elderly Chinese man?" the inspector queried.

She hurriedly checked with Mark Shortley and her own colleagues. The arrest of Lehia Said was delayed whilst additional officers were summoned. When they arrived, the police action resumed in the form of invading the room ostensibly occupied by Lehia Said's two henchmen.

"So what's going on?"

The police had discovered an ill-assorted little group in the room. It was away from the action. It was taken in the name of Amin Abdullah, although the passport of that individual had another name. The inspector got no answer from the Chinese thugs.

"There's something definitely going on here," she muttered to herself in the absence of any response. "The Arabs are more at ease than the Chinese."

But the inspector didn't have time to wait and find out. The two Chinese heavies were arrested, but the two Arabs were only detained until they could be deported. The police moved on, checking the Hotel Manager's room manifest.

"The Chinese woman's taken the room next to Said," reported the inspector's accompanying sergeant.

"We'll go for the Said woman's room first."

Entry was simple; the door was open. The two Chinese minders there put up a more spirited resistance than their colleagues guarding the Arabs had done. Of Hector Xu there was no sign.

"The balcony!" snapped the inspector.

Two of her armed officers hurriedly checked the balcony. One returned; the other moved to mount guard on the fire escape.

"Miss Wong, where is Miss Wong?"

She pointed at the next room as she made the demand of the Chinese minders.

The two men shrugged; it was answer enough. The sergeant burst through the door just as Pearl had achieved ascendancy in her battle with Lehia.

* * *

"Hold it," said the sergeant again.

"What the hell? This is a private party. We don't need the police."

307

In her excitement Pearl had failed to appreciate what was happening. She instantly assumed that the police had come to break up the fight at the instigation of the hotel, or some other guest.

"Pearl," said Leonard Wong tentatively, conscious of his cousin's short fuse. "Pearl, take it easy!"

She had angrily advanced on the small party of police. Leonard's warning and the forbidding figure of the inspector stopped her short.

"Ah, so what's the problem... um... Inspector?"

All the attention was on Pearl momentarily. Inspector Wilke and two other officers had followed the sergeant into the room. One of them had moved to search Leonard; the other, a WPC, stood beside Pearl, ready to take action if need be. This officer was a metre or so from Lehia, who still lay crumpled on the floor, dazed, silent, but nonetheless watchful. Her pain suppressed by a greater need, she tried to bring her shattered mind to bear on this new turn of events.

It only took seconds for the cameo to form around Lehia. And it only took split-seconds for her survival instincts to then take over and formulate her next action.

"Watch out!" exclaimed the startled inspector. "Watch out."

As she raised the alarm, the inspector saw Lehia Said propel herself from her prone position towards the balcony door, becoming upright and running in one movement. The WPC moved to intercept her but collided with Pearl. The suspicion that she had deliberately obstructed the policewoman persisted for some time after the incident was over.

"Stop her!"

The police officers were all telling each other what to do. Lehia, meanwhile, her knife now painfully held in her right hand, and her left arm hanging awkwardly useless, scurried across the room and out of the glass door. As she left, she turned and projected the knife underarm at Pearl. Her aim was not good. The weapon lodged harmlessly in the surprised WPC's body -armour.

Outside, the action was sharp and brief. The armed officer on the fire escape called on Lehia to halt. She ran straight at him, forcing him aside. Recovering, he called her to halt a second time. A single shot ended Lehia's flight.

* * *

It took the inspector another half an hour to sort out the formalities. The Chinese thugs were charged with assault on the two Lebanese terrorists. Leonard Wong was charged with possession of an illegal firearm. Pearl posed a more difficult problem.

"She's certainly guilty of assault," the inspector reported to her superiors, "but beyond that she has committed no other crime. And beating up Lehia Said's wasn't so big a deal. It was the police who shot her resisting arrest."

Eventually, after lengthy consultation, the inspector was instructed to release Pearl pending further questioning the next day.

The death of Lehia Said when reported occasioned little regret. Having been shot in the leg by the officer on the fire escape, she had flung herself from the building and died later of severe head injuries.

* * *

Pearl rendezvoused with Hector Xu, Leonard Wong and Marcus Ho at her country house near Canterbury. The trip in the car had given her time to think, and she arrived at her home composed and ready to move on.

"It's over," she told her henchmen, "she's dead; we're revenged, even if we didn't kill her ourselves."

Mr Xu was relieved both that Pearl had not compromised the Wong organisation by committing such a blatant murder and that the spirit of his old friend could now rest in peace.

"Update?" Pearl then demanded.

"The ship arrives in Port Harcourt around lunch-time Friday."

"OK, Hector. What more is there to be done?" said Pearl.

"We have just to hand over the arms. Our friend Falinde is demanding we formally hand over the containers before they'll pay the rest of the money. Heaven knows why. That means one of us going to Port Harcourt."

Knowing something of the Nigerian climate, Mr Xu was not himself very keen to undertake the duty.

Not so Pearl; but Hector Xu argued that she shouldn't get involved.

"It will give entirely the wrong impression if the head of the organisation performs such a chore," he said.

He had never been in favour of Jason Wong going to Russia originally to set up the whole deal.

Pearl never got to responding. The bomb that ripped the house apart was said by the anti-terrorist squad to have been big enough to have destroyed a whole row of such premises. The explosion was caused by a large packet of elderly Semtex material, whose origins the police declined to publicly speculate about. In addition to the Wong organisation's principals, seven other servants and bodyguards were killed.

* * *

"Oh my God!" exclaimed Janine.

Alerted by the tone of her voice, Mark hurriedly joined her and read the dismal stories of Lehia's suicide and the death and the destruction of Pearl and her establishment on Janine's media monitoring system.

"The two events have got to be related. The bombing's got all the hallmarks of Lehia Said and her group."

Janine agreed with him.

"'New Truth' was almost destroyed by the Wongs last year, now the Wongs have largely been destroyed by 'New Truth,'" remarked Mark.

There was also another item of news that had attracted Janine's attention; she pointed it out to Mark.

"An Iranian cleric, hell, that's provocative!" he said.

"The Middle East News Agency reports the proposed trip to Kaduna of one of the old- time radical and expansionist Iranian religious leaders."

Planetcover was first with the news again.

"The visit is clearly intended to put the Nigerian Government under pressure. To agree would anger the southern part of the country and alienate the northern traditionalists. To refuse, which was what the Iranian extremists hoped for, would give the Fundamentalists and their followers an excuse for massive protests."

Needless to say, the media moguls had no advice to offer on which choice the Nigerians should make.

"What was that you said about the pot really boiling, Janine?"

Janine would have been the first to admit that her impending return to her country of origin, civil unrest apart, was causing her much apprehension. And the visit was only a few short days away.

Mark in his turn, although he didn't fully understand the intensity of the antagonism between 'New Truth' and the Wongs that had so violently erupted, was glad such a violent confrontation was no longer interwoven into what he saw as the main action. And it was the main action that he, like Janine, but in a rather different way, was equally apprehensive about.

FORTY-ONE

The following day, Janine was more like her normal exuberant self, but her concerns about her visit to Nigeria stayed just below the surface.

'I can do this!' she had told herself for the umpteenth time when she had gone to bed.

Now, as departure approached, she was still sure that she could, but the moment of truth, the precise moment when she stepped off the aircraft, still had to be confronted.

"Good morning, on Tuesday sixteenth April, and the morning that Nigeria teeters once more on the brink of disaster."

Janine, ever cheerful herself in the morning, loved the bright and breezy opening to the current affairs and music programme. Mark hated the all-pervading bonhomie. However, startled from sleep at the unusually late hour of eight o'clock, he was, for once, instantly conscious when he heard the opening headline. If it was intended to grab the listener's attention, it certainly grabbed his.

"Hey, Janine!"

Mark called her back from the bathroom.

"Demonstrations, which in many cases turned into riots, took

312

place in dozens of towns and cities across Nigeria yesterday when the proposed visit of the Ayatollah Rafhangeh to Kaduna and other Islamic centres in the north of the country was rejected."

Following the introduction, the BBC's Africa correspondent, already in Abuja reporting for BBC/CNN *Planetcover*, took up the story.

"The Moslem Fundamentalist's campaign to convert Black Africa to its cause took a step forward yesterday. As was widely expected, the Federal Nigerian Government refused to accept the Ayatollah Rafhangeh's visit on the grounds that it would cause civil unrest. This was seen as playing into the hands of the Fundamentalists. On national television, the Federal Minister for Home Affairs, Mr Aminu, who is known to be an opponent of the Fundamentalists, justified the exclusion by stating that the Nigerian Security Service had uncovered plans to use the visit, and the speeches that the Iranian cleric would make, to cloak attacks on the property of prominent traditionalists and to stir up the poorer classes in northern Nigeria to demand the universal introduction of Sharia law."

The correspondent then went on to say that the decision to refuse the Ayatollah entry had been a calculated risk.

"The history of these present troubles," he continued, "is markedly different from the previous political upheavals in the country. The unrest has been largely confined to the north, although there is evidence that this is changing. At the same time the upheavals have been founded on clear external interference. The Fundamentalist zeal has long since spread from its original core power bases in Afghanistan/Pakistan, and now Somalia, and is infecting the whole of the Moslem world. The conversion of Nigeria to their cause would be a coup of massive proportions."

Although he found the rather pompous BBC-speak irritating, Mark was listening for any nuances that were likely to affect his plans for the next few days.

313

"Two things have emerged as the Fundamentalist campaign has progressed. Firstly, the traditions of northern Nigeria and the unique laissez-faire approach of the British in the colonial past have led to forms of democratic government that have proved to be remarkably robust. Despite strong tribal overtones and the see-sawing between military and civilian rule, the basic institutions on which the government of the Federation is founded have been very resistant to the Fundamentalist's efforts to create chaos. The northern Nigerian traditionalists are proving able to draw a clear line between politics and religion in a way that the leaders of many other Islamic countries have not been able to do. This has allowed them to counter the Fundamentalist ideology with practical politics."

"Come on, for Christ's sake," said Janine. "Never mind the theorising; what's happening?"

Mark chuckled; Janine had crept back into bed beside him.

"But secondly, whilst there has so far only been sporadic reaction to what is happening in the north from southern politicians, there is plenty of evidence that some of the factions in the south are preparing to take advantage of the situation. That would turn the clock back decades and expose both the divisions between north and south, and within the south."

There followed the usual illustrations from Nigerian history.

"As an indicator of the likely trend for the future, the only disturbance which took place yesterday not in the north or in the middle belt of the country, was in Port Harcourt, one of the major cities of the south."

Both Janine and Mark focused on this. Port Harcourt, the centre of the oil industry, was probably as a result the most cosmopolitan city in Nigeria. The racial, tribal and political mix there was more complex than anywhere else in the land.

"Two demonstrations took place on Monday afternoon. The largest and initially the best behaved was at the football ground and was ostensibly a straightforward display of support for the Federal Government in their decision to exclude the Ayatollah."

Chief Adeko had addressed the crowd, his message had been camouflaged, but the meaning was clear enough.

"We'll support the Federal Government, but there's a price, so look out…" said Janine as she resumed to her preparations for her business day.

Delightful as it was luxuriating in bed with Mark, life had to go on.

When she got downstairs into her office, she immediately interrogated her new Nigerian media monitoring system.

"So our friend the Chief didn't have it all his own way," she said as she began to digest what had happened. "Supposedly a peaceful rally, my arse. Bit stupid of the police to let the other lot near the football stadium. Must have known they were supporting the Ayatollah's visit. Civil Rights issue… that's a bit of a novelty. Got the rabble rousers going, though. It doesn't take long to forget what you're protesting about when the bricks start flying. Smash up a few shops, loot a few more. And you can bet your bottom dollar that old shit Adeko didn't do a whole lot to stop anything!"

Once looting started, the police intervened on a large scale. The Nigerian riot police were not noted for their subtlety of approach, but they soon found controlling the crowd beyond them. The Rivers State Police Commissioner was forced to call on the support of the army. By dusk, things showed every sign of getting completely out of control; but as the evening progressed, the violence seemed to have peaked.

"The only troops in Port Harcourt are from an Infantry Brigade recruited entirely in the north." Janine reverted to a transcript of the BBC's Africa correspondent's report. "It's still quite common for the army to station units around the country with tribal origins different from the local people. By firing over the demonstrators' heads, and then into the body of the crowd, the army and police combined finally restored order. The death toll was not high, as only a proportion of the individual soldiers were firing live rounds. The atmosphere was, nonetheless, very tense throughout the night. But by morning it was calmer, and the police patrols were reporting signs of things getting back to normal."

"And we're going there on Thursday!"

Janine's apprehensions broke surface again. Mark was less worried. His experience told him that these things blew up and died down very quickly, although he recognised that Chief Adeko might not want that to happen in this case. But with action in prospect, Mark's excitement and adrenalin levels were triggering, and he was entirely confident that they could cope with the problems.

"Don't worry," he said, putting his arms around Janine from behind and giving her a gentle bear hug. "We'll be OK. And we'll have Victoria, and Okeke and his lot behind us."

She wasn't especially comforted by the thoughts of help from Victoria.

'Still,' thought the ever-practical Janine, 'I can't worry about it now; there's far too much to do before Thursday.'

FORTY-TWO

With Thursday approaching fast and the action shifting to Nigeria itself, the various parties involved were all showing signs of anxiety. Whilst Fid Okeke sat back with a mixture of African fatalism and practical common sense, knowing that having engaged Mark Shortley he had to trust him, his principal field agent, for her own reasons, was growing increasingly and uncharacteristically nervous. Experience told Victoria Akinbode that once the action started she would in her turn switch into action mode, but as ever, with such a complex and stressful situation, it was the waiting that was so difficult. With even more experience, Mark recognised the signs in Victoria and sought to mitigate her stress by increasing the communication that he and Janine had with her.

"Mark, it's good to hear from you!"

It was only a few days since they had last spoken, but Victoria made it sound like a conversation between long- lost relatives.

"How's it going?"

"Great, we have a final briefing tomorrow. Mr Okeke has set up a meeting with a couple of Ministers. We'll need some high-level support if anything goes wrong."

"Victoria, nothing will go wrong!"

'I'd better be right,' he thought. 'This last stage is the most difficult to predict, and there's you, my dear!'

Janine's wariness over Victoria had proved insidiously corrosive to Mark's mind, and her present signs of nerves only enhanced his concerns.

'You might have trusted me, but I've only partially shared my plans with you.'

But his niggles over Victoria's loyalties weren't why he had called.

"You heard about Pearl Wong?" he said aloud.

"I heard she was killed when her house was bombed. What about this Arab terrorist?"

"Lehia Said, an operative of the 'New Truth' group."

Victoria knew who she was.

"It seems they, Pearl and Lehia, had a meeting to settle the feud that's been running between them since some spat in Beirut last year. They were having one hell of a scrap when the police interrupted them. When she couldn't get away, Lehia threw herself off the building. Died later."

"So did these terrorists really have anything to do with all this, Mark?"

"I'm not sure they actually did," he responded. "We made all sorts of assumptions about Lehia Said and her group; I guess it was much simpler. I reckon they were just out for revenge against the Wongs."

Having no idea that Lehia was actually working for Alhaji Sullag specifically to cause mayhem amongst the Nigerian Security Services, Mark could only piece part of the story together.

'I doubt we'll ever know,' he thought.

Victoria wasn't interested in Lehia. If the Arab woman had killed Silvanus Akinbode, then she was pleased that justice of a sort had been done. But that was all she cared.

"I guess Pearl's death will be the end of the arms shipments," she said; but she hadn't counted on the resilience of the Wong empire.

"I wouldn't bank on it. Pearl's got cousins, and her old uncles still have power in the organisation," replied Mark. "Nothing's changed, as far as I'm concerned. And we'll worry about the next shipment when we've dealt with this one."

There had been a very brief but chaotic pause in the affairs of the Wong organisation, but as Mark had anticipated, it didn't take the surviving members long to get things back on track. Even the despised Messrs Falinde and Oje would be contacted again before the current arms shipment had even been landed in Port Harcourt.

* * *

"We should get started."

The briefing took place in the offices of the Nigerian Security Service. It was one of the older buildings in the Nigerian capital, not that any building was ancient in Abuja. The more traditional government buildings left over from the colonial era, with large louvered windows and soul-less whitewashed walls, had fortunately not been repeated in the new Nigerian capital. This one at least had some pretence of architectural merit. The room chosen for the meeting was spacious and bright, and morning sunlight flooded in through the windows down one side. The constant low moan of the air conditioning provided an almost soothing background noise.

Mr Kunle Aminu, the Minister for Home Affairs, was the Minister responsible for the security services, and the person to whom Fid Okeke was ultimately responsible. He introduced Okeke to the other minister present.

"Mr Ojoto, very pleased to meet you."

Emesi Ojoto was the Justice Minister.

"Mr Aminu, Mr Ojoto, this is…" Fid Okeke didn't actually name his two colleagues to the Ministers. "They have been responsible for penetrating the southern business consortium and the northern Trades Unions. The Trades Unions haven't supported the Fundamentalists, but they have many contacts and have proved much easier to infiltrate than any of the religious groups. We've got a good handle on grassroot feelings in the north from them."

The two Ministers present were both ardent Nigerian nationalists and in the present situation they saw eye -to -eye on most of the issues confronting the government. Fid Okeke had great confidence in both of them.

In anticipation of their visit to Nigeria, Janine had briefed herself and Mark on most of the key Nigerian figures. Messrs Aminu and Ojoto figured very strongly in this briefing.

"This guy Aminu is a key player," she'd reported. "An austere, devote Moslem, but a bit of an odd one for a northerner. Youngest of three sons of a Fulani schoolteacher, he escaped to London and worked his way through night school and the LSE. Good political science degree. He sees Nigeria from a totally different standpoint from most northerners; thinks much more like many southern politicians by all accounts. As a young idealist and activist, he fell foul of General Abacha just before he died, but eventually became a Minister when civilian government was successfully re-established under President Obasanjo. He has proved to be both a decisive and an efficient administrator of unimpeachable integrity."

She continued.

"Mr Ojoto, the Justice Minister, is a southern Christian. He's a lawyer from a family of lawyers. He knew Aminu in Britain when he worked for a firm of solicitors in Brixton. He entered politics more traditionally via the Rivers State Government. It wasn't an easy trip, apparently. He's an Ibibio, one of the smaller southern tribes. His talents were, however, recognised by the present civilian government. The northerners opposed his appointment as Minister for Justice at first, but now he's universally well respected."

Emerging from the cold words of Janine's report, these were the two men who were responsible for preserving the integrity of Nigeria in the present crisis. And they were the two men that Fid Okeke was about to brief on all that the security service knew about what was going on behind the more public displays of violence and political intrigue.

"Mrs Akinbode?" asked Mr Aminu; he had been expecting Victoria to be at the meeting.

"She'll be here later. There are things to discuss which make her presence inappropriate."

"Very well, proceed."

Okeke did so. Most of what he said was about the penetration of the public service and government itself by Fundamentalist sympathisers.

"Alhaji Sullag," said Aminu.

Both of the Ministers were shocked. Fid Okeke was prepared. He presented the evidence accumulated by Professor Jordane and his Kuwaiti research student for Mike Shortley. The shock remained as Okeke continued and as the scale of the infiltration unfolded.

"We must act," said Mr Ojoto, only too aware that the timescale was shortening as the extent of the unrest in the country increased.

They discussed what needed to be done. Arrests were proposed. The Minister for Justice undertook to prepare the necessary authorisations. Neither Minister was anxious to go to the Nigerian Parliament yet to seek emergency powers; the outcome was likely to be too uncertain.

"Before we move on," said Fid Okeke, "I have to advise you that even the security service is not immune to this canker."

"There are Fundamentalists in your organisation?" said Aminu.

"We believe so, and supporters of the southern consortium," Okeke said.

He named names. Messrs Falinde and Oje were the principal defectors to the southern consortium. Okeke also identified the Fundamentalist supporter.

"So what, Mr Okeke, do you propose to do about these traitors?" demanded the Justice Minister.

Both Ministers were surprised by the admission. The ethos of the Security Service was founded on British rather than Nigerian traditions, and had in the past withstood the pressures of tribe and religion.

"I would like to do nothing," said Fid Okeke. "That is, until the arms shipment that Mrs Akinbode will talk to you about is delivered and seized."

He explained why.

"OK, let's hear about these arms shipments then," ordered Aminu.

Victoria was called from a distant part of the building. After the necessary introductions, she gave her presentation.

"So this group of businessmen from across the whole of the south has formed this consortium to import arms. And this group is led by Chief Adeko?"

Okeke confirmed his Minister's understanding.

"One shipment was intercepted by the British, you say," said Mr Ojoto, "but the second has been let through in order to expose the whole undertaking?"

"That's the idea," said Victoria.

"And," interjected Mr Aminu, "the arms are for the youth group that Adeko has formed to help protect the south if the Fundamentalists succeed and trouble spills over?"

"That is what we're supposed to believe," said Fid Okeke, "but there's evidence that their purpose is more sinister. We believe that they plan to exploit the instability in the north to increase the south's influence in the Federal Government; to the extent of dominating it."

It was something of an understatement – it was a coup. Chief Adeko was out to take over the Federal Government, but Okeke didn't want to be too alarmist.

"But it's even more serious than that," Okeke went on. "We believe the consortium's plans are known to the Fundamentalists and they found out through leakage in the security service."

Both Ministers looked from Fid Okeke to Victoria and back again, clearly trying to digest this information against the background previously given by Okeke before Victoria had joined them.

"Mrs Akinbode, two things. When is this next arms shipment due and why did we recruit this man Shortley?" asked Aminu.

"The shipment is due on Friday. As for Shortley, it's a matter of colour. We would simply have been too conspicuous if we had tried to operate covertly in the UK. Mr Shortley doesn't have the same problem! And, as an ex-SAS officer, he has close contacts with the British security services and is well regarded by them. That has allowed us to use official resources unofficially."

"But why not just ask the British service directly?" asked Mr Ojoto, who was less sensitive than his colleague about depending on their former colonial masters.

It was Okeke who answered.

"The High Commissioner is a relative of Alhaji Sullag and the information would have leaked back immediately."

They were interrupted by a heavy pounding on the meeting-room door; the Justice Minister was called out.

In his absence, there was no conversation between the remaining three people.

"Mrs Akinbode?" the Minister said when he returned in a clear signal that Victoria should leave.

"Alhaji Sullag has demanded that Chief Adeko be arrested for inciting a riot in Port Harcourt."

"Showing his colours?" said Aminu thoughtfully.

"I believe we should leave the matter to the Rivers State authorities," continued Ojoto, well aware that that would not satisfy the Alhaji.

It didn't. But it hardly mattered. The response from Chief Adeko's followers was openly hostile, the demand having been carefully leaked to the media in Abuja as well as in Lagos and Port Harcourt. Groups of the Chief's supporters were immediately out parading in the streets of Port Harcourt, protesting against what they claimed was interference into the affairs of a southern state. This was something of a turnaround since only hours earlier they had been demonstrating in favour of the Federal Government.

All of this public demonstration of the rapidly changing facets of Nigerian politics was noted, digested and largely found unintelligible back in London as preparations for their journey were completed by Mark and Janine.

"The police took no action at first, according to Nigerian News Agency," Janine said as she reported this latest flare-up. "When the groups began to coalesce, however, they sought to disperse them. Running battles developed and once again the troops had to be called out," she continued, reading from her computer screen. "Since the demonstrations were genuinely spontaneous and disorganised, the protesters allowed themselves to be dispersed into the area around the old hospital. The police didn't pursue them into the nearby residential areas."

That part of Port Harcourt was a chessboard of streets and blocks of houses, an impossible area for the police to control without far more resources than they and the army had. By late on the Wednesday evening, all was quiet on the streets, but behind closed doors, preparations were being made for a more concerted protest the next day and on the Friday.

* * *

"Welcome to Nigeria, Janine and Mark, then!"

"Indeed!" agreed Fid Okeke.

Whether Mark or Janine would have felt welcome was debatable. Janine's feelings were a little more basic: apprehension in the face of an unknown that she somehow felt shouldn't have been unknown.

Victoria Akinbode and Okeke were travelling to Port Harcourt on the lunch-time flight the day after the briefing. Victoria had been reading about the previous evening's flare-up in the *Eastern Nigerian Post*.

"The plane's full. It must be the local holiday. Lot of women and children, though, Ibo speaking." Fid Okeke was talking more to himself than to Victoria.

The composition of the passenger load looked more like an evacuation to him than people tripping south to see family.

Victoria didn't respond. Her relations with Okeke were at an all-time low. She was too headstrong to keep her thoughts to herself. Her challenge to his involvement in the action that was about to unfold when he had reviewed her plans with her after the meeting with the Ministers was almost an insubordination too far. But Mr Okeke knew that things couldn't go ahead without Victoria.

"This is field work," she had said. "It's action; people get hurt."

Okeke's response was irritated.

"Mrs Akinbode, it's hardly for you to decide who should run this operation. While the responsibility rests with me, I'll exercise it however I see fit!"

Having served in the Nigerian Army and with the United Nations in some pretty demanding circumstances, Fid Okeke was inclined to resent the imputations of this brash young woman's remarks.

"It's my patch," she responded, not hearing the ice in his voice. "I need maximum freedom to make my own decisions when the action starts on the Friday. I can't keep deferring to higher authority; it's inefficient. You've got to trust me. With Shortley and the woman to look out for, the last thing I need is to be told which bit of the book to go by."

"Enough!"

For once, Victoria had the wisdom to hold her peace.

* * *

Victoria's little spat with her superior had taken place later on the Wednesday. On the flight to Port Harcourt the next day, relations were business-like but barely civil. They had time to fill before Mark and Janine's flight from Lagos arrived, but even an hour in the airport bar failed to mellow their attitude to each other.

Half an hour later still, the flight from Lagos finally arrived. Mark was the only white man on board.

"Over there!"

Mark spotted Mr Okeke long before Janine did. Hooked tightly onto his arm and startled again by the rowdy scrum of arriving passengers and the enthusiastic welcoming of friends and relatives, Janine allowed herself to be steered towards their own welcoming party. The chaos and loud intensity of their arrival at Lagos, and the unfamiliar smells of the atmosphere, terminal building and surging masses of people, had disconcerted Janine, and Mark had had to pilot her through it carefully. And the gamut of sounds, smells and sensations reawakened old images. To Janine's relief, the image that endured was that of an anxious Moslem sergeant and not that of his lecherous trooper.

In Port Harcourt, things were on a smaller scale to Lagos, and the sight of Fid Okeke and even the rather surly-looking Victoria soon dispelled any feelings of anxiety after the initial impact. Their progress through the arrival processes, unlike at Lagos, was quick and efficient. They had arrived.

'She's tense,' thought Okeke as they all exchanged affectionate embraces. 'Hardly surprising, I guess.'

Janine had been tense ever since they had headed for Gatwick. But with so much that was new and different around her to experience, first in Lagos and now Port Harcourt, her curiosity was increasingly excited and her natural exuberance began to prevail. Much to Mark's relief, the grin reappeared in Port Harcourt and it wasn't just in greeting of her cousin, Fid Okeke.

"I need to disappear for a while," she had said to Mark the previous day in London. "I've loaded the laptop and sorted access back here; all I'll need is a mobile connection."

The expanding Nigerian economy had led to the installation of a comprehensive nationwide communications system; the reliability of the power supplies was world- class. Janine would have no problems.

* * *

"Wow, Janine, that's wonderful!"

Mark's reception when she had returned from her London excursion was enthusiastic and vocal.

Janine had been to visit her ethnic hairstylist. Conscious that her skills were rather limited, she had again chosen a hairstyle that was fashionable but simple to maintain. And as far as she could establish, it was fashionable in Nigeria rather than fashionable in London, and this was what she was seeking for. As with the Seychelles trip, her hair had been pulled into a series of plaits and the partings formed into patterns. The patterns were complicated and geometric. The interwoven plaits were enhanced with coloured ribbons and beads. It was going to be uncomfortable to sleep on, but it was stunning to look at. With her hair pulled back from her face again, her true beauty was on display. Mark had been enchanted.

And so they had set off for what Janine steadfastly refused to think of as a homecoming.

FORTY-THREE

"This is Inspector Okezie."

Mark later learnt that the inspector had been instrumental in their unexpectedly speedy progress through the formalities at Port Harcourt Airport.

The presence of the inspector also speeded up the completion of formalities at the hotel.

"Victoria won't be with us for dinner this evening," Fid Okeke quickly said once the two visitors were checked in. It was clearly an agreed absence. "She has arrangements to see to."

Much hung on the success of the action the next day, for Victoria as well as the rest of the party, and she was as keen as her superior to see that the plans that had been laid were properly in place.

"Shall we meet for dinner around seven o'clock? The inspector will join us."

Fid Okeke laid out the arrangements for the evening.

"Great, how about we meet in the bar at six-thirty? You too, Victoria, if you can make it?" said Mark.

"OK," said Fid and Victoria together.

The inspector promised to try and get there.

"Don't forget, it's jacket and tie," added Mr Okeke as they dispersed.

Mark and Janine had been warned about the dress code.

* * *

On the way to their accommodation Mark was thoughtful.

'The tension between Victoria and Okeke isn't good news. The required action is about close co-operation and careful timing. Still, I guess failure for Fid Okeke means the end of a promising career; it would be just another posting for Victoria. Easy to see how they might grate.'

Mark and Janine had been given separate rooms. Mark had barely unpacked his few belongings when there was a gentle tapping on the door. But it wasn't Janine; they'd agreed a coded knock. He prepared for action in case it was Victoria. It was Fid Okeke.

"Sorry to trouble you," he said, "but there's something you need to know, and it would be better if you were told before we gathered again."

Mr Okeke sat down in the indicated chair; he was clearly uncomfortable.

"So what's bothering you?" Mark asked.

His Nigerian colleague explained. The tale wasn't long in the telling, but Mr Okeke seemed relieved to have shared his burden. Mark agreed, with some reluctance, to keep the information strictly to himself, but the revelation left him significantly less confident about the outcome of the next day.

* * *

The inspector, by then in a civilian suit, only managed to join them as they sat down to dinner.

The bar was even colder than the bedrooms. Furnished as a typical British pub, customers collected their own drinks across the counter. Since he was more familiar with the style than the others, Mark purchased the first round.

Conversation was minimal before their attention was attracted to the inevitable television suspended behind the bar counter.

The news item was brief, since it had to be sandwiched between the two halves of the football match between Nigeria and Zambia, but it caused a murmur of surprise amongst those who bothered to take any notice of it.

"Two Government Ministers, Alhaji Mahomet Sullag and Alhaji Ibrahim Akilu, and twenty-seven civil servants, all northerners," the newscaster said, "have been arrested in Abuja on charges of corruption, specifically of using government funds and resources for political purposes."

The Minster for Home Affairs and the Justice Minister then appeared briefly to issue a statement.

"You knew about that," said Victoria to her superior accusingly.

"Do we know when the ship is actually due to dock?" asked Janine quickly, seeking to defuse any awkward situation before it developed.

"It's off Bonny now; it'll dock in the morning," said Victoria, distracted as Janine had intended.

Large vessels often waited at the coast in the deep water off Bonny, the oil terminal on the edge of the Niger delta. Navigating the complex of channels through the mangrove swamps in the dark was a tricky business, and the vessel's timetable was calculated to avoid that. Victoria gave the information as if her previous outburst hadn't happened.

* * *

After Inspector Okezie had joined them and Victoria had departed, the details of the action for the next day were outlined by Fid Okeke over the dinner table. The movement of the arms from the docks and their delivery to the agreed handover point were explained, as far as they were known. Locating the warehouse handover point had been the most difficult part of the exercise so far.

"And Mr Shortley will control the communications from here?" said the inspector.

"Until the trucks get to the warehouse," Mark responded. "I'll join you there when it is safe to do so."

Fid Okeke knew that the local police had to be in charge and was grateful that the Rivers State authorities were allowing him to take control from the background.

'Good of him to acknowledge my role,' thought Mark, 'considering the politics.'

A second briefing after dinner went over the same ground in more depth but also included feedback from the police and military about their dispositions. Inspector Okezie was joined by two other senior officers, both of whom were late as a result of another outbreak of rioting. An army major and two lieutenants came with them.

"The demo wasn't planned. It was just a bunch of youths protesting about Federal Government interference. It all fizzled out when the news broke that Sullag had been arrested."

The information was offered by one of the newly arrived officers as an explanation of their lateness rather than as a contribution to the meeting.

"The Commissioner has agreed to another march tomorrow," said Inspector Okezie.

This, however, was a contribution to the meeting; the route to be taken by the container-lorries was likely to have to be changed to avoid their getting mixed up with the marchers.

"It's supposed to be a rally in support of Chief Adeko."

"But you think it's a diversion?" asked Mark.

"It would make sense from the Chief's point of view. Draw

off as many police and troops as possible. Make it easier to distribute the arms undetected," replied the inspector.

Fid Okeke took the opportunity of the inspector's mention of the troops to introduce the major and his colleagues.

"Major Oyelade is not from the Port Harcourt garrison. The soldiers involved in tomorrow's operation will be from Warri."

Warri was the home of the Nigerian Special Forces Regiment, although at no time was this fact mentioned.

At midnight everybody dispersed. Everything was in place, nothing more could be done to improve the chances of success.

* * *

"Let's go for a walk outside," suggested Janine.

"OK," said Mark, "but we hadn't better be too late."

"I know, I know, we've had a long day."

She laughed. It was pure delight. She was alone with Mark at last and she just wanted to share some new experience of Nigeria with him. She didn't care what it was, so long as it was unique to them only.

"Come on!"

She took hold of his hand and dragged him to the front door of the hotel. She was only half ready for the shock.

"Wow," she gasped as they emerged from the revolving door straight into the oppressive humidity and heat of the atmosphere outside.

Mark peeled his coat off as the heat struck him and the sweat started down his back almost as urgently as it did down Janine's. The vicious cold of the hotel had conned their bodies, and instant sweating was the reaction.

"I don't think I'll ever get this smell out of my brain," Janine said.

"You will."

As they walked away from the hotel and out of its immediate patch of light, the smells and sounds changed. Janine had a sense of moving away from civilisation, but she felt no fear in the situation, just a pleasurable excitement.

"Let's go over there."

The flickering lights of fires in the yards of the houses opposite attracted Janine's attention. She walked towards them. Mark held her back, uncertain where she was headed, and even more uncertain of their welcome if they intruded.

"Look... there!" Mark said by way of distracting Janine.

The little points of light from the fireflies jerked erratically about. Janine watched enthralled, both with the light display and with Mark's careful explanation of all the wonders of the night around them. They meandered along the hotel approach road.

"We'd better turn back."

Janine was reluctant to go. The night around them was magic and she didn't want to be reminded that they were there to do a job. She was deeply aware that all of her anxieties about returning to Nigeria had evaporated. She was bubbling with excitement inside and wanted to savour every minute of it that she could.

FORTY-FOUR

Janine was showered and dressed by seven o'clock. An hour later she crept along the corridor and tapped out the recognition code on Mark's door.

"Hell-fire!" Janine's foray onto her balcony during her idle time had been short and salutary. "I thought yesterday was bad enough... but this!"

She felt that she could almost touch the brooding dark clouds. The rainfall was warm, steady, and persistent. The heavy vapour-laden atmosphere was oppressive.

"Some climate!" she said to Mark as they headed for breakfast.

Mark's SAS experiences told him that dosed up with protective drugs as they were, they would come to little harm.

"Take your time at things and drink lots of water. You're going to sweat whatever you do. Make haste slowly like the Africans," said Mark.

With the temperature in the mid-thirties Celsius, one hundred per cent humidity, and no air conditioning where her day's action was going to be, it was sound advice.

* * *

"Good morning," Fid Okeke joined them.

Okeke's greeting was friendly enough, but his demeanour was more reserved than on the previous night. His thoughts were very much on Mark and his role.

'It's all down to this guy Shortley now. If he's misread the situation, a hell of a lot of arms and ammunition are going to fall into the hands of some seriously dangerous people.'

As he sat down, he looked thoughtfully at the fit, lean and seemingly composed man opposite him, and then at his newfound cousin.

'Well, it's too late now. Whatever's going to happen is going to happen.'

"Victoria left early to make some final checks. She'll be back to pick us up," he said aloud.

And as the time for action approached, Mark felt the surge of excitement and anticipation that was so familiar to him from his SAS days. He thought of himself as quietly efficient, but always tenacious, always seeing the job through. And now was the time to demonstrate these characteristics.

"I've talked to Abuja," Okeke went on. "The police in eight northern states have arrested and expelled about two hundred people of Middle Eastern origin. Two more Federal Ministers, albeit junior ones, have also been arrested, plus a few civil servants. It's been a busy night."

"There was a fracas at the barracks at Benin," Mark said. "Officers arrested in Ibadan; is something beginning to develop in the south?"

"No, no. Northern officers, that's all. Two were relatives of Alhaji Akilu; the others were known to have been in touch with the Fundamentalists. Small beer, I think you would call it. We're only talking eight people."

"One of the Benin officers comes from the brigade in Port Harcourt," said Mark.

"Yes. That's what makes us distrust them; and why

we've replaced them with the Warri troops. We know they're reliable."

"Beats me, Fid, how you can tell how anybody's reliable in all of this lot," said Janine, entering the conversation for the first time.

She got no answer from her cousin.

* * *

Inspector Okezie had commandeered a top-floor suite of the hotel. Mark in his turn spent some time familiarising himself with the communications facilities. Janine interrogated her media monitoring system. Fid Okeke rehearsed the details of the day's activities yet again in his mind and then left to confer with Victoria who had arrived back from her early-morning expedition.

"Pretty well as Fid said," Janine confirmed to Mark as she began to digest all the available information. "Plus some reports of late-night unrest amongst students at Lagos, Ibadan and other universities. Several western towns in Oyo and Osun States are in turmoil as Adeko's supporters demanded more arrests and a bigger share of the power for southerners in the Federal Government now that the northern Ministers have supposedly proved untrustworthy."

"Now what?" Janine said as she read on.

She paused to read before reporting more of the detail.

"Protests are building in many northern areas, attacks on Ibo businesses, gun battles with the Ibos defending them. This is dire. Attacks on both Fundamentalists and traditionalists; businesses, homes as well! There doesn't seem to be any pattern, just random escalating violence."

"What are the authorities doing about it?" asked Mark, now all attention on what Janine was saying.

"Seems like some form of martial law or curfew in most

northern states. Things are spilling over into the Plateau State?"

"Caught between the north and the south," the inspector said, answering Janine's unspoken query.

"The Federal Parliament's going to debate a State of Emergency. Eight o'clock in the morning, things must be getting pretty desperate!"

Janine, like Mark and the inspector, sensed that the country was approaching some sort of a crunch point, but it was far from clear how the situation was going to be resolved.

The inspector had been listening to the briefing.

"I've only a few more months to do," he said sadly. "Most of my career's been taken up with upheavals like this. We don't want another coup. It'll only end in pain and suffering for the ordinary people, and not much else. It always does."

Neither Janine nor Mark had any response to the inspector's comment.

"The rally in Port Harcourt's widely reported."

Janine was showing something of her own latent and still unresolved anxieties.

"The media are certainly expecting more disturbances."

"Can't worry about all of that," interrupted Mark. "It's eleven o'clock, Janine, we'd better get started."

Barred by his colour from any serious involvement, for the moment Mark could only watch, advise and wait. But inevitably he was worried about Janine being so close to the action. And his concern, much to Janine's surprise, was showing.

FORTY-FIVE

But the action wasn't due to start quite yet. Janine set off with Victoria and Fid Okeke from the hotel to the Port Office overlooking the docks. The journey was a revelation to her.

"Amazing…" Her excitement was clearly manifest to both of her companions.

'The place is teeming,' she thought. 'I've never seen so many people.'

Janine was almost overwhelmed by the sheer numbers as they entered the outskirts of Port Harcourt. Trucks, overcrowded buses, cars and taxis careered past them in both directions driven with aggression, on many occasions with foolhardy courage, but always with the raucous noise of horns and hooters. The vibrancy of everything almost intoxicated her.

Fid Okeke watched her absorb her surroundings with affectionate pride.

'Perhaps she'll get some sort of feeling for the place.'

He couldn't realistically expect her to do more with her background.

"How many…?"

She didn't get to ask the question.

A huge 'Mammy-wagon', the once-universal but now fast-disappearing form of commercial transport in West Africa, shot out of a side street across their path. Victoria, used to such displays of erratic driving behaviour, braked. The antique and gaudily painted vehicle complete with a tattered sign, 'God will provide', surmounted by a row of grinning faces came perilously close to them as she swerved. Speaking a different local language from Victoria, Fid Okeke would have been unable to translate her stream of invective in response even if he'd wanted to.

"We've plenty of time," he said hurriedly, anxious to get out of the mêlée before they were involved in any incident. "Why don't we give Janine a brief tour around the centre of Port Harcourt? The traffic won't be so frantic if we move off the main route into town."

They spent the next ten minutes driving around the civic buildings, the market, and the commercial and industrial areas.

"I'd no idea Port Harcourt was such a thriving industrial centre," Janine said.

"It wasn't just to get out of the traffic," her cousin said in response. "You should have an understanding of the geography of the place."

"Half -past eleven, that's good timing," Fid Okeke said as they finally arrived at the Port Office.

They were met by one of the two policemen that Inspector Okezie had had with him the previous evening. The officer of the Marine Police was a much younger man than Okezie and took a lively interest in Janine and Victoria. Janine greeted him like a long-lost friend in her usual exuberant way. Victoria was more restrained; she hadn't met the man the previous day. Janine nonetheless sensed that Victoria's manner was uncharacteristically subdued, and it didn't seem to be because of the presence of her superior.

"What's the matter with her?" she asked Fid Okeke when she had the opportunity.

He had a pretty good idea but was not inclined to share his thoughts with Janine.

"The ship will be here at mid-day," the Marine police inspector said.

From the Port Office, they had a clear view of the docks below and of the berth reserved for the arriving vessel. Janine looked at the bustle on the quayside with considerable interest. She soon grasped the patterns of activity. Both laden and unladen vehicles were arriving all the time. The empty trucks were marshalled into a parking area. The loaded trucks were unburdened and the stacks of containers grew alongside the crane tracks. Mobile cranes carrying the containers between their legs scurried about, ordering and re-ordering the ship's return load.

'Like giant spiders,' thought Janine.

"They will only be in port for eight hours, if they can't get all of the containers on board in that time, they'll leave without them," Janine remarked by way of conversation.

None of her companions were particularly interested.

Using field glasses, Victoria and Okeke were scanning the dockside and particularly the vehicles arriving all the time. Janine watched them watching.

A crackling on the port radio alerted the police inspector. He listened. Janine couldn't understand what was being said. Once people spoke quickly she was lost; the accent and their use of pidgin was way beyond her. The inspector replied and then went to the window.

"Over there," he said to Janine, recognising her as the one most likely to be interested.

He identified the superstructure of a ship apparently moving through the forest of mangrove trees that grew away from the built-up area and which covered every available patch of mud. The vessel had another loop in the channel to navigate, but it would be arriving pretty well on time.

"The vessel's approaching," she said into her radio.

Mark at the Inter-State Hotel acknowledged.

But the inaction was set to continue and to continue uncomfortably. Janine was sweating. Her tee-shirt was clinging to her body and she could feel little rivulets running down between her legs. She was regretting the loose calf-length wrap-over cotton skirt and desert boots, practical as they might have been.

'At least she's sweating too.'

Victoria's tee-shirt was equally wet, and her knee-length denim skirt was clinging to her as well. Janine felt better. Fid Okeke showed wet patches on his shirt but, like Victoria, no signs of anxiety over the impending activity.

"It's arrived," Janine told Mark.

"Keep calm, girlie," he replied. "I know the tension's rising; just keep calm."

Neither he nor Janine was entirely sure that that would be possible.

* * *

The cranes were working almost before the final mooring rope on the vessel was secured and certainly before the customs officers were halfway up the gangway. A period of frantic activity commenced. As the cranes overhung the ship like giant birds of prey, and the clamps descended onto the first container, Fid silently drew Janine's attention to a small group of men standing by a parked car at the end of the stacking area.

"Our southern friends have arrived to take charge of their merchandise."

Victoria, with careful and sometimes surreptitious sweeps of her own field glasses, had also identified the other watchers that she was expecting to see.

'If the containers are bait in the game then it's been taken,' thought Okeke. 'The players are gathering. All Mark's careful planning is coming to fruition.'

The telephone rang. The Marine Police inspector listened and then hung up.

"Two more hours before our containers are unloaded. The customs fellow on deck will signal when they're ready."

All they could do was wait.

They waited the two hours and some more. The atmosphere in the office was oppressive, both from the heat and from the inaction. Even a lunch-time sample of the local delicacies, sent out for from a roadside market stall, didn't relieve the tedium. The idling ceiling fans moved the hot damp air from place to place but lacked the power to draw any fresh into the room.

"How can Victoria and Fid just switch off like that?"

But she knew that it was the difference between their African and her European upbringing.

And then there was action at last, just under four hours after the ship had first appeared.

"Here they come," said the Marine Police inspector with sudden urgency, the weird hand signals of the customs official at last stirring everybody from their torpid state.

Janine repeated the information to Mark.

"Victoria and I will follow. Fid says he'll meet you as planned. He's away now."

"OK."

Fid already knew where to go.

"OK, Victoria, let's get going."

Now that the waiting was over and things were beginning to happen, all Janine wanted was to get out there and join the action. But she still had much to learn about the pace of African activities.

Victoria showed no signs of departing.

"There's time enough; best to stay out of sight for as long as possible."

Familiar, where Janine was not, with her countrymen and the way that things got done in Nigeria, she knew that there was no hurry.

"Be another half -hour before the containers are loaded and the formalities complete."

She was wrong; it was another hour and a half. The process of unloading these particular containers from the ship and onto the trucks seemed to Janine to take much longer than the others that had been unloaded. But at least the documentation was quickly done in the seclusion of some office underneath them. Victoria and the Marine Police inspector laughed at Janine's exasperation. At six o'clock, as the short twilight approached, the trucks were finally ready to move. Only then did Victoria head for their car.

FORTY-SIX

"We're on our way. At last!" radioed Janine.

Once again Mark acknowledged.

"The rally at the stadium's just starting," he said. "Maybe you'd do better to get in front of the trucks and wait for them out of town."

Now that things were moving, Mark's thoughts raced ahead as he sought to anticipate the actions of the various parties involved. The demonstration was a problem.

"If they don't buck their ideas up, the trucks are going to get caught up in the crowd. Hurry up, for God's sake!'

But Mark knew only too well that nothing he was likely to say would change the unhurried approach of the truck drivers, whatever his concerns for Janine's safety were.

"Not good, not good," Inspector Okezie muttered as he listened in on the open police channel. "Adeko's followers aren't going to take the pressure off the Federal Government; things are going to get nasty!"

The thought of Janine stranded in the middle of a riot did nothing for Mark's peace of mind.

As Mark finished speaking, Victoria asked Janine to check which stadium he was talking about; Port Harcourt had more than one. Mark consulted.

"It's the main one by the Aba Road roundabout according to the inspector."

Victoria and Janine knew the area. As Victoria headed the car out of the dock gates into the dimness of the poorly lit streets, Janine settled to concentrate on the more immediate activities that were going on around them.

Victoria took a turning off the main road; they had only gone a few hundred metres.

"We'd do better to avoid the old market area with a riot brewing," she said.

"OK."

After their experiences when entering Port Harcourt earlier, Janine was quite happy to avoid areas of traffic congestion, but to her surprise they very quickly ended up in one of the older and more run-down residential areas.

"Victoria!" said Janine.

"Oh shit," breathed Victoria; but it was more exclamation of frustration at having to slow down than any manifestation of concern.

The streets were clogged with disorganised groups of people, with dogs and children running everywhere, and cars and vans lining the carriageway. With the lighting at best poor and at worst non-existent in places, they had no choice but slow down to a walking pace.

The arrival of two reasonably smartly dressed women in a shiny new car was greeted with jeers. No translation was necessary to understand what the nature of their business was thought to be. However, when they proved unable to respond to the challenges in the local language, the jeers turned to hostility. As non-Ibo-speaking, they were definitely not welcome.

"Jesus, Victoria, what are you doing?"

Janine began to feel distinctly uncomfortable.

It was her first brush with the realities of tribalism. She had long since overcome any feelings that she had about being treated differently because of her colour, but this was something else. As she looked at her, Victoria's face was slowly registering a look of contempt.

'She's not worried at all,' thought Janine.

Nor was she; Victoria, like all Nigerians, was well aware of her tribal origins and was not ashamed of them.

"We'd better get out of here," she said rather obviously.

* * *

'What the hell's going on here?' Janine asked herself. 'She frightens me almost witless and then she gets us out of the place with no trouble at all. We weren't lost; even if she did try to make me think we were.'

They had wasted nearly a quarter of an hour; they were now well behind the trucks, and they still didn't know which road north the vehicles had taken. Worse, it was now fully dark, and the demonstrators were beginning to spill down the road from the stadium.

'What's going on here?' Janine asked herself again. 'Such incompetence isn't Victoria style; it's totally out of character.'

"We're behind them; Victoria got lost," Janine reported to Mark and the inspector as they began to get bogged down in the groups of marchers. "And now we're caught up in the rally."

Her cold, terse tones told Mark, and Fid Okeke, who was also listening in, that Janine was not happy. Since she had driven the route at least twice, Fid, like Janine, concluded that Victoria had got 'lost' deliberately. With his knowledge of his subordinate, that worried him.

"See if you can catch up," said Mark as he closed off the radio channel.

He was beginning to get seriously concerned; leaving Janine alone with Victoria looked like a bad idea. He and Fid knew that Victoria was playing to her own agenda, and it was important to know what she was up to, but it didn't make sense for her to lose contact with the trucks.

"This looks like fun," Victoria said as they were overwhelmed by a mass of people.

What happened in the next fifteen to twenty minutes was hardly what Janine would have described as fun.

'I do believe she's worried now,' Janine thought to herself.

'Bet she didn't bargain on being caught up in an ill-tempered demonstration.'

As every group of marchers passed the car, forced to a halt with a string of other traffic, they shouted at the two women. Janine had no way of knowing what they were saying, but she knew that the crowd was definitely hostile. And, as earlier, if they didn't respond in the local language, the demonstrators pounded on the roof and sides of the vehicle with their fists, or with lengths of wood, or, more frighteningly, with machetes. Victoria's side window was splintered by one such blow and the wind-screen was crazed by several efforts to break it.

"Nothing we can do," Janine said to Victoria, unexpectedly finding herself the calmer of the two. "At least the pressure from behind forces them on before they can do too much damage. And I guess it's not personal."

The police and troops looked on, not wanting to intervene unless lives were threatened. Eventually, as the end of the rally tailed away, the queue of vehicles was shepherded past the stadium by a couple of military armoured vehicles.

"That was exciting," said Victoria as she headed after the trucks along the road towards the Inter-State Hotel.

Janine shrugged the experience off. But it did occur to her that Victoria in her own eyes had 'lost face' with her over her fear, and that might not be such a good thing.

Janine checked in with Mark. Mark's anxieties were not allayed by his partner's avoidance of any conversation about Victoria.

"The trucks went by the hotel five minutes ago. They're being followed by at least two other cars, according to Inspector Okezie. They'll be at the suspect warehouse in around half-an-hour. Other vehicles are beginning to converge on the site. Police patrols have picked up several parked lorries along the A3 Port Harcourt-Aba Road."

Janine checked her map. The fact that the trucks were using the 'A' road and not the dual carriageway gave them more confidence that the warehouse that they had identified was the true destination.

"You should be able to catch up. The road's under repair for much of the way so they won't be going fast."

"OK, I'll tell Victoria."

"We're into the endgame," concluded Mark. "Talk to you later."

Janine gave Victoria the latest situation but made no mention of Mark's closing remark. She supposed that Victoria was well aware of the state of play, having, Janine somehow felt, engineered a large part of it.

* * *

"It's fortunate we don't have to rely just on Janine's surveillance of the trucks," Mark remarked to Inspector Okezie when the pursuing car seemed to have got itself lost.

They were really only there to see the containers out of the docks and on their way to the warehouse. Mark and the police had set up other avenues to track the vehicles when they were moving north.

Discovering the location of the warehouse had been a task undertaken by the security service. It hadn't proved easy. The security service had also established the identities of the major players likely to be involved from the consortium. The only risk that Fid Okeke and Mark could see was if the identified warehouse was a blind and another site for unloading the arms was planned.

"Not very likely," was Okeke's opinion. "There aren't that many options outside of the immediate Port Harcourt area."

"But why did Victoria let the trucks out of her sight then, Fid?"

It was a question that none of Okeke, the inspector or himself could find an answer to. Some of Mark's anxieties reawakened.

* * *

"The warehouse is used for storage of palm oil and belongs to a local co-operative."

Fid Okeke had provided the information to the police and military at the briefing the previous evening.

"The chairman and manager of the co-operative are supporters of Chief Adeko. The building is on a side road from the older A3 north-south trunk road that leads to Akwete. It's about five kilometres from the junction with the Port Harcourt road. And it's about thirty kilometres from the docks. It's not a long or hard drive and avoids the main highway to Enugu"

"We expect the vehicles coming to collect their share of the weapons to arrive from the north, as well as from Port Harcourt. We don't expect anything to come from the east along the side road, so the military will come that way, from the direction of Akwete. Everything will be done on the ground; no helicopters. Once the soldiers are in place, the police will close the road and set up a road-block, reducing the escape routes to only the two principal directions."

"The last phase of the plan is the most difficult," Mark had picked up the narrative at the earlier briefing. "The objective is the capture of as many of the southern conspirators as possible."

The soldiers had reconnoitred the warehouse as soon as they were told of its location. The cover around the building was very limited, it had a large open parking area, it was well floodlit and only had one access road from the public road. Apart from a small gatehouse there were no other buildings on the site. The bush had originally been cleared back, leaving a track around the outside of the perimeter fence, but with the passage of time and absence of maintenance it was now overgrown again. This made access to the fence difficult, although there were several nearby paths and tracks. It was a well-chosen location.

"You'll have to move your men through the bush and get them into position early. Once the trucks and other stuff arrive, there'll be too many headlights and people moving about."

Mark had stressed this at the briefing.

"We won't know how many other vehicles will be involved or when they'll arrive, early or after the arms are delivered."

Major Oyelade understood the problem. He and his officers and his senior NCOs had spent the earlier part of the day checking out the surrounding area and moving their equipment into position. From his point of view, it was not a difficult target to attack.

Now, with the trucks heading inexorably towards the warehouse, the major reported his status.

"Our groups are in position and ready. The fence will be cut in three places at the last minute. We'll keep radio silence until after the signal."

"OK, the police are in position in the old oil mill opposite. The ETA of the trucks is ten minutes."

Mark had the map spread out in front of him on his knees as he and Inspector Okezie made their way towards the rendezvous. The battered old van that they were travelling in would have attracted little attention; there were thousands like it. As far as he could judge, they were less than half a kilometre behind Janine and Victoria.

* * *

"Why are we stopping now!" demanded Janine as Victoria pulled over into a small cleared area at the side of the road.

Janine's feelings of discomfort had been forming into something more tangible as the journey progressed.

There was a coach already parked in the lay-by, its drab military colours briefly lit up as other vehicles passed by on the main road.

As they came to a halt, Janine tensed. Victoria had become almost hyperactive as they had moved further and further away from Port Harcourt, as if she was preparing herself for something that she knew was going to happen next. And now as she was challenged by Janine, seemingly taking confidence from the sight of the coach, she metamorphosed into a Victoria that was totally foreign to Janine.

"I think I'd better have the radio," she said, opening the rather battered door beside her.

The interior light came on. She had turned to face Janine. Janine didn't at first notice the small handgun that was pointing at her. Janine glanced to her right and out of her own side window. All she could see was the anonymous torso, in military fatigues, of the man who was now standing close to the car.

FORTY-SEVEN

"Oh, man!"

The two trucks came to a halt at yet another set of roadworks. The lead driver shrugged; such holdups were a part of his life. At least he was at the Akwete turning. Not that the turn into the side road was made any easier for the long vehicles by the narrowing of the carriageway.

At the roadside, in a ramshackle plastic and wooden shelter, the home of the inevitable and often unnecessary night watchman of any Nigerian public works, a policeman watched.

"The second wagon's turned the corner," he reported to his inspector by radio. "Two cars and two vans have followed."

"Is that all?" muttered Mark.

Two of the smaller trucks parked on the A3 had pulled away from the roadside parking as the huge six-axle trucks went by. What Mark didn't know was how many more such vehicles, like the elderly Mercedes truck that had been following them until they pulled off onto the Akwete road, might be heading for the warehouse.

"We have to take the risk," said Inspector Okezie. "We need to be out of sight at the old mill by the time the trucks reach the warehouse."

There was another anonymous car-load of police behind the ancient truck. If it, or any other vehicle, did take the turnoff, they would be shepherded carefully away from the warehouse if they didn't prove to be a part of the action by approaching it. To Mark's relief, the Mercedes continued on its way onwards along the road towards Aba.

The scene was set.

"They've arrived," muttered Fid Okeke, feeling something of the same tingling of excitement that was suffusing Mark Shortley.

As the headlights of the first truck, flickering as it bounced over the potholes, came into view, the doors of the warehouse were rolled back. With the usual accompaniment of squeals and hissing of brakes, the two trailers were backed into the building. It was a tight fit and much manoeuvring was necessary before the two containers were finally in place inside the warehouse. The motor units remained outside the building.

"OK, standby, here we go," said Mark.

He and the inspector had joined the group of waiting policemen at the old oil mill opposite the warehouse. From the upstairs windows of the derelict office building, they had a good view across the road and into the warehouse yard. A constable handed Mark and the inspector night-vision field glasses.

Fid Okeke had already made his way to the old mill. He updated them.

"The trucks have just got themselves into place in the warehouse. They've blocked the front entrance. There are nine vehicles altogether, and we reckon twenty-two people. Falinde and Oje..."

Okeke seemed pleased that his security service colleagues were amongst the conspirators in the warehouse.

"Recognise anybody else?" asked Mark.

"The guy who manages the warehouse; at least three of Adeko's particular cronies; three or four people I don't know. The rest will probably be there to do the hard work."

'OK,' thought Mark, 'everything's ready for the final showdown; and not just this shindig at an obscure warehouse in the middle of nowhere.'

The seizure of the illegal arms was to be the trigger for much wider action against the southern consortium. They were putting down a potential coup.

"Standby," repeated Major Oyelade quietly to his officers.

The troops prepared themselves.

FORTY-EIGHT

One of the containers was open, and in a series of frantic, short dashes, a forklift truck was stacking the crates around the walls. As always, there seemed to be too many people involved. The ubiquitous Mr Falinde vainly tried to impose some order.

The blackness was sudden and instant. It was overtaken by multiple flashes of magnesium intensity and a series of the loud high-frequency explosions that were shattering to the eardrums and addling to the brains, so overwhelming was the volume of noise and light.

A choking smoke filled the building and then was swirled away by the very force that had created it. Two or three short bursts of gunfire followed, and then a silence and a darkness that almost hurt. The conspirators mostly froze where they stood, disoriented, denied control of their limbs and incapable of coherent thought.

The firm tread of ordered feet broke the disordered quiet and then there was the sound of people being unwillingly moved about. Gasps and whimpered protests added to the growls of sound.

As there was light again, the smoke drifted up to form a haze that gave the atmosphere a ghostly yellow glow. Someone amongst the shattered group set up a terrified wail until silenced by a soldier.

* * *

"Stand still!"

The order was repeated in several local languages to avoid misunderstanding.

Ranged around the warehouse, their night-vision goggles and their black uniforms making them look like the sinister mechanical warriors of some futuristic space-fiction movie, stood a dozen soldiers, their weapons trained on the groups of stunned and frightened figures in the middle of the open area. The forklift truck stood impaled in the metal sidewall of the warehouse, the driver motionless. He seemed to be the only physical casualty.

Outside, more soldiers awaited the order to join the action. It didn't come, they weren't needed.

"Over there," ordered the lieutenant.

His goggles removed, he scanned his prisoners contemptuously. Aided by some none- too- gentle prods, the occupants of the warehouse were herded into one corner and searched. There was no resistance.

"OK," said Major Oyelade into his radio, "we have the warehouse secure; one casualty amongst the civilians, none on our side."

Mark acknowledged.

"Well done. Inspector Okezie and his men will be over immediately."

"Shall we reload the crates?"

"No, not yet. And stay vigilant – there's a piece of the jigsaw still missing."

* * *

"OK," said Inspector Okezie, signifying that all the occupants of the warehouse had been formally arrested. Feeble protests began to emerge from the hardier souls, but they were ignored.

"Well now!"

Fid Okeke joined the inspector and confronted his two fellow security service officials. The conversation was bitter and heated. They knew that they could expect no mercy for their perceived treachery.

"Three elected members of state assemblies, two businessmen from Lagos, a couple local," the inspector checked off the list as it was presented to him. "Apart from the drivers, the rest are Adeko's intended shock troopers."

The policeman judiciously refrained from calling them thugs.

"Quite a haul," said Mr Okeke.

'Glad that's over,' Mark said to himself, 'but Victoria and Janine should be here by now! What are they up to? They know they have to radio in regularly.'

The police control van, with Mark in it, was driven into the warehouse yard.

"No trace of them, or their car, Sir." The constable manning the communications had just checked with his Port Harcourt headquarters.

"For God's sake, where are they?"

Janine would have wanted Mark to maintain his professionalism, but it was going to be hard to keep his mind on the job.

* * *

"Inspector!" said Mark rather sharply. "It might have been better if you'd waited."

By the time that he entered the warehouse, curiosity had

taken over and one of the soldiers had levered open a crate; the inspector was peering inside with a bemused expression on his face.

"What's this?" he demanded.

The arrival of a white man caused a discernable stir amongst the disconsolate group of detainees in the corner. But it was the inspector who was attracting attention. He reached into the open crate.

"What is this?" said the inspector again.

The soldier stood back to watch the unfolding scene with increasing interest; he had seen what the policeman had seen.

"Mark?" said Fid Okeke tentatively, backing up Okezie's question.

Because of his concerns about leakage of information from the security service, Mark had only confided part of his plan to Okeke. He had been privy to the plans to expose the members of the southern consortium but not to what was now emerging.

Mr Okeke moved to join Inspector Okezie at the open crate.

"When the planned shipments were first known about," Mark said, "the priority was to prevent the weapons getting through. But that didn't implicate anybody."

He gestured towards the huddled group, several of whom were now rather better focused on what was going on.

"So, whilst the arms dealer's warehouse was on fire…"

Mark gestured at the offending crate.

There was enlightenment at least for Messrs Falinde and Oje, and then consternation.

"And?" said the inspector.

"And then we baited the trap that you kindly set for us."

Mark raised his hands to signify that that was it.

"For God's sake, Mark." Fid Okeke's first reaction was anger. "If something had gone wrong, it would have been me for the chop, not you, you should've told me!"

He had now seen inside the crate.

He was about to say something more when he realised that the inspector was laughing. Okezie was holding up a section of ancient and rusting metal pipe as if it was a gun and was pointing it at the huddled detainees; he was laughing, loudly and gleefully.

First the major, and then Okeke himself, joined in. The detainees, who now generally understood that they had been hoodwinked into exposing themselves, looked on in dismay.

The weapons and ammunition were being held safely in a British military armoury.

FORTY-NINE

As the laughter died down and the four principals took stock, they each had separate worries of their own. Mark was still concerned about Janine. Fid Okeke was unable to explain to himself what had happened to Victoria Akinbode. Major Oyelade still wasn't sure of the extent of the measures that he might have to take. The inspector wondered whether he had enough men to process the detainees and whether the parallel action that was supposed to accompany the activities at the warehouse was underway.

With the uncertainties and complexities of Nigerian politics, the inspector's worries were well founded. Self-interest was a powerful driving force. The limited penetration of the ethos of the 'Club' and the rising middle and professional classes meant that the possibilities of loyalties changing as the success or failure of the activities of the Fundamentalists and the southern consortium became apparent was an ever-present concern to both Fid Okeke and the inspector.

The inspector retreated to the communications vehicle.

"I've talked to the Commissioner," he said when he returned. "He acted within minutes of the army assault."

Following a plan proposed by the security service, and

initiated by the Rivers State Police Commissioner, the authorities in half -a -dozen or so southern States began simultaneously to round up known plotters.

But there was another worry. As they had learnt at the previous evening's briefing, Fundamentalist supporters were known to be in Port Harcourt to try to hijack the arms.

By making his announcement deliberately loudly, Inspector Okezie ensured that the detainees were aware of the developing situation. The murmurs of concern and anger indicated that the message had been heard.

"OK," said Mr Okeke, "let's get this lot sorted."

The 'sorting', however, had to wait.

* * *

"What!" exclaimed the inspector.

Major Oyelade, who recognised the sound at once, gestured to his lieutenant. Rapid commands were given and a sergeant cautiously crawled out under the trucks into the warehouse yard to investigate.

"Down, down," yelled Mark, waving to the detainees and soldiers alike to crouch below the level of the one-metre base brick wall of the warehouse.

His action was none too soon. A drum-roll of sound, accompanied by a two-metre perforation in the aluminium skin of the warehouse, marked another burst of machine-gun fire. The major cursed, it was his own fire that had peppered the building.

The sergeant returned, bringing the frightened constable from the communications van with him.

"We're under attack," he said. "One of the perimeter guards returned fire."

"Who's attacking us?" asked the inspector.

The sergeant did not look happy. Major Oyelade's expression demanded an answer.

"Njoku thinks it's the Bauchi battalion, sir."

Njoku was one of the troopers who had returned fire. The Bauchi battalion was from the Port Harcourt garrison.

"But I thought we'd stood them down," said Fid Okeke.

This was not good news; renegade troops supporting the Fundamentalists was something that Okeke had feared most; now it was happening.

The major, with no arms now at stake, was only interested in preventing a bloody clash with uncertain results.

"Lieutenant, do we have their frequency?"

It wasn't needed. Mark's radio flashed; somebody was calling him.

"Hello, Janine?"

"This is Victoria."

Mark's reaction got the attention of Okeke, Okezie and Oyelade.

Switching his radio to mute, Mark reported to the surrounding group. He was angry that it wasn't Janine. Each of the other three went into overdrive as they digested the implications and reformulated their plans. After a lengthy pause, as much designed to unsettle Victoria as anything, Mark resumed contact.

"So what do you want, Victoria?" he demanded.

"The arms, Mark, the arms , what else would I want?"

Victoria clearly was not yet unsettled.

"You're surrounded; we know you've only got a few special forces troopers. We don't want any bloodshed. Why don't you just let the drivers bring the trucks out into the road?"

Mark retailed the gist of Victoria's demand. His negotiating experience kicking in; he began to prevaricate.

"OK, but they won't be much use to you," he said, signalling his companions to be quiet.

"Why not?" she demanded; Victoria was instantly suspicious.

"The Wongs seem to have sent the firing pins separately," replied Mark.

'I hope she doesn't know anything about these new American rifles,' he thought. 'I certainly don't. I haven't a clue about their design. I'm probably talking total nonsense.'

"I don't believe you, Mark!"

Fid Okeke, with his greater knowledge of Victoria, might have detected a hesitancy in her response.

"Why aren't I surprised by that?" he muttered.

"Then you'll have to come and see for yourself, won't you?" he said in response.

There was a pause. Mark wondered whom Victoria might be consulting with as the radio went dead.

"What about Janine?" whispered Fid Okeke.

Mark hadn't forgotten about Janine.

Major Oyelade, his sergeant and lieutenant went into a huddle. The detainees, who could not hear the radio exchanges, looked on with rising concern, although the more perceptive of them began to think that a problem for the police and soldiers would more than likely be a relief for them.

"Drive out one of the trucks and make an entrance. I'll come and inspect the rifles. Any tricks and we'll attack."

Victoria's return to the conversation again was what Mark would have expected. Victoria really had no choice but to check or unleash the sort of uncertain violence that the major was so keen to avoid.

"OK, but bring Janine with you. If you're alone, we'll shoot you down," replied Mark.

Inspector Okezie's look of outraged consternation contrasted with the curt nod from Fid Okeke. The police and security service played to very different rules.

"Janine's not here," said Victoria, her voice now rising in anxiety at the risk that was being forced on her.

"Where is she then?" demanded Mark.

"I don't know Mark, truly I don't. She ran off earlier, I don't know where she's gone."

Mark was incredulous as he shared the information about Janine with the others.

"That's nonsense, there's no way they'd have let Janine escape!"

Again they didn't get the opportunity to consider what this latest information meant.

* * *

"Now what?" exclaimed Mark in surprise.

Two rifle reports, followed by a burst of automatic gunfire, shattered the relative calm. Moments later, there were two further rifle shots but no returning fire.

"Not us," said the Major, sounding worried. "We don't have any normal service rifles."

The exchange of fire was followed by another interruption, but this time from inside the building.

"What the hell's going on?"

It was the manager of the warehouse. Having recovered more than some of his fellow conspirators, and being tired of watching the pantomime between the white man, and the police and military officers, he demanded to be given information.

"We're being attacked," said Okezie bluntly.

"Who by?"

"No one friendly to you!"

Further conversation was interrupted by the sound of a scuffle and then angry curses in a language that Mark at least couldn't understand. As two of the troopers cautiously pushed open the back door of the warehouse, their weapons at the ready, the jumbled figures of two of their fellow soldiers, and Janine, spilled into the light.

"Janine! Shit, Janine!"

Mark rushed over to her.

"Mark, Mark!" came Victoria's disembodied voice over the radio again. "We're getting impatient, Mark."

"OK, OK, we'll move a truck out."

The inspector called for one of the drivers, but having heard the shooting outside, neither was very enthusiastic. However, surrounded by armed soldiers and a squad of policemen, they were quick to perceive that an option was not on offer.

"Janine, what happened?"

"Victoria... oh, hell, never mind. I escaped."

FIFTY

Time was running out and Victoria knew it. The soldiers with her were nervous and she suspected ready to creep back to their barracks in Port Harcourt with hopefully no questions asked. She clearly had to do something. And Mark's threat to shoot her if she couldn't produce Janine had to be confronted.

'The police won't let him shoot me,' she told herself.

Her confidence, even if well justified, didn't reflect both that the special forces would shoot first and ask questions later and that her boss had already authorised deadly force against her if it proved necessary.

* * *

Janine's story wasn't told there and then. In fact, it was told backwards and selectively, as Janine knew that any information about the dispositions of the soldiers with Victoria would be valuable. And since shock had yet to set in, it was told with a fair degree of coherence.

But as Mark and Okeke pieced it together later, many of the question marks over both Victoria's behaviour and the leakage to the Fundamentalists from the security service were resolved.

Somewhat surprisingly, Victoria, through her mother, turned out to be the Moslem equivalent of the god-daughter of Alhaji Sullag.

"She's been working for him all along," said Janine, "and very proud of her cleverness in hiding it too."

"But what happened?" Mark had demanded; he was far less interested in Victoria than in Janine.

"Ah, well, we pulled off the road a few miles back from the turning. There was a coach-load of soldiers and civilians, and other vehicles. Victoria had a gun, so I didn't argue. They tied my hands."

She'd had a strand of coarse rope still attached to one of her wrists when she'd been grabbed by the special forces troopers.

"They didn't seem to know what to do with me. They just took me into the bush with them. Victoria was obviously in charge, the soldiers did whatever she said. That was a surprise. Then they started to disperse. You could see a little glow of light reflected on the clouds, so I knew the warehouse couldn't be very far away.

"Once the attacking force was in place, Victoria got on the radio to you, Mark. They tied me to a tree, which said something about their numbers if they couldn't afford a guard. It was whilst she was roping me to the tree that she did her gloating. She couldn't resist it. And that was when I found out about her Fundamentalist credentials."

Janine had chuckled at the recollection, which Mark had taken as a good sign of her well-being after the incident.

"I soon managed to free myself; that wasn't so difficult. But then it dawned on me that I had to get through the attacking soldiers and find the warehouse. And I had to do it in the dark. And worse still, being a city-dweller, I'm hopeless at knowing which way to go in the street, let alone in the jungle."

Mark's concern had begun to dissolve into respect when it was manifest that she had coped astonishingly well with the problems.

"I crept out of the back of the little clearing and set off in what I hoped was a great big circle. I came to a track eventually. It seemed to be heading towards the glow in the sky… so I followed it.

"That was the easy bit. It was when I got to the road that the panic really set in. The track I was following went to the old oil mill, I clearly didn't want to go there, but the bush was really thick, and I had to force a way through to get to the road away from the floodlit area around the warehouse. And then there was the chance of both sides taking potshots at me!

"In the end, I had no choice. I was spotted.

"Then all hell let loose. I crashed through the last of the bush and leapt across the road, bang into this guy all done up in black and covered with weapons. And that was it!"

Janine gestured at the special forces soldiers who had brought her in.

There was wonderment and praise later at the time of the storytelling, but earlier, safe in the warehouse, Janine was conscious that the information that she had garnered needed to be handed on at once.

"There are about twenty-five of them, as far as I could tell. About half are soldiers. I didn't recognise any as officers. Nor any weapons like these."

She pointed at the automatic weapons that the black-clad soldiers were carrying.

She told them all that she could, jerking out sentences as things occurred to her. The major asked a few questions and then gave his orders. He was relieved. Even allowing, as he did, for Janine's limited military knowledge, the attacking force was greatly diminished as a threat by what she was saying.

* * *

The heat inside the warehouse was intense, and the atmosphere was still clogged with the smoke of the stun grenades. The after-effects of her escapade were still distant for Janine as she surveyed the groups watching her in the oven-like ferocity of the building. The sullen group of people, guarded by a few soldiers, were obviously the captured consortium people; Okezie and the major she already knew. Other soldiers and policemen milled around.

"What's going on?" Janine asked after her debriefing to the major.

Clearly something was expected to happen and everybody was waiting.

"Victoria's coming; she doesn't believe the weapons aren't any use to her!" Mark said.

Janine burst into a nervous, overloud, gurgling laugh at this, knowing the truth as she did.

"Ma'am!"

A soldier gave her a water bottle to drink from and the military medic dealt with her scratches and cuts. One was a bullet wound, although she didn't seem to be aware of it. Her main concern, as she began to unwind, was that her skirt was in tatters as a result of her journey through the bush, and although her tee-shirt was long, she was showing more bare skin than she thought appropriate amongst strangers. Nothing could be found to cover her legs.

"Probably saved her life," the major remarked. "The trooper who first saw her couldn't believe his eyes."

The trooper's reprimand from his sergeant for failing to fire on sight was somewhat tempered in the circumstances.

"My poor darling!"

Mark, despite his focus on the job in hand, was sensitive enough to Janine's situation to put his arms around her and give her a gentle hug.

"Now is not the time, is it?" she said.

From past experience, he knew that she would have to talk out her feelings at some length before she came to terms with what had happened to her, but since she could hardly do it where they were, he was concerned to buoy her up until they were in more congenial surroundings.

They were interrupted by a choking blast of exhaust fumes as one of the trucks was moved forward and away from the warehouse doors. The detainees were then herded again, this time into the dead end formed by the remaining truck and the front corner of the building.

"I've spoken to the Commissioner," said Inspector Okezie, who had reoccupied his communications van in the pause whilst Victoria made her way to the warehouse.

"We're to avoid violence. He's sending reinforcements, but they're not for fighting with the Fundamentalists; they are for dealing with the southern troublemakers. Since the Bauchi battalion CO doesn't know where his men's loyalties lie, the Commissioner hasn't asked for more troops."

"I'm on the road, about fifty metres from the warehouse entrance," said Victoria over the stolen radio.

Without Janine to provide her with insurance, she was now extremely nervous. She genuinely didn't know where her former prisoner was.

"Come slowly. When you make it to the gatehouse, just stand still in the spotlight. I'll tell you when to move," ordered Mark.

The major, standing next to Mark in the shadow of the second truck, murmured an acknowledgement into his lapel microphone. His perimeter guards had just reported.

"She's alone."

"Walk straight forward, Victoria," said Mark.

Once she was inside the warehouse, the soldiers partially closed the front door and mounted a guard in the gap.

"Over here," said Mark coldly, directing Victoria to the open crate.

She began to pick her way through the scattered pile of

ironwork around the crate. Then she stopped, almost not daring to look inside it.

Body tensed, Victoria immediately understood what had happened, as she, like the inspector had, pulled out a piece of misshapen ironwork. Her face contorted into probably the most venomous expression Mark had ever seen, she rounded on him.

"You bastard. You filthy, two-timing bastard."

Victoria's command of English failed her after her initial outburst. Very few of her countrymen present were capable of understanding the stream of foul language that followed. Those who could shuffled uncomfortably from hearing such a flow of invective from a woman.

"You switched the guns at the Wong's warehouse!" she spluttered. "That was what the fire was all about."

She took a pace forward. The simultaneous raising of several weapons gave her pause. Neither the inspector nor the major showed any signs of entering the conversation. The look of utter contempt that passed across the face of Fid Okeke confirmed that he too had nothing to say.

But others had.

"Seems so obvious and simple now, doesn't it?"

Victoria stiffened. It was Janine's voice.

'If she's grinning, I'll kill her,' Victoria thought viciously. She turned around. Janine was grinning!

Janine was also alert to Victoria's possible reaction. But neither spoke or moved.

The standoff was brought to an end by Fid Okeke.

"So what'll you tell your friends?" asked her superior officer.

"You can hardly tell them how much you've been made a fool of," said Janine sweetly.

"Janine!" said Mark in warning.

She was definitely overexcited and still on an adrenalin rush following her escape.

But Janine wasn't listening. Suddenly all her anger, jealousy, and submerged rivalry came to the surface. She wanted Victoria to be angry and she wanted revenge for the heartache that she'd caused her.

The open crate was alongside the left-hand wall of the warehouse. Victoria was surrounded by Janine, Mark, Fid Okeke and one of the special forces lieutenants. Inspector Okezie and Major Oyelade had moved over to the other side of the building to discuss their next steps out of earshot. The southern consortium prisoners were away in the corner. Apart from the soldiers on guard duty, the major and the lieutenant were the only other military personnel still in the warehouse, the sergeant having gone to support the other lieutenant and his patrol. Between the groups was the open space that had been partly filled by the departed truck.

"I've seen enough," Victoria announced, and moved towards this vacant area.

Having recovered something of her composure, she knew that she had to escape.

Only Janine was between her and the part-open door.

Outside there was a sudden explosion of sound, dominated by the sharp coughing noise made by the automatic weapons used by the troopers. Clearly the special forces unit had located the Fundamentalists.

"Hell!" exclaimed Janine.

Now more in control of herself, Victoria took the initiative.

With space around her, she launched a fierce attack on her one-time friend. Half expecting the kick, Janine ducked and was only grazed by the blow. Still on balance, she leapt at her opponent and grasped her outstretched left arm. Taking a two-handed hold, she started to pull Victoria around, intending to throw her onto her back. Some deep-buried instinct in her told her that she should use her judo skills, where she was superior to Victoria, rather than allow her to use her kick-boxing skills.

"Janine!"

Mark's anguished cry was almost lost in the squealing grunts that the two girls were emitting.

Perhaps sensing what was in Janine's mind, Victoria was too quick for her. With only limited leverage, she was still able to land a powerful punch to Janine's right jaw as her body moved down and round. The blow was enough to slacken the grip on her arm. She was free and, having regained her footing, she prepared her next attack as Janine staggered away.

Victoria's second kick, had it landed, would have done permanent damage, but it sailed harmlessly over Janine's head as she dropped to the ground. Kicking backwards and upwards herself, Janine, like Pearl Wong had done, aimed for the kneecap. The powerful blow was effective. Forcing her legs from under her, Victoria landed on her side with a loud scream.

"Enough!"

Having seen what was going on, Inspector Okezie moved back into the open space and demanded the fight stop. Mark, seeing Victoria fall, moved to restrain Janine from further action.

But they were far too slow.

Despite the fall that she had taken, and perhaps fed by her desperation, Victoria was instantly on her feet, and able to avoid Janine's attempts to grapple with her. However, she didn't renew her attack. Seeing the warehouse entrance in front of her, she set off in a rapid hop-and-skip run, sidestepping the startled soldier guarding the doorway, and heading for the gate.

The single cough of the lieutenant's weapon filled the sudden silence. As Victoria had propelled herself into the circle of light at the gatehouse, the officer had fired. It was a cold and calculated execution.

"My God," said Inspector Okezie when he realised what had happened.

* * *

Police buses and army trucks poured into the warehouse yard.

It was all over. Janine, Mark and Fid Okeke were helped into a police Land-Rover and ferried away. The clearing-up took the rest of the night.

FIFTY-ONE

"I didn't want it to end like that," said Janine rather sadly.

She'd crept in with Mark when they returned to the Port Harcourt Inter-State Hotel.

"No," he said simply.

He was certainly shocked, but then he had been away from the rather brutal and instant decision-making world of special forces long enough to have regrown something of his more normal sensitivity.

They slept late, luxuriating in the air conditioning. Janine's jaw was very stiff and she had difficulty with talking when she first woke up.

"Peaceful day," remarked Mark with a chuckle.

Taking the remark as a slight on her normal early-morning chatter, Janine leapt onto him and began pounding his chest in mock anger, but they were interrupted by a knock on the door. It was Fid Okeke.

"Oh, sorry, I'm not dressed," said Mark hurriedly as he answered the door.

Fid came in and walked over to stare out of the window whilst Mark pulled some clothes on. Janine scurried into the bathroom, showered and later reappeared, wrapped in a towel.

"Success, Mark! Real success."

The Nigerian was in high spirits. He had been up early and had spoken to Mr Aminu, his Minister.

Mark grunted his encouragement.

"Yes, indeed. It was a coup that wasn't. The army stayed in their barracks. The only troops on the streets were backing the police. There was huge support for the Federal Government and the status quo. The north's still seething, though; a few Fundamentalists have been beaten up. A few windows in the Iranian Embassy in Abuja got broken. But the worst trouble was over by midnight. About two hundred people have been arrested."

"Fid, that's great, absolutely wonderful," said Mark. "So what happened in Port Harcourt in the end?"

"It seems the battalion commander and the brigadier got wind that something was going on and called the whole Bauchi unit on parade. It was a bit risky; foolhardy, you might say, based on past history. In the end, a couple of officers and half a dozen NCOs were arrested and a few ordinary soldiers."

"But did they do anything about the troops who had already mutinied?" asked Janine, who had now appeared.

"The brigadier eventually sent a couple of platoons to help Major Oyelade. Most of the dissidents were rounded up. Eight soldiers and four civilians, including Victoria, were killed."

Fid Okeke's mention of Victoria rather dampened the atmosphere, but he'd said what he'd come to say, so he excused himself.

"See you on the 'plane," he promised as he departed.

Janine and Mark had a belated breakfast in the hotel roof garden. They were still sombre.

* * *

"Even Port Harcourt's quiet now, and most people are concentrating on the holiday break and a carnival that's been organised by the oil companies," Fid Okeke told them on the flight to Abuja.

As they drove to the Abuja Inter-State Hotel, the streets were quiet, and the business and diplomatic quarters almost deserted. The taxi driver, as everywhere the source of local news and gossip, was full of the latest government appointments.

"They've replaced Alhaji Sullag with a Yoruba from Ogun State, another Effiong."

A Moslem himself, the taxi man seemed to approve of the decision to replace one of the two arrested northern Ministers with a southerner.

"Don't think you're related," said Fid Okeke when Janine showed interest in the new Minister. "It's a fairly common name."

"It would be!" said Janine with a chuckle.

"I've arranged a little dinner party," Fid said as they were dropped off at the hotel and before he set off for his home. "Seven -thirty."

He didn't say who else he had invited.

The preparations for the dinner were hectic. At least they were for Janine. To Mark's total astonishment, she went into the sort of feminine hustle of preparations that he had never ever seen before. On this occasion, they had adjacent and interconnecting rooms; Mark was banished to his own and banned from returning until called.

* * *

"OK, Mark, let's go!"

Janine had part opened the interconnecting door and was inviting him in.

"Oh, my goodness, Janine, oh, wow!"

Mark was completely taken aback. Janine's inevitable infectious grin was chased by her deep, gurgling laughter as she enjoyed his surprise to its utmost.

She was wearing a full-length dress with the straight but fairly full skirt and the tight bodice and wide-pleated waist sash that were currently in vogue amongst the fashionable of the Nigerian capital. The sleeves were elbow-length, and both her wrists were festooned with an array of silver and gold bracelets. The dress was boldly patterned in blue and white with small red flowers picked out in some of the swirls of the design.

"The hat, Janine, what a wonderful hat."

Mark was entranced.

He had seen the elaborate turbans of various shapes and sizes at the hotel in Port Harcourt, but the one that she was wearing struck him as positively exotic by comparison. It was wider at the top than at the base, where it fitted her head, and the ends of the layers of wrapped-around material, starched and stiff, stood out like two flared cockades. The hat was made of identical material to the dress. Janine's earrings underneath were enormous and very noisy.

"I'm glad you like it," she said pertly.

She took his arm. Mark shook his head; this was a whole new Janine whose existence he'd never even suspected.

Their effect as a couple was immediate. As they entered the restaurant, the head waiter descended upon them and enquired if they were of Mr Okeke's party. He led them to a private room where Fid, and a lady dressed as gorgeously as Janine were already waiting.

"Wonderful, Janine!"

Fid Okeke was delighted that she had gone to the trouble of wearing the dress, and that she had wanted to. He introduced his wife.

Janine and Mrs Okeke embraced in the way that Mark had seen other Nigerian women do in greeting. It was as if she had been living in the country all her life. The change confused Mark.

"There are only two other guests," said Fid, doing his attentive host act.

'I wonder whether he'll show up?' thought Okeke, 'Victoria's relationship seems to have been far more relaxed and flexible than Janine's and Mark's. Since she's dead, I suppose he'll at least mourn her.'

Fid's anxieties on the subject of Victoria's boyfriend were noisily relegated to the background as Janine burst into excited squeals that were met by those of the other young woman who had just been shown into the room. It took Mark no time at all to understand what the Okekes of course already knew. This was Janine's sister.

"This is Mark."

Once she had finished hugging her sister, all she wanted to do was share her with Mark and show Mark off to her.

Her sister looked very much like Janine; she was slightly shorter and younger, but otherwise they were the proverbial two peas. Having introduced Mark to her sibling, Janine went off to excitedly thank Fid Okeke for inviting her. She stood and watched Mark and Patience with shining eyes and great surges of love and affection. Unheard and unseen, the final guest approached her from behind.

"Hello, Janine."

It was Victoria's boyfriend. Unlike Fid Okeke, he was wearing a western suit and a black tie. He had just arrived and was taking in the scene.

"Daniel! Daniel Onifade! What a surprise; you're the last person I would have expected!"

The dinner was a rousing success.

REFERENCES

Africa, Richard Dowden
Nigeria – Bradt Travel Guide, Lizzie Williams